TIED UP IN KNOTS

"I could put a gag on you," she warned Ian.

"Damn!" Pretty Boy said over the headset. "Did I just hear her say she was gonna put a gag on you? How could she do that?"

"Because she knocked me out with a rock and tied me up…ankles and hands."

Pretty Boy must have heard the amusement in his voice because he laughed.

"You're going to get laid tonight, aren't you?" Pretty Boy accused him.

"I don't think sex is on this puss's agenda."

"You can be certain of that," Yasmine said hotly. "And remember what I said about my talent." She waved her fingers toward his crotch.

"Wait till I tell the other guys about this," Pretty Boy said.

"Listen, she's no prize. In fact, she says she's been kicked out of nine harems because—"

"Harems?" Pretty Boy sputtered.

"…because she claims to have a talent for turning hard-ons into wet noodles."

"Hasn't anyone told her it's supposed to be the other way around?"

Other *Love Spell* and *Leisure* books by Sandra Hill:

WET & WILD
A TALE OF TWO VIKINGS
THE VERY VIRILE VIKING
MY FAIR VIKING
THE BLUE VIKING
TRULY, MADLY VIKING
THE LOVE POTION
BLUE CHRISTMAS (anthology)
LOVE ME TENDER
THE BEWITCHED VIKING
THE LAST VIKING
SWEETER SAVAGE LOVE
DESPERADO
THE NIGHT BEFORE CHRISTMAS (anthology)
LOVESCAPE (anthology)
FRANKLY, MY DEAR . . .
THE TARNISHED LADY
THE OUTLAW VIKING
THE RELUCTANT VIKING

RAVE REVIEWS FOR *ROMANTIC TIMES* CAREER ACHIEVEMENT AWARD-WINNER SANDRA HILL!

WET & WILD

"Sandra Hill is a master of the romantic comedy for a reason, and *Wet & Wild* proves it beautifully."

—*A Romance Review*

"Irreverent, sexy fun." —*Affaire de Coeur*

A TALE OF TWO VIKINGS

"Quintessential Hill—outrageous, side-splitting, funny-bone-tickling entertainment."

—*Booklist* (Starred Review)

"Hill is known for the fresh, funny, contemporary feel of her Viking romances.... Each page is bawdier than the last."

—*Publishers Weekly*

THE VERY VIRILE VIKING

"With its boisterous humor and lovable characters, [*The Very Virile Viking*] will charm the socks off readers."

—*Publishers Weekly*

"*The Very Virile Viking* has all the outrageous humor and sizzling sexiness for which Sandra Hill is well known.... This very virile Viking puts your libido into overdrive. A fabulous read!"

—Newandusedbooks.com

MY FAIR VIKING

"A singular blend of humor and romance."

—*Publishers Weekly*

THE BLUE VIKING

"This book was hilarious. Another keeper!"

—*Paranormal Romance Reviews*

MORE PRAISE FOR SANDRA HILL!

TRULY, MADLY VIKING

"Once again the ingenious Ms. Hill brings a megadose of humor to her captivating and fun-filled time travels. Another winner!"

—*Romantic Times*

THE BEWITCHED VIKING

"*The Bewitched Viking* is just the book for that night you absolutely must have a story that skillfully incorporates rollicking humor with sensual romance."

—*Reader to Reader*

THE LAST VIKING

"This book is priceless.... Ms. Hill is superb! She makes you laugh out loud with her humor... Whatever you do, don't miss this book."

—*The Belles & Beaux of Romance*

THE LOVE POTION

"The very talented Sandra Hill adds to her already impressive list of reading gems with this delightfully funny and sexy tale."

—*Romantic Times*

LOVE ME TENDER

"Leave it to Sandra Hill to take this modern fairy tale and make it a wildly sexy and hilarious romp. Her fans will be delighted."

—*Romantic Times*

SWEETER SAVAGE LOVE

"A fast-paced, sensual yet tongue-in-cheek story peppered with plenty of dynamite dumb-men jokes and riddles. This funny and uplifting read will brighten any day!"

—*Romantic Times*

DESPERADO

"Humorous repartee and a high degree of sensuality mix well in Hill's tale of a wisecracking poor boy and the aristocratic woman he loves."

—*Romantic Times*

SANDRA HILL

HOT & HEAVY

LEISURE BOOKS NEW YORK CITY

A LEISURE BOOK®

July 2005

Published by

Dorchester Publishing Co., Inc.
200 Madison Avenue
New York, NY 10016

ISBN 0-8439-5160-5

Printed in the United States of America.

This book is dedicated with great respect and fondness to my longtime editor, Alicia Condon.

She has worked with me on sixteen books and two anthologies, which is an amazing record in this world of changing editors and disappearing authors. She has given me the freedom to write the most outlandish stories, and her editing has made them better. She bought my first book, which in itself is something for which I will be forever grateful.

This is not the only book I have dedicated to Alicia, but it is the one most special to me.

Thank you, Alicia.

HOT & HEAVY

A life most lordly,
we led, my hall within:
dearth was there never
of noble athelings;
well stocked were our stables
and in state lived we,
had great wealth of gold rings
which we gave to many...

Woman's lot is worsened
...by warriors' recklessness:
the oak's strength is stunted
when stripped are its branches,
the tree will topple
when torn are its rootlets:
in all mayest (man)...
thy own will follow.

—The Greenlandish Lay of Atli

(Translation: Woman is always the sufferer by men's deeds.)

Chapter One

The motley crew . . . and then some . . .

Navy SEAL Lieutenant Ian MacLean looked over his Last Will and Testament . . . and began to laugh.

His policy before any mission required every man on his squad to get his affairs in order. Bills, wills, good-byes, any loose ends. With each subsequent mission, all those things needed to be updated or renewed.

Ian headed the Force Squad that was part of the 8th Platoon in SEAL Team Thirteen at the Naval Special Warfare Training Center in Coronado, California. There was a risk of not returning from any military mission, but his squad's impending Operation Rodent in northern Iraq would be particularly dangerous because it was a silent op, meaning it would not be publicly acknowledged by the U.S. government. Translation: No help from Uncle Sam if they screwed up.

Getting Jamal ben Hassan would be worth it,

though. The notorious terrorist leader and his slimy rat cohorts were hiding out following a recent suicide bombing in Mosul that had killed ten people. The SEALs would gladly risk their lives to bring him in.

That was their job. As an old commander once said, "A ship in the harbor is safe, but it's not what they were built for." The moral: SEALs were trained to be out in the field, facing danger, not dry-docked on base.

There was a time when SEAL teams did a lot of Mickey Mouse jobs while waiting around for active deployment, like security for high-level government big shots. Even MacLean had served a duty billet three years ago as instructor here at Coronado before going active again. Since 9/11 most of them were designated "quick response" teams, on call for duty whenever and wherever a terrorist threat popped up. And the training for SEALs had changed dramatically, too, to meet the times. What used to take months now required three years of training.

"Hey, Mac, come here. Look at those poor fools out there," Petty Officer Justin LeBlanc said from a nearby window in the SEAL headquarters.

Ian got up and walked over. The new SEAL class was doing "sugar cookies" out on the beach. It was a long-standing practice in BUD/S (Basic Underwater Demolition/SEALs) to make the grunts wear full fatigue uniforms and heavy boots or boondockers to run for miles and miles, usually with IBLs (Inflatable Boats, Large) on their heads, but to make the exercise more torturous, the instructors demanded that the trainees intermittently run into the surf, then roll around in the sand, before resuming their runs. To make matters worse today, a gray haze hung over the Pacific waters, which would make it cold despite the heat of a California summer.

"Boy, does that bring back memories," Ian said. "Bad ones. It's been ten years since I was a trainee, but I can still feel the cold, wet and pain like it was yesterday."

"Me, too, but it's only been three years for me."

"The only easy day was yesterday." Ian liked to toss out motivational quotes now and then, but that one was familiar to every SEAL and it usually brought a groan.

"Ain't that the truth?" Cage grinned. "What were you laughing about before?"

"It's like this, Cage." Cage was short for Cajun, which LeBlanc was. "I'm trying to figure out who to leave all my 'worldly goods' to, and, one, my 'worldly goods' aren't all that plentiful. Two, I have no idea who I should leave them to if I get offed. My sister is married to a guy whose family is richer than God. My two brothers will inherit from my old man; I'm on dear ol' Dad's shit list, *again*." Ian shrugged. "It's pitiful, really. I'm thirty-four-friggin' years old with no kids, no wife, no significant other. The perfect Navy SEAL. No strings."

"Except for Sam."

Ian arched his brows at his petty officer. "My beloved cat from hell? Oh, yeah, I'm writing Sam into my will . . . *not!*" Ian smiled inwardly at the mental image of his roommate, who at this very minute was probably reclining on his bed, which was a no-no. Sam was the only thing left behind when his fiancée Jennifer dumped him three years ago . . . the same fiancée who was now a divorcee and having second thoughts about him. *Not going to happen. Only one chance, and you blew it, babe.*

Cage grinned at him. "Would you want them?"

Ian had been so lost in thought that he had no idea what Cage referred to. "What? Cats?"

"No! A wife and kids."

Ian thought for a moment, then grinned back at Cage. "Hell, no!" *Once burned, twice shy.*

That wasn't quite true. Ian did like the idea of kids. He'd come to that amazing conclusion this past weekend when attending a party at Blue Dragon Vineyard, family home to his sister Alison's in-laws. There had been lots of rug-rats scampering about, and one particular toddler who tugged at his heart strings. Who knew that a hardened fighting man like himself could be so touched by a gummy grin? Or a tiny, tiny hand placed in his callused palm? Not that he was planning on doing anything about it, but it was like one of those light-bulb moments, realizing how much he yearned for children of his own.

"Hey, you're better off than I am," Cage said. "I hardly have two dimes to rub together. *Mon Dieu!* Me, I doan even have a gumbo pot, and that's a sacrilege to us Cajuns. Plus, I doan have any family at all . . . 'cept my Maw Maw and Paw Paw."

Ian hadn't intended his remarks to make Cage feel bad and attempted to make up for it by saying, "Yeah, but you have every hottie in the world chasing after you."

"There is that," Cage admitted unabashedly. "You could have hotties, too, if you wanted them. SEAL groupies abound, like crawfish on a willow branch wherever we go."

"Pfff! I'm too old for that crap."

"What? Thirty-four is over the hill now? Talk about! You're only five years older than me."

"Five years is forever in lust land, buddy."

"Are you shittin' me? You lost your lust?"

Ian shook his head at the senselessness of their conversation. "No, I haven't lost my lust. I just don't feel the need to boff every willing person with breasts. You and one-night stands have become synonymous, my friend." *After you've done it several dozen times, Cage my boy, one-night stands lose their appeal. Believe me, you'll find out . . . eventually.* But he wasn't about to reveal his thoughts to the smirking petty officer. Then he'd have to endure a lengthy grilling about those three dozen babes-of-the-one-night-stand, most of whose names and faces he couldn't recall. Just body parts.

"Me, I'm discriminating." Cage actually looked affronted.

Ian laughed.

"Just 'cause a chicken has wings doan mean it can fly."

"What the hell does that mean?"

"Appearances can be deceiving."

Ian laughed again.

"Well, okay, there was that Russian chick, but who knew how potent vodka could be? And besides, I was tryin' to pump info from her."

"More like hump." They both laughed.

"What you need in your life are more *meaningful* one-night relationships," Cage advised.

"What I need is for you not to give me sex advice. Besides, 'meaningful one-night stand' is an oxymoron, if you must know."

"You callin' me a moron?" Cage ducked when Ian threw a crumpled wad of paper at him.

"What are you two talkin' about?" Pretty Boy asked as he came into the room. Lieutenant (jg) Zach Floyd, a former race car driver, had earned the nickname Pretty Boy because he was, frankly, pretty . . . even with the black eye he was sporting today. Prettiness aside, Floyd would be their radio operator on this mission. There wasn't anything the Florida native didn't know about machinery.

"Sex," Cage answered Pretty Boy before Ian could stop him. "That's what we were talkin' about."

Ian put his face in his hands briefly, knowing what would come next.

"What else is new?" Pretty Boy waggled his eyebrows in a manner that probably made women melt. It did nothing for Ian.

"In particular, the lieutenant's loss of lust, bless his heart."

Both men turned to look at Ian then, their eyes on his crotch. *The clowns!*

"Since you love those stupid motivational sayings," Pretty Boy said with a twinkle in his blue eyes, "here's one for you. 'Sex is like a misdemeanor. The more you miss it, the meaner you get.' And, man, you are one mean sonofabitch lately."

Cage groaned. "I doan think I can take *two* teammates quoting corny proverbs."

"You can tell by his skin whether a guy is getting any," Pretty Boy announced with seeming irrelevance, disregarding Cage's remark.

Pretty Boy sure does have a running mouth today. Probably nervousness over this mission from hell.

"And our squad leader is looking mighty pale these days."

Yep, a real blabbermouth!

"Is that really true . . . that you can tell whether someone is sexually active by their skin tone?" asked Geek, who'd come in while they were talking. Merrill "Geek" Good was twenty-four years old but looked fourteen. He was a genius, having received his doctorate at age eighteen, but he knew zip about sex.

"Absolutely," Pretty Boy replied with a straight face. "In fact, sex is one of the safest sports around. It stretches and tones just about every muscle in the body."

Geek looked transfixed with that bit of information, while Pretty Boy and Cage just grinned. Geek would probably be adding it to his computer tonight in a file marked Sex Secrets of Navy SEALs. *Unbelievable!* One time Pretty Boy, under the influence of too much beer, had been pontificating on the G-Spot, and Geek actually thought it was a local bar. *Unbelievable!*

Amazed at the gullibility of some people, Ian offered, "Maybe the Navy ought to eliminate the O-course and just prescribe sex for all the SEAL trainees."

"There's a thought," Pretty Boy said. "Skip the obstacle course and instead provide lots of sex for Navy SEALs. Hopefully kinky . . . to get out the kinks, dontcha know." Then, turning to Geek, he added, "Maybe you should suggest that in a letter to the XO."

Deciding to give Geek a break, Ian quickly said, "Don't you dare."

The other members of the squad started to drift in then, some of them carrying styrofoam cups of steaming coffee, some looking as if they were hung over, and a few like JAM, Jacob Alvarez Mendozo, a former Jesuit priest, who had probably just come from confession. But most of them, even JAM, had probably had their ashes hauled, good and proper, last night . . . or through the night, if they were lucky. For many of them, it was a pre-deployment ritual.

What a scruffy-looking bunch they were! Mostly unshaven. But all of them, himself included, were as physically fit as any man could be. They wore T-shirts, shorts and heavy combat boots. After their final planning session this morning, they would join the SEAL trainees for a ten-mile jog, run the O-course, and do a few rotations of terrorist training over at the Kill House. Having graduated to the teams, or serving on multiple ops, didn't preclude a SEAL from continuing his physical training. In fact, it was required.

A few years back the Navy had relaxed the requirement that SEALs sport the usual "high and tight" military haircuts and that they wear standard uniforms so they could blend in with the indigenous people of foreign countries when they engaged in covert operations. As a result, they usually had long hair . . . at least over the ears. In addition, he and Pretty Boy . . . and now Geek, too . . . often had to dye their hair and eyebrows black. He had reddish-brown hair, Pretty Boy blond and Geek red, which would stand out like neon signs in some places. Some even went farther than that, like JAM, whose black hair was pulled back into a ponytail.

Then there was Ensign Omar Jones. Half Muslim, half Native American, he could pass for an Arab, an Italian, a Hispanic, a Greek or an authentic Indian chief, all of which he had done on numerous occasions. He was an invaluable member of the team, especially for his Arab-language fluency. His hair, too, was pulled into a pony tail. While the others looked as if they'd been up all night, Omar, a linguist and former college professor, was bright-eyed. At thirty-two, Omar shared Ian's lack of appetite for the SEAL groupies. Omar had probably stayed home with his five-year-old daughter, the product of a failed marriage.

"What's with the black eye?" Omar asked Pretty Boy.

Pretty Boy blushed, which was a rare occurrence, and said nothing, which also was a rare occurrence.

Cage spoke for him. "We were at the Wet and Wild last night, and hot-shot Floyd here went up to this Berkeley babe who was wearin' a NOW T-shirt, which shoulda given him a clue." He grinned at Pretty Boy, who gave him the finger, before resuming his tale. "Anyhow, Hot Shot says to her, 'So, you're a feminist, huh?' And she says, 'Yeah, what of it?' And Dumbo here, bless his heart, says, 'Did you hear the joke about the feminist and the Navy SEAL?' After which, she belted him. Did I mention she was built like Queen Latifah?"

Pretty Boy reached over to swat Cage, but he ducked. "It was no worse than your sorry line to that waitress." In an exaggerated Southern drawl, Pretty Boy mimicked Cage, saying, "Honest, darlin', I really am an angel. Those itty-bitty horns on my head are there just to hold my halo on."

"Know what I think?" Cage said, also red-faced now.

"Here's a news flash, buddy. I don't give a pig's ass what you think," Pretty Boy replied and turned his back on his squad mates to talk with Sylvester "Sly" Sims who had just walked up to them. The chief petty officer was a tall, slim black dude from Manhattan who used to model men's underwear for *Esquire* magazine. You'd think he would be considered a girly guy for that modeling gig, but no way! Sly, who'd grown up on the streets of the Big Apple, had joined the SEALs because of his hatred for terrorists. His brother had been one of the many killed on 9/11 in the Twin Towers. Sly was their munitions expert.

The last one to straggle in was Luke Avenil, better known as Slick. An odd bird, Slick was quiet and kept to himself. He was a man with secrets, but a helluva SEAL. Slick had a knack for breaking and entering, a skill presumably learned as a teenager in one juvie hall or other.

Ian went to the podium to get their attention. Once the men were seated and quieted down, Ian asked, "We'll be wheels up at oh-five-hundred tomorrow. Are you men good to go?"

"Hoo-yah!" they all yelled out.

Ian pulled down the map over the blackboard behind him and said, "Let's go over this terrain one more time. First, where we do the HALO drop, then the pickup location."

A communal groan resounded through the room. They'd gone over this map of Iraq a hundred times already. Hell, some of them probably had latitude marks on their eyeballs.

"Iraq is a triangle of mountains, desert and fertile river valley, bounded on the east by Iran, on the north by Turkey, on the west by Syria and Jordan and on the south by Saudi Arabia and Kuwait. It's the mountainous area we'll be hitting."

"Repeat how far the LZ is from the target." Omar was taking notes on a small pad.

"The landing zone is about five miles from Jamal's enclave."

After reviewing the geography one last time, Ian reminded them, "Gentlemen, this is a very important mission. Our goal here is to kill or preferably capture Jamal and the other thugs."

"Did you see this morning's Intel report?" Geek interjected, looking down at the laptop on his knees. "Jamal was bragging on Aljazeera how he and his tangos are now personally responsible for the deaths of five hundred and thirteen men, women and children, and many thousands of injuries, tortures and rapes. All in the name of Allah." Tango was a SEAL word for a terrorist bad guy.

"His death would be a blessing," Sly said in a deadly soft voice. "I hope I get to do the honors."

"No, no, no! The secrets he might spew out during interrogation could be invaluable," Ian cautioned.

"In other words, bring the loser back alive, if possible," Pretty Boy remarked with disgust.

"I cannot emphasize enough how dangerous this op is going to be. In effect, we'll be inserting ourselves into the middle of a rats' nest."

He was not surprised that there wasn't even a flinch at that news.

"Despite the odds, I have confidence in you all, and your SEAL abilities. Remember that SEALs are sent down rough paths, but the Navy, through your training, has provided us with good shoes." Even Ian sometimes cringed at his own motivational sayings.

"Well, holy hell, shoes won't mean squat where

we're going," Omar quipped. "A camel would be more welcome."

They all laughed at the logic of Omar's observation.

"Remember those SEALs who got themselves in hot water a few years back when news photos showed them leading a bunch of Afghan friendlies on horseback," Sly added.

"Yeah, and the Defense Department had a shit fit over it. SEALs are supposed to be water warriors, and we sure as hell aren't supposed to call attention to ourselves. Those hotdogs thumbed their noses at the brass." It was JAM speaking now.

"Hey, those are friends of mine you're referring to as hotdogs," Ian said, smiling.

"Frogs and alligators have it easy," Cage drawled out. "They just eat what bugs them."

"What? You want us to eat terrorists?" Pretty Boy replied.

"Only if they're female," Cage countered, waggling his eyebrows lasciviously.

"What does that mean?" Geek wanted to know.

Laughter rippled through the room.

"Speaking of women," Ian said, "I got an alert from Intel this morning. Jamal's longtime mistress is supposedly with him. If we could nab her, she might have significant information. Plus, Jamal might be smoked out of hiding if we get her first."

They all nodded.

"Her name is Yasmine. Not sure if she's Arab. Maybe Pakistani or Lebanese. Hell, she could be an Eskimo, for all we know."

"I take it we have no physical description," JAM said dryly.

Ian shook his head. "Just that she's thirty or so and extremely beautiful."

"Oooh, I like the beautiful part," Cage said. "Can I interrogate her?"

"Get a life," Pretty Boy told him.

Cage told Pretty Boy something pretty explicit, even for Ian's ears.

Ian would have reprimanded the two of them, but he was willing to give them leeway today. Everyone was nervous. The adrenaline level in the room was sky-high, a mixture of fear and exhilaration in the face of extreme danger.

After their exercises this morning, everyone would break down their weapons, clean and lube them and then go out and test fire them. Despite the joking, this was deadly serious business.

In conclusion, Ian told his men, "Be safe. We're entering their land. We're a small squad . . . only eight men, compared to their dozens."

"Never underestimate the power of stupid people in large groups," Omar commented.

"Besides, we're SEALs, we're at an advantage, no matter the odds," Pretty Boy boasted.

"Hoo-yah!" seven men yelled back at him.

All the SEALs left then, leaving Ian to his own thoughts.

He decided to pray.

(The Norselands, a.d. 1013)

Strong women survive . . .

Madrene Olgadottir, noble granddaughter of Eric Olafsson, once high jarl of Norstead, walked through her great hall, which was filled with hundreds of laughing, drinking men.

She was being led by a neck tether, her hands bound behind her back, a short rope connecting her two ankles.

She was naked.

And she was madder than a hornet caught in a spider web.

She stopped before Steinolf the Vicious, the chieftain who had invaded and captured Norstead and its surrounding estates a sennight past. All her fighting men were gone to Valhalla or scattered to the far mountains awaiting word from her to come back and fight . . . something she could not in good conscience command.

Her family, once huge and powerful, was gone now, and that was the crux of her problem. She'd done her best to hold Norstead intact, even fighting side by side with her soldiers. Many invaders considered Norstead fair game because all the men of the family were gone. But she was strong and stubborn and had held on since the last of her family—her brother Ragnor—died a year past. Until now.

Steinolf hoped to shame her into compliance by parading her through the hall nude. *Hah! I am the daughter of many generations of Viking warriors. I cannot let them down. I cannot let my people down.* Lifting her chin haughtily, she eyed the brute who was staring at her nudity with mild interest, as if she were a piece of meat offered at the high table. She had not been raped . . . yet . . . as many of her kitchen maids and village girls had been, but that was only because Steinolf hoped that she would wed with him. She had been whipped, however . . . repeatedly. Her back would bear scars for the rest of her life, she would warrant, as would her wrists and ankles and neck from the abrasive ropes.

If that weren't bad enough, Steinolf had tried to kill her precious pet cat, Rose, to teach Madrene a lesson. If her hands had been free, she would have throttled the miscreant gleefully for that sin alone, to say nothing of all the sword dew he had spilled amongst her people. Luckily, Rose had escaped and was in the hands of one of the village cotters.

"Kneel, wench, and kiss my boot as a sign of your surrender," Steinolf's deep voice boomed out.

Is the man barmy? She spat on his boot.

The ruffian who held her tether shoved her to her knees, but she refused to lean down to the boot. Instead, she glared up at the monster who had overtaken her keep.

He was a huge man, at least a head taller than she and twice as wide under his fur mantle. His stringy hair was blond and hung down to his shoulders; war braids framed his scarred face.

"Kiss . . . my . . . boot," he repeated in an ominously soft voice.

"Kiss . . . my . . . arse!" Madrene surprised herself by saying. It was an expression she'd heard her brothers use on many an occasion, but one she'd never used herself.

Steinolf's eyes went wide with surprise, but then he threw his head back and laughed uproariously. "Mayhap later," he said when he was no longer laughing.

I wish my brothers were here. They would wipe that lackwit smile right off your face. "I hope you choke."

"You are a feisty one, I give you that. Much joy will I get in breaking your wild spirit."

Madrene rolled her eyes. *Men are such braggarts, always thinking they are so superior. As if the dangly part betwixt their legs gives them greater intelligence. Hah!* "You are a pig, Steinolf. Look at you. Bread crumbs in your beard. Grease stains on your shert. You reek of stale mead and unwashed skin. Methinks you and all your herd of soldiers need a good bath and delousing. You should sleep in the barn at my farmstead, instead of on the clean rushes here at Norstead." Madrene couldn't believe she'd criticized the chieftain so. Ah, well, she was as good as dead anyway. Despite her dire situation, she had to smile. Her father and brothers would hoot with laughter because her nagging spirits couldn't be held back, even when kneeling afore her conqueror stark naked.

Actually, she probably reeked as well, not having been able to bathe this past sennight. The blond braid hanging down her back had been plaited before the assault and was half undone now.

"You find humor in your predicament?" Steinolf asked incredulously.

"I find humor in you." She was getting a kink in her neck from looking up at him.

Instead of running her through with his broadsword as Madrene half expected the man to do, he just studied her, stroking his unkempt beard thoughtfully. "I have heard you are a shrew, no doubt due to the free rein given you by the men in your family. Fools they must have been. Everyone knows that women are meant to serve men, not stab them with their sharp tongues."

Blather, blather, blather. Why don't you just kill me? I have nothing to live for anymore. Oddly, Madrene felt a sense of peace come over her.

"Are you ready to come to my bed furs . . . as my bride?"

Oh, yea, I am ready. Best you keep your manpart away from me. Even if I have to use my teeth, Steinolf, you will have no dangly part by dawn light. "You already have two wives and several concubines. I have been baptized by a Christian monk and do not accept the *more danico* practice of multiple wives." *Why am I attempting logic with such a dolt?*

Anger blazed in his gray eyes. "Wouldst join with me in wedlock if I put those women aside?"

Oh, for Valhalla's sake! Even I, lowly woman that I am, can see that is a ruse. "You would not want me. I am barren, you know. 'Tis why my husband put me aside ten years ago."

She saw surprise on his face before he masked it. "That matters not to me. I have whelps aplenty. What does matter is all your soldiers and housecarls who escaped our battle-axes. They must come back and pledge fealty to my banner. Otherwise, they will be like pesty gnats."

She hated the fact that she was carrying on a conversation naked whilst everyone else was clothed. But she understood Steinolf's reasoning. He hoped to shame her into compliance. It would not work. Madrene valued Norstead and her people more than her pride. She knew without a doubt that her people would be slain once they returned. There was no dishonor at being paraded naked before one and all. The dishonor was on Steinolf and his men for subjecting her, a lady of noble birth, to such humiliation.

In fact, she saw some of them turn their gazes away in guilt. Not Steinolf, though.

"I ask you again. Will you wed with me?" The warrior's impatience was evidenced by his mottled face and clenched fists.

"When all the fjords in the Norselands freeze over," she answered tiredly.

Apparently, this final insult was the last straw for him. He leaned down and backhanded her across her face.

She flinched, and tears welled in her eyes at the pain, but she held her ground, still kneeling upright. "Coward!" she gritted out through the blood that seeped from her cut lip.

"So be it," he said then and motioned for a man to come forward. She recognized Toki the Trader. The poor man, who had oftimes been a guest of her father, Magnus Ericsson, tried his best to avert his eyes from her nakedness. "Take her as far away from here as possible. To the Arab lands. Yea, that is it. Take her to the slave marts and sell her to some lustsome caliph for his harem. Far from her home and the trouble she would surely brew."

The trader gazed with sympathy on Madrene.

Noticing that stare, Steinolf told Toki, "Heed me well, Toki. If I find that you have helped this woman to escape, I will skin you alive and hang your carcass on the ramparts for all to see."

"I will do as you demand," Toki said, and he meant it.

Madrene's spirits sank. As long as she was here, there was hope that she could escape and regain her rightful lands. An appeal to the high king or a gathering of warriors might have been successful. But separated from the Norselands by vast seas, she would be lost.

Should I agree to wed the beast in order to stay here?

Nay, I would rather be dead. Leastways then I can join my much-missed family in the afterworld.

As Toki led her off, she decided that she had only one recourse now. She began to pray.

Chapter Two

Are we having fun yet? . . .

Ian and his SEAL squad were flying in a C-130 over the night skies of northern Iraq. It would soon be daylight.

In the next fifteen minutes they would HALO jump into their insertion point, a small, flat area in the midst of a very hilly region. High-altitude, low-opening exercises always carried some measure of risk, especially in a mountainous region like this, but they were all experienced jumpers. Geek was the only one who hadn't been "blooded," but he'd been as well trained as any of them. A piece of cake!

Even so, there were eight collective sphincter muscles that were tight right now. The pucker factor was sky high. Some people likened it to riding a bucking horse in a rodeo. It took balls to get on the freakin' horse, but then all a cowboy had to do was just hang on. In skydiving, it took a leap of faith to go out that door, but then the ride took over.

A superstitious lot, SEALs did the oddest things for good luck . . . odd to civilians, that is. Instead of a rabbit's foot, Cage carried an alligator tooth in his pocket. Omar did this odd chanting thing under his breath. Pretty Boy ate oatmeal and only oatmeal the morning of a jump. JAM, of course, had a crucifix hanging from his neck, despite regulations that SEALs wear no jewelry, including dog tags; at the last minute he would stash it in his boot. Sly, who swore a blue streak on most occasions . . . effin this and effin that . . . abstained till his feet hit the ground. Slick chewed gum . . . spearmint only. Ian personally insisted that he always be the last guy off the stick.

They wore helmets, breathing masks, night-vision goggles, fingerless Kevlar gloves and jump suits, some of which would be discarded once they completed their insertion. Those items would be hidden from sight till the extraction a day or two from now when a chopper would come and lower rappeling ropes to them. Under their suits, they wore camouflage, and they would cammie up their faces, too.

The oxygen was needed because they would be free-falling through the atmosphere, starting at 25,000 feet and not opening their stealth chutes till they were at about 2,500 feet from the ground. The greatest advantage of HALOs was that they allowed the plane and the teams to pass below the enemy radar.

In full combat ruck, they each carried roughly seventy-five pounds of provisions, everything from top-of-the-line weapons to radio equipment to GPS (Global Positioning System) locators to NVGs (night-vision goggles) to MREs (meals ready to eat).

The noise of the engines precluded any conversation, so, they mostly communicated with hand signals or through headsets fixed to an inter-team channel. Two minutes before they hit the drop zone, the jump master mouthed and at the same time signaled by raising his arm, "Stand up." Then, "Hook up."

The eight of them hooked up to the static line, a cable running the length of the cargo bay. Some of them made the sign of the cross, even those who were not Catholic. They stood practically ass to belly, wanting to go out and land as close as possible to each other.

"Stand in the door!" was the next order. The whole stick shuffled forward and the point man, Cage, stood with palms on the outside edge of the open doorway, feet slightly apart, one foot a little behind the other, legs bent slightly. When the jump master yelled "Go," Cage went out with a wild whoop, immediately followed by Pretty Boy, JAM, Geek, Omar, Sly, Slick and then Ian, who was always the tail.

The plane's engine droned off into the distance. They were on their own now.

Belly dancing was not her thing . . .

After two years and nine different harems, Madrene knew, even if the various caliphs and sultans did not, that she was not cut out to be a houri. And, truth to tell, her belly button wouldn't hold a jewel no matter what they tried.

Women of the harems were supposed to be sweet and beautiful and compliant, none of which described Madrene. And she certainly did not know how to dance, or want to learn, with or without a bloody ruby stuck in her navel. *Yech!* It was silly, really, and she'd told the eunuch teachers so, earning her the first of many switchings with an olive branch. At least those didn't leave scars as Steinolf's leather whips and rope ties had.

She should be insulted that she'd been discarded by one Arab potentate after another. Not so! Although being sold a sennight ago to this bedouin tribe in the Arab mountains after two years of swallowing sand in the Baghdad region was a bit of a blow to her pride. Especially since the men . . . and women . . . here smelled ripe betimes, like the back end of a camel, an animal she had come to loathe. Sheikh Fakhir's large tribe did not follow the Norse practice of frequent bathing; in fact, she'd yet to see one of them set soap to skin. Not like the city Arabs who bathed and perfumed themselves daily, men and women alike. She was less than aromatic herself, being forced to follow the nomadic tribe's practices.

"Tell me again how you came to be here," demanded Zena, Fakhir's fourteen-year-old third wife. Madrene was only his fourth concubine, which meant that Zena could order her about. The little half-brained maggot!

When she'd first arrived in this land, Madrene had been able to speak bits of the Arab language because of the trading she'd done as mistress of Norstead. After living here for two years, she'd become proficient. Thus, she was able to understand Zena's words.

Right now, Zena . . . short and very plump . . . was admiring herself in a piece of polished brass that

Fakhir had given her when she'd pleased him particularly well in his bed rugs. Madrene knew he was pleased because they all slept on rugs in the same tent, all seventeen of the family and workers, and everyone got to hear all of Fakhir's grunts and Zena's squeals of pleasure. *Holy Frigg! You would think a pig was being stuck.*

Instead of obeying Zena's order, Madrene said, "I cannot understand how you can bear to have Fakhir slake his lust on you. What any man needs with three wives and four concubines is beyond my comprehension."

"It is a sign of his wealth," Zena said in her usual condescending manner. If she only knew how ridiculous she looked when she turned up that hooked nose of hers. "You envy me, that is why you speak so disparagingly of my husband."

Oh, yea, I envy sharing bed furs with an old man who has seen at least fifty summers. A repulsive, hairy man who has stomach problems which cause him to break wind at the most inappropriate times. Like during prayers . . . or lovemaking . . . or riding his favorite camel. That was what Madrene thought, but she did not dare share those sentiments with Zena, who would report back to her beloved spouse. Fakhir was already angry with Madrene, feeling that he had been duped in his purchase of an accomplished concubine . . . her. *Ha, ha, ha!*

Zena picked up a date from a wooden bowl and popped it into her mouth. "Entertain me, or I will tell my husband that you displease me. He will have you beaten . . . or something."

It was the "or something" that worried Madrene. While she pondered the threat, she continued to work the wooden churn which would eventually, after great strain to her arms, turn the camel's milk into a loathsome form of butter. Better this than the curdled camel's milk she'd made yesterday, which hung inside the tent in a large leather pouch. To the Arabs' delight and her dismay, one camel, even without drinking any water, could produce five buckets of milk per day.

You'd never know that she was supposed to be a pampered concubine, not that the leisurely life mattered a whit to her. Madrene had run her father's large farmstead for years, and milking a cow had always given her an earthy feeling of satisfaction. Milking a stubborn, spitting camel was a whole other matter!

"Did you hear me, you lazy wench?" Zena whined. "I want to be amused."

Madrene gave Zena a sweeping look that clearly showed which one of them was the lazy wench. Zena totally mistook her survey, and preened as if Madrene had been admiring her.

Madrene sighed at the uselessness of insulting the silly girl. "I come from a noble family in the Norselands," she said, even though she'd told Zena this story in one version or another several times before. "My holding was invaded and I was taken to your Arab lands."

"Why did your family not come to rescue you?"

"They are all dead."

"Ahhhh," Zena said with as much honest sympathy as the empty-headed girl could garner.

"Toki the Trader sold me to Caliph Abdul Abba in the Baghdad marketplace." *An experience I would not want to repeat . . . ever.*

"I have heard of him. Why would such an important caliph be interested in such as you?"

Zena's incredulity should have been insulting, but Madrene was beyond caring about such trivial concerns. All she cared about was escaping, something she'd been unable to do thus far. Besides, her appearance probably *was* dreadful. Her blond hair hung in a single, disheveled braid down her back, not having been washed or combed since she'd left Baghdad. She wore an ankle-length, hooded gunna of coarse linen with a rope belt. She could hardly remember the times when she'd worn embroidered silk and jewels. Well, this garb was better than the transparent garments she'd been forced to wear before coming here. "To answer your question as to why any man of importance would want me, it could be because Toki, the traitor, told everyone in the slave mart that I was a Norse princess, accomplished in the bed arts." *Blather, blather, blather. Betimes my tongue outruns my good sense.*

Zena's little mouth formed a circle of surprise. She did not question Madrene's lineage, having more interest in other matters . . . like sex. "Do you have such talents?"

"Hah! I never noticed any art in the bed furs of Karl, my former husband, and he is the only man with whom I ever coupled. To further enhance my desirability, Toki claimed I could do exquisite things with my mouth, whatever that meant. Needless to say, the bidding was enthusiastic."

Zena frowned with confusion. "You said your former husband was the only man you have lain with. How can that be? Did the caliph not purchase you for his harem?"

"Yea, he did. The slimy weasel! As did the other seven caliphs and sultans who purchased me after that, including your husband, who brought me here."

Zena's dark eyes went wide at that number. Then she resumed frowning. "Does my husband know this?"

"He did not when he purchased me. He does now." Madrene now knew how a man could holler and break wind at the same time.

"Why did those men not use your body? Are you diseased?"

Madrene smiled to herself in remembrance. She had never been one to believe in luck, but that was the only way she could describe all that she had escaped. Oh, her capture by Steinolf had been unlucky, but she had not suffered too badly these two years since. Except that she wanted her freedom. She wanted to return to Norstead. And she would do so . . . somehow, someday. Mayhap she should pray to the Christian Mary, mother of the One-God, and Freyja, the Norse goddess, to deliver her from this wretched land.

"Why are you smiling?" Zena whined. "Are you laughing at me?"

"Nay, I am not laughing at you." *Leastways, not on the outside.* "And, nay, I am not diseased."

"Then continue with your life story . . . and cover that smelly butter. It turns my stomach."

I would like to give you a life story . . . one about a dimwitted maid being knocked over onto her fat buttocks. "That first night I was pampered in Abdul's luxurious home. Abdul's harem girls bathed and perfumed my body and forced me to wear a garment which was so sheer my nipples and nether hair were visible to one and all. I would have run away, but there were always guards about to make sure no one escaped from his harem."

In fact, the same was true today. She could not even go to the bushes to relieve herself without Gadi the goatherder following after her. She glanced over to where he leaned against a tree watching her. He winked at her, and Madrene almost gagged. She feared, with good reason, that Fakhir would eventually tire of her and hand her over to the big man who made no secret of his lust for her. Gadi would take her; willing or not; she just knew he would.

"Go on, and stop daydreaming."

Madrene made a face at Zena, who didn't have the sense to know she was being mocked. "That first night, dressed in those sheer garments, I was led to an opulent room of marble walls, velvet cushions, soft carpets and low tables overladen with food. The room was filled with men only, except for the serving girls. The men reclined on rugs and ate whilst listening to music from a harpist behind the curtains. I was led in front of the men to sit at Abdul Abba's feet, which was apparently a great honor." *If the men in my family, or in my troops, ever lay about on the rushes afore the hearth and demanded that girls on bended knee serve them food, they would have been laughed out of the hall.*

Instead of being repulsed as Madrene was by that image, Zena sighed with yearning.

"Abdul fed me grapes and other delicacies like a lapdog, not allowing me to use my own hands. When he gave me a fig in honey sauce and it dripped down my chin, he and the other men thought that was a great jest. Abdul even drizzled some of it over each of my breasts; that, too, was considered a mirthsome feat." *Men and breasts! Really, what a fuss they make over bodily appendages.*

The giggle that escaped Zena's lips did not amuse Madrene. "And then what happened?"

"Later, they led me to Abdul's bedchamber and disrobed me. There lay Abdul on his silken bed, naked as a newborn babe, with his dangly part . . . well, not dangling." *Whoo! What a sight that was. And hairy balls! I have ne'er seen the same before or after.*

"Huh?"

Madrene rolled her eyes at the thick-headed girl. "His manpart was standing up like a knight's lance. As small as Abdul was in stature, that part of him was . . . well, huge . . . if one was wont to be impressed by such things." *He, for one, certainly thought he was Allah's gift to women.*

"And then?"

"And then I pointed at *it* and said, 'If you dare to put that thing in me, may the gods and goddesses frown down on you and turn your staff to butter.' "

Zena gasped at her temerity.

Madrene had been surprised at her own temerity at the time. She hadn't planned to say what she did; the words just came to her in the moment. Luckily for her, as it turned out.

"Did Abdul's guards smite you down?"

Hell and Valhalla! I am here, lackwit. "Nay. They were too appalled by what they saw. No sooner had I spoken than Abdul's manpart wilted . . . like a lump of butter in the hot sun. And no matter what

Abdul did . . . or what Abdul did to me . . . and no matter how his eunuchs beat me, they could not get his manpart to rise again. Day after day, night after night, they tried, but nothing happened. They swore I had put a spell on his dangly part . . . dooming him to eternal dangling . . . and that is why Abdul sold me to another caliph."

Zena's eyes were wide with wonder, and her lips turned up in a barely suppressed grin. Perhaps she was not as dumb as she appeared. "And the next caliph?"

Madrene shrugged. "Once I realized what men feared most, I had a powerful weapon in my hands. I began to develop a performance, perfecting it with each caliph or sultan to whom I was sold. Not only did I say the words, but I waggled my fingers in the direction of their manparts. Betimes I would hum as I said my curse. 'Uhm, uhm, uhm!' I even twirled about one time whilst cursing, but I tripped and did not try that again."

"That is an amazing story," Zena said, eyeing her with admiration for the first time. But then her eyes narrowed with suspicion. "Did you do the same to my husband?"

"I did." *And, unlike Abdul, his was not huge.*

"And did he wilt?"

Madrene nodded. *Like a candle wick.*

"But he has bedded me since you have come here."

"I told him the curse only involved me, but if he forced me, it would wilt forevermore, with all women. 'Tis the same story I give them all."

"And Fakhir believed you?"

"Listen, Zena, you are young, but there is one

thing you will learn in time. When it comes to their manparts, men will believe anything." *I recall the time a dairy maid told Ragnor that dousing his staff in honey would make it grow thicker. He had every bee from hides around chasing after him.*

"Aren't you afraid I will tell my husband, and your sham will be over?"

"Nay, I am not. Because if you do, and if Fakhir takes me as his concubine, and if I please him, then it will be I who gets the trinkets, not you."

Zena studied her for a long moment. "Mayhap I will wait before disclosing your secret."

Smart girl!

Later that evening, after evading Gadi's lusty hands on several occasions—he was getting bolder and bolder—Madrene found herself on her knees outside in the bushes where she was supposed to be taking care of her bodily needs. "Dear God . . . father of the Christ whom my grandmother worshiped . . . I beg you for your help. Two long years have I suffered. Please deliver me from this captivity." It was a prayer Madrene had said on many an occasion, and she no longer had much hope. Still, she felt compelled to try.

But then, loud claps of thunder shook the skies and the earth trembled and quaked. The wind rose with a vengeance. Fakhir's tribe was running hither and yon, screaming with dismay as the skies opened with loud explosions of sound . . . thunder and lightning as she'd never seen before.

This is your chance, a voice in Madrene's head said.

She looked up at the roiling skies. Stunned, she whispered, "Thank you, God." Then, lifting her robe up to her knees, she ran and ran, off into the hills.

The skies continued to explode with light and sound. Madrene ran till she could run no more, a pain throbbing in her side, her breath coming in pants. For more than an hour she ran, even though she heard no one following her. They would eventually.

She saw a cave up ahead and knew she had to stop and rest. Settling into the darkened chamber, which was luckily empty of any wild animal, Madrene laid her head down to rest. She was not back home, not even close to Baghdad, where she might find a Norse longship willing to take her back to Norstead, but for the first time in three years, she felt safe.

A deep sleep overtook her then, and in her dreams she floated and floated and floated.

I'm fallin' for you, baby . . .

The entire team landed flat on their feet, their legs acting as springs to absorb the shock.

They dropped, rolled over and got up quickly. Then they collapsed their stealth chutes, balled them up and ran at a crouch toward a nearby stand of bushes. Within minutes they removed their helmets and jumpsuits, buried them and their chutes under a pile of leaves and rocks, then cammied themselves up. Later, they would also put on black balaclava hoods with only their eyes showing, but the hoods were hot and not necessary yet. Some of them wore floppy hats. Others, like JAM and Omar, pulled their hair up under an olive drab, triangular bandana tied behind their heads. They all wore night-vision goggles, or NVGs, which wouldn't be necessary much longer since the sun was starting to come up.

Pretty Boy carried state-of-the-art Motorola SATCOM radio equipment in his backpack. The satellite-based communication system, with its ability to encrypt messages, provided instant contact with anyone in the world, thanks to the Milstar satellite. Thus they were able to communicate with the chain of command at NavTel, at CentCom in Baghdad and SEAL headquarters in Coronado. In addition, for inter-team communication, each of them carried short-range Motorola radios with belt packs, lip mikes and ear pieces.

Each of them had infrared American flags on their sleeves which could only be seen with night-vision goggles. It was a good method for recognizing each other in the darkness of a covert operation.

All his men were geared up with a full loadout of weapons and ammunition. Many of them carried Colt M4 carbine rifles with all the bells and whistles of Special Operations Peculiar Modification (SOPMOD) accessories.

Ian had an assault rifle in a sling over one shoulder, a Beretta handgun in a low-slung holster on his thigh, and a K-Bar knife in his boot. They all carried two sets of flexible plastic handcuffs to secure their prisoners . . . a bit of optimism there. JAM, their sharpshooter, also carried an MK11 which could take a tango out at one thousand yards. And, of course, they all wore assault vests and hard body armor.

Ian looked over each of his men. Satisfied that they were as prepared as they were going to be, he said, "Okay, let's party! Go, go, go!"

With those words and a directional signal from Geek, who had a compass and GPS in hand, they moved off silently toward their target zone five miles away, where they were to find the terrorists, take them by surprise, and capture and secure them for the extraction to Baghdad for interrogation. In the most successful military operation, no shot was fired. Ian could only hope that would be the case this time, but reality suggested that lethal force would be necessary.

They progressed in "leapfrog" movements, whereby two SEALs alternately covered each other's advance . . . one crouched and covering his partner till he moved forward, and the second took his turn. Ian was up front, leading the way.

They were silent as shadows, barely discernible even to themselves. Every item of gear on their bodies had been taped down or padded. Not a sound could be heard. Not the crunch of their boots underfoot. Not the rustle of clothing. Not even breathing. SEALs were so attuned to each other that they even knew each other's scent.

When they'd traveled about a half mile, Ian stopped and put up a halting hand. His men looked at him. "Some movement up that hill. I'll go check," he said softly into his throat mike. "Go ahead. I'll catch up." It was probably just a small animal, but just in case, he pulled the safety off his weapon, ready to fire if necessary.

"You sure I shouldn't go?" his partner, Cage, asked.

Ian thought a moment. A squad leader really shouldn't leave his men, but they were far from the target zone and unlikely to meet any tangos in this kind of terrain. "Okay, you stand watch down here. Don't come up unless I direct you to."

Cage nodded.

"JAM, you take over till I catch up."

"Roger," JAM replied.

When his other men were out of sight, gone about ten minutes, he spoke softly into his headset, "Any problems?"

"Negative," someone answered. Sounded like Sly.

"Nothing here, either," Cage said.

Ian crept up the hill slowly, hiding behind a bush every couple steps to inspect the area. Nothing. But wait. That looked like a cave up there. Into his mike, he whispered again, "Cave. Going in."

"Watch your back," Cage whispered back.

Stepping into the dimness of the silent cave, Ian made sure the safety was still released on his rifle. Too late he sensed a presence behind him at the cave opening. He glanced over his shoulder and saw a figure in a long robe with a rock raised high in two arms. A woman! Surprise . . . the enemy of any soldier . . . caused him to hesitate. A huge mistake. Pain hit him in the back of the head like a hammer to the skull, and he fell forward to the ground.

After that, there was only blackness.

Chapter Three

Playing possum . . .

Ian blacked out for only a second, but he remained still, flat on his stomach, arms stretched forward, one hand holding his assault rifle. He deliberately kept his eyes closed to bare slits.

He waited while the woman circled him tentatively, checking for signs of life, he would guess. First, she toed him in the side to see if he would move, which he didn't. Then the nutcase pinched his buttock . . . as if that would cause him to move. He barely felt a thing.

He'd only got a brief glimpse of her before being struck, but, man, she was some kind of wild thing. She would scare the bejesus out of someone in the dark, for sure. Plus, she reeked to high heaven.

He could easily jump her now, but decided to wait and see what she was up to. More important, who she was, out here in the middle of Arab nowhere.

"Cat Two to Cat One. Contact? Contact? Cat Two to Cat One." Cage kept saying into Ian's earphone.

When in hostile territory, real names were not used over radio lines which could be intercepted. Since this was Operation Rodent, the members of Ian's squad had named themselves Cat One, Cat Two and so on. The upper chain of command had names of well-known cats, such as Garfield and Sylvester. It was a joke among the teams that none of the flag ranks would take the name Puss, as in Puss in Boots.

When the woman moved to his legs, he whispered into his throat mike. "Cat One here. Do you read? I'm okay."

"Roger. I'm watchin' your six. Need help?"

"Not yet. Woman here. Watch for others. Alert team."

"Did you say something?" the woman shrieked, coming back to his head area.

He made a soft groaning noise to cover up. Then went back to silence.

"Bloody hell, I'd best hurry afore he wakens," the woman said in an odd accent.

Ian decided to play possum for a while to see what was up.

My cave is your cave, honey . . .

Madrene started to drag the man farther into the cave by his outstretched arms. He was still face-down.

"Loki's lips!" she swore under her breath. "He must weigh as much as a warhorse. Must be I am weakened by my escape . . . and lack of food." In the end, it took her a considerable time to pull and shove his large body, huffing and puffing the whole while.

The villain appeared to be as tall as the men in her family. Lean, but well muscled. Instead of Arab garb, an odd fabric covered his wide shoulders, narrow waist and long legs. It was a mixture of browns, green and blacks . . . a combination that would blend well in a wooded area. His hands were covered with fingerless gloves. In one of those hands had been a strange, molded object made of iron or some similar product; it had slipped from his fingers when she'd started tugging. Was it a club?

I should just kill him, one part of her said.

Yech! the other part countered.

It would be done in self-defense . . . of a sort, her hardened side argued.

Hmpfh! Killing is killing.

Mayhap I will kill him later.

Yea, later is good.

Madrene had no idea why she hesitated. She had killed in the past. She was not proud of the fact, but it had become a reality of her life after being left alone to safeguard Norstead. Fighting men needed a leader, and she'd been forced to take on that role. But usually it had been done to save her life or that of one of her *hird* of soldiers. She sighed with resignation. She needed to know more about this man before dispatching him to the afterworld.

Was he one of Fakhir's men, come to take her back for punishment? If so, he would merit death. Or some other man with ill intent? Then, too, he would merit death.

What a fool I am! I should have killed him outright. But she could not bring herself to do so until she discerned his intent. It was a weakness of hers, she supposed. Her father and brothers would not have hesitated.

I should turn him over and see if he has any hidden weapons. Nay, I must needs restrain him first lest he awaken. With quick efficiency, she removed the large cloth pouch with shoulder straps off the man's back. Then she tore two long strips from the hem of her robe, thus leaving it only mid-calf length. Wrenching the man's arms behind his back, she bound his wrists tightly. She did the same for his ankles. After that, she went outside the cave to survey the area for any of his comrades that might be lurking about. There were none. She swept the ground with a leafy branch to hide his footprints.

When she came back inside, she saw that he still lay face-down in the same spot. She rolled him over with a bare foot.

"Eeeeek!" she screamed. It was a monster she had captured. Not only was his face black, with only his eyelids and lips showing white, but there was an appendage coming out of his ear and around his face to rest in front of his mouth, like a grasshopper. A man-beast, that was what he must be. A troll. She had heard of such in the sagas spun by the skalds of old, but never believed in them. Till now.

Bending over, she touched a fingertip to his cheek and saw that some of the black came off. *Ahhh. Face paint, like the Scottish warriors wear when going into battle. So, this must be a soldier of some sort. A troll-soldier. Hmmmm.*

Just then, his eyes shot wide open, which made his appearance even more bizarre, with the whites of his eyes surrounded by all that black. He tried to lurch upward but soon realized that he was restrained hand and foot.

She jumped backward, just in case.

He let himself fall back to the ground and looked up at her. He seemed just as surprised and repulsed at her appearance as she was at his. "Jesus, who are you?" he asked.

English. The troll-man spoke the Saxon English. *Just my luck to be saddled not only with a troll, but a bloody Saxon as well.* "Nay, I am not Jesus," she replied. The man's head wound must have rendered him senseless.

"Jes . . . what?"

"I . . . am . . . not . . . Jesus," she said, very slowly, so he could comprehend her meaning.

"Holy hell! I know you're not Jesus. Who are you?"

"Madrene," she said, before she could hold her tongue. 'Twas not wise to give the enemy too much information.

"Yasmine?" he repeated, mishearing her. His eyes went wide with wonder.

"Yea, that is who I am. Yasmine." *What a dolt!*

Narrowing his eyes, he reverted to the Arabic tongue and asked, "Are you Yasmine?"

"I already said I was," she snapped back, also in Arabic. *A double dolt, that is what I have here.*

"You speak Arabic." The troll-man smiled then, which made him look almost appealing, and at the same time ridiculous in that black face with white eyes and teeth. "Sonofabitch! Talk about wandering in a field of shit and landing in a gold mine," he muttered to himself.

"What is *your* name?" she inquired in English, a language which came easier to her tongue than the Arabic, since it was more like her own Norse.

He hesitated, then disclosed, "Ian MacLean."

"A Scotsman! I should have known," she said, throwing her hands up with disgust.

"What's wrong with a Scotsman?" he asked, working himself into a sitting position, then wiggling his arse back so his head rested against the cave wall, his long legs outstretched.

"Hah! Sneaky thieves, that's what they are. Always stealing cattle and such. And they eat that horrible haggis."

He shook his head as if he couldn't believe what she was saying. Betimes she had that effect on men. "Are you the one who knocked me out?"

She nodded.

"Why?"

Questions, questions, questions! Does everything have to have an explanation? She shrugged. "Every soldier knows to take the offensive. Attack before being attacked."

"You, a soldier?" he scoffed.

"Betimes." *I should have knocked him harder.* She could tell that her answer surprised him.

"What makes you think I would have attacked you?"

Now, that is a silly question. "You were carrying a club."

"Huh?"

She pointed to the iron object.

"That's a weapon, for chrissake. An assault rifle, to be precise."

Madrene hadn't a clue as to what he'd just said.

"Let me go," he demanded.

Does this man truly not understand that I am the one in charge here? "Are you demented? Nay, I will not release you. In fact, I am thinking about killing you."

He arched his eyebrows. "What's stopping you?"

How do I know? "That is not for you to know."

He seemed to accept her answer . . . for now.

The man is extremely calm, considering his position. "Are you not fearful of death?"

He pondered her question a moment. "I'm not afraid to die . . . but I don't want to."

A logical answer, she decided.

"Your English sounds . . . odd," he remarked.

"Nay, *your* English sounds odd."

"Now that we have established that we're both odd, what is that ungodly stink in here?" He sniffed several times, then looked pointedly at her.

Her face heated with embarrassment. "Well, you would smell, too, if you had not bathed in more than a sennight, especially in this heat," she said indignantly. In truth, her underarm scent was enough to turn her own stomach.

"A sennight? What's a sennight?"

"Seven days."

"Why didn't you just say a week?"

"Huh? Were you sent by Fakhir?"

He frowned in confusion and repeated back to her, "Was I sent to fuck her?" Then, "Fuck who?"

"Oh, you vulgar beast! I said Fakhir, not . . . that other word."

He smiled again.

And Madrene felt an odd flutter in her stomach, not unlike butterfly wings. She supposed it must be hunger pangs.

Just then, she could swear she heard talking coming from his ear/mouth appendage accompanied by a sort of buzzing noise. Rather like a bee buzz, she decided. He really was not human, then. "Are you a bug?" she blurted out. The buzzing, as well as the talking, stopped.

"No, I'm a SEAL."

"That is ridiculous." *I'd better watch him closely. The blow to his head must have turned him barmy.*

"No more ridiculous than asking me if I'm a bug."

Should I just humor the man? "Where is your glacier? Did it melt in this excessive heat? Ha, ha, ha."

"I am not a bug. I am a SEAL," he said, not at all amused by her little jest.

I have had enough of this nonsense. The lackwit is trying to make me out the fool when it is clear that he fits that description better than I. "You buzz like a bee. You have a buglike appendage sticking out of your ear. You're ugly as a . . . bug."

"Are you for real?"

"What? You think you are dreaming me? Methinks you might be an idiot."

"There's only one idiot here, and it's not me." He exhaled with a whoosh as men are wont to do when women have outwitted them. "Have you ever heard the proverb 'Silence is golden'?"

"Are you saying I talk too much?"

"If it walks like a duck and talks like a duck, it must be a duck."

"Is that another proverb? If so, it is lackwitted."

"I like proverbs, and that's a very good one. By the way, how long have you been living in this cozy cave?"

"Since this morn," she answered.

"Are you alone?"

"Dost see anyone else here?"

He bared his teeth at her sarcasm. "Does anyone else know about this cave?"

"I hope not."

"Why are you here?"

"I am running away." *Now, why did I tell him that? Why am I telling him anything?*

"From whom?"

"That bloody Arab who calls himself my master." *My tongue must have a mind of its own.*

"Really? That's interesting. So, you're not with him by choice?"

"Of course not. Do I look like a harem houri?"

"Not like any whore I've ever seen." He gave her a sweeping head-to-toe scrutiny, and it was not complimentary. Her grimy feet and exposed calves got special attention.

"I do not appreciate your insult." She put a hand to her head. Her hair must look like a haystack.

"What insult?"

"Calling me a whore."

"Hey! I'm not the one who mentioned a whore first."

She tilted her head before understanding came to her. "You halfbrain! I said houri, not whore."

He grinned then. "Someone tried to make you into a harem girl?"

The oaf! Apparently he'd known what a houri was all along.

"Pfff! Nine men tried these past three years. None succeeded. I have developed a knack for making a sultan's manpart wilt. So, best you not try any of that bedplay with me." *If I had a needle and thread, I would sew my mouth shut. Be quiet, Madrene. He is quite possibly an enemy. Stop giving him information.*

His jaw went slack with astonishment. "This is the most incredible conversation I've ever had with a woman. Let me get this straight. You escaped from some Arab sultan, and—"

"The last one was a sheikh." It was a flaw in her personality that she always needed to correct mistakes.

"You escaped from an Arab sheikh, in fact nine different Arab sheikhs—"

"Three were sultans, two were caliphs."

"Stop interrupting."

"Interrupting is one of my talents, or so the men in my family always complained."

She could swear she heard laughter coming from his appendage.

He exhaled with exasperation, just like her father used to do when she nagged him endlessly. "You escaped from nine different Arabs who tried to make you their harem girl, and you were passed from one to the other because you can make their cocks wilt."

"Precisely." She smiled at him before she caught herself, then frowned some more.

"How did you wind up with the first . . . sultan?"

"Ah, that is a long and painful story."

He glanced at his bound legs. "It doesn't appear as if I'm going anywhere soon."

"I am a noblewoman in my own country."

"You're not Arab?"

"Nay." Why he was surprised she could not say. Surely she did not resemble Arab women, not with her light hair and fair skin. Mayhap her complexion had darkened during her sojourn in this land.

"Where *do* you come from?"

Once again, she cautioned herself not to disclose

too much information. She thought a moment and then said, "The Rus lands."

"You're Russian?" Shock showed on his face, and he muttered something about the Pent-dragon going to be interested in that information.

One thing stood out in his mutterings. The word *dragon*. Yea, he must indeed be a troll who lived in the land of dragons.

Just then, there appeared to be a lot of chatter coming from his appendage.

"Lower the volume on my headset," he ordered her.

"Huh? Who are you to give me orders?"

"My headset—turn it down, dammit."

"Why do you want me to turn down the set of your head? Does it hurt?"

"Adjust the frickin' volume, here, near my ear." He jerked his head, indicating the part of the appendage that came out of his ear.

Peering closer, she decided it might not be a part of his body, but a part of that thing in his ear. But she was taking no chances. "Nay. It might bite me."

"Bite you? I have landed in a loony bin. No, bite me!" he said with chagrin. If his hands were free, he would probably be tearing at his hair as her father had been wont to do on occasion when exasperated with her. She guessed she knew what his expression meant. 'Twas like Askil the Angry, who used to say "Eat my nose!" when he was especially angry.

"Bite me? Is that another of your ridiculous sayings?" She raised her chin haughtily and said something she never in her old life would have dared say. "Nay, I will not bite you. Bite *me!*" She felt herself blush like a young maid.

His brown eyes—and, yes, she could see in the

dim light from the cave's opening that they were brown as clover honey—almost bulged with astonishment. She was astonished herself and wished she could take the words back, especially since she belatedly suspected a different meaning to those words. But she was ne'er one to back down once she'd taken a stand.

"You are priceless, sweetheart," he said and began to laugh . . . and laugh . . . and laugh.

"Mayhap I will kill you after all," she said.

The brute continued to laugh.

Caving in . . .

Ian took one last look at the screwball in front of him, then turned his attention back to his headset, which was staticky for a couple seconds more. That was why he'd wanted her to lower the volume.

"Cat One here. I say, Cat One. Do you read me?"

"Damn, where've you been?" asked Pretty Boy, who carried the satellite radio equipment. From his hushed voice it was obvious he was in a position where stealth was required. In fact, Ian could hear gunfire in the background.

"What's your position?"

"We set up a perimeter about half a mile from the target. Cat Three and Cat Four"—meaning JAM and Sly—"went in for a look-see. There are hostiles coming and going . . . at least three dozen. No Big Rat yet, but he's there. I'd bet my . . . uh, tail he is."

"What's the gunfire I hear in the background?" Ian recognized the stuttering sound of an AK-47 and other rifle fire.

"A couple of jerk-offs doing target practice. Guess

they're bored. They appear to be waiting for something . . . or someone."

"How about munitions?"

"A stockpile. Everything from Uzis to rocket-propelled grenades."

"Hmmm. Did you alert Garfield?" General Adams at CentCom was Garfield.

"Yep. Will fill you in later." Which meant, in person, or when they had a more secure line. "Seems there's some intel that a big-time roach is coming in, even bigger than the Big Rat." Roach was code for Al Qaeda. "They figure we can nab the whole bunch at one time."

"That's just sweet. Rats *and* roaches. What do they think we are? Supercats?"

"Nope. Just frogs." SEALs were traditionally known as frogmen from the old days.

Ian grinned. "Same thing. Both super."

"Yeah," Pretty Boy agreed. Ian guessed he was smiling, too.

"Should we come rescue you?" Pretty Boy asked, laughter in his voice. Apparently, not just Cage, but all the guys had been listening in on his conversation with the wild woman, or as much as they'd been able to overhear.

"In a while. For now, tell the other cats to hold their position till I tell you to come back here to the bat nest for further orders." He hoped that Pretty Boy understood that he meant *cave* when he mentioned bat nest. "Tell Cat Three to continue as point man in my absence."

Pretty Boy must be wondering why Ian, leader of this squad, wasn't planning to join them immediately. Instead, he asked, "What bat nest?"

"The one I pointed out to you cats near our drop."

"Ahhhh. Are you sure you're not in any trouble?"

"I am in a little bit of trouble."

"A little bit?" Yasmine exclaimed from across the cave. He'd almost forgotten she was here, but there she stood, hands on hips, tapping her filthy foot on the dirt floor. You'd think she was some kind of friggin' princess, instead of a straggly-haired harridan. "You are in *big* trouble, I assure you."

"What's going on?" Pretty Boy asked.

"I'm in the bat nest near our drop zone, like I said, and I've got a . . . um, friend here."

"Are you referring to me? I beg to differ. I am not even close to being your friend," Yasmine squawked. The woman did like to talk a lot.

"Are you sure you don't need backup?" Concern resonated in Pretty Boy's voice.

"Nope. Nothing I can't handle."

"You'd better not be planning to handle me. Dare to touch me and I will lop off one of your body parts." Her voice was getting shriller and shriller.

Man, she is a bloodthirsty wench. No wonder she and Jamal are lovers.

Not surprisingly, Yasmine continued to prattle on. "Why are you talking to yourself?" She stepped closer, but not too close, to see what he was about. "I knew a man once who talked to himself . . . Dar the Dumb. He was demented. Are you demented? Huh? Huh?"

"So what's with the pussycat?" Pretty Boy inquired.

"That's debatable . . . whether she's a pussy . . . cat, or not." Ian chuckled.

"Oooh, I am getting closer and closer to killing you," she said.

"Get this," he told Pretty Boy. "She just might be the Big Rat's cheese. And she speaks Arabic."

"Oh, my God! You hit paydirt?"

"In spades."

"Is she as beautiful as the intel said?"

He looked over at the glaring woman, who seemed to think he was talking to himself. She must have been totally cloistered all her life not to recognize a headset . . . or kept in some harem, like she claimed. But no, no way was this chick ever selected for a harem. She was tall, probably five-ten. Her long, dirty hair, which stuck out every which way, was a nondescript color because it was so stringy and greasy . . . probably a mousey brown. Her eyes were pretty, though, sort of an icy blue. And her mouth . . . holy shit! . . . why hadn't he noticed her mouth before? Angelina Jolie had nothing on her in that department. But even with that mouth, she was not a babe by any means. He laughed and answered Pretty Boy, "Beautiful is not the word I would use."

"Are you talking to yourself about me?" she demanded to know. "If you are, stop it."

He just waggled his eyebrows at the shrew.

"I could put a gag on you," she warned.

"Sonofabitch!" Pretty Boy said. "Did I just hear her say she was gonna put a gag on you? How could she do that?"

"Because she knocked me out with a rock and tied me up . . . ankles and hands."

Pretty Boy must have heard the amusement in his voice because he laughed.

Ian still had the K-Bar in his boot and could slit his ties at any minute. He preferred to wait for the right time.

"You're going to get laid tonight, aren't you?" Pretty Boy accused him. "That's not fair."

"I don't think sex is on this puss's agenda."

"You can be certain of that," Yasmine said hotly. "And remember what I said about my talent." She waved her fingers toward his crotch.

"Wait till I tell the other guys about this," Pretty Boy said. "You're the only one on this squad who isn't horny enough to bang any babe in sight . . . well, almost the only one . . . and of course you're the one who gets the prize."

"Listen, she's no prize. In fact, she says she's been kicked out of nine harems because—"

"*Harems?*" Pretty Boy sputtered.

"—because she claims to have a talent for turning hard-ons into wet noodles."

"Hasn't anyone told her it's supposed to be the other way around?" Pretty Boy chuckled and said something to one of the guys who must have come up beside him. "You won't believe . . ." was all Ian heard.

He glanced over at Yasmine, who was crouching down and fiddling with his backpack, unable so far to undo the clasps. There were things in there he did not want her to see. "Gotta go," he said hurriedly. "Tell Garfield and Sylvester who I have and ask for further orders. She says she was being held against her wishes. Maybe she can be offered asylum in return for some information. On the other hand, she might be lying through her teeth."

"Got it. Over and out."

"So, sweetheart," he drawled out then, causing her to stand quickly and look down at him suspiciously, "wanna play a game?"

Chapter Four

She-bang, she-bang . . .

Madrene shot the warrior-troll her "You-are-an-idiot" look—the one she'd often used with her father and brothers when they did something particularly halfbrained, as men were wont to do.

He just grinned at her, as if she would melt at one of his smiles. *Hah! That will never happen, even if he does have an engaging smile. Too bad it is ruined by his black face and arrogant attitude.* "What kind of game?"

"The Exchange Game."

She raised her brows in question. *What kind of fool does he think I am?*

"I tell you a secret. You tell me a secret. It'll be fun."

Fun? That is a word I no longer know . . . if I ever did. She narrowed her eyes at him. "Why would you want to play such a game with me? And why, pray tell, would I be interested in playing games with you?"

"To gain something you want?"

"Pfff! There's nothing I want but to get to Baghdad."

"See. I could take you to Baghdad."

"You could?" *Have a caution, Madrene. It is no doubt a trick.*

He nodded.

"How? Do you have a camel nearby?"

He laughed. "Nah! A bird will be coming for us tomorrow."

"Are you mocking me?"

"Me? Uh-uh! You will be in Baghdad tomorrow, that I can almost guarantee."

One day to Baghdad? Even a fast camel could not get us there so quickly, let alone a bird. Even so . . . "And what would you want in return?

He smiled.

Oh, now I understand. Another randy male looking for a nest for his dangly part. My nesting days are over. "I am *not* going to couple with you. So forget about that."

"Lady, let's understand one thing. I have absolutely no interest in sex *with you*. Don't reject what hasn't been offered."

His obvious disdain for her rankled Madrene, not that she wanted him to be attracted to her. Still, no woman liked to think she was repulsive. "I have nothing to offer in exchange." *Well, I do have that navel gem which I pilfered last year from Sheikh Yasir . . . and, all right, there are those nine other jewels I happened to pick up from the others . . . but I am not about to give any of them to the likes of you.*

"Yes, you do."

He could not have discerned the large stones which she'd sewn into her sleeves. Could he? "And that would be?"

"Information."

Whew! "Information about what?"

"Your . . . uh . . . master."

Huh? The man really is demented. I would tell him all about Fakhir without any recompense. "He was not my master, he just thought he was. No man is my master. Besides, he has three wives and three concubines to call him master or whatever the bloody hell he wants to be called."

"Three wives and three concubines? No shit?"

"There is no need to be vulgar."

"Sorry. Concubine? That's an outdated word, dontcha think?" He shrugged, as if it didn't matter, which it didn't.

"I was the fourth concubine, or so he planned when he purchased me. That is, until—"

The dolt grinned and finished her thought. "—until you waved your magic fingers and lowered his flag."

That is one way of describing that thing. "Yea. Plus I have added other things to my bedchamber performance."

"Like?" His lips twitched with mirth he did not even attempt to suppress.

The loathsome lout! "Spinning about three times whilst waggling my fingers in the direction of . . . well, you know. And I hum. Uhm, uhm, uhm."

"This is unbelievable," Ian—that was the name he had given her—said. "Then what happened?"

"Since he couldn't swive me with his dangly part, he gave me work to do. For the love of Frigg! I had to milk his bloody camels. Believe you me, that was almost as bad as bedding the old bag of wind. Camels are not pleasant creatures, you know. They spit and snap and snort and smell. Like men. That is part of what you smell on me. Camel spit."

The troll's jaw dropped practically to his chest at her long discourse. "He's old. How old? For some reason, I thought he was fairly young. You called him a bag of wind. Odd way to describe your lover."

"Aaarrgh! Did you not hear me say I never coupled with the maggot? And, yea, he is old. He has seen more than fifty winters, I would guess. Mayhap even sixty."

"Hey, fifty isn't old. I'm thirty-four myself. How old are you?"

"Thirty-one and do not dare make a jest about my being so old my female parts have no doubt dried up." *Which they probably have.*

His mouth dropped open again.

Good thing there are no flying insects in here.

"Did someone actually say that to you? Never mind. Don't answer. You do know that the rumor mill has it that the two of you have been lovers for years?"

"That is the thing about rumors. They are rarely true. First, I have only been here one sennight. Two, I have had no lover since my husband put me aside ten years ago. Three, if I were going to take a lover, it would not be a crude man who breaks wind constantly, day and night."

"You were married? To whom?"

How like a man to home in on the least relevant thing I said! "To Karl Ivarsson, if you must know. And that is all I will say on the subject."

"About that farting thing . . . maybe the tango has a stomach ailment. Hmmmm. That's one thing we didn't know about him."

"What's a tango?"

"A terrorist. A bad guy."

Then say what you mean, troll. Calling a bad person a

tango . . . dumb, dumb, dumb. "He does strike terror in those around him. Not me, though."

"Of course not. You are such a brave woman."

Is there perchance a rock nearby that would fit in his mouth? "I find your sarcasm insulting. I am not talking to you anymore." She walked away from the beast and picked up the metal object.

"No!" he hollered.

Is my prisoner daring to order me about . . . again? Incredible! She turned her head, holding the object in her right hand. He seemed very upset that she would touch his . . . thing. *Hmmm. Does it have some special value? Mayhap there is a gem in there.* She held the metal part to her face and peered into the barrel.

"Oh, damn! Put . . . the . . . gun . . . down!" he yelled.

"You are going to burst a vein in your forehead if you are not careful. You remind me of my father the time he suffered under an absurd vow of celibacy. Grouchy all the time, he was."

"Gun! Down!" he demanded.

Of course, she held it all the higher. "What is a gun?"

"A weapon, you fool."

"Well, it could be a weapon . . . a club wielded to inflict bodily harm."

"A cl . . . cl . . . club," he sputtered.

As she continued to handle the . . . gun, he threw himself down on his side and took a knife out of his boot with his hands, even though they were tied behind his back. He starting sawing at the cloth that bound his feet.

Madrene was caught off guard. At first. "Nay, you will not escape from me." She started to rush back and take the knife from him, but when she dropped the club . . . uh, gun . . . to the ground, the air around them exploded with the loudest noise she'd ever heard. Like a thousand strikes of lightning all at once. Dust and rock shards flew from the area near the cave opening where the loudest part of the explosion seemed to take place. Apparently, the weapon had been aimed that way when it dropped. Her gunna protected most of her body, but some of the bits of rock hit her exposed face, and she could feel blood running there. But Ian . . . oh, my gods! Was he all right?

When the dust settled, she saw her prisoner, who was apparently not a prisoner anymore. He stood with hands on hips, pieces of rag dangling from his wrists and boots. And he was glaring at her.

"I guess it was not a club," she said weakly. "How was I to know it was a magic stick?"

"I told you it was a gun," he said with cold fury and started to walk toward her.

She backed up toward the cave opening. "And how was I to know what a gun does? I know what a gunna is, of course, but ne'er have I heard of a gun. Stop frowning at me. It makes you even uglier. And if I were you, I would worry about that big vein in your forehead."

With every step he took forward, she took a step back. Forward, back, forward, back. Once she was outside the cave, she took off like a deer, running as fast as her bare feet would take her . . . which wasn't far. He threw himself in the air and caught her ankles. They both went down with a thud, faces in the dirt.

Then he turned her over onto her back and lay on top of her. Before she could understand what he was about, he put white arm rings on each of her wrists. At first, she was puzzled that he would give her jewelry, but she soon realized they were not adornments, but objects that would restrain her, much as her cloth ties had restrained him. Only then did she look up at the troll-man.

His eyes were hard. His lips a thin line of anger. Blood drizzled from various cuts on his face and neck. But all he said was, "Gotcha!"

When trolls go trolling . . .

The first thing Ian did was signal Cage to back off.

Of course, Cage had run to his aid when he'd heard the gun fire. Luckily, Jamal and his cohorts were five miles away and couldn't hear. Cage stood ten yards or so behind the woman, grinning. The shrew couldn't see him there. "Go," he mouthed.

Cage left, still grinning.

"Get your bloody damn body off of me, troll!"

Not bloody damn likely! "No, I don't think so," Ian said, laughing despite his anger. The witch could have killed them both with her carelessness, and still she thought she could give him orders. Amazing! "And if I'm a troll, you for sure are a trolless, if there is such a thing. Your face is grimy, your hair is greasy, and you stink. Haven't you ever heard that cleanliness is next to godliness?"

"Do I look like a goddess?" The woman bucked up against him with uncommon strength. She was unable to move him off of her, but she did move him. He was impressed. And just a teeny tiny bit aroused. *How pathetic is that? Hot for a hag. Must be a battle hard-on. Sort of like battle fatigue, but the opposite.*

She made a mewling sound of distress, having presumably noticed his teeny tiny arousal, which was no longer teeny tiny. She closed her eyes and inhaled as if for strength. Then she looked him straight in the eye and said, "You won't take me, troll. I won't let you."

At first he didn't understand what she meant, but then he did, and he was offended. "I do not rape women."

She shrugged to indicate she wasn't so sure about that.

"And I am not a troll. I am a U.S. Navy SEAL." Usually, women were impressed when he told them he was a SEAL. Not this babe.

"Ha, ha, ha!" she mocked him. "And I am a whale."

Ian had the woman pinned to the ground by his body weight. Her hands were cuffed in front. He could kill her in an instant by pressing his thumbs just so on her neck. And yet he saw not one ounce of fear in her blue eyes. Instead, she was angry. Hey, he was the one who had cause for anger.

"You and I are going to have a talk, Yasmine, but first we're going to establish some ground rules. You are not going to run away again."

"Oh? And why is that?"

"Because I will catch you."

"Sure of yourself, are you?"

"Damn sure."

"Stop poking me with your . . . uh, poker."

He grinned. He couldn't help himself. "Keep moving, and it keeps poking. Basic biology. Sorry about that."

"Make it stop being hard."

"Lady, there isn't any man alive who could talk

down a hard-on . . . when he's lying on top of a soft body."

"My body is *not* soft."

"Some parts are."

"Aaarrgh!"

"That's what women always say when they've lost an argument."

"You said it, too, before."

"Ah, but when men say it, they have just cause."

"My father always said there are only two ways to argue with a woman. And neither of them works."

"Smart man, your father."

"Not so smart. He had thirteen children. Get off me, you oaf. You are as heavy as a warhorse."

"Did anyone ever tell you that you talk too much?"

"Plenty of people. All of them men."

"And you lie like a rug. Tell the truth and shame the devil, babe."

"You are the devil, in my opinion. Yea, best you be careful you do not trip over your tail."

"Didn't anyone ever tell you that you catch more flies with honey than vinegar?"

"Why in the name of Frigg would I want to catch flies?"

But then she had no more chance to complain because he stood in one smooth movement, bringing her upright with him. Before she had a chance to squawk—and, yes, she began to squawk—he tossed her over his shoulder and carried her back into the cave, kicking and screaming. If there were any tangos in the area, he and the shrieker were dead meat. Cage was probably watching him through his scope and laughing his ass off. "Either shut up or be gagged."

Where's the duct tape when a guy needs it? If ever a mouth needed duct tape, this is the one.

She shut up. *Thank God.* Smart lady.

"Is there any water in this cave?" he asked as he put her down on the dirt floor, away from the shards of rock left by the gunshot. It was a miracle that the weapon had been pointed toward the cave opening. Some angel must have been watching over them.

Yasmine immediately tried to get up, but he shoved her back down, probably a little too hard, but, really, he'd had enough of her nonsense. He quickly attached the plastic cuffs to her ankles to further restrain her.

"I asked you a question. Answer me."

She zipped her lips. Just what he'd expected her to do.

"That's okay, cupcake. Let's just take these clothes off and see if you have any injuries that aren't visible." He proceeded to lift the hem of her filthy garment, exposing long and well-shaped legs, something he should not be noticing at the moment.

She suddenly found her tongue, as he'd expected she would. "Nay! I'll answer you. I have no injuries under my gunna. No need to remove my clothing."

"Suddenly shy, are you?" He smiled at her in a mocking way. He could tell that she'd like nothing more than to clout him over the head with another rock.

"Damn you to hell," she swore.

"I'm already well on my way there, without your help, sweetie. About the water?"

"There is no water, other than the drippings on the back of the cave wall, down that short passageway." She motioned with her head toward the back of the cave. "It satisfied my thirst today, but it tastes like dragon piss."

"You've got a foul mouth on you," he said as he took out his first-aid kit and wet a piece of gauze with a small amount of precious water from the drinking tube leading to the hydration bladder on his back, then held the tube to her mouth. "Here. Take a couple of small sips."

At first she resisted. Surprise, surprise. She was the kind of woman who resisted everything, even what was good for her. Once she realized that it was not poison, she gulped the water greedily. He had to pull it away. Who knew how long it would have to last them?

He forced her to lie back and knelt at her side. Taking the wet gauze, he began to clean the cuts on her face, some of which were still seeping blood. "Most of the wounds are just superficial, but the one above your left eye probably needs a butterfly clip," he remarked as he worked, dabbing and applying antiseptic.

"I have no idea what you said. Just do what needs to be done."

He took a metal suture from his kit and leaned forward. "This is going to hurt."

"You cannot hurt me any more than others have done." She closed her eyes and did not even wince when he clamped the pieces of skin together. He finished cleaning up the blood as best he could with the small amount of water.

"That'll have to be good enough for now."

"You have cuts on your face, too. Release me so I can minister to you."

"No way!"

She made a tsk-ing sound of disgust, then remarked, "You look ugly with that black on your face."

"Thanks for the compliment." Ian was sensitive about his receding hairline, but he had a passable face and a superior body, thanks to SEALs training. No one had ever called him ugly before, and it rankled a bit.

It was then that he noticed the thin welt around her throat. It was not a new scar. Suddenly he recalled something he'd seen but not taken note of in passing. Looking down, he saw the same welts around her wrists and ankles.

"Sonofabitch!" he muttered under his breath. "Who did this to you?"

"A man," she replied flatly. Her eyes were wide open now. And she clearly put him in the same category as the kind of man—or men—who'd done this to her.

He shook his head. "Not a man. A beast."

She shrugged. "It has been my experience that all men fall into that category."

"Then your experience hasn't been wide enough."

"Just like a man, defending his own."

"I am *not* defending this," he said, tracing the scar on her neck with a forefinger.

She shivered and turned her face away from his touch.

"Was it Jamal who did this to you?"

She frowned. "I know no Jamal."

"Whatever you say, honey." *Even now, she protects the bastard. Is it love or fear? Not my problem. The CIA guys will get all the info they want from her . . . one way or another.* For some reason, that prospect bothered him. Not that they would hurt her physically, but they would play with her mentally, and if she was one of the tangos, God help her.

He stood and began to put the first-aid supplies away.

"Were you able to escape my ties from the beginning?"

"Yes."

"Much as I try to be a leader to my men at Norstead, I am still a woman and not made for battle games." She exhaled loudly with disgust at herself. "I must do better. When I get back."

Ian had no idea what she meant, but he empathized with her feelings of failure at not living up to some standard. In his case, it was his father, Rear Admiral Thomas MacLean, who set the bar too high for him. Who was it for Yasmine? Jamal? Or someone else? Perhaps a cause . . . like a religious jihad? "Don't feel bad. You tied me good. I should know. I'm an expert at these things."

"Because you are a seal?" she said, no longer mocking, just tired. "I am going to close my eyes for a moment . . . just for a moment. Are you going to ravish me whilst I sleep?"

"I promise I'll restrain myself."

His dry humor was lost on her. "Swear it on your sword . . . uh, weapon."

He laughed. "I swear it on my rifle."

"Nay, your knife."

"Okay, I swear it on my K-Bar."

"Good," she said and fell into an instant, deep sleep. She must have been exhausted. Probably hadn't slept at all, hiding out here, worried about being caught.

He sat back on his haunches, hands on his thighs, and for several long moments just studied her. She was a mess. Bruised, dirty, disheveled. There was nothing attractive about her.

And yet . . .

And yet . . .

Ian's heart squeezed and he felt breathless just looking at her. What did it mean?

Shaking his head to clear it, he stood, put the safety on his rifle, put his knife back in his boot and prepared to leave. He was here on a mission, which would not wait, not even for a woman who might very well be one of the rats herself.

He clicked on his headset and said, "Force, Force." It was the code word for their op, as well as the name of their squad. "Can you hear me?"

"Cage here."

"I'm heading out."

"What about the tango's honey?"

"Restrained."

"Be careful."

"Always." He clicked off.

Outside the cave, he cut several bushes and put them in front of the cave opening to hide it from any passers by. The whole time he kept worrying about Yasmine, which was not only ridiculous, it was dangerous. There was always the chance that he wouldn't be able to come back . . . in which case, Yasmine would die of starvation in the cave, restrained as she was. But he couldn't in good conscience release her, either. He should not care. If he followed strict Navy and SEAL policy, he would consider the mission and only the mission.

At the last minute, he sighed in surrender, pulled

the bush aside and went back inside. It was the scars on her neck and wrists and ankles that had done him in, or so he told himself.

No woman should be so mistreated, one side of his brain said.

Unless she is a terrorist, the military side of his brain said.

There is no proof yet.

You are kidding yourself.

My instincts urge caution.

It's your funeral, buddy.

Squatting down to his haunches, he set his water bladder a few feet away from her still sleeping body. She must have been bone-deep exhausted. The tube was near her mouth. She would recognize it when she opened her eyes. In addition, he unwrapped a granola bar and put it near her face, too. Then he put his knife several feet away. It would take her a long time to get to the knife and even longer to manage to slit her ties. He should be back long before then. But if not . . .

He hoped he wouldn't be sorry.

Then he took off to join his squad.

Even trolls have a good side . . .

Hours later, Madrene awakened.

It took her several moments to recall where she was. It was still daylight; she could see that, although something had been placed in the cave opening . . . probably a bush. Her wrists and ankles were restrained by the white armlets. Her shoulders ached from lying in one position for so long.

She turned over on her side, and the first thing she noticed was that the troll was gone. *Good,* she thought, but she missed his presence. *How odd!*

The next thing she noticed was the water tube, which the troll must have placed near her face. *A considerate troll? How odd!* She sipped, but did not overindulge, recalling his warning to conserve the liquid.

Next, she noticed an object next to the water bladder, lying on a scrap of colored parchment. She sniffed it and concluded that it must be food. *The troll has left me food? Why? To fatten me for the kill?* She decided that it mattered not what his motive might have been. She had been fasting for two days. Rolling onto her face, she got up on her knees, her buttocks in the air, and nibbled on the food like a dog in the rushes. The food was delicious. Sweet. With nuts and raisins. Eating like a dog was not so easy, she soon discovered. The bar kept moving away from her till she pushed it up against the wall.

Once replete, she wiggled her body back to its resting place. She'd noticed the knife on the other side of the cave, and did not doubt that the beast had left it deliberately. He was too much a soldier-troll to have been so careless. Later, she would think on why he had done so . . . there had to be method to his madness.

She was too tired now to crawl over to the weapon. Later. For now, she wanted just a little more sleep. It seemed like years—three years, to be precise—since she'd last felt safe enough to succumb totally to the peace of a deep sleep. Though why she felt safe now, she could not say. She was restrained. Fakhir and his men would no doubt be tracking her. It was a long, long way to Baghdad, and an even longer trek back to her homeland.

Putting her hands together under her cheek, she yawned widely. Just a few minutes and she would get up, escape these ties, and be on her way. Just a few minutes . . .

Strange dreams came to her then. Her father. Her brothers and sisters. They were all smiling and beckoning to her. Was it some kind of message? That she should just give up and join them in the otherworld?

Then she noticed something else. *Oh, for Odin's sake!* Ian the Troll was there, and he was beckoning her, too. She could not see his face clearly in the haze of her dreams, but she would have sworn he was grinning at her.

So, should she just lie here, make no effort to escape, and possibly die? Or should she fight for her freedom? One thing was clear: If she was to escape, she might very well have to kill the troll, despite his kindness to her. That prospect brought a tightening to her heart that she had not felt since the disappearance of her family.

Later, she decided. She would decide what to do later.

Chapter Five

The best-laid plans . . .

"Houston, we have a problem," Ian said into his mike.

"I copy you," Geek said.

"Son . . . of . . . a . . . bitch!" Pretty Boy added.

"*Mon Dieu!*" Cage offered.

"My God!" JAM repeated.

Omar said something in Arabic that Ian assumed was an expletive.

Slick made a growling sound, then, "Let me at 'em."

Sly made the crude observation, "The Big Rat is one sorry motherf—"

"Shhh," Ian cautioned.

The eight of them were lying on their bellies about thirty feet apart, balaclava hoods in place. High-powered scopes on their weapons were trained on Jamal's hideout, a good half mile away.

The object of their consternation had just come out

of the largest tent and slumped against a tree. A young Arab girl, no more than sixteen, Ian would guess. She wore only a tattered man's shirt. One eye was blackened shut. The stains on her outstretched thighs could only be blood. She had obviously been raped . . . repeatedly.

"Riyad's granddaughter," they all guessed at once. A month ago, the son and daughter-in-law of the Iraqi Ambassador to the United States, Musa Riyad, had been brutally murdered by terrorists. Their daughter Altaira Riyad had simultaneously disappeared, and Aljazeera television had claimed, since there had been no ransom demands, the teenager must be dead. Instead, it appeared that Jamal was taking a particularly cruel form of revenge against Riyad, his sworn enemy. There would probably be pictures, horrible pictures, sent to Riyad sometime soon.

As they watched, a man in a turban and long white robe walked up to the girl and grabbed her by the upper arms, shaking her. He seemed to be yelling something at her. Then he let her drop back down to the ground, like a rag doll.

Eight sets of teeth could practically be heard grinding with frustration. The SEALs would like nothing better than to rush in and save the girl, whether it was Altaira or someone else. Impossible. Not yet. A civilian in the rats' nest changed the whole game plan.

For one blip of a second, Ian remembered Yasmine's scars. *Is this brutal treatment what she's running from? Or is she like those women terrorists you see on CNN with bombs strapped to their bodies?*

"This changes everything," he said into his intersquad head phone. Moving quickly but carefully, he crawled over to Pretty Boy, who carried the radio satellite equipment. Pretty Boy already had General Adams at CentCom on the line.

"Garfield, this is Cat One," Ian said.

"Garfield here. Cat Five briefed me. What's your take?"

"Tricky situation. Depending on how we play it, it could be a hallelujah mission or a major goat fuck."

"I read you. We must assume you've caught a bird." Ian didn't know much Arabic, but he did know that Altaira was the Arabic word for bird. "Do not . . . I repeat, do not . . . go in with the original 'Shock and Awe' plan."

"I copy." The second Ian had seen the girl, he'd known a new strategy would have to be developed. The original plan had been to go in with stealth from seven different directions, taking the tangos out one at a time, except for Jamal.

"There's always the danger of crossfire," the general reminded Ian, as if he didn't already know that. They all did. "Too dangerous to the bird."

Aside from the basic human concern for an innocent victim, the U.S. already had an image problem in the Arab world. Killing that girl, even accidentally, would be a colossal mistake. "I hear you," Ian said.

"Stand down," the general ordered.

"Delay the mission?"

"Correct. Do not engage. I repeat, do not engage."

"Roger."

"Retreat back to your prior location." Ian read that to mean the cave. "Leave two cats behind, to be relieved every three hours. Keep this line open for further directions. Wait for final orders." Ian suspected that it would be a nighttime raid now. "Big Bird will be alerted and on standby for extraction." That meant the chopper, of course.

"Yes, sir. And our priorities?"

"Number one, the Big Rat. Two, the safety of all you cats. Three, taking out as many of the other rats as possible. Four, the Big Rat's cheese."

Even though he'd already known what the general would say, his heart sank a bit. Yasmine, aka the cheese, would be sacrificed at the least notice, that's what the general was saying.

Once they disconnected, Ian ordered Geek and JAM to stay behind for first shift. There would probably be two more shifts before they attacked the site.

Ian was point man, leading the way back to the cave. It was mid-afternoon now. He'd been gone since that morning.

It took them more than an hour to get back to the cave, because they had to take care they weren't spotted along the way. Once they got to the site, Ian raised a halting hand. The bush was still in place in front of the cave, but that didn't mean anything. "No firing," he said into his headset, "no matter what she does."

He pulled the bush aside and tried to see inside, without actually entering. She was lying on the floor in the same place, except she was facing the wall. Her body, under her hooded robe, was deathly still. Something wasn't quite right. He could sense it.

He took out his pocket flashlight, shone it inside as he entered. And was attacked by some whirling dervish with a raised knife. Ian made neat work of stepping aside, but still the knife hit his chest . . . or rather his assault vest and body armor. It could have been worse . . . much worse. When he didn't fall to the ground—dead, for chrissake, if this idiot had her way—the whirling dervish threw herself at him, pummeling him about the chest and head as he lifted her by the waist so that her bare feet dangled off the dirt floor. He lowered his hands to get a better grip.

"Oh, my God!" With a gasp of surprise, he stared at the now screaming dervish in utter astonishment. Because the dervish was butt naked . . . and said butt was in his hands. He smiled. He couldn't help himself.

Glancing to the far end of the cave, he saw on closer inspection that her robe was covering piles of leaves and sticks. Ergo, she had to be naked to attack him.

"Listen, sweetheart, you'd better stop squirming and scratching so I can go over and pick up that robe to cover you. Otherwise, you're going to be doing the full monty for not one but eight men."

She drew her head back from where she had been attempting to bite his shoulder and yelped, "Eeeek!" on seeing him in the balaclava hood. All he could think of, though, was the view he got of her breasts when she leaned back. *I am not looking. I am not looking. They are not pretty. Nope. Not even close. Hell, who am I kidding? We're talking Pamela Andersons here. Practically.* He didn't even care that she had B.O. out the wazoo.

But then, the harridan with practically Pamela Anderson breasts looked over his shoulder toward the cave entrance and did a double eek, "Eeeek! Eeeek!" at all his squad mates in full military gear gawking at the picture of him holding a squawking, naked shrew. She yanked his hood off his head and glared at him, as if he were at fault. "Get my robe, you lackwit. And stop leering at my breasts. I'm not a cow."

No, baby, you are not. He walked her over to her robe, her sweet breasts pressed against him; he could swear he felt their firmness all the way through his vest and body armor. He leaned down, with her clutching his neck and her legs wrapped around his hips so that he wouldn't turn and show her to the rest of the guys. It was clumsy work easing down to a squat and pulling her robe over her head. Thank God for all those duck squats in PT.

"Can we come in now?" Cage asked. "Or is this a private party?"

All five of them were pulling off their hoods and taking off their weapons and vests as they walked in. And they were all grinning.

"You are a beast," she said and punched him in the arm.

"What did I do now?"

"Bringing all your troll friends here."

"Hey, it's not your cave."

"I was here first."

"So that's the cheese, huh?" Pretty Boy remarked. To Yasmine, he said, "Pleased to meet you, pretty lady."

Someone made a snorting sound of disbelief at the pretty-lady observation. It might have been Yasmine.

"I'm Lieutenant (jg) Zach Floyd, but you can call me Pretty Boy. Everyone does."

It was definitely Yasmine who snorted with disbelief now. This time at Pretty Boy's conceited self-assessment.

Pretty Boy extended a hand to shake with her, but she backed away.

Ian grabbed her forearm and pulled her back. "This is Yasmine, fellows. Yasmine, these are my fellow Navy SEALs."

She rolled her eyes and muttered something like, "The seal business again!"

One by one, he pointed to and introduced Pretty Boy, Cage, Sly and Omar. They all nodded at her.

Omar said something to her in Arabic, and she replied in the same language. She turned her back to them all and walked a short distance into the back tunnel of the cave and plopped down to a sitting position.

"What did she say?" Ian asked Omar.

"I asked how she was doing, and she pretty much told me to 'Drop dead!' "

"What's with the Phyllis Diller hair?" Cage asked.

"She sure is a mess. Poor thing!" Slick observed.

"Are you nuts?" Ian rubbed his chest as if it hurt. "She tried to kill me."

"With your own knife, I noticed." It was Pretty Boy who pointed that out to him. *The jerk!*

"Did you get a whiff of her B.O.?" Sly asked. "Phew. Even the street people in Harlem smell better than that. Bet she hasn't taken a shower in a month."

"Hey, we smell a little ripe about now, too," Ian pointed out. Even though they'd all probably showered this morning, the stress of a mission in all this heavy gear in the hot sun brought on a lot of perspiration. *But, hell, why am I coming to the shrew's defense?*

"Her hair does look like a haystack," Omar said. "Sort of like my ex-wife on a bad-hair day."

They all laughed at that.

"She reminds me of my old girlfriend, Lisette," Cage said and sighed. Cage had more old girlfriends than God had angels.

Five sets of eyes turned as one to look at Cage. Ian wasn't sure if he meant there was a resemblance because of her wild appearance or the breasts from outer space.

"Man, did you see those knockers?" Cage whispered.

Yep, that was what he meant.

"That's enough, guys. We have plenty of serious business to discuss." They pulled the bush back to the entrance, built a small fire for light, then sat in a circle discussing today's events and what they should do next. A call from General Adams or Commander Harding back at Special Operations Command in Coronada would seal their final plan.

They decided to have one man stand guard outside the cave, and alternate every hour till the call came. Slick took the first shift. With Pretty Boy, Sly, Omar and Cage settling in for short naps, Ian walked back to their "prisoner."

"Are you all right?" he asked Yasmine. "Do you need to . . . uh, relieve yourself . . . or anything?"

She looked up at him and said, clear as a bell, "Drop dead, troll!"

"Okaaay," he said, then turned and went back to the fire. He lay down on one side, head on his backpack. He'd slept in far worse situations.

Pretty Boy, across the fire from him, said, "Shot down, eh, lover boy?"

"She couldn't have done better with an AK-47," he responded with a laugh. "Can you see my tears?"

Despite his lighthearted words, Ian did feel something for the wretched woman. And he wasn't sure what it was. There was a very strange connection between them.

More important, Ian realized suddenly, *I've seen her face before. But where?*

Then he slept, one of the short catnaps SEALs were taught to take on a moment's notice, often in the oddest places, like in a tree, or in between PT evolutions. And he dreamed, too. Of Yasmine, of all things.

You snooze, you lose . . .

Madrene sat for a long time in the back corridor of the cave. She was thoroughly disgusted with herself.

She had awakened several hours ago and, after much work, had managed to reach the knife and to cut her bonds. If only she hadn't wavered in her decision to flee, she could have been long gone by now. But nay, she kept thinking about the troll and his promise to take her to Baghdad. *Should I leave? Shouldn't I leave?* Over and over she'd argued with herself. Now it was too late.

"Why are you scowling?" Ian said, slipping down to the ground to sit beside her.

"I always scowl."

"I noticed."

"Troll."

"But you look particularly annoyed now. Is it because you failed to kill me?"

"Nay," she said with a sigh. "If I had really wanted

to kill you, I would have used a rock again . . . and ambushed you from a hidden spot outside the cave. I have not trained to be a soldier for naught. Some skills, I do still have. Alas, I wavered, and that puts a soldier at peril." She could tell that her words surprised the oaf. He probably thought all women were helpless, cow-eyed maids.

"You would not have been able to trick me this time."

She shrugged. "Little did I know that you would come back here with a *hird* of troll-soldiers."

"We are not soldiers; we are sailors," he corrected her.

How like a man to home in on the most irrelevant facts. Soldier, sailor, same thing. "But you are trolls, eh?"

"I have been known to behave like a troll on occasion," he admitted.

"You had to bring all those other trolls along, didn't you? You, I could have handled, but eight trolls! I am not that good a she-warrior." She folded her arms over her chest with disgust. "And all of them carrying those exploding clubs and enough weaponry to fill a king's armory."

"You sure do talk funny," he said.

"I thought we already established that you are the one who talks funny."

"Female illogic is an amazing thing. You hear only what you want to hear. There's an old saying that goes—"

"Oh, spare me from your meant-to-be-inspiring sayings. We had a skald one time who did that all the time till everyone was nigh asleep from boredom. Did anyone ever fall asleep whilst you were pontificating endlessly?"

"Has anyone ever called you a shrew?"

"Plenty of times. You say shrew as if it is a bad thing. I say a shrew is a woman of intelligence."

"Amazing!"

She almost smiled at him, but caught herself in time.

He did smile at her, though, and her stomach clenched. It was probably a reaction to the food he had left for her. Or hunger pangs. Other than the bar of grain and nuts, she had not eaten all day.

"Are you hungry?" he asked.

Did he hear my belly talking? Ah, I am too tired . . . and, yes, hungry . . . to be embarrassed. But what she said was, "Nay."

"You're lying."

"Why would you care?"

"I like to fatten up my captives."

She considered arguing the notion that she was a captive, but decided to wait till later for that. "Is that why you left me that bar of grain and nuts?"

"Your stomach was rumbling louder than your snores, so I took pity on you."

At first, she just stared at him. "Are you teasing me?"

He waggled his eyebrows at her.

"I have not been teased since my brothers . . ." She shook her head to stop painful memories. "*Do* you have food?"

"Yeah. Just MREs but they're filling."

"What kind of food is that? If it's anything unrelated to a camel, I would eat it."

"MREs are portable provisions. You know, quick food on a mission."

"Like dried lutefisk?"

"Huh? No, things like beef ravioli, chicken cacciatore, jambalaya."

It was her turn to say, "Huh?"

"Listen," he said, rising to his feet and extending a hand to help her up, "are you hungry or not?"

She ignored the hand. "Yea, I am a mite hungry."

He made a snorting sound.

"But I do not want to go by the fire. Bring it back to me."

"Why don't you want to . . . oh, is it because you're embarrassed 'cause the guys saw you naked?"

"You really are a dumb dolt, aren't you? I was led naked through my great hall by a neck tether before two hundred enemy warriors. If I could survive that, I can certainly survive snickers from a few trolls."

Ian's jaw dropped practically to his chest. "You are making that up," he accused, but then he glanced at her neck, and wrist and ankles, and said, "I'm sorry."

She shrugged. "It was a long time ago."

"Then why do you avoid my teammates?"

She looked at him as if his head must be particularly thick. It was a look she'd perfected years ago with the men in her family. "Because I smell, you lackwit. I would not want to expose others to my stink."

His jaw dropped again. "But you don't mind exposing me to your stink?"

She stood up. "You deserve it."

Women! Go figure! . . .

Ian couldn't figure Yasmine out.

Okay, he'd obviously not been a rocket scientist in

the past when it came to women; otherwise, Jennifer wouldn't have been screwing her personal trainer behind his back. But Yasmine was something altogether different.

First of all, she behaved like a bleepin' shrew, nagging and complaining about every little thing. And she looked and smelled like an old hag. Cripes, you could build a bird's nest in her hair. Yet he felt an odd attraction to her. And, no, it had nothing to do with his glimpse of those world-class breasts . . . or almost nothing.

Second, she was childlike in her ignorance about everyday things. Like thinking a rifle was a club. Like believing he was talking to himself when he was communicating on his radio headset. Like being ecstatic over MREs—she had eaten three of them before her hunger was satisfied, not to mention two fudge brownies, a handful of hard candy, peanut-butter snack crackers, and a dairy shake. You would have thought the barely palatable rations were a gourmet meal.

She was wide-eyed with wonder at all the things she saw or was told about. Cage especially had made a big impression when he talked to her about his Cajun people. He even sang her a freakin' Cajun song. The dolt!

Ian reminded himself how sheltered some women still were in the Arab lands. Wearing the traditional chador or burqa, which covered them head to toe except the eyes. Rarely leaving their homes. Not exposed to TV or radio. But Yasmine didn't strike him as the type who would tolerate that kind of life. And she sure as hell wasn't meek.

Third, she was mean enough to be a terrorist.

Hadn't she tried twice to kill him? Hadn't she punched him several times? But did that mean she really was a terrorist, or in cahoots with them?

Fourth, she continued to call them all trolls. At first, he had thought she meant that they—he, in particular—behaved like trolls. But he was beginning to think she believed they were actual trolls . . . part of some troll society or something. *Geeesh!* Which must mean she was a mental case.

Fifth, it was hard to tell under all that grime, but Ian did not think she was Arab. At least, she didn't look like any Arab woman he'd ever seen. Not that he was an expert on such things. But Omar had remarked on the same thing.

They were still waiting for final orders from CentCom, although he'd spoken to his contact several times since leaving the tango site. Cage and Omar had gone back to relieve JAM and Geek. After taking a short nap, JAM came out to relieve him from guard duty outside the cave. Coming inside, he saw that Yasmine was still talking with Geek and Pretty Boy in her stilted English. He might not be sure if she was Arab, but it was clear that English was not her first language.

"Tell me again why you need to get to Baghdad, darlin'?" Pretty Boy lay on his side in front of the fire with his head propped on a braced elbow.

Yasmine, from the opposite side of the fire, sat on crossed legs. "Do not call me dearling. I am not your dearling."

"Sorry," Pretty Boy said with a smile that said he couldn't care less if she objected to his endearment, which he didn't mean anyhow.

"In Baghdad, I might be able to find a ship traveling to my homeland. Once there, my people will give me aid."

"Where is your homeland?" Geek asked. He looked up from the mini-laptop he was studying with logistical information about their mission.

"Norsemandy," Yasmine said.

"I thought you said you were from Russia," Ian said.

Yasmine jumped, not having realized he'd come up behind her. "Must you always sneak about like a . . . a . . ."

"Troll?" he inquired.

"Yea, a troll."

"Normandy, huh?"

Under all that dirt on her cheeks, he detected a blush.

She was lying through her teeth. "What a tangled web we weave when first we practice to deceive," he remarked, almost to himself.

Her response was to raise her chin haughtily. "What matters it to you where I go once you take me to Baghdad?"

"Uh . . . about Baghdad," he started, easing down to his haunches beside her.

"What?" She was immediately alert.

"There's been a change in our original plans. We expect to have an additional person on our flight back. And our extraction site might have to be closer to the terrorist hideout. There's a chance we will have to leave you behind."

She gasped in outrage, then turned and shoved him backward. Climbing over him, she began to pummel his chest and face. "You . . . will . . . not . . . abandon . . . me," she shrieked, punctuating each word with a punch.

He put his hands over his face, laughing. Geek and Pretty Boy were laughing, too. "You hit like a girl," he accused her, which was a silly thing to say.

"A girl, you say?" Rising up on her hands, she hit him in the balls with her right knee. "Do I kick like a girl, too?"

He saw stars before he rose to his full six-foot-four and glared down at her. He barely restrained himself from cupping himself to ease the pain. "If that's the way you try to get your way, no wonder you're lost in the middle of camel nowhere. Big mistake, sweetheart!" With those words, he picked up his backpack and walked down the back corridor of the tunnel. Throwing it to the ground, he lay down, facing the wall. He was so angry he probably wouldn't be able to sleep, and he needed all the rest he could get before they started out again.

He sensed her following him before he actually heard her.

"I am sorry," she said, standing at his back.

"Go away."

"Sometimes I let my temper get the best of me. Hah! I always let my temper rule. My father used to say . . ." He could swear she gulped then.

"I don't give a rat's ass about your temper or your father or any other bloomin' crazy thing you say or do. Just leave me alone."

"I cannot." Now she dropped down to her knees.

"Look, I don't hurt women, but I'm afraid I'll give in to the urge to throttle you if you keep bugging me."

"I have a proposition for you."

"This oughta be good," he muttered, turning over to face her. "You are a piece of work, lady."

"Is that good or bad?"

"What's the proposition?"

"If you and your men will get me to Baghdad . . . and from there to my homeland . . . I will reward you generously."

He gave her a once-over survey which pretty much said she had nothing he wanted.

"Don't be a lackwit," she said. "I didn't mean *that*. I meant that I would pay you in coins . . . gold coins . . . chests of gold coins. All you have to do is deliver me back to my people. My fighting men will come out of hiding to help me rid my estates of Steinolf and his evil warriors."

Ian rolled his eyes.

She stared at him expectantly.

"Where did you say you come from?"

"Uh, Jorvik."

"Jorvik?" *Liar, liar!*

"Yea, the Saxons call it York."

He burst out laughing. "So far, you've said you live in Russia, Norsemandy and England. Which one is it?"

She waved a hand airily. "It does not matter which. I can get home from any of those places."

"And then you will hand over a pigload of gold. Just like that."

"Yea. Now you understand."

Delusional, that's what she is. Or a scheming witch who will change sides as it suits her in the war on terror, regardless of ethics. "No, you understand this. I will take you to Baghdad *if I am able to*. But it won't be so you can fly off to Leningrad or London town. You will be considered a terrorist suspect, subject to the interrogation of my superiors."

Her mouth—the mouth he'd been trying hard to ignore—formed a perfect O of surprise. "You think I am a terrorist?"

"Damn straight I do." *Maybe.*

"What is a terrorist?"

He rolled his eyes again. "A person or group who uses violence, usually in a cowardly way, for political or ideological purposes."

She frowned, as if she still didn't understand. "What kind of violence?"

"Like 9/11. Like those Islamic terrorists who've killed thousands of men, women and children, even their own people."

She gasped. "You think I would kill innocent women and children?"

He hesitated, then nodded. "For a cause, yes."

"You vile troll! Even to get back to my beloved Norstead, I would not kill innocents."

He was saved from further discussion, or her punching him again, by a soft signal from Pretty Boy's satellite phone. They all rushed forward to get the news.

Except Yasmine, who stood in place, tears in her eyes.

Chapter Six

Time to get out of Dodge . . .

Ian and his squad were running as fast as they could just before nightfall, dragging a bound and wounded Jamal and carrying the terrified Arab girl. They were headed toward the extraction site.

It had been one of the moments SEALs live for. Ian would never forget the moment he'd entered the big tent and leaned over the sobbing girl to say, "Lieutenant Ian MacLean here. U.S. Navy SEALs. We're here to take you home, baby." She clung to JAM now, arms clutched tightly around his neck, as they raced toward freedom.

"The package is secured," Ian said into the satellite phone as he ran. "And the bird is in hand."

"Good work, Lieutenant," General Adams responded. "Casualties?"

"None on our side. At least two dozen of the tangos are down and dirty. No time to collect or destroy weapons and munitions. Some of Jamal's men escaped and are heading this way with reinforcements from another terrorist cell. They'll be on our tail soon. Time is of the essence." Ian was breathing hard when he finished his report.

"Be careful, Lieutenant."

"Over and out." He handed the phone back to Pretty Boy, who ran beside him.

Soon a Skyhawk chopper was hovering over the small clearing where they'd inserted and would now extract. Rappeling ropes were dropped. The SEALs would free-climb up on their own, but harnesses had to be lowered, first to raise Altaira, and then Jamal. They had twenty minutes, max, before the tangos caught up.

"I'll be right back," Ian told Cage, squeezing his shoulder.

"No!" Cage shouted at his back. "Don't do it. We have Jamal. She's not worth it."

I beg to differ. Shit! Where did that thought come from? Heart hammering in the oddest way, as if it were chanting, "Go . . . go . . . go," Ian waved without turning and ran toward the cave where they'd left Yasmine hours ago. He saw her running toward him, apparently having heard the gunfire and the whup-whup-whupping of the chopper blades. He'd ordered her not to come out, no matter what. Surprise, surprise, she hadn't listened to him.

"You came back," she said, smiling at him.

With utter idiocy, Ian registered the fact that it was the first time the shrew had smiled at him . . . and he liked it. "Yeah, but we've got to hurry." He grabbed her hand, and they raced toward the chopper.

"Oh . . . no!" Yasmine wailed and dug in her heels once they got near the site.

Jamal and Altaira were already in the aircraft, along with Pretty Boy, Omar, Geek and Sly. JAM and Slick were rappeling up one of the ropes now, with Cage on the ground, beckoning him wildly with shouts of "Hurry, hurry, hurry!"

"Please don't tell me you are going to fly away on a bird? No, no—"

Ian picked her up like a sack of flour and tossed her over his shoulder, running. "No time to panic. Just shut the hell up and do what I say." *Like that's ever going to happen.*

They got to the site. Cage was already climbing up, faster than a monkey up a tree. Ian pulled the harness over on the other rope, secured a screaming Yasmine into the leather straps, then held on to the ropes above her head and wrapped his legs around her body. As soon as he gave the signal, the rope was lifted upward.

Yasmine buried her face in his neck just as the tangos arrived and began shooting wildly, luckily from some distance yet. Despite the noise of the chopper blades and the sound of gunfire, he could still discern Yasmine's words against his neck, "I . . . am . . . really . . . going . . . to . . . kill . . . you . . . now!"

"Yeah, yeah!"

They no sooner crawled inside the chopper than it was flying away, not even waiting to close the doors. As darkness settled over the land, Ian secured Yasmine and himself in seat belts. Jamal was unconscious but still alive, thank God. Altaira, realizing that she was finally going home, smiled tentatively through a cracked lip at Slick, who had his arm over her shoulder. He and his fellow SEALs looked at each other and yelled, "Hoo-yah!"

After they'd settled in for the short trip, Ian turned to Yasmine and asked, "Cat got your tongue?"

She muttered something under her breath that sounded like "bloody idiot proverbs."

"Are you all right?"

She wouldn't look at him, just stared straight ahead, her white-knuckled fists clutching the hand rests. In the dim interior light, he saw that her face looked white as a sheet. "Nay, I am not all right, you dolt! You've put me in a bird the size of a longship, for the love of all the gods! I'm flying. Flying, do you hear me?"

Everyone from here to Afghanistan heard you. "Hey, I saved your life. You could at least be grateful."

"Grateful? Grateful?" she sputtered. "More like you *risked* my life. Oooh, does it have to go so fast? My stomach is churning."

Ian put a paper bag under her chin.

She shoved it away. "Where are we going, by the by?"

"Baghdad. I already told you that."

"Oh." She thought a moment and said, "I thought we might be going to your troll kingdom. If we are going to Baghdad in this thing, we may as well go all the way to my homeland."

Troll kingdom? "And where might your homeland be . . . this time?"

She hesitated . . . which showed him that she would lie, once again. "Birka."

"Where the hell is Birka?"

"The Danish lands. Don't you know anything? Birka is a well-known market town. Even dumb Scotsmen know that."

Okay. Russia, Norsemandy, England . . . and now Denmark. You are a real pistol, lady.

After that, he turned to his other side, where Omar was tugging at his sleeve. "Uh, Mac, I think we might have a problem."

He raised his brows in question.

"Have you noticed that Yasmine hasn't looked at Jamal . . . not even once?"

"She's probably doing that deliberately."

"Maybe. But look at Jamal."

The terrorist had opened his eyes and was glaring at them all. Except Yasmine.

"He hasn't given Yasmine a second look."

"What's your point?"

"I'm thinking she's not who we thought she was."

Uh-oh! "Who else could she be, here in the middle of Jamal country?"

"I don't know."

He should leave her interrogation to the experts in Baghdad, but still he couldn't resist asking her, "Is Jamal your lover?"

"Who is Jamal?"

He and Omar murmured at the same time, "Uh-oh!"

"Is your name really Yasmine?"

"Of course not!"

I think I will pull out my hair. No, maybe I will pull out her hair. No, I wouldn't want to touch that flea nest. "What is it, then?"

She hesitated.

Another lie incoming.

"Ailine."

"Yikes!" Omar said.

Ian said something way more explicit, but it amounted to the same thing. "We are in big trouble."

"Whoa! What's this *we* business? *You* are in big trouble."

Welcome to the Magic Kingdom . . .

The magic bird landed on a large field where there were many other birds at rest. Madrene could finally unclench her fists and let out the breath she had been holding.

I just flew. Holy Thor! High up in the air. Holy Thor! Now that they were on the ground again, Madrene was able to smile at the experience she'd just had. Not that she ever intended to do it again. *I wish my family were here so I could tell them about this. Torolf and Ragnor would be so envious.* It was sad, really, that there was no living person with whom Madrene could share her excitement.

Except for the troll.

How exciting is that?

Ian and the other "seals" jumped out of the bird onto the field, where they were hugging other similarly attired men and clapping each other on the back. Just like men in her country. On return from battle, they liked to boast of all their feats of bravery. Male exaggeration flowed like mead at a Frigg's Day feast.

Madrene gazed out the window of the bird. The skies were dark, but the field was well lit, almost like daylight. Everywhere she looked, she saw people in uniforms, men and women alike. Some of the uniforms were made of the same woodland fabric as Ian's and his fellow "seals." Others were a drab light brown or all blue. And the women . . . by Odin! . . . many of the women wore *braies*.

She had to admit that she'd half expected the metal bird to land in the cold north seas where Ian and his men would then turn into the seals they claimed to be. She was not disappointed that they hadn't.

None of these people had blackened faces like the "seals" who'd brought her here. Were they a separate clan of fighters?

Jamal, the now cursing terrorist restrained at wrists and ankles, was handed down to stern-looking, stiff-postured soldiers in brown, carrying magic clubs—guns, Ian had called them. They walked him slowly toward a large building to one side of the field.

Altaira, the poor Arab girl, was put on a rolling bed by white-clothed men and women. They also headed toward the building, which apparently housed a hospitium.

Madrene was the last person to exit the bird. Ian held out his arms to help her down the short ladder.

"I can walk myself," she snapped, and almost tripped over herself getting down.

Ian snickered.

The troll!

"Come this way," he said, taking her by the elbow, even though she would have liked to shrug him off. "That's General Adams up ahead. And those are the CIA boys who will have a few questions for you."

"What is a general?"

Ian groaned. "A general is a high-ranking military officer."

"Higher than you?"

He laughed. "Way higher."

"And the see-eye-aye?"

"CIA is Central Intelligence Agency. You know, um, information gatherers."

"Spies?"

He shrugged. "Sometimes."

"Why did you not just say spies, then?"

He squeezed her elbow in punishment for her sass. "Settle down and behave yourself. Don't speak until you are addressed first."

"What kind of male jest is that?" She mimicked his deep voice, repeating, "Don't speak until you're addressed." The man was too full of himself by half. Then she said, "Ha, ha, ha!"

"Believe me, there's nothing funny about this."

The seriousness of his face and tone forewarned her. She looked from him to the group ahead. Of a sudden, she understood. This was not a welcoming group about to offer her hospitality. They regarded her as an enemy.

"Stay with me," she said. Almost immediately, she regretted pleading st with the man.

"I can't," Ian said.

She shot him a sideways look. "You are going to abandon me?"

"It's not my call. You're an alleged terrorist, and as such I've got to turn you over to the authorities." To give him credit, he did look sorrowful. But sorrowful counted for naught if her life was in peril.

"Are they going to lop off my head?"

His eyes widened with surprise. "Of course not."

Then he grinned and teased her, "They might lop off your tongue, though."

Now he makes a jest. "You brought me here," she accused him, refusing to yield to his mirth. "Why did you not leave me behind if this was your intention?"

"It's my duty."

"Your first duty is to yourself. What honor is there in giving a mere woman over to enemy forces?"

"Are you questioning my honor?"

"Oh, go away. I will fight my own battles . . . as I always have."

Ian looked as if he wanted to say more, but all he said was, "I'll see you later, if I'm able."

"Do not do me any favors." Raising her chin high, she walked up to the leader, leaving Ian in her wake. For some reason, her heart felt crushed at his betrayal, but she could not think of that right now.

Ian came up to stand next to her. She'd thought the traitor would have scooted off. He gave the general a sharp salute from the forehead and said, "Lewd-tenant Ian MacLean of Force Squad, Eighth Platoon, SEAL Team Thirteen, reporting as ordered, sir."

The commander did the same salute back at Ian and said, "At ease, Lewd-tenant."

Ian, who had his hands linked behind his back, stood just like the commander, as if he had a lance up his arse. Which looked really silly with that black face paint.

"Why are you all standing like you have lances up your arses?" she said under her breath.

"Shhhh!" Ian said.

She would like to shhhh him.

"Good job, Lewd-tenant," the general said. "I will

expect a full report in my office in an hour. That gives you time to shower and settle in."

"Yes, sir."

Then the leader turned to her and asked in a stern voice, "Yasmine Bahir?" His body remained rigid as he stared down at her.

"Nay."

"Oh, shit," Ian murmured beside her.

"Nay?" he and the men beside him asked.

Thick-headed lackwits! "That's what I said. Nay."

"You are not Yasmine Bahir?" the leader said, his voice a trifle shrill with distress.

"I already said I was not. Dost have a hearing problem?"

"*What?*"

Definitely shrill.

She heard a tsk-ing noise beside her from the troll. She reached behind him, discreetly, and pinched his buttock.

"She just pinched the lieutenant's ass," one of the spies remarked to the general with a smirk.

Apparently, she hadn't been as discreet as she'd intended.

"Will they lop off my hand for that sin?" she asked Ian sweetly.

"Get serious," he warned.

"Your name, young lady?" the general demanded.

I have not been called young in many a year. Should I laugh or kiss the man? Instead, she decided it was time to be truthful . . . or somewhat truthful. "I am Madrene Olgadottir." In the Norselands, women took their last names from their mothers, and she was the daughter of Olga.

Ian muttered something that sounded like, "Another friggin' name!"

She muttered back at him, "Turn so I can pinch the other side of your arse. Methinks you need matching cheeks."

Ian burst out laughing.

The general and his spies frowned at him . . . and at her. Apparently, laughter was not allowed in this country's military.

"Ensign Wilson. Ensign Baxter," the general said loudly.

Two women dressed all in brown came forward. They looked as if they had poles up their arses, too.

"Take Ms. Badir—"

"I told you that is not my name."

"Take Ms. Olgadottir to the women's quarters for a shower, then bring her to my office, and call General Assim and Commander Kelly to be present as well. Do not let this young lady out of your sight."

"Are we ever going to eat?" Madrene asked as her stomach growled.

"After our . . . meeting, you will eat. But before that, you will have to go to the women's quarters for a shower." The general sniffed dramatically. "I don't think the cooks would let you near their food."

She felt her face heat with embarrassment. "You would smell too, if you were covered with camel spit."

The general fought a smile, though what mirth he found in her words, she could not tell.

The women came forward, walking stiffly, then flanked her on either side. When they put a hand on each of her elbows to lead her forward, she shrugged out of their grip. "For the love of Frigg, I can walk myself."

"They want to prevent you from escaping," Ian told her. He had stepped aside to make way for the women.

"I am not such a halfbrain that I would attempt to flee in the midst of the troll kingdom. I will wait till later."

Ian rolled his eyes, then turned to the general. She followed the two women to whatever fate held for her.

The last thing she heard Ian tell his commander was, "With all due respect, sir, don't hurt her."

That made her feel a mite better; so she asked the women warriors, "Perchance, could I have a horn of mead? My throat is drier than a dragon's tongue. No doubt it is due to the ride I just had in a bird up in the sky. Son of a god! That would dry the spit out of even a hardened warrior. Is that rouge on your lips? I like it. Better than the harem houris who rouge their nipples. Oh, mayhap you rouge your nipples, too. Do you two need to use the privy? I only ask because you walk just like Baldr the Blacksmith when he has the roiling bowels and must needs find a bush quickly. Leastways—"

"Ms. Olgadottir," the woman on her right said. "Shut up!"

Can't Get You Out of My Mind . . .

Ian took a long, hot shower.

And thought about Yasmine.

He thought about shaving, then didn't bother.

And thought about Yasmine.

He put on a clean camouflage uniform.

And thought about Yasmine.

He spent an hour with his squad in the routine after-mission briefing with the general, his staff and half a dozen CIA ops. They would do a more detailed critique once they returned to SpecWar Command at Coronado.

And he thought about Yasmine.

The general complimented them on their good work. "You men have done the world a favor bringing in Jamal. We hope to get intel out of him, but be prepared. We're going to announce his capture to the news media tomorrow in hopes of scaring more of his scum-of-the-earth comrades to turn themselves in."

"Will we in Force Squad be required to deal with the media?"

"Yes."

All eight of them groaned. Dealing with the press was a SEAL's nightmare. One female reporter from AP was particularly hard on the SEALs. Every single time, she tried to bait them with stereotypical questions about elite commandos. If they had done half of what she'd asked them about, they would have to be Supermen.

"I also want to commend you on the skill with which you rescued Altaira. Ambassador Riyad is on his way from D.C. and will want to thank you personally. Good job!"

"Now for the bad news." The general turned to Ian. "What were you thinking, to leave your team? I'm sure your commander will have more to say about that, but, good Lord, man, it could have been a disaster."

"But it wasn't," Ian interjected, unwisely, then added, "sir."

"Next, what were you thinking, going back for that woman during the final extraction?"

Ian thought about explaining why but decided that nothing he said was going to make any difference.

"No matter your good intentions and no matter how successful the outcome, those were risks a SEAL leader should not take. You know better. It will go in your record." He scowled at Ian, who was biting his tongue. Then the general relaxed and smiled. "But luckily, the good accomplished on this mission will far outweigh the bad. Congratulations." The general came around from behind his desk and shook each of their hands in turn.

It wasn't the first time Ian had screwed up and probably wouldn't be the last. And, actually, this mission would probably mean a medal for him, and promotions for him and all his men. Jamal was one of the most hated terrorists in the world. His capture was important to the United States and its allies.

"The CIA has Jamal in one of the interrogation rooms as we speak," the general told them just before they left. "I expect to talk with the female any minute now. Lieutenant MacLean, are you sure she's Jamal's lover?"

Ian felt his face heat up. "Pretty sure . . . sir."

"I beg your pardon, Lieutenant. 'Pretty sure' is not a term we accept in this Navy, as you well know."

The admonition annoyed Ian, especially since it came on top of the criticism. Bristling, he defended himself. "The woman was in Iraq . . . in a remote region known to be Jamal's hiding spot. She said her name was Yasmine . . . at that time. She spoke Arabic. With all due respect, General . . . sir, I would have been remiss if I hadn't assumed she was the tango's . . . uh, cohort."

"That remains to be seen." The general hadn't cared for his tone, any more than Ian had cared for his superior's. But the Navy was not a democracy, and Ian had to remind himself to pay the proper respect to a higher-ranking officer.

After they left the briefing and headed toward the mess hall, he was still thinking about Yasmine.

What the hell is wrong with me?

"What the hell is wrong with you?" Cage elbowed him in the side to get his attention. "It's Yasmine, isn't it?

"Yeah. Crazy, isn't it? She has Phyllis Diller hair. She nags so much she give shrews a bad name. She smells. She talks funny. She freakin' tried to kill me. Twice."

"Beauty's only skin deep," Slick said, throwing a proverb at Ian for a change.

"Yeah, if you're drunk out of your mind and willing to dig down to her liver," Ian countered.

Cage put a finger in the air as if to interrupt him. "She does have nice breasts, though, bless her heart."

"Breasts aren't everything," Ian observed, with a straight face yet.

Cage and the other members of his squad exploded with laughter at that remark. Ian laughed, too.

"To some people they are," Geek pointed out.

"Oh, yeah?" Pretty Boy said. "You got statistics on that, Mister Brainiac?"

"Actually—"

"Don't let him needle you," Ian advised Geek. To

the rest of them, he explained, "I know it's crazy, but I feel guilty about turning her over."

"Maybe it's a bit of Stockholm Syndrome," JAM offered. "You know, where the captive falls in love with the captor."

"I am *not* in love with that witch. Besides, I was the captor, not the captive," he protested.

"Stranger things have happened. Besides, they say that ugly women try harder to please." It was Slick speaking and waggling his eyebrows at him.

"There is that," Sly said. "Maybe she's the Avis of the female species."

"Actually, I'm getting kinda tired of beautiful women," Pretty Boy commented.

They all stopped and gaped at him.

"Gotcha!" Pretty Boy said with a laugh.

JAM said something as they entered the mess hall that got Ian thinking. "I wonder what Yasmine looks like under all that grime."

"Before, she looked like a dirty witch who swallowed her broom," Omar said. "I suspect that after her shower she will look like a clean witch who swallowed her broom."

Ian thought a moment, then said, "Yeah, you're probably right."

She was no swan, but . . .

In some ways, Madrene felt as if she'd died and gone to Asgard, so heavenly was her experience in this new world.

Her robe had been tossed in a basket to be taken out later to their midden. The two lady soldiers, whose names turned out to be Amber and Dough-lore-ass, took her to a bathing chamber where she enjoyed the most bone-melting all-over wash. Without even sitting down in a tub! Madrene had thought the bathing pools in the Baghdad harems were luxurious, but even they could not compare to the showers of hot water that came out of a metal sprayer in the wall.

And the soap! The hard bars of rose-scented soap were a luxury she would have thought reserved for the highest royalty. For the hair, there was a scented liquid called sham-poo. Amber and Dough-lore-ass claimed even the lowest classes had access to such special soaps and sham-poos. If the scented soap and sham-poo were not enough, they also gave her an object called dee-odor-ant to apply in her armpits. She would smell like a bloody rosebush by the time they were done with her.

Afterward, they stood her before an enormous mirror, a luxury most kings could not afford in her country, and helped her comb all the tangles out of her waist-length blond hair. Her hair was the same color as it had been when she'd left the Norselands three years ago, but her skin had darkened somewhat because of her exposure to the hot Arab sun.

Amber had helped her in the bathing chamber. Dough-lore-ass, on the other hand, stood with a weapon in her hand the entire time, guarding her. As if she might run off naked to the gods-only-knew-where!

"I like the name Amber," Madrene remarked. "My father and my brothers traded in amber."

The two women just stared at her. Then Amber said, "You told the general your name was Madrene. Do they call you Maddie for short?"

Madrene had forgotten that she'd divulged her real name. That had been careless of her. She blinked several times, then said, "Yea, they call me Maddie."

"I don't think we have a bra that would fit you, Maddie. You've got to be at least a 34C, maybe even 34D," Amber said, once they were out of the bathing chamber and in the sleeping chamber known as a bare-racks. Other women in the room or passing by gazed at her with interest, but they did not intrude.

"What is a bra?" Madrene asked. She had a large, plush towel wrapped around her body, covering her from chest to thighs.

Amber and Dough-lore-ass looked at each other, then at her.

At the same time, Amber lifted her *shirt*, revealing the oddest garment. Made of an almost transparent lace fabric, it covered the breasts and had straps over the shoulders and a band around the chest.

"Well, hell fires, what is the purpose of that attire?"

"To hold up the breasts," said Amber, who had no breasts to speak of.

"Like a harness?"

The two women laughed.

"You could say that," Dough-lore-ass replied. "Plus, they make a woman feel sexy. And they turn men on." She raised her eyes meaningfully.

"If by 'turning on,' you mean what I think you do, well, I doubt me that the men in my country would turn lustsome over that skimpy attire. If given a choice, methinks they would prefer the udders bare and hanging in the wind, though I am no expert on the subject."

Amber helped pull a green, collarless, short-sleeved *shirt* over Madrene's head. The letters U.S.

Navy were on the front. Like most women in her country, Madrene had never been taught to read, but she was able to make out some words and letters.

"Going bare-chested in public is not an option, Maddie, especially here on a military base," Dough-lore-ass pointed out with a smile.

"I know that. Bloody hell, didst think I would ever consider such scandalous behavior?" Madrene shook her head at their foolishness. "I referred to your remark about men liking . . . what did you call them? . . . bras. Besides, judging by my brothers' past conduct, men's staffs rise at the least provocation. And if they have been imbibing too much mead, they need no provocation at all. Their dangly parts have a mind of their own. Leastways, that is what Ragnor used to say."

Both women were staring at her, slack-jawed with amazement. She affected people like that on occasion.

"I talk too much betimes," she admitted with a shrug. "And I tend to be blunt of tongue. I do not mean to offend, though often that is the case."

Amber patted her on the shoulder. "No, no, that's all right. You just surprised us."

"And you talk oddly," Dough-lore-ass added. She was still guarding Madrene but did not seem to consider her a real threat.

"Hah! Why does everyone say that my speech is strange? It is all of you who talk in an odd fashion."

"What country are you from?" Amber asked as she pulled out a flesh-colored bra from a chest. She held it up in front of Madrene and nodded her opinion that it would fit.

Madrene considered telling them the truth, but decided that caution was the better path. After all, she had been taken from her homeland and forced to stay in the Arab land for two long years. And she was still in the Arab lands, for all she knew. Best to be careful of how much she revealed, she decided. "North of here," she said.

"Syria? Turkey?" Dough-lore-ass inquired with seeming shock. She and Amber exchanged looks again.

What was it about this land that everything has something to do with animals? Seals, birds and now turkeys. I am certainly not a turkey, last time I checked. She was about to tell them just that, but another woman soldier came up and told them, "General Adams wants to see the prisoner as soon as possible."

"Which prisoner?" Madrene asked. Then realized that the woman was referring to her. "I am not a prisoner," she started to say, then realized that perchance she was.

Quickly, Amber found her *braies* made of the woodland fabric that the "seals" had worn, dark calf-length hose, and heavy boots. But first, they showed her how to put on an undergarment called panties. They were flesh-colored, like the bra, and barely covered her belly, buttocks and nether hair. She giggled at the feel of the garment on her body.

Soon, flanked by the two women soldiers, she was walking toward the general's chamber. She could not wait to get this meeting over with so she could eat, her stomach being nigh empty.

"Those SEALs from Force Squad are going to get a rude awakening when they get a look at this babe," Amber remarked to Dough-lore-ass.

"Oh, yeah! I can't wait to see their faces," Dough-lore-ass replied. "I heard Seaman LeBlanc refer to her Phyllis Diller hair."

"Are you speaking of me?" Madrene asked.

"Yep. You are beautiful, and I'll bet my stripes they didn't have a clue," Amber explained.

"I am *not* beautiful," Madrene said with consternation. She hated it when people felt the need to pay false compliments.

"Maybe not beautiful exactly," Dough-lore-ass said. "More like knock-'em-dead attractive."

"Tsk-tsk! What nonsense you spout!"

"Honey, you're tall, you're slim, you have to-die-for hair, and you have breasts that would stop even a gay guy in his tracks."

"Gay guy? Why would my breasts make a happy man stop?"

Amber and Dough-lore-ass erupted with laughter. When they explained what "gay" meant, she laughed, too. Thus the three of them were laughing as they entered the general's chamber.

Chapter Seven

Surprise! . . .

Ian and the guys were sitting in the mess hall, drinking coffee and shooting the breeze. The only one missing was Slick, and God only knew where he'd disappeared to.

They'd all been invited to a party, hosted by some Air Force babes that Cage had met within fifteen minutes of landing here . . . surprise, surprise! Ian wasn't sure if he would go, but maybe he should at least make an appearance to avoid the ragging he would get about his libido, or lack thereof. Besides, after the reprimand he'd gotten from General Adams, he could use a beer . . . or five.

It was almost nine p.m., so the large room was mostly empty. The SEALs of Force Squad were full, relaxed and rehashing their mission for about the tenth time, not counting the unpleasant meeting with General Adams. Ian didn't like being called on the carpet; it reminded him too much of his father, always criticizing him, never praising. Even when he'd finally given in and gone to officers candidate school, that hadn't been enough. Even when he . . . oh, hell, what difference did it make?

"What do you think will happen to Jamal?" Pretty Boy asked.

"My guess is that security around him will be tighter than anything we've ever seen before," Omar said. "That man is one mean mother, up there with Bin Laden and the other super terrorists."

Ian agreed. "Uncle Sam, *and* the Iraqis, will want to make an example of him, punish him for all the deaths he's ordered. Did you hear about that mass grave they found last week in Fallujah? I have a friend with the marines who were first on the scene. He said the jarheads couldn't stop vomiting, it was that bad."

"Yeah, but the pussies in Washington will want to be politically correct," Pretty Boy pointed out. "His trial will have to be squeaking damn fair or the ACLU and Amnesty International will be on the military like dogs on a bone."

They all nodded, having no liking for the ultra liberals who made their work harder.

"It feels good to have brought the creep in, though," Geek said, echoing the satisfaction they all felt. As for Geek, he'd done real good for his first mission. Now he could say he'd been "blooded."

"Did you see that little Arab girl when her granddad came to get her?" Sly asked. "Man, I had tears, and I hardly ever tear up."

"Yeah. She'll probably need a shrink for a long time, but she'll be okay," Omar said. "Now, if she were living in an Arab culture, she'd be ostracized for the rapes, even though they weren't her fault. But she's westernized, and her family lives in the U.S. most of the time. She'll be okay . . . in time."

"What do you think will happen to Yasmine?" Geek wondered.

That was what had been worrying Ian, though he berated himself for even thinking about her. "Hell if I know! If she *is* Jamal's lover, she'll be in big trouble. Prison, for sure."

"I find it hard to believe that even Jamal would want to screw that . . . shrew," Pretty Boy said, then laughed at his own joke. "Screw the shrew. I like that."

There was a communal groan at Pretty Boy's warped humor.

"Yeah, but there are those breasts," Cage reminded them, as if any of them needed a reminder.

"Man, I could have pissed my pants when I saw her launch herself at you," Omar said. "She was like a nude missile or something."

"She is . . . something else," Ian agreed.

"She seems to have latched on to you, Mac," JAM said, "like you're responsible for her or something."

"I know, and I actually feel guilty for turning her over, terrorist or not," Ian confessed. "That's all I need in my life . . . a cat with an attitude and a hag with an attitude."

"I think I know what country she comes from," Geek said. "I recognize the accent."

They all turned to him with interest.

"Iceland."

Some of them laughed, even Ian, who said, "Aw, shiiiit! A freakin' Eskimo."

"I said Iceland, not Alaska." Geek looked at him as

if he were dumber than dirt. But then, Geek looked at everyone like that, him being so much smarter than the average guy.

"Iceland, Alaska, North Pole, whatever. It's colder than a witch's tit up there," Cage said.

His use of the word tit reminded them all of a pair of those they'd seen recently.

Geek went off on one of his usual tangents then about the statistical probability of Yasmine being from Iceland based on factors and exponents and international language codes and modern Icelandic being similar to Old Norse and numbers and numbers and numbers and numbers and other crap.

Cage spoke for them all when he said, "Geek, you make my head hurt."

Luckily, something happened to interrupt the flow of Geek's brainy discourse . . . or perhaps not so lucky.

"Sonofabitch!" Omar's jaw dropped practically to his chest.

"Hot damn!" JAM added.

"Holy crawfish! I think I've died and gone to heaven." Cage put a hand over his heart and sighed dramatically.

Omar, Cage and JAM were sitting on the opposite side of the table from Ian, Geek, Sly and Pretty Boy, who had their backs to the doorway.

The four of them turned on their seats, looking back to see what had caught their buddies' attention. Three women were walking toward them, two of them dressed in traditional Navy uniforms—Ensigns Amber Wilson and Dolores Baxter. The one in the middle—the statuesque blonde—wore fatigues with an olive drab T-shirt.

Ian's brain morphed into slow-mo then. He couldn't quite grasp the scene unfolding before him. His men were talking with excitement, but he filtered out their words of astonishment and appreciation.

First, he took in the fact that the woman in the middle was gorgeous. Well, not gorgeous. Her nose was too straight and her face too thin for that. Stunning would be a better word.

Her blond hair hung down her back in a long braid, like a twisted skein of spun silver. Except it wasn't gray; it was platinum.

She was tall, at least five-ten. With legs that were as long as a Coronado mile. Despite her slim frame, her breasts were nothing short of magnificent. Probably due to some push-up thing or other that women used to fool men. Even so, the favorite part of his body jump-started into full-tilt testosterone overload; if it could say howdy, it probably would.

When was the last time I was this attracted to a woman?

Never.

Her chin was lifted high like some friggin' princess looking down on all the lesser beings, including him. No, in particular, him. *Why me?* Ian had no illusions about his sex appeal, compared to some of the other studs sitting with him. Hell, he even had a receding hairline.

Hold the train! Something strange is going on. He frowned in confusion.

Why were her blue eyes directed at him with haughty disdain? He didn't even know the woman.

Yes, I do.

It can't be.

I must be the blindest guy in the universe.

It was the hag . . . Yasmine.

Except she wasn't a hag.

His eyes went back to her breasts, which were clearly outlined by the drab Navy T-shirt. *Yep, it's her. And there's nothing common about her. Nosirree!*

"Oh . . . my . . . God!" he said as all the implications hit him in the gut like a sucker punch. His squad members were exclaiming as well, all talking at once.

He stood and started to walk toward her, dazed. It was probably a testosterone trance. So obvious was his reaction to the woman that the guys behind him hooted with laughter. He couldn't care less what they thought.

"Yasmine?" he said.

She blinked several times, then said. "Nay. Maddie."

Another name. He rolled his eyes.

She punched him in the stomach.

"Hey, why did you do that?"

"One, you abandoned me. Two, you did not tell me how bad I looked. Bloody hell, I almost scared myself when I looked in the mirror. Three, you are not a troll, but a real man. Four, you failed to inform me that you are handsome as all the gods under all that face paint. Five, your hair is rusty brown, not black. Six, I asked you to take me to Baghdad and you bring me to this military fortress. Seven, you put me in a flying bird and almost frightened me to death."

Slowly he grinned. "You think I'm handsome?"

"Pfff. As if you didn't know, you puffed-up son of a lout. Go get me some food. My stomach is screaming, and after arguing with those lackwits in the general's office, I have a megrim that would down a dragon. I will sit over here." She waved a hand airily and sat down at the next table. Her two guards sat, too . . . looking a bit poleaxed. He knew how they felt.

He still grinned, though. When had her nagging started to have an appeal? Shaking his head to clear it, he went over to get her a tray of food, like a bloomin' lackey.

When he came back, he sat down across from her. Amber and Dolores kept a constant eye on their "prisoner" but went over to the next table. Immediately they began to talk with the guys on his squad, who were mouthing suggestions to him and making hand gestures, all of which were obscene.

He noticed that Yasmine was sniffing her arm. She even lifted her arm and smelled her armpit. Subtlety was not her strong point. "Yas . . . I mean, Maddie, what are you doing?"

"Smelling myself."

"Why?"

"Because I smell good, lackwit."

Considering how she'd stunk to high heaven before, anything would be an improvement.

"My skin smells like flowers and my hair smells like apples. If I run into a swarm of bees or a hungry horse, you may have to rescue me."

Was she actually making a joke? Wonders never ceased. Meanwhile, she continued to sniff herself.

"Can I come over there and smell you, too?" he teased.

She gave him a look that pretty much said, *Do and die!*

"Yasmine, . . ." he started to say.

She glared at him.

He propped his elbow on the table and rested his chin in his hand. "Maddie . . . I keep forgetting. You sure do lie a lot, don't you, Maddie?"

She studied him for a long moment. "Yea, I do."

He raised his eyebrows.

"But only these past two years. Lies have been my only tool for survival."

"Well, you sure pulled one over on me today."

"I did?"

"Who knew that the ugly duckling would turn into a swan?"

She threw her hands up in air. "I swear, you have an obsession with animals. Seals, birds, turkeys, swans."

"Turkeys?"

"Not turkeys. Turkey. Amber and Dough-lore-ass asked me if I came from Turkey."

"Oh." Talking with her was like going through a maze. You never knew what turn you would take next.

She sat playing with the jello on her tray with a butter knife. She did the same to the corned beef hash and tossed salad. The roll was the only thing she ate, gobbling it down as if it were gourmet food. Then she just stared forlornly at her tray of food.

"What's the matter? I thought you were hungry."

"I am." She sighed. "I do not know how to eat this food." She jiggled the jello again to demonstrate.

He got up and went around the table to sit next to her. Yep, she did smell like flowers and apples. It wasn't a bee or a horse that should worry her. He might just take a bite himself.

"That's jello," he said, picking up a spoon and

scooping a small amount up and putting it in his mouth. "Yummm." *God, I hate jello!*

She took the spoon from him and did the same. Smiling, she took one spoonful after another till it was all gone. "Jello," she said. "I like it."

She licked her lips.

His cock thought her gesture was talking to him, and raised its head. *Do that again, honey.*

"What's this?" She stared with dismay at the entree on her tray.

"Corned beef hash."

"It looks like vomit."

She must be an alien or something. Nothing here seems to be familiar to her. "It's beef and potatoes and onions. It's not bad." *Liar!* he told himself. *I hate corned beef hash almost as much as I hate jello.*

At first she was awkward with the fork, but then she got the hang of it and ate all the hash, which indeed did look like barf, especially after hours under the steam warmer. She concluded, "Interesting." She smiled at him then, as if he'd done her some favor.

It had to be the first time in the world that hash affected a person so, but her smile touched him. He didn't know why, it just did.

She took a long drink of water then, after picking up one of the ice cubes and studying it carefully. With each swallow her chest moved. In, out, in, out.

Amazing! Her simple drinking was an erotic exercise. For sure, you-know-who agreed and twitched in his pants.

Now she was eating the salad and started in on the brownie. "Ummmm," she said. "I am not so fond of the dish of weeds, but the brown thing is delicious." Replete, she raised her hands above her head and stretched. Mid-yawn, she turned on him. "Stop looking at my breasts."

"I can't help myself. Are you wearing one of those push-up things?"

She frowned. "I do not think so, but I *am* wearing a lace harness. Leastways, I don't jiggle anymore." She reached for the hem of her T-shirt and started to lift it.

Holy shit, she was going to show him her "harness." Laughing, he took her hands and put them and her hem in her lap. "That's okay. I know what you mean."

"I am also wearing a silk garment to cover my arse and female parts," she confessed to him. "Pan-teas they are called."

He made a gurgling sound, which she must have interpreted as encouragement to go on.

"Whenever I walk, the silk moves against my body in the most sensuous way. And my breasts feel as if someone is holding them up. I have ne'er heard of a country where people wear silk under their clothing where it cannot be seen. Can you imagine that?"

He groaned. *I'm imagining, all right.*

"Do you wear silk pan-teas, too?

"No."

"Never?"

"Well, once." He waggled his eyebrows at her.

She frowned. Apparently, his eyebrow waggling did nothing for her. "Are you married?"

Where did that come from? "No. Are you interested?" *Where did that come from? Honest to God, they oughta nominate me for dumb man of the year.*

"Pffff. One marriage was more than enough for me. How about you? Are *you* interested?"

"In what?"

"You are rather thick-headed, aren't you?"

He smiled.

"Stop it."

"What?"

"Smiling."

"Why?"

"It does fluttery things to my stomach."

He put his face in his hands. His cock was doing the hallelujah dance. And he . . . well, he was in big trouble if this conversation went any further. "You shouldn't be telling me things like that . . . Maddie." He had trouble remembering what her name of the moment was.

"Why not?"

Because I might just jump your bones, that's why. "You shouldn't tell a man that he turns you on . . . unless . . ."

"Turn on? Turn on? Turn on?" she repeated the words over and over, as if trying to understand the expression. He was just about to explain when she slapped him on the arm. "You think I want to fornicate with you?"

Well, yeah! He felt his face warm up. "You did say you got all fluttery when I smiled." He smiled just to see if he got a reaction.

She put both hands to her stomach.

Oh, boy!

"That's not what it means. It can't be *that!*"

Yep, it's that. He felt about ten feet tall.

Then reality began to creep in to testosterone city. "We can't do anything about it anyway. I'll be leaving tomorrow afternoon."

"Leaving? For where?"

"Home."

She tilted her head in question.

"Coronado. California."

"You are *not* leaving me here."

He had no chance to respond because, despite his glares and silently mouthed "Go away!" the guys and two women came over to sit with him and Yas . . . Maddie. The guys grinned at him. The women looked confused. He understood both the humor and the confusion.

Pretty Boy had plopped himself down next to Maddie. *Geesh, I have trouble with that name.* Cage sat on his left. The other guys sat on the facing bench with the two women.

"Why don't you introduce us, Mac?" Sly suggested, ignoring his glower and smiling at Maddie.

"You already met Maddie back at the cave," he grumbled.

"That wasn't Maddie," Cage said. "That was Phyllis Diller on crack." He winked at Maddie.

Ian elbowed Cage for his remark and the wink. Cage elbowed him back.

Reluctantly, Ian introduced them all, ending with Pretty Boy.

Maddie frowned. "Why do they call you Pretty Boy?"

Everyone laughed except Pretty Boy, whose face had turned red. Pretty Boy had been given that nickname—all SEALs got nicknames—because his last name was Floyd, but also because he was exceptionally good-looking, or so women said . . . lots of women.

"Because I'm pretty?" Pretty Boy said. The overconfident ass. When Maddie still appeared confused, he added, "Don't you think I'm pretty?"

"Well, I suppose some might say so, but, of course, you are not near as handsome as the lackwit Scotsman."

At first, Ian didn't know that she referred to him . . . not till the guys laughed and teased him about his prettiness. Everyone in the world thought Pretty Boy was God's gift to women, including Pretty Boy. No one, *no one*, ever said Ian was handsome when Pretty Boy was in the room. Everyone at the table looked as astonished as he felt.

"I have a receding hairline," he said. *Why don't I just shoot myself? I have the finesse of a twelve-year-old.*

"You need to get out more," Sly said.

"I could give you lessons," Cage offered.

Maddie studied his hairline, than asked, "Do you have much hair on your chest?"

Ian's jaw dropped open.

"My father always said that a man's virility could be measured by the amount of hair on his chest. The less, the better. Now on the manparts, hair is an entirely different matter."

Several males looked down at their chests, then below.

"Maddie, you shouldn't say things like that."

"Why?"

"Women are supposed to be demure and—"

"Oh, bloody hell! Not that demure business. I am tired to my teeth of men requiring meekness in a woman. The men in my family were like that. And the sultans in the harems where I served were even worse. Do you know what those lackbrain houris did to please men? They plucked—"

Ian put a hand over her mouth. "We get the picture, Maddie."

"You were in a harem?" Amber asked. She and Dolores had been silent so far, but now they were clearly interested, along with a bunch of horny sailors.

Maddie went on to regale them with a long spiel about all her experiences in harems. Ian had his face in his hands, unsure whether to laugh or cry over this strange, strange woman who had fallen into his life like a meteorite.

Once she'd talked herself out, and everyone was suitably dumbfounded, he told the guys, "Remember, you have to be present tomorrow for the press conference. CentCom wants to brag to the world how they captured Jamal by parading a bunch of presumably hunky SEALs as part of the program."

They all groaned, except Pretty Boy, who liked that kind of crap.

One time a Pentagon PR person had actually suggested that they might come shirtless. As if! Although some of the guys probably would have. Then the clueless PR person had suggested they wear lots of medals. Unbelievable!

But, for now, the squad members nodded, although they weren't happy about making nice for a bunch of reporters.

As an afterthought, Ian added, "And make sure you are dressed appropriately."

"What? You didn't like my 'Save a Horse, Ride a Cowboy' T-shirt the last time in South Africa?" Cage, ever the clown, pretended to be offended.

"More like our commander at Coronado, and about twenty frickin' admirals in D.C., were not amused to see that on CNN," Ian said.

"It's just the title of a Big and Rich song," Cage said with the innocence of one of his native alligators.

"What is a cowboy? Oh, do not tell me. Another animal!" Maddie was shaking her head at them.

"A cowboy is a man who handles cows . . . out on the open range," Sly explained.

"Except if you're in Nashville, where everyone pretends to be a cowboy," JAM pointed out.

"What is Nash—" Maddie started to ask.

Ian ignored them all. "We will have plenty of time after the press conference to catch the plane back to the States."

"We are going to the . . . states?" Madrene inquired, her brow furrowed with her usual confusion.

"*We* are not going anywhere. You are staying here," Ian said. "Unless they send you to prison somewhere else. But I don't think they'll do that to a woman."

"I don't know about that. Remember Tokyo Rose," Geek said. "And Hanoi Jane."

"They didn't put Jane Fonda in prison, did they?" Sly asked.

"No, but they would have liked to," JAM answered.

"You would abandon me here in this strange land?" Maddie was looking at Ian, not the group as a whole.

"Hey, you asked me to take you to Baghdad. You're in Baghdad."

"This is not the Baghdad I meant."

"Honey, there's only one Baghdad," JAM interjected, even though she hadn't been addressing him.

"I'm telling you, this is not the Baghdad I meant." She inhaled and exhaled several times as if to calm herself. Then she looked at Ian like he was a yucky pill she had to swallow. "I suppose I will have to go with you . . . till I find a ship to take me home."

That made him sit up a little straighter. "One, you are *not* going home with me. Two, I am not responsible for you. Three, you can find a ship from here to take you to Iceland. You don't have to go to California to get a ship."

"Iceland? Why would I want to go to Iceland?"

"Don't you live there?"

"Nay. I have visited there, of course, but it is not my home. Where did you get that idea?"

Geek blushed and ducked his head.

Ian said, "Never mind."

"Tomorrow afternoon, you say? I will have to make sure your general is done questioning me. He seems to consider me a prisoner. I am not really a prisoner, am I?"

"More like a forced guest." Why else would the guard over her be so loose?

"I am going with you."

"No, you are not."

"We shall see."

"Every time a woman says that, it means she will get her way. Well, you won't this time, sweetie. Besides, you need a passport to enter the U.S.A. Do you have a passport?"

"What is a passport?"

He spread his hands in a "See!" manner.

"Get me a passport."

"I can't do that."

"There is one way they give passports on short notice here," Omar said with a grin.

Ian flashed Omar a glare. "You are barking up the wrong tree, buddy."

"Who barked?" Maddie asked.

Ian ignored Maddie's question and glared at Omar. "*That* is out of the question."

She narrowed her eyes. "What?"

"Marriage," Omar the traitor said.

She let out a whoosh of disgust.

Hey, marriage to me is not whoosh-worthy. Not that I'm interested. Damn, damn, damn! How did I get involved in a marriage question? "Don't worry. The general's staff will take good care of you. *Provided you aren't actually a terrorist.*

"If that is the only way, I guess we will have to do it."

"*What?*" he practically shrieked.

"Get married. Of course, you can put me aside, like my first husband did, once I am on a ship heading home."

"No, no, no, no, no! We are not getting married." He thought a moment. His heart was racing hard. He shouldn't ask, but when did he ever listen to his own sound advice? "Why did your husband divorce you?"

Her face turned white as a sheet, and her fingers clenched and unclenched her paper napkin. "I'm barren."

"Huh? You're bare and what?"

"You are the world's biggest idiot. I'm barren."

Everyone, especially the women, were looking at Maddie with compassion. Cage even patted her arm.

Ian felt like a louse. "Oh. I'm sorry. What a creep . . .

to walk out on you for such a thing! Hell, it was probably his fault anyway."

Her eyes welled up with tears, which she wiped away. " 'Tis nice of you to say so, but he has four children now with his second wife."

"If it had been me, I would have performed a Lorena Bobbit on him before I danced out the door," Amber said.

"Except I would have used a butter knife," Dolores added.

"What is a Lor . . . that thing she mentioned," Maddie asked him.

Why me? Ian sighed at the impossible situations this woman kept putting him in. "Lorena Bobbit was a woman who whacked her husband's pecker off while he was sleeping."

At first Maddie's eyes went wide; then she clapped her hands with glee. "I wish I had thought of that."

Time to get back to the subject they'd been on. "Yasmine . . ."

"Aaarrgh!"

"Maddie. Are you a terrorist?"

She gave him a long, considering look. "No."

"Then you'll probably be freed tomorrow, and you can go anywhere you want."

"How will I get there? Will you take me home?"

Ian had no idea where "home" was, but it really didn't matter. His silence was his answer.

Her shoulders slumped. "It would do no good anyway. I must needs raise an army first. Steinolf will not give back my estates willingly."

Ian refused to ask who Steinolf was. The woman

must be a little bit crazy. "An army? You don't ask for much, do you?"

"In truth, you and your hird of seal soldiers would suffice. My people would follow you if you taught them your fighting skills. What a sight that would be! Norstead would be mine once again."

Norstead? I won't even ask what country that is in. "Listen, we're putting the cart before the horse." At the questioning tilt of Maddie's head, he elaborated, "We're jumping to conclusions. First the general has to release you."

Her eyes said he was lower than a snake's belly. "And once he does, then what?" she inquired in a voice dripping with sarcasm. "You are not leaving here without me."

He had no answer to that.

But JAM did. "I could help, if it came to that."

Ian refused to ask, but the others had no compunction about hearing JAM's solution. "God save me from my friends," Ian muttered, throwing his hands up in disgust. He had a sinking feeling he was not going to like JAM's answer.

And he was right.

"Even though I left the seminary, I am still able to perform baptisms, last rites and . . ."

Ian groaned.

The others grinned.

". . . civil marriages."

"So, you could do a quicky wedding if you had to?" Sly asked. He was grinning so wide, you could have stuck a plate in his mouth.

JAM nodded, entirely serious.

"And I could go on the Internet to get all the legal documentation, including the emergency green card application." Good ol' Geek. Always had the answers.

"But who would she marry?" Amber asked, excited to be planning a freakin' wedding. Some guard she was!

Everybody turned to look at Ian.

"No!" he said. "No, no, no, no, no!"

"What a lackwit," Maddie said.

"You shouldn't call your groom . . . uh, potential groom . . . a bad name," Dolores advised Maddie. Some guard she was, too!

"Dearling"—Maddie said the odd endearment with sugary sweetness—"I would rather lie with a three-pronged goat than be your bloody bride."

Now, there's a picture.

At first there was silence, and then Cage pronounced, "I think they make a perfect couple."

Ian had the sensation of drowning in quicksand.

Chapter Eight

The sucking sound of a man drowning in quicksand . . .

Later that evening, Ian was at the party, half blitzed, heading for a total, knee-walking drunk. As if that would help anything!

Just then, an old acquaintance of his walked up. Dan Sullivan was a pain-in-the-ass CIA agent he'd met years ago at some Pentagon cocktail party hosted by Ian's admiral father. Dan liked to needle him every chance he got. Actually, Ian usually did a good job of needling back.

Ian glared at Dan, but did the man take a hint and vamoose? Nope. He looked like the proverbial cat that swallowed the canary. His smirk boded ill for Ian.

Taking a long swig from his longneck, he braced himself.

"How's it hanging, spy guy?" he asked. Judging by his continuing smirk, Dan must have heard about his "predicament." Hell, everyone at the party had, thanks to his big-mouth squad members. "Long and hard, Kermit." Dan thought it was cute to call him Kermit, as in frogman, what SEALs used to be called in the old days. "And you?" Dan was still smirking.

"Hot and heavy," Ian replied. It was their usual back-and-forth greeting, but it seemed to have more significance for Ian now. Why he was attempting to make small talk with the jerk-off was beyond him. Must be the beer.

"I just came back from a late-night meeting with the boss. You are in deep shit," Dan informed him, with glee.

What a loser! "What else is new?"

"Oh, this is new, all right." Dan deliberately failed to go on.

But Ian wasn't going to give in and ask.

Finally Dan couldn't help himself. "Madrene Olgadottir, or whatever the hell her name is, is not Jamal's bed bunny. Nope. Yasmine Bahir was spotted this afternoon in Kabul."

Ian felt the blood drain from his head. He'd suspected as much—that Yasmine wasn't . . . Yasmine—but somehow confirmation came like a sledgehammer to his thick head. "So, who is she?"

"Damned if we know. Not yet. She has no social security number in the U.S. Interpol has no data on her. She's still suspicious. Hell, she keeps giving a cock-and-bull story about harems and raising an army to get back her estates, but exactly where those estates are, we can't figure out, and she's not telling. Not yet."

"Where does that leave her?" *Or me?*

"We can't hold her. Oh, we'll put a tail on her, once she's released, but for now, sayonara."

They're releasing her? Wow! "Do you plan on relocating her . . . somewhere?"

"No. Why would we?"

Because she's lost. Because she'll never get to her destination from here. Because it's the right thing to do. "Well, maybe because we are responsible for her being here."

"*We* are not responsible for her being here, Rambo. *You* are."

Don't hit him. Do . . . not . . . hit . . . him. "You can't just dump her here in Baghdad. It's a snake pit right now. And she doesn't have a clue about this city and its dangers."

"We offered to transport her back to northern Iraq, but she refuses to go there. Something about milking camels and harems and camel spit."

Ian barely stifled a grin. So, he wasn't the only one being subjected to her wild stories. "Then find her a safe house here," Ian demanded.

"I don't think so. We'd rather drop her and see where she goes."

She won't last a week. With her mouth . . . and, yeah, her beauty, she'll be raped or dead in no time. Probably both. "She's not my responsibility."

Dan raised his eyebrows at Ian's vehemence. "Who said she was?"

Yas . . . Maddie, that's who. She's like a barnacle on my backside, determined to make me feel guilty. Well, I won't.

"Of course, the word is already out. Even if she's not affiliated with any terrorist cell, I suspect they'll want to talk to her. Just in case."

And we all know how tangos talk. Ian suddenly recalled a woman they had found in an Afghan terrorist camp last year. Her breasts had been cut off, and a vile object stuck into her vagina . . . all while she was still alive and before they chopped off her head. "You would subject her to that?"

"We'll be watching her."

Just like you took care of the Afghan woman? "Bullshit! You and I both know that the tangos might get hold of her anyhow. Did you see that Arab girl we brought back? Her only crime was having a powerful father. What do you think they might do to a woman they suspect has spilled some secret information to the feds?"

Dan shrugged.

Ian blinked several times and unclenched his fists. *Life sucks, and I am not friggin' Superman.* "I'm outta here tomorrow. She can be toast, or not toast. I don't care."

Oh, God! Yes, I do care.

I shouldn't care.

Yes, I should.

A numb feeling came over him as Dan swaggered away, off to needle someone else. The prick!

His teammates came up to take Dan's place. Apparently, they had overheard it all.

"Are we really going to leave her here?" Geek asked. He was an innocent, despite having been blooded on this mission. He still believed the good guys always won, Prince Charming rescued the princess, all that crap. Not that Ian was a prince, not by a long shot.

"Hell, no!" the other team members said as one.

Then they all looked at him.

And JAM took a piece of paper out of his pocket that Ian knew without being told was a marriage license.

Ian was not a wuss. He could very easily hop on that plane tomorrow . . . actually today since it was two a.m. There had been many times in his career when he'd had to make decisions for the greater good, even when something or someone had to be sacrificed. But in those cases, there had been no other choice.

Besides, there was something about this woman . . . something that tugged at his memory. He could swear he'd seen her somewhere before. And, honestly, she drew him to her, even when he had thought she was an old hag. Hell, she thought he was prettier than Pretty Boy. He made her flutter. There were worse things in the world.

His shoulders slumped with resignation.

"I think I smell wedding cake," Sly said.

What you smell is smoke coming out of my ears.

"Dum dum dee dum," Pretty Boy sang.

How would you like to no longer be pretty?

"I know where there's a little chapel we could use," Omar offered.

I know where there's a hole I could stuff you in.

"I could sing," Cage offered.

Yeah. If we want to drive all the dogs in Baghdad nuts.

"Do you have your dress whites here?"

I am not making an event out of this fiasco.

"Can I be your best man?" Cage looked at him hopefully.

"No, me." "No, me." "No, me," the rest of them said.

"We can all be best men," Cage offered, and they all smiled their agreement. Except Ian.

This is going to be a sideshow.

"I'm going to go check the Internet to make sure it's all legal and everything," Geek said and left the party.

Oh, yeah. Gotta make this stick.

JAM saw the dismay on Ian's face and and assured him, "It's only temporary. You can get an annulment when you get home."

That's for damn sure.

Avenil came out of nowhere and put a hand on his shoulder. The guy was like a ghost. You never knew when or where he would show up. Into Ian's ear, he whispered, "You're doing the right thing."

Ian, deep down, believed that to be true, too. Otherwise, he wouldn't be allowing himself to be railroaded.

"If this is my wedding eve, I guess this must be my bachelor party, except there's one thing missing," he said, resigned to whatever fate held for him. "Where are the strippers?"

The troll takes a wife, the troll takes a wife, high ho, the . . .

"Do you take this man to be your lawfully wedded husband?" JAM asked.

"If I must," Madrene replied.

Her prospective husband snorted his disgust. Then he whispered into her ear. "I'm doing you a favor, lady. Shape up or I'm out of here."

She looked at JAM, the SEAL who was acting as minister; he had been a priest or almost-priest at one time. "Yes."

"Yes what?" JAM asked.

"Yes, I take the lout to be my husband." Then she turned to the lout. "Now are you happy?"

"No, I'm not happy," Ian told her, disgust thick in his voice. But when JAM asked him, "Do you take this woman to be your lawfully wedded wife?" he said "Yes."

After a bunch of words, most of which Madrene

did not understand, JAM announced, "By the power granted me by church and state, I now pronounce you man and wife."

I cannot believe I am wed-fast again. I vowed never to take another man into my life. It hurts too much. Ah, but I have no choice. No choice at all. And that is ever a woman's lot. I thought I was different.

JAM had been serious throughout the short ceremony, but now he winked at Ian. "You may now kiss the bride." The other SEALs, the two female soldiers and many other military friends present to bear witness clapped and chanted, "Kiss, kiss, kiss!"

Ian was as surprised as Madrene by that suggestion, but she was the first to react by snorting her revulsion and stomping down the steps of the makeshift altar. She had only gone down two steps when Ian grabbed her by the upper arm and pulled her back.

"If I'm going to be leg-shackled to a shrew—" Ian said for her ears only.

Wait just a bloody minute. I am the one being leg-shackled here.

"—I am going to get some recompense."

If I had coins, I would not be in this predicament.

With his words, he hauled her flush against his body, one hand around her waist and the other buried in her hair.

Oh. That kind of recompense.

Their eyes locked for one long second.

She wanted to protest, but her limbs and tongue were frozen. His mouth spoke anger, but his eyes—brown as clover honey—entreated her to surrender.

And then he kissed her.

Nay, kiss was too weak a word for what he did.

His lips were not rough on hers, as Karl's had been most times, especially when he had the alehead. Instead, his firm lips moved back and forth till he found just the spot he wanted. Then his lips coaxed hers in the most compelling way to return his kiss.

And she did. Blessed Frigg! She did.

It was too much, and not nearly enough.

With a soft moan against his open mouth, she raised her arms around his neck and pressed her body even closer. For the first time in her life, she relished the difference between man and woman. For the first time in her life, she did not disdain the softness of a woman's body or the hardness of a man's. When he teased her mouth with his tongue, she gasped, and he used that opportunity to slip his tongue inside. She was not sure whether to be outraged or excited.

No contest. She was excited. In fact, her knees buckled.

With a chuckle, he caught her, and only then did he draw away from her. But he still held her in a close embrace.

They both stared at each other with shock. What had just happened? The brute had hoped to punish her with a humiliating kiss. But instead, they had both been overcome with . . . what? She could not say, having never experienced such a pull toward another human being. And she could see that Ian felt the same. They were in their own small world, and it was a blissful place.

But then the rest of the world intruded. All around them, people were offering congratulations, as if this marriage were something to celebrate. The men suggested coarse ideas for Ian to use in the bed furs, as if there would be bed play between them. Amber and Dough-lore-ass had tears in their eyes, as if this joining came from love. But it was done, and Madrene was safe, for now. She should be thankful.

Turning to her new husband—*what a thought!*—she said, "Thank you."

He just grumbled.

Boar! "Once I get my bearings, I will be off, believe you me. I have friends in high places."

He rolled his eyes.

Boar! "If I could have found a way home without your help, I would not have . . . inconvenienced you."

"Inconvenienced! Lady, you are a huge boulder in my life."

Boar!

After that, JAM brought a document for them to sign. Ian scratched out some words with a most ingenious pen—it had ink in its body—then turned to her. "I cannot write," she confessed.

All of them looked on her first with surprise, then pity. Why? Few men and even fewer women learned to read in her land. They were too busy trying to survive. Chin lifted with pride, she put a mark where JAM indicated, then led the way to the back of the rude metal building, where a small repast had been set out. A sweet cake with frosted words on top. Small pieces of bread with meat in the center. That bitter brew known as cough-he. And a red liquid that resembled weak blood; 'twas called punch. She had no appetite, but tried each of them. It would have been impolite to Amber and Dough-lore-ass not to. The men had no such reservations, gobbling the food and drink as if they hadn't had a break in fast a mere two hours ago.

The man known as Cage came up to her then, took her by the waist and twirled her about. "Best wishes, chère. It's time to kiss the bride." And he did just that. On the mouth.

The rogue!

Next came the man named after one of the apostles, Luke, also called Slick. He was a serious man, and the look he gave her was somber. Kissing her on the cheek, he said, "Give it a chance, honey, and this marriage just might work."

Hah! When fjords turn to mead!

Pretty Boy smiled before he gave her a warm hug. "Are you sure you don't find me unresistible?"

She laughed. *Not while the lout is in the room.*

Omar of the dark coloring—part Arab, she would guess—gave her an odd message after his light kisses on both her cheeks: "May Allah bless your pillow tonight."

Nobody better be coming anywhere near my pillow.

JAM squeezed her hands. "God bless you, Mrs. MacLean."

I am to be called Miss-us MacLean now? Ah, in the seal world, women must take their husband's name, unlike my country, where the woman retains her mother's name.

"I would not have performed this ceremony if I didn't think it was the right thing," JAM continued.

She nodded. It felt right to her, too.

Sly the Black—or so she thought of the tall man in her mind—grinned and lifted her high in his arms. "Make the sucker beg, sweetheart. Make him beg."

I have no idea what that means, nor do I want to know.

Geek, the young man of great intellect, pulled her into a hug and said into her ear, "Come to me when you're ready. I'll help you find your country."

That was the most hopeful thing she'd heard all day. She smiled her thanks.

Ian saw Maddie smile at Geek and gritted his teeth. *She doesn't smile at me that way. And why should she? I've been a world-class horse's ass.*

So, what did he do, bumbling idiot that he'd become? He said, "Are you done sucking tongues with my teammates?"

She gasped at his crudity, and several of the guys protested his words, including Cage, who suggested to him, "Lighten up, *mon coeur*. It's just a custom."

He knew that. Although Maddie had her nose pointing to the ceiling, he saw the hurt in her eyes. Or maybe it was fear. This had to stop. He had to stop.

Twining his fingers with hers, he pulled her over to two folding chairs at the side of the quonset hut which served as the chapel. She resisted, of course. He pushed her down into a chair and sat beside her, still holding her hand.

She tugged.

He tugged back.

She growled.

He growled back.

Ian realized suddenly that he enjoyed sparring with the shrew. She wore the same outfit she'd had on last night . . . not the usual bridal fare, but then, he wore a cammie uniform. She looked magnificent. He probably looked like a dork.

She thinks I'm handsome, he reminded himself. And smiled.

"Do not think you can melt me with a smile."

Melt? Oh, my God! "It never occurred to me that I had the power to . . . melt you."

"Hah! You are a man. Men think with their dangly parts."

No way am I going to react to that. Dangly parts, indeed! "Listen, this is a scintillating conversation, but we have to talk. The shit is going to hit the fan any minute now, when CentCom hears what I've done. I'm sorry if I've been rude, but I've got a lot on my mind."

She tilted her head and studied him. "Could you lose your command over this?"

Maybe. "Nah!"

"I am sorry, too, if I have been ungrateful. 'Tis just that I ne'er expected to wed again. I have been on my own these past thirteen years, with neither father nor husband to control me."

"I can't imagine any man being able to control you."

She shrugged. "Well, they tried." She gave him a slight smile then.

And his heart lurched. "We must come to an understanding here while we have this minute alone."

She nodded. Then sniffed first one arm, then the other. Apparently, she was still fascinated with scented soap. In fact, she looked as if she was considering sniffing him, as well.

Lordy, Lordy! Distracted for a moment, he shook his head to clear it. "There will be no sex between us." He felt his face turn hot, but the words had to be said. *An annulment will never be given if we do the deed.*

"And you think that will disappoint me?" She glanced up from her sniffing. "Karl is the only man I have coupled with, and it is not an experience I yearn to repeat."

He should have been surprised, but he wasn't.

"And do not be trying to convince me that you would be more virile in the bed furs than Karl was. Better men than you have tried. I am not interested."

I could make you interested. He just stopped himself from speaking those words aloud. She would cut him off at the knees . . . or somewhere else. But he knew without a doubt that it was true. That hot kiss between them moments ago had convinced him if nothing else did that the two of them would make sparks in the hay. "Okay, that's settled. No sex. There are a couple other things. You can't be telling anyone that this is a temporary marriage. They'll make us stay and get it annulled here, meaning you won't be able to leave the country."

"What reason will we give for the quick marriage?"

His face flushed again. "Love. Red-hot passion. Whatever. Just don't act like you usually do."

"How do I usually act?"

"Like I repulse you."

"I only wish that were so."

Uh-oh. She's about to torpedo me, I just know it.

"If ever I were going to reverse my loathing for the bedsport, that kiss of yours would have convinced me. Glad I am that you do not want to mate with me. I am not sure I would be able to resist you."

Sonofabitch! You can't tell a guy that he turns you on, then expect him to control his libido, as if it has an off-on switch. He would have taken back his earlier words about no sex, but his nemesis came up then. Dan the Slime Spy.

"Congratulations, Ian. Is this the lucky lady?"

If he dares to try to kiss her, I'll knock his teeth out.

But Dan just shook her hand, a gesture that seemed to puzzle Maddie.

"What are you doing here, Dan?" Ian asked bluntly.

Not at all fazed by his rudeness, he handed Ian some documents. "The general sent these."

He frowned. *The general knows I'm here? In the chapel? Getting married?* "What are they?"

"Travel papers. For you and the little lady." Ian smiled smugly.

Ian took hold of the schmuck's arm and pulled him a few feet away from Maddie. Then he cocked his head. "General staff knew about my wedding plans?" Then an unbelievable suspicion entered his mind. "Did they have a hand in this?"

Dan shrugged. "Not exactly. Let's just say your wedding to Ms. . . . uh, Olgadottir . . . fits into the government's surveillance plans."

"Dammit! No matter how you spin it, I've been railroaded."

"Hey, man, take it easy. You get to enjoy a beautiful wife . . . for now." Ian was eying Maddie like she was a popsicle and he'd like to lick her up one side and down the other. "And you get to serve your country at the same time."

"This was your idea, wasn't it, dickhead?"

"Tsk-tsk-tsk! Sticks and stones, Kermie. No one made you do this. But we didn't put up any opposition either."

"Get out of here, slimeball, before I kick your ass up to your tonsils."

Dan smirked at him.

"Do not threaten my husband, you worthless piece of dung." Maddie had come up beside Ian and heard at least some of their conversation. "If my father were here, he would skin you alive." She had her hands on her hips and was glaring at Dan with belligerence.

All Ian could think was, *Look at her breasts in that shirt when she puts her hands like that. I am in male chauvinist heaven. Hope I'm not drooling.* Belatedly, he pondered her words. *I can't believe this. I am being defended by a woman.*

Dan gave Maddie another vulgar once-over, then turned and walked away.

"Would your father really skin a man alive?"

"Well, not this fellow, but Steinolf, the man who stole Norstead and degraded me so . . . yea, my father would skin him alive and feed his heart to the pigs. This man he would probably throw into the sea."

Unbelievable! Ian inhaled and exhaled several times to calm himself down.

"Even if he is not as vile as Steinolf, I do not like that Dan person, not one bit," Maddie went on.

"You and about a zillion other people."

"He kept staring at my breasts."

"Maddie, everyone stares at your breasts."

"Not really. Leastways, not in my country. Karl called them udders."

He gave her a look of disbelief. "Karl was a jackass."

She smiled then. At him. A full-blown smile which came from the heart and made her eyes dance. He felt the smile in every cell of his body.

Then she put a hand on his forearm and said, "Sometimes you are not such a troll."

Give me your tired, your poor . . .

One day later, Madrene was so tired and confused and lonely and disheartened that she felt like crying. But she had not wept for two long years, since the fall of Norstead, and she refused to succumb now.

She had ridden in an enormous bird known as a jet plane across the ocean for hours and hours, more than half a day. Most of the others inside the bird, at least two hundred, had worn military uniforms of one kind or another. Meals had even been served to the passengers, and there had been a privy. All this inside a bird.

It frightened Madrene to realize how much farther advanced this country was over her own. Even with all the adventuring that Norsemen did, none had ever reported such a civilization.

She had not wanted to cling to her new husband, but she had. When the bird had taken off. When she had seen clouds outside her window. When she had realized how far she was traveling from all that was familiar to her. When she smelled his man-scent or when he looked at her just so.

Then, late afternoon on the day after her wedding, they had landed in Ian's homeland, called Ah-mare-ah-ca. There, she'd been subjected to still more marvels. They rode in a horseless boxed cart with wheels, called a car, to Ian's keep in Sandy-egg-go. Everywhere she looked, there were people, hundreds and hundreds of people, all scurrying somewhere or other on important business. And the buildings were so close together here. No landed estates as in the Norselands, but small buildings with small plots of grass in front and behind.

Ian had told her that everyone was equal in this country, that there was no royal class. She could not fathom that. Even the Saxons had royal families, tradesmen, cotters and thralls. Her father had been a jarl, comparable to a Saxon earl.

She and Ian had come to somewhat of a truce.

Theirs was a marriage of convenience which would be ended sooner rather than later. She was agreeable as long as she could work on a plan to return to Norstead. Ian gained naught from their arrangement, except his honor, but she might just have a way of raising coin to repay him.

When they arrived at Ian's home, he helped her out of the tax-he car and said, "Be it ever so humble." He paid the tax-he car man, then led her up a stone walkway by putting a hand under her elbow. He slung his cloth carry bag over his other shoulder.

His home was modest by Norstead standards . . . as small as one of the stables, and there were no upper levels. He had told her that he lived alone in this cottage, with no servants; so it was no doubt big enough for his needs. There was a grassy section in front, like the other cottages had, but the back led to a sandy beach and the ocean. At least the smell of salt air was familiar to her.

When they got to the doorway, he put his bag down and inserted a key in the lock. He turned then and grinned at her. "Should I carry you over the threshold?'

"Whatever for?"

"A bridegroom is supposed to carry his bride over the threshold, for good luck." Before he even finished his words, the brute picked her up in his arms, kicked open the door and walked inside.

Madrene was not a small woman. "Put me down. I am too heavy for you."

He chuckled and nuzzled her neck. "Think again, sweetheart."

She could not recall any time in her thirty-one years that she had ever been lifted in anyone's arms.

Her mother had died when she was three. If her father had ever carried her, she did not recall it. There were always so many children about.

For just a moment, she allowed herself to enjoy the experience. She wrapped her arms over his shoulders and buried her face in the crook of his neck. She could swear he issued a soft moan. His skin smelled of pine and man. She could grow accustomed to that scent.

Nay, I could not, she immediately corrected herself. *This is a temporary arrangement. I should not become too comfortable here.* "Put me down," she demanded.

"Prickly already?" Ian laughed and set her down. It seemed as if he deliberately let her body slide over his, but she was no doubt wrong about that. He did appear to be in some discomfort.

"Are you in pain?" she asked.

He coughed and barely choked out, "No," though she thought she heard him mutter under his breath, "Hell, yes."

She looked around a small room which had comfortable stuffed chairs, a fireplace and low tables. Pale brown carpeting covered the floors, even to the walls. It was so clean and plush, a person could sleep on it, unlike the rushes in her home, which were a constant chore for her to rake clean and sprinkle with sweet rosemary. The smooth walls were white, and on them were framed paintings, like the one over the fireplace that she would study later . . . a roiling sea with a ship in peril. There was also a black box with knobs on it; she would ask Ian about its purpose at another time.

For now, this was his great hall, unlike any she had ever seen. She liked it.

He had been watching her closely for a reaction to his home. No doubt modesty had caused him to refer to it as humble, which it definitely was not. Everyone knew that only the very wealthy could afford to have paintings on their walls.

"Welcome to my home," he said.

She could not tell if he was teasing her, or serious. She chose to take him seriously. "I thank you for your hospitality."

"My pleasure." Once again, he muttered under his breath, this time saying, "Or pain."

He took her hand and showed her a bathing room, two large bedchambers, one of which held a bed big enough to hold a small army and the other a desk for doing business, and then to the kitchen, which garnered her greatest admiration.

Madrene had managed the affairs of a vast estate. She had been a warrior leading fierce fighting when Norstead was attacked. She had been a shrewd trader of goods in the marketplaces of Birka and Hedeby. But at heart she was a woman who could appreciate a good kitchen.

"Oooooh!" she said, putting both hands to her chest. "What a wonderful kitchen! I could live my entire life in this space alone and be happy."

"It's only a kitchen, for God's sake! Don't have a freakin' orgasm over it," Ian said.

"What's an orgy-asm?"

His tanned face flushed at her question, leading her to assume orgy-asm had something to do with sex. That was the only thing she knew that could bring a blush to a man's face.

Before he could answer, she knelt down to the floor to touch the gold-marbled tiles. They were not stone, but some other material. Like the carpet in his solar, it was exceptionally clean.

Ian was leaning against the doorjamb, watching her with amusement.

She did not care if she appeared foolish. This kitchen was a marvel.

There were wood doors and drawers above and below what Ian told her was a countertop, which had real tiles of a lighter shade than the floor. Inside those compartments were dishes and pots and pans and cutlery and foodstuffs. "I know a few kings who would swoon at all this luxury."

"Know a few kings, do you?" Ian inquired lazily. Obviously, he thought she lied.

"I do, you doubting oaf. But that is not important. How do you maintain your keep so spotless?" While she talked, she was fiddling with some metal contraptions from which hot and cold water flowed into a metal basin. It was like the showering apparatus she'd used back in Baghdad.

"I have a cleaning lady come in every two weeks," he said. "And I'm away a lot."

"But you must do some work yourself in between."

He shrugged. "Coming from a military background, I tend to be neat."

"This is beyond neat," she observed. Now she stood before a large white object built in between the wooden compartments. "What is this?"

"You know, this game of yours is getting old. I could buy your being so sheltered that you didn't recognize an airplane or common female underwear, though those are a stretch, but a stove? No way!"

"A stove? This is a stove? What is its purpose?"

"Give me a break! It's for cooking, and you very well know that."

She frowned. "I thought . . . what do you do with the fireplace in your solar, then?"

"It's for building a log fire and sitting there on a winter evening."

"For warmth?"

"Holy shit, no! It's supposed to be cozy."

"A fire just to sit afore with no purpose? You jest."

"No, I don't."

"Show me," she demanded, pointing to the stove.

He exhaled with disgust, but he turned on a knob, put a pan of water on top of a round implement, and waited. Soon the water came to a boil.

"This is wonderful! No smoke. No mess."

"If a stove makes you swoon, I wonder what you'll think of this." He opened the door of a very large box made of the same white material as the stove. Out came a blast of cold air.

She jumped back, frightened at first. "What is it?"

"A fridge for keeping food cold. So it won't spoil." He took out a piece of cheese from the lower section to show her. Then he pointed to the frozen meat in the top section.

"I am so confused," she said, sitting down on a wooden chair.

"You can say that again."

"Where am I?"

"San—"

"Not that," she interrupted. "I mean, what strange land is this? I ran away from an Arab man whose family lived in a tent, and end up here in a land of magic. I just do not understand."

"Me neither." Once again, disbelief and disgust

rang in his voice. "Well, I'll leave you here to drool. I've gotta go next door and get my roommate." He was opening the back door.

"A roommate? Someone lives here with you?"

He laughed. "You could say that. Her name is Samantha."

"Will Samantha object to my being here?"

"We shall see." The brute had a mischievous gleam in his eye.

Madrene was in shock.

He has a woman.

But he told me he was not married.

He married me.

It must be his lover.

Oh, what am I going to do? I must needs find another place to stay.

She walked through the house again, touching polished woods, and fine bed coverlets, admiring the showering stall in the bathing chamber, lying down on the solar carpet to see if it was as soft as it appeared. But her heart had gone out of her newfound joy.

He has a woman.

Worst of all, Madrene realized it wasn't just for practical reasons that she was so devastated. Somehow, somewhere these past few days, she had become attached to the lout. Not just attached. Attracted.

Should I leave?

Where shall I go?

Just then the back door opened, then slammed. He was back. With Samantha. Madrene stood in the hall corridor near the front door, waiting.

Ian came in and with him was . . . *a cat!*

A big fat cat that could be the sister of her own Rose. A lump formed in her throat. The man had a cat. How would she ever resist a man who cherished a cat?

"Maddie, I would like you to meet Samantha. The most ornery cat in the universe. Sam, this is Maddie, the most ornery woman in the universe."

Sam hissed at him as if she understood, jumped out of his arms and walked over to rub against Madrene's legs.

"Samantha's the only thing my fiancée left behind when she walked out three years ago. We called the cat Sam until I discovered that he was a she and . . ." His words trailed off as he realized that she wasn't listening to him at all.

Madrene picked up Sam, which was a feat because the cat was huge, just like her precious Rose back at Norstead. She held the cat up to her face for a kiss. Tears welled in her eyes.

Finally, when she'd cuddled the cat and petted her and showed how much she liked her, she turned to Ian, who was leaning against the wall, watching her with amazement.

"That cat never goes to anyone," he marveled.

"She reminds me of my cat, Rose. What a gift your cat is to me . . . I mean, your cat's presence here on this day!"

He raised his eyebrows at her.

"It is an omen, I think. A sign from the gods that everything will work out for me," she said.

"Don't you think that's reading a little bit much into a cat?"

She shrugged. "There is another thing I should forewarn you about."

"Omens and warnings," he scoffed. "What?"

"I think I could love a man who loves a cat."

Chapter Nine

She loves me, she loves me not, she loves . . .

"No, no, no!" Ian put his hands up in the air to halt her words. "You are wrong, wrong, wrong."

"How so?" she asked, walking into the living room and sitting down on the sofa, cradling Sam in her lap.

"Two things. One, this pain-in-the-ass cat is not an omen or a gift, or anything else. Sam is a high-maintenance, stubborn, in-your-face, hair-shedding, hair-ball-puking animal who doesn't know her place."

"Shhhh," Madrene hissed. Sam hissed, too. "You will hurt her feelings."

He rolled his eyes. "You cannot insult this cat. Believe me, I've tried."

"Poor little cat," she cooed, giving Sam another kiss on her ugly little cat lips.

Little? Sam could be the poster cat for Chubbettes Cat Food.

"What was the other thing?"

"Huh?" he said. Then, "The other thing is, you are not falling in love with me. Uh-uh! No way! Not over a cat or any other jack thing in the universe."

She looked at him with skepticism. In fact, she was licking her lips—the same lips that had just kissed a cat—and looking at him as if she were a nymphomaniac, and he'd just invented sex. *What a thought!*

"Look, it's seven o'clock, and we're both beat. Jet lag and all that. Why don't you take a shower while I fix us something to eat? I've got to be up early to meet with the Commander." *And get my ass chewed to smithereens.*

She agreed, putting the cat on the floor with reluctance. Sam immediately jumped up onto the sofa, which was a no-no. He could swear that was a smirk on the cat's face, daring him to try to dislodge her now that she had a new friend. He decided to wait till Maddie left the room before booting the feline into the kitchen where she belonged. There was a cat bed there, which Sam rarely used.

After that, he made some grilled cheese sandwiches and tomato soup, which was about all he had in the house till he went grocery-shopping tomorrow. He had heard the shower turn off about fifteen minutes ago, so he went to see what was holding Maddie up.

In the bathroom, her shirt, fatigues, panties and bra lay on the floor. He thought about picking up the lingerie, but decided that might be a bit perverted. But, uh-oh, what was Maddie wearing, if these items of apparel were here?

His head shot up and he looked toward his bedroom. There was a ringing in his ears, and his heart started racing. His cock had already been at half-staff, just ogling her undies. Now it was full-tilt boogie. He held a towel up to his middle and walked into his bedroom, flicking a lamp on in the darkened room.

Then he stopped dead in his tracks.

The reason Maddie hadn't come to eat was because she was asleep. In his bed. And she was NAKED.

Ian's eyes nearly popped out of his head.

She was covered with a sheet from her groin to the top of her breasts, but that didn't matter. He saw more than enough. Her damp pale blond hair was spread on the pillow under her head. Her eyelashes were honey-colored and long, curling naturally against her flushed cheeks. Her legs ran on forever. Her waist was small, flaring out to the curve of her hips. The shape of her firm breasts was crystal clear.

Jessica Simpson had nothing on her.

How could I possibly not have seen this magnificent body on that hag back in the cave?

What the hell am I going to do?

He was only a man. He could not live in the same house with a woman who looked like this, a woman who claimed she could love him, a woman who came from nowhere and claimed his cat was a frickin' omen, a woman who was still under suspicion of being a terrorist. He would have a nonstop hard-on in her presence from now on.

He decided to do the thing that most SEALs did when they were stressed out. Run. Changing into a pair of nylon shorts and running shoes, he went jogging on the beach. He ran five miles. It was totally dark when he came back to the sandy stretch behind his back deck. Bending over at the waist, he panted to get his heartbeat down. Then he looked up and realized that Maddie stood in the bedroom doorway, which led onto the deck. Backlit by a lamp, she wore one of his white T-shirts. And only that.

"Shit!" He groaned and decided to run another five miles.

You run, and run, and run, why? . . .

Madrene had a new concern to add to her long list of concerns. She had cast her lot with a barmy man.

There he was, running. Not just running, as in running from an enemy, or running to get something, but he appeared to be running for the sake of running. Up and down the sandy beach, for an hour or more.

He was a nicely built man, she would give him that. *Very* nicely built. But then, the men of Norseland were much the same, tall by birth and well muscled by necessity, being warriors always on the alert for a good fight. Still, she got that fluttery feeling in her stomach when she looked at his body as he ran.

He stopped once, down by the water. So riddled with exhaustion and probably pain was he that he was bent over at the waist. But what did he do? He looked up toward his house and began to run again.

Sam came out and rubbed herself against Madrene's bare leg. "Meow, meow, meow!" Madrene could swear the cat was saying, "What a lackwit!"

Yea, he must be demented.

HOT & HEAVY

Sweet temptation . . .

When he came in from his run, Maddie was on her hands and knees, butt in the air—very fine butt, by the way—licking his kitchen floor.

I swear to God, my life is going down the toilet. What next? "What the hell are you doing down there?"

Maddie hadn't realized that he'd come back. Her head shot up and she fell over, first on her side and then into a sitting position.

At least she's wearing fatigues and a T-shirt. I'm not sure I could resist her bare butt. I'd probably be down there licking, too . . . but not the floor.

Meanwhile, Sam, who had been licking beside her, let out a howl of outrage as Maddie apparently sat on her tail.

"Oh, it is you."

What? You'd think I was some intruder. I live here, for chrissake!

"You scared me. You scared the cat," she accused him.

Said cat, belatedly deciding to show a little fear, shot up into the air and landed on Ian's bare chest.

"Ow, ow, ow, ow, ow!" he cried as he tried to pry Sam's claws from his flesh. He had about fifteen pounds of fur ball mauling him. "I'm going to have this cat declawed. First thing tomorrow."

Sam dug in deeper.

Maddie got up and came over to help take the cat off of him, cooing at the beast like it was the injured party. "Poor cat. Did you get scared by the big man? Everything is fine now."

Finally the cat was off of him. Sam stood on the floor for a moment, arched her back to show how fierce she was, gave him "the look" which she'd perfected so well, and sauntered off to do what she did best—sleep. "Poor cat? I'm the injured party here." He walked over to the sink and wet a dish towel. He was about to wash the scratches when Maddie took the towel from him.

"Let me."

No way! "I can do it myself."

"I can do it better, you stubborn lout. I've tended wounds much worse than this for my fighting men." With that, she began to dab gently at the blood seeping out of the wounds, and, yes, she did seem to know what she was doing. "As for my siding with the cat. She did not know any better. You scared her."

She is standing so close I could kiss her without . . . Get a grip, man, get a grip! "Hah! That scaredy-cat probably gave me rabies, or blood poisoning or something."

"Huh?"

"Never mind. I was just kidding. She's had shots."

He could tell that Maddie didn't understand.

"I do not think that I need to sew up any of these scratches, deep as some are. I do wish I had my special healing ointment here. It has cured many an injury, including a festering sword wound on Dar the Deaf one time. Mayhap you could take me out in a forest sometime and I will gather the herbs I need."

Sword? Dar the Deaf? Herbs? I am not going to ask. He could take only so much of her standing close to him—*she smells like Irish Spring soap*—and touching him. *Even in my pain, I can imagine those hands doing something else, and not just to my skin.*

Quickly, before he embarrassed himself, he went

into the bathroom and took a cold shower. When he came back, he wore a tank top and sweats; his feet were bare. He usually slept nude, but these would have to suffice for pajamas tonight. Which brought to mind something he needed to discuss with her. But first, he should feed the wench.

"Maddie, where are you?" he yelled from the kitchen.

"Right here." She was standing behind him. "You don't have to bellow."

"Do you have to sneak up on me?" he griped.

"Do you always blame everyone else?"

"Aaarrgh!"

"That is what men say whenever they have lost an argument."

"Aaarrgh!" he said again.

Within minutes he had reheated the tomato soup in the microwave, made fresh grilled cheese sandwiches and poured them both glasses of Pepsi with ice. He put the food in front of her at the kitchen table, then plopped down on the opposite side. He was already halfway through his food when he noticed that she hadn't started. She was just staring at her dinner.

"What?"

"I'm not sure how to eat this. The cheese bread I can handle. I see you using your fingers. But I'm not sure I could use a spoon and get this thin liquid from the bowl to my mouth. And what is this beverage with ice floating in it?"

"It's Pepsi. Try it. You'll like it."

She took a sip and smiled.

"How would you eat tomato soup where you live?"

"What's a tomato?"

He laughed. "A tomato is a fruit."

"This broth looks like blood. Are you sure it is not blood?"

He crossed his eyes at her continual questions.

"This is what we would do in my land." She picked up the bowl in both hands and took a drink.

He laughed again. "Well, that's one way to do it. But if you were out in public, it wouldn't be appropriate." He used his spoon in his own bowl to demonstrate. "See?"

She frowned with skepticism.

He shook his head at her cluelessness. Was it an act? Or was she really that ignorant of normal everyday table manners? He got up and went behind her, showing her how to hold the spoon and bring the liquid carefully to her mouth. "No, don't lean over the plate. Bring the food to you."

There were a few dozen SEALs over in Coronado who would get a kick out of the idea of Ian teaching anyone table etiquette.

"Why must you make eating so difficult here?" With that, the stubborn woman lifted the bowl to her mouth and drank it down. Then she polished off two sandwiches and chugged down her Pepsi. She must have been as hungry as he was.

Now he leaned back in his chair and said, "Maddie, we need to have some house rules here." *Rules are made to be broken. No, no, no, I did not think that.*

"Oh?" Her body tensed. Someone must have done her wrong real bad for her to be so distrustful.

"When I went to my bedroom earlier, you were sleeping in my bed."

"Was I not to sleep there? I did not see any other bed in your keep."

"It's not that." He could feel his face heat up. Dammit, he'd developed a pattern of blushing around her, and he hardly ever blushed. "You and I can't sleep together and then get an annulment, if you know what I mean."

She just looked at him, incredulously. "Do you mean we could not resist each other?"

Well, yeah! He was a little bit insulted by her incredulity. "I don't know about you being tempted by me, but I sure as hell am hot to trot for you."

She smiled. *The witch!* "Ian, your bed is big enough for twelve people. You stay on your side. I stay on mine. Good Lord, we would probably hear an echo if we spoke to each other in bed."

He had to grin at that. It *was* a king-size bed.

"And actually I *am* tempted by you, much as I fight it."

Uh-oh! He stopped grinning. "You have got to stop saying things like that to me."

"Why?"

Because I like it too much. "Discretion is the better part of valor."

She furrowed her brow. "Another of your sayings! Do you not value honesty?"

"Of course I do, but some things are better left unsaid. Why take unnecessary risks?" *I sound like a total dweeb.*

"Is that all?"

"No, that's not all." He exhaled loudly. "You were *naked* in my bed."

She put her hands out in a "so what?" fashion.

"People in my land sleep naked. It saves wear on clothing and there is less sweat to be washed out by the house carls. Plus, it is more comfortable. Except when I have my monthly flux; then I wear bedclothes. And betimes when Karl was *drukkin* and I did not want him to touch me. Do you sleep in your clothing?"

Way more than I needed to know. He felt himself blush again. "I usually sleep naked, but I'll be wearing clothes for damn sure if you're in the same room, let alone the same bed."

She shrugged. "I can do that. Anything else?"

Yeah, there's a lot more. "No, I'm going to bed."

"Me, too."

Oh, boy!

Do men really think they can order women about?

Madrene awakened at dawn as she always did, but she was alone in the big bed.

In the darkened room, she had heard her seal bedmate tossing and turning throughout the night before he finally fell asleep.

Finally she'd turned his way in the dark and advised him, "Why don't you pleasure yourself to gain release? 'Tis the best thing to do when sleep eludes you and coupling is not a possibility. Leastways, that's what Karl used to do."

From across the bed, she'd heard a choking sound, then laughter. "You are a piece of work, Maddie. Why don't you say what you really think sometime?"

Now she heard water running and concluded that Ian must be in the showering room. Again. He had showered the night before. What need was there for another showering? She sat up at the side of the bed and shook her head with wonder. Vikings were known for their cleanliness, but this was excessive.

He came into the room with a towel wrapped around his middle. And stopped abruptly at the sight of her. His eyes, before he turned away, surveyed her body and liked what they saw. She was wearing a long white tea *shert* of his over a pair of tight *braies*, made of a fabric called lay-tax. She knew that because Ian had told her yesterday when she'd seen some girls running down the street wearing similar garments.

He opened some drawers and pulled out dark hose and a white undergarment similar to her panties, but different. Before he returned to the bathing chamber to put them on—though she suspected he would normally do it here—he remarked, "I've got to go in to the base for several hours this morning and probably part of the afternoon. Maybe we can go buy you some clothes after that . . . and stop somewhere for dinner."

She nodded. "What am I to do all day? I would like to be useful, but your house is so clean and organized, there is no work for me. That was what I did all my life . . . until I was sold to the harems, of course."

"You cleaned and organized for a living? Like Molly Maids?"

Her brow furrowed, as had become her habit around him, and she continued, "Before I was sold to the harems, I ran a vast estate."

"How vast?"

"One hundred hectares of land. Two hundred

fighting men, fifty cotter families, twenty-five house carls and maids, ten thralls, and—"

"Whoa, whoa, whoa. You sure do know how to tell a whopper, lady."

"I do not even see any gardens for food." She ignored his words because, frankly, she did not understand what a whop-her was. It sounded painful. "And there is not a cow for milk. Nor chickens for eggs. I could weave a tapestry if there is a loom about. Or polish swords. Or . . ." She let her words fade out as she noticed his gaping jaw. "I have never relished idleness."

"Idle hands are the devil's work."

"For a certainty. That is one of your lackwit sayings I can agree with."

He shook his head as if to clear it and said, "Just stay here till I get back. Watch TV. Take a bubble bath. Do your nails. I don't care. Just don't leave."

"I will do as you command," she said to him, but inside she said, *I must needs explore this new land to find out how to return to Norseland. I wonder where I could find a horse.*

I smell a rat . . .

Ian started to feel suspicious the moment he entered the Naval Amphibious base at Coronado. Everyone was rushing him through to headquarters.

Within a half hour he knew why, and he was not a happy camper.

Commander George Harding was there, along with his XO Jack Bell; Lawrence Sanders, a high mucky-muck in the CIA; a representative of the Pentagon; and—the biggest surprise of all—his father.

Commander Harding told him to sit down when he threatened to leave the room. Good thing it wasn't his father who gave that order. The mood he was in, he would probably have told him to go screw himself.

He inhaled and exhaled to calm his temper, but it did no good. A short time later, he said, "Let me get this straight. You know that Maddie isn't a terrorist. You don't know who she is, but that doesn't matter . . . not for the sake of whatever goal you have for this half-assed brainstorm that can probably be traced to Dan the Prick Sullivan. You expedited my marriage to her and made her departure from Iraq a piece of cake. From the minute I got off that chopper and brought Jamal in, this plot was being brewed. Sonofabitch!"

"Watch your tone," his father advised.

Ian ignored the bastard. How could he do this to his own son?

"Let me reiterate," the commander said. "This woman can lead us to a whole network of Jamal's operatives."

"She doesn't know jack shit, if you ask me."

"Doesn't matter," Sanders, the CIA guy, told him. At least this bunch of dodo birds knew enough not to send Dan Sullivan. "We've already put the word out that we've got in custody a woman who infiltrated the terrorist camps and has been there the past year. We'll let an 'unnamed source' slip a tidbit or two about this modern-day Mata Hari to the *Washington Post*. We'll say she has enough data to bring down the entire Al Qaeda network. And that she's in a safe house on the West Coast. Aljazeera and the major news media in this country will eat it up."

"Ian, we need to draw out these tangos once and for all," his commander tried to convince him.

"They'll know she's with me. I didn't make any secret of the fact I was bringing her back. My home address is unlisted, even here on the base, except to my direct chain of command, but still, you know damn well they're going to find it . . . and Maddie."

"That's the point," Sanders said.

"You want to set Maddie up as bait."

Sanders shrugged. "She won't get hurt."

"The hell you say. You can't guarantee her safety."

"Yeah, I think we can. You'll be guarded at all times, surreptitiously, of course. In fact, you've been tailed by at least two men since you got married."

Ian closed his eyes and clenched his fists.

Commander Harding came up behind Ian and put a hand on his shoulder. "It's for the greater good."

"That sounds like something a politician would say when he's done something slimy. How long do you expect this operation to last?"

"Two . . . three weeks at the most."

"And the marriage?"

"Annulled as soon as you two file the papers after that. As long as—"

"Forget it," Ian interrupted. Geesh! Now they were interfering in his love life, too. "Ain't gonna happen." *I hope. I pray. I hope.* "How about Maddie? What happens to her after this is all over?"

Sanders said, "Either a safe house and new identity here in the States, or we'll fly her wherever she wants to go. Give her a little money to help her get adjusted, too."

"Are there guards watching my house now?"

They all nodded.

"If I agree to this . . . and I am only saying *if* . . . I demand that this be a SEAL operation. No CIA within a mile of me or my home."

"You have no right to make demands," his XO said.

"We have to be involved," Sanders protested.

"Why are you being so difficult?" his father demanded. "You don't have any feelings for this woman, do you?"

He gave his father a scorching look. *You traitor. What kind of man are you that you would sacrifice your child for some "greater good"? Ah, hell, it's the same old thing. Loyalty to country comes first, even above family.* His father didn't even wince.

"Actually, it might work better if this is a SEAL op. If men are seen anywhere near his house, people will assume it's just a friend or teammate dropping by for a beer." Commander Harding's face turned red with excitement. "It could work. What do you think, Ian?"

"I don't know," he said. "I'm so pissed right now I can't think straight. Let me think it over."

Harding said, "I could order you to do it."

"But you'd rather you didn't have to. Right?"

Harding nodded.

"Give me twenty-four hours to give you an answer. And let me talk it over with the other members of my squad. Then . . . we'll see."

Just then, a cell phone buzzed in Sanders's pocket. "Excuse me," he said. "They wouldn't call me here unless it was something I needed to know." He put the small phone to his ear. "Sanders here. Yes, yes. Uh-oh!" Sanders looked over at Ian when he said "Uh-oh!"

Uh-oh! Something's up. And it involves me. Oh, maybe one of my guys got in trouble, and he needs my help. Probably got picked up at the Wet and Wild for disorderly conduct last night. Needs me to bail him out.

"I see. Okay. Just stick with her."

Her? Alarm bells went off in his head. He stood and tilted his head in question.

"Your wife is strolling the shops in San Diego. And she has a big cat with her."

Chapter Ten

Norsemen go a-Viking, Norsewomen go a-shopping . . .

Maddie and Sam were strolling, as if they hadn't a care in the world, along a strip mall about two miles from Ian's home when he finally caught up with her.

Ian pulled his red Mustang convertible into a parking slot and started after the errant pair. Sam saw him first and had the good sense to duck between Maddie's legs. Maddie had no sense at all, just waved at him as if she had a perfect right to wander off.

The first thing he said to her when he walked up, practically nose to nose, was, "What the hell are you doing here?"

She cocked her head as if trying to puzzle him out, and answered him tit for tat. "What the hell are *you* doing here?"

He took a deep breath and warned himself to be

polite . . . until he got the willful witch home. "Maddie, *dear*, I'm curious. What are you doing here?"

"Looking in the market stalls, *dearling*."

Do not lose your temper. Do not lose your temper. She's just being sarcastic. Like I am most of the time. Do not lose your temper. "I distinctly ordered you to stay home."

She looked at him as if he were dumb as toast. "Dost really think that I would take orders from you . . . or any other man? You have not been listening to me, if you are of that opinion. Mayhap you are deaf . . . or leastways, deaf where women are concerned. Some men are. Bloody hell, *most* men are. And, by the by, that vein in your forehead is throbbing again. Best you be careful or it may explode."

"Aaarrgh!" He took her by the upper arms and barely restrained himself from shaking her. "Did it ever occur to you that I might have a reason for wanting you to stay indoors? Did it ever occur to you that you don't know this city and could get lost? Did it ever occur to you that someone other than yourself might have a brain? Did you even think, period?"

"Did it ever occur to you that you are not my real husband, nor my master? You have no rights over me. I do not like your tone. Not at all. I am not one of your seals that you can speak to like that. If you must know, I was bored. After washing your clothes and hanging them to dry, there was nothing else to do. And take your hands off me. I did not give you permission to touch my body."

"Lady, if I want to touch you, I will, and by damn, I'm not going to say 'Pretty please' first."

"Be careful, troll, I could wave my magic fingers at your male parts and render them useless."

"Bullshit!" He laughed and released his hold on

her. Guilt struck him then as he noted the marks he had made on her fair skin. "I'm not afraid of your fingers, sweetheart, magic or otherwise. You give me a hard-on that couldn't be brought down by a hammer, let alone your piddly little fingers."

She gasped with indignation. "I know what a hard-on is, you oaf. I asked Pretty Boy when I heard him use the word back in Baghdad." A smile flickered on her lips then as she asked, "I give you a hard-on?" She appeared pleased at the notion. Probably because she enjoyed torturing him so.

"This is not a conversation we should be having. Not in a public place." *Not anywhere else either.* "Another thing, people don't go out walking with a cat. Cats run away. Cats get run over by cars."

"Sam does not run from me. She is a good cat."

He rolled his eyes.

"Really, even when I entered these shops, the traders would not let her come in, but I told Sam to sit outside on the pavement and wait for me. And she did just that. Didn't you, sweet cat?"

Ian glanced down at the cat, which was indeed sitting next to Maddie like a docile pet. "How come she never behaves like that for me?"

"You handle her incorrectly." The implication was that he handled Maddie incorrectly, too. *If she only knew how tempted I am to handle her!*

While Maddie was looking at him and not at the cat, he could swear Sam stuck out her tongue at him. "Well, since we're here, we might as well get you some clothes. You can't wear the same thing every day." She was wearing the T-shirt and latex pants she'd put on this morning. *Lordy, Lordy!*

Her face lit up. "I love to buy . . . and trade. Would

it be immodest of me to say I have a talent for trading? The merchants at Birka and Hedeby know me well, and respect the hard bargains I make with them."

Okaaaay. Birka and Hedeby again. I'll have to ask Geek where they are.

So a-shopping they did go.

She went nuts over some weaving loom or whatever the jumble of wood was in the window of an antique shop. "I had a hand loom like that one time. I did not have much idle time, but when I did, I loved to sit and weave." She sighed.

He was getting used to her sighs. Not!

They continued walking, but she kept looking over her shoulder at the loom. And Ian did not miss the fact that, while they were walking, lots of people—*mostly men, dammit!*—did a double take when glancing at Maddie. Her pale hair hung in a long, single braid down her back. Her facial features were sharp. Her lips were full and sexy . . . really sexy. She walked like she was the queen of the strip mall on long, long legs. And he wasn't even going to look at her breasts . . . though a couple dozen men were.

"That forehead vein is throbbing again," Maddie pointed out.

Something else is throbbing, too. "You bring that out in me."

"I do not!"

He shrugged. "By the way, what did you mean about washing my clothes? I didn't think there was any detergent left by the washing machine."

"Deter-gent. Mash-sheen." She sounded both words out, and when he just shook his head at her continuing game of "What is that?" she replied, "I washed your garments in that metal trough in your kitchen. I used the hard soap that was there. Then I hung them out to dry."

The dingbat washed my clothes. "I'm afraid to ask. Where did you hang them? I don't have a clothesline."

"Out on the railing of the wooden platform behind your house."

Oh, good Lord! "The deck?"

"Yea, the deck. And what a problem I had with your pant-teas and mine, not to mention my breast harness. The wind kept blowing them out onto the sand." Her face brightened. "But I took a rod down from your window covering in the kitchen and anchored it between two chairs. With the garments strung along the rod, they are drying nicely."

"My pan-panties?" he sputtered out. "Holy hell, Maddie! You washed my jockey shorts? By hand?"

"Yea, I did." She must have noticed the stormy expression on his face, because she glared at him, hands on hips, and said, "Say thank you."

He barely choked out the words, but he said, "Thank you." *Man, we'd better get this shopping expedition over quick. One of the guys might come over early for our meeting tonight. I'll never hear the end of it if they see my tighty whities blowing in the wind, next to her "harness."*

For the next two hours, Ian enjoyed the wonderful pleasure/torture of watching Maddie try on tight jeans, revealing shirts, short skirts, sandals and sneakers, all of which she marveled over like a kid in a toy store. In the process, he saw up close and personal that Maddie had been telling the truth. Her "harness" had been left at home on his deck rail.

The lingerie section was particularly embarrassing to him. Maddie held up one sexy bra after another, continually referring to them as harnesses. "I wear a 34-see," she told him. *Like I need to know that!* As for panties, they settled for hip-hugging silk scraps, which he was not imagining on her body. Uh-uh. Not him. When he suggested that she try a thong, she examined it closely, then made a scoffing sound. Looking up at him impishly, she said, "I'll wear a thong if you will." They didn't buy any thongs.

Now they were headed toward their last stop . . . the grocery store at the end of the strip mall. Maddie's eyes went wide, even wider than they had on first seeing an aircraft, or all the clothing items in the boutique, or his freakin' kitchen.

"This must be heaven." She sighed orgasmically. *No, no, no! I did not think that word orgasmically. She sighed—that's all. Oh, God, this is a losing battle. I am dead meat.*

First they went to the produce department, where Maddie had to touch and smell everything. Grapes that she declared bigger and more succulent than those on her father's farmstead, wherever that was. Apples that were redder and firmer than those she'd seen in Birka, wherever that was. Pomegranates more inviting than those eaten in the Arab harems, wherever they were. She claimed to have never seen a banana before. He bought several of those. Oranges she was familiar with, but the ones she'd tasted had been far smaller and bitter. He gave her a sample section which was set out on a tray. She declared it food of the gods. They tossed a bag of oranges in the cart. Then a bag of lettuce mix, potatoes, tomatoes, peaches, blueberries, watermelon and so much more, each of which required another of those sighs which he was not categorizing in a sexual way, like he had before, though he was thinking it.

Dammit. A man has to be dead below the waist not to want a woman to sigh like that over him. I can hear it now. "Oooh, it is bigger, and firmer, and more succulent than any I have seen before."

"Why are you grinning?"

He zipped his lips. "Never mind."

He had to pull her from the produce department after half an hour and a half-full cart of produce alone. The meat department was equally tantalizing to her. She just couldn't accept that there were no cows or pigs or lambs being slaughtered behind the counters to yield all these packets of meat. They bought hamburger, hot dogs—*and didn't that raise her eyebrow?*—steaks, bacon, sausage, a couple of frozen pizzas, frozen French fries, butter, bread, rolls, ice cream, milk, eggs, soda, beer, nail polish, dish and clothes detergent, a brush, comb and mirror, soap and shampoos, each of which she had to sniff. Even as they left, he with a sigh of relief, she with a sigh of regret, he had to promise they would return. They ended up with two carts full of groceries and a three-hundred-dollar bill.

Outside, one exasperated-looking cat greeted them with a loud, whining, "Meow!"

"We bought you some cat food, sweetling," Maddie told Sam, reaching down to ruffle her fur. Sam purred her thanks.

"Hey, thank *me*. I'm the one who paid for it."

Sam thanked him by pissing on the sidewalk near his boot.

"Damn cat!" he said under his breath as he led them toward his convertible.

"I heard that," Maddie said. But she wasn't mad at him, he could tell. He'd taken her to a magic mart—her words—and he was in her good graces. For now.

They were cruising down the streets in his neighborhood, top down, the late-afternoon sun warm on their heads. Ian was feeling oddly at peace. And happy. He couldn't say why for sure. He just was.

Maddie was holding on to her seat for dear life. Claimed she had never ridden in a horseless red box with no roof before. "Do you have to go so fast?

"Are you kidding? I'm going fifteen miles an hour. Relax."

Maddie sat back and seemed to loosen up. That was when she threw him one of her zingers. "Ian, is one hundred thousand dollars a lot of money?'

"You could say that. Yeah, it's a lot. Why?"

"The man in the jewel mart offered me that much today."

"No way!" *Oh . . . my . . . God! Prostitution now. I don't believe it. No, no, no! It can't be that. Even Maddie wouldn't be worth that much money for a roll in the hay.* "No way!" he repeated.

"He did. I assure you, he did." She held out a business card to him. It read: *Abraham Kranich. Fine Estate Jewelry.* Then, handwritten on the card was, "$100,000. Eight-carat emerald."

He had just pulled into his driveway and was about to punch in the remote for his garage door when he turned to her. "You have an eight-carat emerald?"

She nodded, and took a big green stone from her

pocket to show him. What did he know? It looked like a big green stone.

"The man said this is a rare jewel and of superior quality."

"I'm going to hate myself for asking, but where did you get it?"

Her face flushed. "I might have taken a jewel . . . or two . . . from the harem treasure chests."

"You stole jewelry?" *This is just great! First she seems to be a terrorist, then a hooker, now a cat burglar.*

She lifted her chin haughtily. "I was sold, against my will, to one man after another. For two long years I have been kept from my homeland. I deserved just payment, and that is what I got. No one ever missed them. I kept them sewn into the seams of my gunna. Ten little jewels! Pfff! I had ten times as much stolen from me when Steinolf invaded my keep."

Steinolf again! "Ten, you say?"

"More or less."

He raised his eyes heavenward. "You're a freakin' millionaire."

"Is that good?"

"Very good."

"Then I will give you one of the jewels for the groceries you bought today. I do not like to be beholden to any man."

He started to laugh and couldn't stop. He could see that she was annoyed by his laughter. "A hundred thou for a bag of groceries?" he choked out through his continuing laughter. "What is that? Like a hundred dollars an orange? A hundred dollars a banana? A hundred dollars for a brush? A hundred dollars for a candy bar? Oh, geez. Oh, man. This is the funniest thing I've heard in a long time."

She looked downright cute glaring at him.

So, what could a red-blooded male—which he was—say but, "Baby, you can pay me in some other way"?

It was a Norse-Arab-Cajun-American Indian pasta dish . . .

Madrene was in the kitchen learning how to cook while the men were in the solar talking about some big secret mission, as men were wont to do. Every time she entered the room, they went silent. *Men! Blowhards, all of them.*

One at a time, each of the men came into the kitchen, where she was watching the red spaghetti sauce cooking on the stove. Every one of them tasted the sauce and added some new spice or grated cheese. They came to get a beer . . . which was similar to mead. She was drinking a glass herself.

They all commented on her new attire. Tight *braies*, called jeans. A sleeveless, hip-length *shert*, which tapered in at the waist, called a blouse. It had odd fasteners on the front called butt-ons, and was made of a light blue fabric. When he purchased it, Ian had said it matched her eyes, which pleased her; he did not toss many compliments in her direction. No doubt he wanted something from her.

Omar, who prided himself on his cooking skills, had spent some time with her in the beginning of the evening, teaching her how to use the kitchen implements. The stove. The can opener. The toaster. The microwave oven. Of course, he had to then explain to her what a can was, or why one would want to brown a slice of bread. He'd also had to explain all the different foods to her, since she could not read the labels. Tomato sauce. More spices than she ever thought existed. Rice. Pop-Tarts. Spa-get-he . . . which was what they were making tonight.

In addition, he showed her the laundry room and demonstrated the two magic mash-sheens there. No wonder Ian had been embarrassed over his under-garments hanging outside. Apparently, people here hid their washing and drying efforts.

She saw Omar studying her at various times when he did not realize she was aware of his scrutiny. He also alternated his conversation between Arabic and Saxon English, as if trying to trick her up with some mistake.

"So, you live with your little girl?" she asked. "Five years old, did you say?"

"Uh-huh," Omar replied while he stirred the mary-nary sauce with a wooden spoon and added some Eastern spice. Every once in a while, he tested it by dipping out a little on the spoon. He made her do the same, though she had no idea how to deter-mine when it was done. He took out a shiny paper with the image of a little girl on it. The red-haired child did not much resemble Omar. "Darla is going to start school in September. Early enrollment in kindergarten." Pride was evident in his voice.

That got her attention. "Girls go to school in this country?"

"Absolutely. It's required of both boys and girls."

"That is wonderful. I have always wanted to learn to read and write, as my brothers did. My father, un-like many, would have allowed it, I think, but there was no time. Running a vast estate, whether it be a farmstead or royal household, left no time for anything not strictly a necessity."

"A vast estate, huh? Tell me what kind of things you did."

Omar was a very interesting man. He had been a teacher at a large university before becoming a seal. He had regaled her with astonishing stories of his brave ancestors on his father's side. They had been red men, known as Indians.

Because he had shared some of his life story with her, she felt comfortable doing the same for him. "I will tell you of Norstead, the royal estate, because that is where I was at the last . . . not at the farmstead."

"Royal?"

"My father's family held a jarldom. We are related to the king's family, though not in line of succession, thank the gods. What a snake pit of greed and intrigue that is! I had been married to Karl Ivarsson for a few years, but he put me aside and—"

"Do you mean divorce?"

She shrugged. "I guess that is your word for it."

"I'm divorced," Omar said.

"Really? Did you put your wife aside?"

He laughed. "Nah. It was a mutual decision."

"But the child stays with you? How odd!"

"Colleen is a magazine writer. She travels all around the world in her job with *Vanity Fair*. It was more expedient to leave Darla with me." He went over to the kitchen table and showed her a sheaf of thin papers, bound together. "This is *Vanity Fair* magazine, he noted.

"You travel, too," she pointed out.

"Yes, I do."

Obviously, the mother did not choose to take on the responsibility of her own baby. For shame! "And what happens when you are gone?"

"My mother helps out."

"I would give anything to have a child. Girl or boy, no matter. But it is not to be." She sighed.

"You were telling me about your duties at . . . Norstead."

She regaled him for a long time with a description of her duties from dawn till nightfall, some of which changed with the seasons.

He was looking at her with amazement when she was done. "I could almost believe you."

Madrene took insult at his words, but did not tell him so. He must have suspected how he had offended, though, because he put a hand on her shoulder and said, "Give us time to get to know you. We'll come around. Or you will." He grinned at that last.

"Hah! You will see."

They smiled at each other, just as Ian came in to put a big loaf of bread in the oven to warm and to put on a large pot of water to boil for the spaghetti. "You never smile at me like that," he griped. "Guess it's true that nice guys finish last."

"Who is the nice guy?" she asked.

Ian stomped out.

Omar just grinned at her.

Geek came next . . . a young man with freckles on his face that made him look much younger than his years. He added a pungent section of garlic to the pot. "You can never have too much garlic," he said with a wink. Then he came over to the table where she was sitting. "What're you reading?"

"I am just looking at the pages. I do not know how to read."

"No kidding? I thought everyone knew how to read. In all parts of the world, I mean."

"Some do in my country, but not many women."

He nodded as if he understood, muttering something about women's liberation needing to reach every corner of the world.

She eyed him closely for a second, then asked, "Would you teach me to read and write?"

He gave her a steady gaze, surprised at her request.

"I could pay you," she added quickly.

A smile twitched at his lips. "Yeah, I heard."

She could only imagine what kind of story the troll had told his teammates.

"I've never been a teacher," Geek said then, "but I can try."

"Another thing. Ian tells me that you know everything about everything, and—"

"He was being sarcastic."

"Hmmmm. I do not think so. In any case, I need to find a way home to Norstead. Would you be able to help me?"

"You mean, a map."

"Yea, a map would be good."

"Probably. Next time I come I'll bring my laptop and we can check it out on the Internet. Or else we can use Ian's computer."

Madrene did not understand all his words, but it appeared that this young man had agreed to help her find her way home, in addition to teaching her to read and write. "Thank you, thank you." She got up and hugged him.

Ian walked in to get a beer, saw the hug and

walked back out. She thought she heard him say a well-known, one-word Saxon expletive.

Geek arched his eyebrows at her in a knowing manner.

Sly, the tall black man, regaled her with stories of his homeland, Man-hat-and, also called the Big Apple, which was odd since he'd told her, upon questioning, that there were no apple trees there. She could hardly fathom his claim that there was a building more than a hundred stories high; a story was one level of a building, floor to ceiling. No doubt he was teasing her, as all the seals were wont to do.

She was laughing at his description of the way people traveled there on underground vehicles when Ian came in again. He looked at her, frowned, then banged some utensils at the stove as he added the thin sticks of spaghetti to the water. "Don't let me interrupt anything," he said. The words should have been polite, but they came out like a criticism.

"Why would he criticize us for laughing together?" Madrene asked Sly after Ian stomped out of the room again.

"He's jealous," he said.

"Impossible," she replied. "He does not care about me."

Sly winked at her and left.

Cage, the mischievous one, came next. He didn't even bother to taste the sauce. Instead, he turned up his nose and said, "If it ain't gumbo, it ain't worth fixin'." He put a little black box on the table in front of her. "You ever heard Cajun music, sugar?"

She shook her head slowly from side to side.

"You're in for a treat." He pressed a red thing on the black box, and loud, raucous music came forth.

She jumped out of her seat and backed away. "What is it? Is there a person in there playing an instrument?"

"Oh, chère," he said with a grin, "you have so much to learn. That, darlin', is Cajun music, the best in the world."

"Well, it certainly is loud."

"That's a backhanded compliment if I ever heard one." He told her a fascinating story about his people—the Acadians, who were driven out of France and then Canada. Finally, many of them settled in Lewis-i-anna. Apparently, there were swamps in this region which abounded with fierce animals called ally-gate-ors. But the strong Cajun people survived there, eating the animals the city dwellers disdained, turning them into spicy dishes. And they were a happy people, as evidenced by their lively music. "Plus," Cage added at the last, "Cajun men are known to be great lovers."

At first she did not realize that he was teasing her. When understanding came, she told him, "'Tis the same thing men of my country claim. Methinks men have an overblown opinion of their prowess in the bedsport. Except for my father, of course. He bred thirteen children on different women and could lay claim to being particularly virile. Is that not outrageous?" Without waiting for an answer, she continued, "Of course it is. And believe you me, I told him so on many an occasion. Some people say that I am a shrew, but I prefer to say I am a strong-minded woman. What say you?"

Cage blinked at her several times, as if she'd stunned him with her words. He was not the first man to do so. Then he smiled at her. "All I can say,

Maddie, is that you are a very interesting woman."

"I will take that as a compliment." *Even though it probably was not meant as such.*

"Would you like to dance?" Cage held his arms open for her.

"I cannot imagine dancing to that music."

"I'll show you. C'mon, baby. A strong-minded woman wouldn't be afraid of a little dance."

She narrowed her eyes at him for throwing her words back at her, but she stepped into his embrace, which was too intimate for mere acquaintances in her opinion. But the rogue never gave her a chance to protest, and he twirled and stomped her about the kitchen to an exercise called the "Cajun two-step." Every time she stepped on his toes with her new sandals, he kept telling her, "Feel the beat, Maddie. Just feel the beat."

"I would like to beat someone, for sure," Ian said, flicking off the radio and glaring at Cage. "In case you've forgotten, dimwit, we are having a serious meeting in the living room." Then he turned and walked away.

Cage followed him, but not before saying, "It would seem that there is more than one shrew in this house."

She was flipping through the magazine again when Luke came in—she preferred that name to his nicking name, Slick. Actually, he was standing in the doorway, leaning lazily on the frame, watching her. For how long, she could not say. This man was different from the other seals. Oh, he was handsome, with his dark hair and eyes so dark a blue they almost appeared black. And his long, lean body was as muscled as all the rest. He did not talk much, though, and there was a danger in his quietness. Like she used to see in her Uncle Jorund.

"I understand you have some valuable jewels," he said finally, after prolonged silent scrutiny.

She nodded.

"If you ever need to sell them, contact me. I can put you in touch with . . . people."

She nodded again.

"Avenil, leave my wife alone," Ian said, coming up on Luke.

"Wife?" Luke inquired in a disbelieving voice. Then he, like the others, walked away.

"I am not your wife," she called after Ian.

"You're not my mother, either, Mrs. MacLean," he called back.

What does that mean?

After the meal, which was messy . . . at least for her . . . the men went back into the solar to finish their meeting, except for Pretty Boy. He noticed the magazine was opened to a page where there was a beautiful woman with scarlet lips and fingernails, posing with her hands upraised, combing through a wild mass of wavy red hair.

"She's beautiful," Madrene observed.

"You could be just as beautiful, with a little cosmetic help."

"I bought some nail paint today at the shopping mart. Is that what she is wearing?"

He nodded.

"Mine is not so red. It is a color that Ian called pink. Do you know how I go about putting it on?"

He flashed her a wicked smile. "Babe, this is your lucky day. I have three sisters who made me help them sometimes when I was a kid and not big enough to refuse. Besides, any male worth his testosterone has tried painting a pretty woman's nails after watching that sexy scene in *Bull Durham*."

Madrene went to the sleeping chamber and got the nail paint. When she returned to the kitchen, Pretty Boy had moved her chair closer to his. "Plant your sweet ass here, honey."

Once he was done, her nails looked beautiful, in her opinion, even though hers were short and a bit ragged, unlike the long-nailed woman in the magazine. She kept holding her hands out to admire them.

"How about a pedicure, too?" At her frown of confusion, he explained, "Your toenails?"

She giggled at the prospect of such an exercise in vanity. Madrene could not remember herself giggling in a long, long time . . . or engaging in such a frivolous activity.

So it was that when Ian came back to the kitchen this time, she was sitting with her legs extended and her bare feet in Pretty Boy's lap. And he was studiously painting her toenails.

"What the hell is going on here?" he grumbled. That vein was sticking out on his forehead again. "You guys are acting like friggin' idiots. She's not the queen, and you are not one of her minions."

Pretty Boy ignored Ian and helped her put her feet on the floor. "We're done, honey. Be careful for a little while. Don't put your shoes on or touch the polish." He kissed her on the cheek then.

Ian made a growling sound.

Grinning, Pretty Boy swaggered by Ian, saying as he passed him in the doorway, "Don't be such a dog in the manger, boss. It might come back to bite you in the butt."

Ian stared at Maddie for a long moment then, taking in her new outfit and her newly polished finger and toenails.

Does he like what he sees? Oh, yes, he does. "Betimes you are a dragon's arse, Ian, but I do not think you are a dog."

He obviously didn't understand what she meant, and then he did. He grinned in a rueful manner and said softly, "I would have polished your nails for you."

After he left, Madrene thought about his words for a long time. And she found herself oddly excited.

Chapter Eleven

She was temptation on the hoof . . .

Ian felt a little bit like Adam in the Garden of Eden. Eve was sashaying around his "garden," swinging her sweet breasts in front of him, doing everything but shout, "Catch me if you can."

I have to be strong. This is just a pretend marriage. She is just another woman. My luck with women stinks. It's not worth the pain. I have to be strong.

"Sit down, Maddie." He pointed to the stuffed chair in the living room, across from the sofa where he sat. Sam jumped onto her lap—*lucky cat!*—and immediately fell asleep, snoring.

Ian's knees were spread and he was leaning forward, absently rubbing his palms down his jeans-clad thighs, from knees to groin, over and over.

She noticed his nervous action.

And his cock—foolish, foolish appendage—grew thick and heavy.

Her eyes widened in surprise.

"Stop looking at me *there*."

"Stop rubbing yourself *there*."

"I wasn't . . . never mind." He closed his knees, steepled his hands before his face, trying to ignore the source of his heated embarrassment. "I brought you in here to talk. It's important."

"So, talk."

So, talk, he mimicked silently. "The reason the members of my squad were here tonight involves you."

Her head shot up, and Sam looked up, too. Seeing that it was only him, Sam immediately went back to sleep. "If it involves me, why was I not permitted to listen?"

I don't think I've ever seen eyes that blue. Maybe it's because her skin is so fair and her hair so light. No, they're just a pretty shade of blue.

"Ian?" she prodded.

He blinked several times. "I needed to explain everything to the guys to see if they're interested in this . . . uh, mission."

"Seals get to approve their missions? They can choose to go or not go where they are ordered?"

Yeah, right. "No, this is a special case."

"Special, how?"

Aaarrgh! "Back to what I was saying . . . it would have served no purpose to tell you about the mission if it wasn't approved. But it was. We're good-to-go now." He smiled, hoping she understood.

"Let me understand you." She stood, dumping Sam, and began to pace the small room. "You needed to have your men's permission afore informing me of a plan that involves me?"

"Maddie—"

"When were you going to ask *my* permission?"

"Maddie—"

"Oh, how like a man! You think women have no brains. You think you are so much smarter."

"Maddie—"

"Do not 'Maddie' me, you stubborn lout. I do not know why I am surprised. My father and brothers did the same. Always underestimating my abilities, unless it came to running the household. Well, I proved just how capable I could be for one year as I led the Norstead warriors in one fight after another to fend off our attackers. Until Steinolf. But that—"

"Shut up!" he shouted.

Which surprised her, of course. "You crude oaf. You cannot speak to me like—"

He stood and shoved her back into her chair. "Just sit and listen for a change. I don't need or want your nagging. This is not the day for it. I'm pissed off at the SEAL commander. I'm pissed off at the CIA. I'm pissed off at my father. And I'm sure as hell pissed off at you. Dancing with a guy who has notches on his belt for all the women he's laid. And putting your feet in the lap of a guy who gives new meaning to the word stud." He stopped suddenly and rubbed a hand across his forehead. Maybe he was turning into a male shrew, as Pretty Boy had muttered earlier tonight. "Hell, Maddie, I sound just like you."

"Me?" But then she changed the subject on him, like she did all the time, probably to distract him. "What has your father—"

No, no, no! I will not talk about my father. He gave her a glower that stopped her tongue. Thank God! "When I went into the base today, I was ordered to report immediately to my commander's office. When I got there—"

"They took away your rank. I feared this would happen . . . because of me. Well, I will go give your commander the straight story. Do not think that I cannot. Tell me his name so I—"

Ian's jaw dropped. Then he said, "Do . . . not . . . interrupt . . . me . . . again."

She must have seen how angry he was, but did that stop her? Hell, no! "Do . . . not . . . give . . . me . . . orders."

He had to smile at her mirroring his own words. "Some wife you are! You don't show proper respect for your husband."

He'd been teasing, but she took him seriously. "Mayhap if you acted more like a husband, I would act more like a wife." He could see that she regretted the words the moment they left her mouth.

The prospect of their acting like a real married couple hung in the air between them. Could they? Should they? Would they?

Finally he shook his head to erase the erotic images that hovered there. "Maybe I should have had you sit in on the meeting. But I didn't. So let me tell you now."

"Your apology is accepted."

"I didn't apologize."

She arched her eyebrows at him.

"You're a hard negotiator." *I'm turning into my father. He could never apologize either . . . even when he'd been proven wrong.* He stood and walked over to her chair, then reached a hand out to shake hers. "I'm sorry."

She nodded her acceptance, but appeared suspicious. As he walked back to the sofa to continue his explanation of the mission, she said, "You have a nice arse."

He stopped in his tracks, then plopped down on the sofa. "I beg your pardon."

"You have a nice arse. I noticed it in those tight jeans as you walked away from me," she explained. "What? Is that another unsuitable thing for a woman to say to a man?"

"Not for a wife to say to her husband, but a woman who says it to a single, red-blooded male is giving a clear signal."

She pondered his message for a moment, and said, "Oh."

"Oh." That is all. She didn't say it wasn't what she wanted. This is probably some female trick. Bait-and-switch, or something. He explained the mission then, telling her that his teammates had agreed to participate, their primary role being to guard her day and night, waiting for the tangos to attempt to grab her. There would be three men there at all times, one inside, one in back of the house, one in front. Hidden, of course.

She'd been surprisingly quiet while he'd explained the mission. "Are you asking for my permission, or telling me what is going to happen?"

It was more like the latter, but he fudged a bit and said, "We *want* your permission."

She smiled slightly, obviously catching his hesitation. "The answer is yes."

Thank God! "It could be dangerous. We'll try our best to protect you. Even so, you'd be a decoy to some mean-ass bad guys."

She shrugged. "I have been in more dangerous spots."

"Someday you are going to tell me exactly who you are."

"When I trust you more. There is still a chance you or your comrades would send me back to Steinolf. He is a powerful man."

"Maddie, I don't know anyone named Steinolf."

"We shall see. I will tell all when the time is right."

"I'm going in to shower, and then to bed. I've got to be up by five to report to the base by six. Do you want the shower first?"

"I bathed this morning."

He smiled. She'd told him her opinion of twice-a-day showers. "Okay. See you later."

Ian did not realize till later . . . a short time later . . . how prophetic his words would be.

When he was in the middle of rinsing the shampoo out of his hair, he glanced through the glass doors of the shower stall, then did a double take.

Maddie was standing there. Watching him.

This is a losing battle. He turned off the shower and stepped out, wrapping a towel around his middle, but not before she'd seen his full-blown boner. What did she expect? When a woman purposely looked at a naked man, his cock interpreted it one way only.

"Maddie, what are you doing in here? You shouldn't go into a bathroom when a man is naked."

"I shouldn't? Why?"

"It's just not done." He glanced down pointedly at the tent in his towel.

"Oh, that! I have seen plenty of *those*. Sometimes, when the housemaids were busy, it was my job to help the visitors or my warriors bathe. I do not take *that* condition personally."

"Take it personally, Maddie. Believe me, take it personally."

She tilted her head in question. "As an insult or a compliment?"

"Definitely a compliment."

"Hmmm. Then, thank you."

Holy shit! This is the first time a woman has thanked me for a hard-on. "Why did you come in here?"

"I came to ask you to shave my legs." He hadn't noticed before, but she had a can of his shaving cream in one hand and his razor in the other.

If he hadn't been surprised before, he sure was now. "Why?"

"The lady in the clothes mart yesterday told me that women shave their legs and armpits in this country. I would like to try it."

Incredible! "I've never shaved a woman's legs before."

"You shave your face. It must be the same thing."

Not in a Navy minute! "Not really."

"I could ask Pretty Boy when he comes next time. Since he painted my toenails, I'm sure he—"

Over my dead body. "I'll do it, dammit!"

Rub a dub dub . . .

Maddie was sitting on the closed toilet seat, with one leg propped up on the edge of the sink vanity.

He had been putting hot water in the sink and laying out a towel when he turned and groaned. "Are you trying to give me a heart attack?"

"Because I took off my jeans? Tsk-tsk! Think about it. How are you going to shave my legs if they are covered?"

How am I going to stop looking at that shadowy area barely covered by your panties? He wet her leg with a hot washcloth, soaped it up with shaving cream, ankle to never-never-land. For just a second, he closed his eyes and relished the sensation of, well, feeling up Maddie's leg. He inhaled and exhaled for strength—which was a lost cause. His favorite body part was practically drooling over Maddie's long, long legs. Then he hunkered down and began to shave knee to ankle. "I don't know why you want to do this. Your leg hair is so light, you can hardly see it."

"But you can feel it."

Damn straight I can.

"You mentioned your father earlier today. Why was he here in Caliph-ornery-ah? Why did he not come to your home?"

At first he bristled, not wanting to discuss the old man. But he had to think about something other than the burning question: Did she want him to give her a bikini cut? "Yeah, my father was there. The bastard!"

"That is an awful way to speak of your father."

"He deserves it. Hell, Maddie, he was partly responsible for this mission we're starting on."

"Is this not what seals do?"

"Yes, but . . . you have to know our history. I'm the oldest in my family, and the biggest disappointment to him. No matter what I do to please him, it's never good enough."

"Like what?"

"Well, I was a senior master chief for years, a

Navy rate that fitted me perfectly. I was successful there, but not by his standards. He badgered and badgered and badgered till I went to officers' candidate school and became a junior-grade lieutenant and then a full lieutenant. Then he decided that wasn't enough. He started badgering me to accept a desk job in D.C." He looked up at her and saw the sympathy on her face, as well as confusion. "You didn't understand a word I said, did you?"

"Not the separate words, but the whole of it, yes, I did. Your father wants you to be something you cannot be. In truth, I would guess he wants you to be him."

He was surprised that she'd been able to cut to the heart of the problem between him and his father. "Bingo!" he said, then put one of her legs down, and lifted the other. *I cannot believe I am shaving the legs of a half-naked woman, and I'm talking about my father. I must have the libido of an earthworm. Well, no, that's not precisely true. I have the libido. I just have iron control. Someone ought to give me a medal. I could pin it right below my Budweiser, the SEAL trident pin. I can see it now. Some admiral or other, maybe even my dad—horror of horrors—would pin the medal on and say something like, "Great job, MacLean. You could teach all the rest of us how to keep it in our pants."*

"At least you are smiling now."

I am? Hell, it takes a lot to make me smile after thinking about my dad.

"Tell me about the others in your family."

She is like a puppy tugging on a pant leg. Tug, tug, tug . . . till she finally gets what she wants. He sighed. "My mother died a long time ago, when I was a kid."

"Mine, too."

"I have two younger brothers. Clay, who is in his last year at Annapolis and will probably become a ring knocker in the SEALs. My other brother, Ross, is an Air Force pilot; you can imagine what my father thinks of that. Then there's my sister Alison. She's a doctor, got married three years ago to a guy who had considered joining the SEALs, but instead turned out to be a real computer genius."

"Like Geek?"

"Yep."

"It sounds to me like each member of your family has chosen his own life path. Your father should be proud of you all."

"You'd think so, wouldn't you?"

"Was it always this bad?"

"Actually, no. He was a little bit autocratic when we were kids, but it's gotten out of hand now. Probably because it's looking less and less likely that one of us will follow in his footsteps."

"If you ask me—"

"I didn't."

She smacked him lightly on the shoulder. "I believe you should reconcile with your father."

"Not that I care, but why would you say that?"

She shrugged. "He is your father. The last words I said to my father were, 'You are the dumbest dolt in all the world to take this voyage. And you risk the lives of all my brothers and sisters you take with you.' I couldn't imagine how Ragnor and I were to take care of all his holdings in his absence. I called him irresponsible, too."

He could picture her laying into her father in just that way. But what was that about Ragnor? His sister was married to a guy named Ragnor. It wasn't a common name, but there had to be more than one man named Ragnor.

"They all died on that voyage, and Ragnor's death followed more than ten years later, leaving me to hold it all together."

"I'm sorry." *I don't believe one word she said. Well, some of it has to be true. That's the technique of a good liar. They take a kernel or two of truth and weave it into a world-class lie.*

"Imagine how you would feel if your father died tomorrow."

Uh-oh! Sucker punched by her again! I should have seen it coming. "I would be sad, but—"

"I think you would be devastated."

He ignored her interruption. She always interrupted. "I repeat, I would be sad, very sad, but your argument goes both ways. How would my father feel if I were to die suddenly, which is a more likely scenario in my line of work?"

"He would be devastated, of course. You bullheaded men need to bend at some point."

"You're an expert on bullheaded men?" He was trying to change and lighten the conversation.

"That I am. Let me tell you . . ."

She went on and on and on then about her experience with bullheaded men, in particular, her father, her brothers, her ex-husband, pretty much the entire male gender. He just let her ramble on. He was actually starting to like her tart personality. Besides, while she rambled on, he was able to concentrate on her legs.

He'd already finished shaving both legs from knee to ankle while they talked, being extra careful around those scars on her ankles . . . the ones that matched her wrist scars. Sometime in her past, Maddie's legs and hands had been shackled with an abrasive rope, either for a long time or so tightly the skin had been rubbed off.

He started working on her thighs now. Under normal circumstances, he would have considered this a highly erotic activity. He had to remember that he needed to keep his hands to himself if he wanted an annulment. But, man oh man, as he stroked and stroked her with the razor, he was for damn sure thinking about another kind of stroking. Good thing he'd pulled a pair of sweatpants on. The towel wouldn't have hidden a damn thing.

"You have nice hands," Maddie said, interrupting his fantasy.

He held his hands out. Nothing out of the ordinary in his opinion.

"They're big but long-fingered and capable-looking. Also, they are not hairy."

Lady, the things I could do to you with these capable hands! "So, you like my ass and my hands, eh?" he teased. "What else do you like about me?"

She smiled at his obvious fishing expedition. "Not much," she said.

Good. I do not want you liking me . . . too much.

"Except for your kissing. Whew! I like your kisses, too."

He closed his eyes and counted to ten, willing his lower body to behave. It hadn't worked in the past and it definitely wasn't working now. "I only kissed you once." *Way to go, cowboy! Could I say anything more uncool?*

"Once was more than enough. I was fluttering so much 'twas a wonder I did not fly off."

He had to smile, dammit. He just had to. "I liked your kiss, too." *Why don't I just throw in the flag and admit I am out of my league here?* "I'm done," he said. *Just in time!* He stood and turned to the sink, rinsing off his razor and letting the water go down the drain.

"You can't be done," she complained to his back. "You haven't done my armpits yet."

No way! I am not putting my hands that close to the breasts from heaven. He turned to let her down easily, and, oh my God, she was unbuttoning her blouse and dropping it to the floor. He should have been ready to jump her bones. She was facing away from him, wearing only a lacy bra and matching hip-hugger panties. But what he saw caused his erection to go down instantaneously, like a pricked balloon. "Sonofabitch!"

Her back was crisscrossed with dozens of old welts, from her neck to her buttocks. His eyes teared up in sympathy for what she must have suffered. He should have guessed after seeing the ankle and wrist welts. He should have guessed.

"What's the matter?" She tried to turn around, but he took hold of her upper arms from behind and pressed her against the wall. With her hands raised above her head and her body pressed against the wall with his left hand, he began to trace each of the scars with his fingertips, then with his lips. He started at her shoulders and began a slow, slow journey down to her lush behind.

"Oh, that!" she said against the wall. "I forgot about my back."

"How could you ever forget such a thing?"

She shrugged. "I do not wish to speak of it. I cannot draw up the memories or they will crush me.

Are the scars ugly? I have never seen them, but I can feel them."

He kissed the curve of her neck and said, "There is nothing ugly about you. *Nothing.*"

"It is nice of you to say so, but I suspect you are trying to spare my feelings."

"Who did this to you? No, don't tell me. Steinolf. Right?"

"The very same."

"I can see now why you would want to raise an army to avenge yourself. In this case, revenge would definitely be sweet. To do that to a woman . . . it boggles the mind." *I wonder . . . hmmm . . . I wonder if she did something horrible to provoke such treatment.*

"He wanted me to agree to a wedding . . . with him. And I would not."

A wedding? That's all? "Most women would have given in. At the first sting of the whip."

"Mayhap I would have if it were only me who was affected. But his offer was a ruse to draw my fighting men out of the hills. He would have ambushed them one and all."

"You did it for your . . . uh, people?"

She nodded.

"So that is why you want to raise an army."

"Will you help me?"

"Probably not, though I do sympathize with you."

"Pfff to your sympathy! I have felt safe here with you, safer than I have felt for years, but that is dangerous to me. If I feel too safe, I will never have the bloodlust to enter the fray again."

Down on one knee with one hand pressed against her shoulders, he kissed the small of her back where there was a particularly livid scar.

She stiffened and tried to struggle out of his grasp. She failed. "What are you doing back there?"

"Caressing and kissing your scars."

She was silent for a moment. "Please do not," she said in a soft voice.

He stepped back. "Why?"

"Because I must remain strong, and you are making me soft."

"I am?"

"Hah! Any softer and I will melt."

Son of a gun! I must be good. Ian grinned. "Are you fluttering?"

"Like a butterfly. Do not try to fool me. You are doing it apurpose."

I didn't even know I had that skill. Hot damn! He stood and released his hold on her. She turned and looked at him. They stood only a foot apart. He could practically touch her with his erection.

A tantalizing silence hovered between them then.

Maddie was tall, and he liked the fact that she was almost eye level with him. In fact, he liked way too much about her.

Maddie was thinking that she liked way too much about the rogue that the norns of destiny had cast her way. She looked at his face, which was often too serious, especially when he spoke of his father. His wet hair was darker than its usual reddish brown hue. Black eyelashes framed honey-brown eyes. There were small lines bracketing his eyes and mouth, whether from laughter or frowns, she could not say. Probably the latter.

She had been telling the truth when she said he made her melt. As he continued to stare at her, her blood slowed and grew thick. Her breasts ached. A delicious flutter lodged itself low in her belly, way too close to . . .

He stepped back slightly and glanced down her body. She had noticed that he had taken great care to avoid looking at her in her panties and bra. But he was looking now, for a certainty.

Her nipples grew hard as pebbles, just at his scrutiny. If her body liked mere looking, what would it do if he actually touched her?

And then . . . oh, blessed gods and goddesses . . . she found out.

Just with the tips of his fingers, he touched the peaks of her breasts.

Her eyelids—suddenly heavy—drifted shut, and she arched her back. A small moan escaped her mouth. What a delicious, delicious feeling! She wanted him to stop. Nay, she wanted him to touch her more.

"Maddie," he whispered.

When she opened her eyes, she saw his face lowering to hers. His eyes were hazy with desire, and his lips parted. "I'm going to kiss you," he murmured, a hairsbreadth from her mouth.

"And if I say you nay?"

"I'm going to kiss you," he repeated.

She could not say nay if she wanted to, so tense was her body with anticipation.

He burrowed his fingers into her hair, to hold her in place lest she wanted to bolt.

Hah! Not a chance!

Only then did he settle his lips on hers, parting her lips in the process. He groaned into her mouth.

Mother of God! I never realized a male groan could be so erotic. She wrapped her arms around his shoulders.

He moved in closer, putting one hand on her nape and wrapping the other arm around her waist. She thought she heard him murmur, "I give up!" The kiss, which had started gentle and searching, turned hard and demanding. Who knew that a man's lips could coax such a response from a woman? Certainly not she. When his tongue entered her mouth and retreated, entered and retreated, she soon realized that he was imitating the sex act itself.

Finally he jerked his mouth off of hers. Panting for breath, he said, "This is insanity."

He was going to stop. He was going to end their kiss. He was going to leave her feeling hot and excited and wanting. *I do not think so!* She grabbed his ears and pulled him back. "Do not dare stop, you brute. Kiss me."

He did not need much encouragement, but this time he put his hands on her buttocks and lifted her so only the tips of her toes touched the floor. When he kissed her now, his manpart was aligned perfectly with her cleft, while his bare chest abraded her breasts.

If he had not been holding her up with his hips pressed hard against her belly, she would have swooned, so intense was her pleasure. Now it was not just his tongue dancing the sex act in her mouth, but his lower body undulating against her, too. With each thrust, her nerves drew tighter and tighter. There was a wetness between her legs. Both her breasts and nether parts throbbed with aching.

At some point, somehow, her legs had become wrapped around his hips.

"This is not a good idea," he choked out, even as

he turned and walked her out of the bathing chamber, her body wrapped about his like a clinging cat. "This is definitely not a good idea."

He did not stop, however.

Thank the gods!

Instead, he tossed her into the middle of his giant bed so she landed flat on her back. Immediately he crawled up and over her.

"Are we going to make love?" she asked.

"Oh, yeah." With that, he undid the front fastener on her bra and eased the lacy garment off her. He looked down at her then. And smiled. "Oh, baby," was all he said.

She felt such joy that he liked looking at her. Then she felt more than joy when he began to touch her. He lifted her breasts from underneath, he kneaded them, he swept his palms over them repeatedly; then he tweaked the nipples so hard it felt good. They became still more prominent.

"You have no idea how long I've wanted to do this," he said in a husky voice. He put his lips to her breast then and suckled rhythmically.

"Aaaaaaaaahhhhh!" she wailed, arching her back. She tried to push him off but he was immovable. It was too much. Too much!

Between her legs she felt herself begin to pulse, then spasm. He lifted his head to watch her face as her female parts shattered in devastating pleasure. She didn't understand. But apparently he did, and he must have liked her response, because he leaned down and kissed her lightly on the lips. Then he shifted to the other breast, which he licked and nipped with his teeth before he began to suckle there, too.

"You are torturing me," she gasped out.

"Good torture or bad torture?"

"Definitely good."

He rolled over on his side and shrugged out of his *braies*, then eased her out of her pan-teas. She tried to sit up, but he pushed her back down. She was about to protest, to say that she wanted to participate in the "event," not let it happen to her.

"Let me," he said. "You are so beautiful."

"No, I am not."

"Shhhh. You are beautiful to me." Placing a hand on her belly, he crept low, brushing her woman's fleece, then inserting his fingers between her legs.

"Noooo," she said, pressing her thighs together.

"Yes," he insisted, and even with her legs clamped together, he thrust a forefinger into her wetness and touched her in a place she had never been touched before. She keened out her ecstasy and loosened her legs, reflexively. He must have considered that an invitation, because he began to caress her folds more boldly, even inserting one finger, and then two, to test her readiness. She could have told him she was more than ready.

And what did he do? He rolled away from her and opened a drawer in a chest beside the bed.

"What? You are stopping *now?*" Her voice was shrill with her need for fulfillment.

He chuckled and rolled back. "No, I am not stopping, sweetheart. I'm just beginning." Lying on his back, he tore open a silver packet and was about to put the object inside on his manpart.

"What . . . is . . . that?"

"A condom," he said, surprised at her question. "Birth control."

"This country has a means of preventing conception?"

He nodded, even as he sheathed himself.

She shook her head. " 'Tis not necessary with me. I am barren."

"Are you sure?"

"Woefully sure."

He unpeeled the sheath from his manpart and arranged himself over her. Pushing her knees up and out, he entered her with a grunt of satisfaction.

She could not breathe. She could not move. Speech was impossible. Had anything in the world ever felt this good? He filled her, then moved, and filled her some more. Her bedsport with Karl had never been anything like this.

His straightened arms were braced on the mattress on either side of her head, but he lifted one arm. His hand reached between their bodies where they were joined. He flicked his middle finger back and forth, playing a part of her that felt engorged and extremely sensitive.

Her lower body bucked against him, of its own volition. The muscles of her inner female channel clutched and unclutched his still unmoving, fully imbedded manpart, which unbelievably thickened even more.

The only indications that he was as aroused as she were the perspiration on his forehead and his heavy breathing. He took both of her hands and raised them over her head, where she grabbed onto the rungs of the headboard. "Hold on, honey," he said, and began long, long strokes in and out of her body, so slow she wanted to scream.

Holding on tight, she arched her back upward, so

intense was the sweet agony. He leaned his head down and licked one nipple. Ecstasy was hitting her everywhere—where his lips suckled, where his lower body hit her special spot when he slammed into her, where her inner folds convulsed over and over and over.

She spread her legs wider, wanting more, giving that special spot greater access to the rhythmic off, on, off, on graze of his body against hers right there.

"Are you ready?" he choked out.

"For what?"

He let out a hoot of laughter, and showed her. His strokes became shorter and harder, slamming into her. Apparently, she had been ready, because her mouth was letting out those embarrassing, whoofing grunts, "Uh, uh, uh, uh . . . !"

Ian was no better. One continual moan was coming through his gritted teeth.

And then . . . and then her body splintered apart, starting where they were joined and spiraling out to all her extremities. Ian thrust into her one last time, arched his neck back, and spilled his seed inside her welcoming body.

For the first time in many, many years, Madrene mourned the fact that she was barren. Because this wonderful, wonderful lovemaking she'd just experienced with Ian ought to have some fruitful result. Alas, that was not to be. But she was happy nonetheless.

The man was sprawled over her heavily, panting for breath. She lowered her arms and caressed his back. "It was never like this for me afore," she told him, not sure if he was asleep or awake.

He raised his head and said, "It was never like this

for me, either. I swear to God, Maddie, that is the truth."

Withdrawing his wilted manpart from inside her with a grimace of pain, or pleasure—she could not guess which—he turned so he was lying on his side. He kissed her lightly on the lips. "Thank you," he said. "No, don't say anything. Any minute now, you will probably revert to your regular shrewish nagging. Before that happens, I want to thank you for the most incredible sex of my life."

"Well, I have only Karl to compare you with, but you were far superior to him."

"Thank you. I think."

"Is it always like this for you?"

"Not even close." He pulled her closer so that his arm was over her shoulder and her face lying on his chest.

She tried to ignore the feeling of her breast nestled in his chest hairs. "Do you think it was a one-time thing?"

"I hope not."

"Me, too." There was a comfortable silence between them as she just listened to the thump, thump, thump of his heart. "Mayhap we should try again."

She felt his body shaking with laughter.

"What?"

"I have a motivational quote for you."

"Now?"

"Practice makes perfect."

She laughed and said, "That is the first one of your silly sayings that I have liked. So, are we going to do it again?"

He pretended to be reluctant. "A man needs some time to . . . regroup."

"Really?" She trailed her fingertips down his chest, over his belly. Then she took his limp manpart in her hand. Like magic, it grew larger and larger in her loose grip.

"On the other hand . . ." he said.

Chapter Twelve

Playboy would be envious . . .

Ian was slam dunk in the middle of the ultimate sexual fantasy, and he wasn't even dreaming.

A gorgeous woman straddled his stomach . . . a *naked* gorgeous woman. She had silver blond hair down to her sweet butt . . . her *naked* sweet butt. Her breasts were big, and firm, and uptilted . . . her *naked* breasts. They were not as big as he'd originally thought, but hot damn big enough; her slender body—narrow waist and hips—made them appear larger.

"Why are you grinning?" she asked.

"Because you are so hot and you're sitting on my lap. Naked." *And because I am hoping for a repeat . . . or two.*

"Is hot good?"

"Definitely." *Better hot than cold, sweetheart. And I've had a few of those.*

"Then I think you are hot, too."

That has got to be the first time a woman has called me hot. Not that he'd ever had trouble getting a girl. Being a SEAL made it easy. But hot? Uh-uh! He probably had a goofy grin on his face.

She raised her arms to push her hair behind her ears.

And his cock jackknifed from zero to ninety degrees in an instant. Well, okay, from forty-five to ninety—he'd already been half hard.

"What do you want me to do?" she asked.

He almost swallowed his tongue at that question. "Everything."

"Be more specific. I'm new at this."

Oh, sweetie, you do not want me to be specific. "You ever heard the song, 'Save a Horse, Ride a Cowboy'?"

She frowned with puzzlement. "What?"

"It would be like saying, 'Save a Boat, Ride a SEAL.' "

He saw the minute she understood. "The seal being you?"

"Oh, yeah." He smiled at her.

"You should smile more often. You have a beautiful smile."

"Yeah?" *Horse, seal, whatever. I'm all yours.* He'd seen a bumper sticker yesterday on a pickup truck that read, *Save a truck, ride a redneck.* He smiled some more.

"It . . . your smile . . . makes me fluttery." She put both hands over her stomach.

Well, holy shit, I can't get a more direct invitation than that. He guided her down onto his cock. Sloooowly. So slowly he feared he might come before the big event.

When she was impaled on him, her eyes went wide and her lips parted with arousal. Then, of all things, she said, "We probably shouldn't be doing this."

No way, babe! You are not backing out now. "*Now* you realize that?"

"We won't be able to get that annul thing, will we?"

"Annulment. No, that won't be possible, but we can still get a divorce." *If she changes her mind now, I might just cry . . . or beg.*

"How is that different?"

"Takes more time." *I cannot believe I am discussing divorce with a naked woman sitting on me.*

"How much more time?"

Enough already! He reached down between her legs and stroked her there. "Yeeek!" she squealed and spasmed around him a few times, which caused him to twitch. But then he answered her: "Months."

"Good."

He did a mental high-five. "Okay, baby, show me your moves." He arched his hips up to get her going.

"I don't have any moves. What are moves?"

Talk, talk, talk, talk. "Just do what feels good. That's a move."

Turned out Maddie had moves aplenty.

No regrets . . .

She was sound asleep when she felt a tickle on the bottom of her foot.

She kicked out, hoping to shoo the fly away. But it persisted. When she opened her eyes, she saw that the fly was in fact Ian standing at the foot of the bed. He was fully dressed, and she was splatted out on the bed, arms on the pillow, legs spread. *Naked!*

"Eek!" she said and grabbed for a bed linen to cover herself.

"A little late for that, sweet pea. There isn't an inch of your body that I'm not up close and intimate with."

"You don't have to say it out loud." She glanced at the window and saw that the sun was fully up. It had to be at least an hour past dawn. She hadn't slept this late since she was a little girl.

As she slowly came awake, she recalled the events of the night before. Her body ached in unmentionable places. Her lips felt kiss-swollen. In effect, she felt sated . . . and wonderful.

Her blush prompted Ian to ask, "Are you having morning-after regrets?"

She thought about saying yes. After all, she did not want him to get too puffed up, but she could see that he awaited her answer nervously. "No regrets." *I might later, but not now.*

He came around and sat on the edge of the bed near her. He reached over and pushed a strand of hair off her face. Then he kissed her gently on the mouth. "I'll be gone all day, but Geek is here. He'll stay with you till I get home this evening. Please . . . *please* don't go be-bopping off to the mall or anywhere else."

What in the name of Thor is be-bopping?

"Sly and Cage have outside duty, but you won't see them."

I have much to do. I must needs find a map in order to return to my country. The jewels have to be sold to raise funds for an army. So much planning to do. I cannot sit back and enjoy life, tempting as that might be. "How long will this go on?"

"Weeks, I would think. Starting today, there'll be little snippets about you planted in newspapers and on television. After that, it will probably take Jamal's cohorts several days to track you here. So you're relatively safe for now. We have to be cautious anyhow."

She nodded. *So the danger won't come for a few more days. Hmmm.*

"Geek says you want to learn to read and write. I told him to bring some materials with him. And you should rest. You didn't get much sleep last night." His voice was thick with meaning at that last.

"Why are you being so nice?"

He laughed. "I'm always nice."

"Hah! Not to me." She looked at his face, and it was impossible to miss the lack of the tension that was usually there. And she knew why. " 'Tis amazing what a little bedsport will do for a man's disposition."

He pinched her arm in a teasing manner. "You're being more agreeable yourself."

"I'm just tired."

"Liar."

She raised her eyebrows at him.

"It's amazing what a good roll in the hay will do for a woman's disposition."

He ducked then when she would have clouted him upside the head, which caused the bed linen to drop, which caused his eyes to widen, which gave her the opportunity to punch him on the arm. He laughed at such a piddly effort. She heard him still laughing when he closed the front door after himself.

Madrene found herself laughing, too, with sheer joy. This euphoria she felt now was probably temporary. But for now, she was happy.

There was hope.

Every time men think they understand women . . . oops! . . .

Ian and those squad members not at his house joined the other team members, and a new SEAL training class, for a grueling day of physical and technical training.

They ran five miles. They went to the "Kill House" to practice breaking down doors and fighting pretend terrorists. They ran another five miles. They practiced gunmanship on the firing range. They . . . yep . . . ran another five miles. Then they went through all the obstacles on the O-course, including the climbing wall and the suicide jump. And that was before noon.

Throughout it all, he kept thinking about Maddie and the incredible night they had spent together. *Crazy* and *irresponsible* were words that came to mind to describe himself, but there were also *lucky* and *happy*. Toby Keith sang a song saying something to the effect that he wasn't talking about forever, he was just talking about tonight. In other words, no promises. *I don't want just one night.* He surprised himself with that thought. What did he want? *Hell if I know. Just more. Lots more.*

As they paraded over to the mess hall, muscles aching as usual after a workout, Pretty Boy looked at him and said, "You look different today."

He didn't answer, knowing what was going to come next.

"Yeah, he seems more . . . relaxed," Omar said, fighting hard to keep a straight face.

"I think he's blushing. Yep, I see a blush," JAM concurred.

"Well, hell's bells, it looks as if the good lieutenant got his ashes hauled," the usually quiet Slick said.

They all turned and looked at Ian. At first with disbelief . . . which he considered insulting, then with mischief.

"I don't know what you're talking about," he said and walked faster to avoid further conversation on that subject.

But they were not going to drop the subject. No way! He wouldn't have, either.

"Let me guess. You brought some babe into your house while Maddie was asleep and did the deed on the couch." They stood waiting in the food line, and Pretty Boy was having a great time tapping his chin in exaggerated contemplation. "No, that doesn't seem right. It must be . . . could it be? . . . our boss nailed the decoy."

Ian tried to punch Pretty Boy in the arm, but he ducked away. Luckily, Ian was spared any further discussion on the subject. His cell phone rang.

"Yo, Mac," Cage said. He could hear the laughter in his voice.

Uh-oh!

"Guess what your wife is doing, bless her heart?"

Uh-oh! "Stop playing games. What the hell is up?"

"Well, me, I am pretty sure . . . but I better check with my binoculars again . . . yep, I'm pretty sure that's your wife out there swimming in the surf."

"I'll kill her," he muttered.

"Oh, did I forget to mention skinny dipping? Yep, your wife is N-U-D-E," he spelled out.

"Fuck!"

"Seems to me you already did that, by the looks of her when she came outside. *Mon Dieu!* She had whisker burns up one side and down the other. And her lips—whooee, they—"

"Shut up!"

"A little testy today, are you, *mon coeur?*"

"Don't give me that 'my friend' crap. Where's Geek? He's supposed to be watching her."

"He was in the head when she slipped out."

Shit! Cage and Geek both looking at my wife's nude body. Aaarrgh! She's not really my wife. But I still don't want other men ogling her. How long has she been out there?"

"About ten minutes."

"You have been standing there watching her for ten minutes?" he asked in an icy voice.

"Yep!"

"I'll be right home."

"Do you want me to go in and get her?"

"*No!* Is that clear?"

"How could it not be? You about melted the wax in my ears."

He hung up then on Cage, who was laughing like a hyena.

Ian was so angry he was shaking. He didn't care how good Maddie was in the sack, he was going to kill her. Well, he did care, but he was still going to kill her.

He slammed his cell phone shut and noticed everyone was looking at him. And every single one of them was smiling.

A far journey was obviously in her future . . .

Madrene was learning to read.

If she had known she would get such joy from the simple task of practicing letters on a piece of parchment, she would have taken time when she was a child to study along with her brothers and their monk teachers. She had started her lessons early this morning until she'd taken a break for a quick swim . . . something she had learned to do as a toddler in the cold waters of a Norseland fjord. Vikings, who were most comfortable in the seas riding their longships, considered swimming a necessary skill.

Geek said she was a quick learner and he gave her homework to do on the days when he was not there. Writing her letters over and over. And practicing simple words like cat and dog.

Now they had a book in front of them called *See Jane Run,* which was helping her to recognize simple words.

"I don't think you need to learn everything," Geek said. "People start learning to read when they're four or five years old and continue studying the language in one way or another for twelve years or more."

"You jest?" she asked with horror.

He patted her arm. "Don't worry. We're going to try to compress all that into a few weeks. Sort of a *Reading for Dummies* kind of approach."

"You jest?" she repeated.

"Really. They use this method in English as a Second Language classes sometimes."

She made a quick lunch for them . . . slices of white bread put together with ham and cheese and mustard, called a sand-which, of all things; there was no sand used. For a beverage, they drank that bubbly drink called Pepsi with ice in tall glasses. She, who had put together feasts for two hundred in the past, was inordinately pleased with herself that she was able to accomplish such a small feat.

While they ate, they talked. Geek told her about his family . . . a mother, father and five sisters who lived in a country called Poo-kip-see. Apparently, he had an extraordinary intellect and had many years of learning. "Why did you decide to become a warrior?" she asked.

He shrugged. "Seemed the best way to put my brain to good use in a just cause." He grew quiet for a moment, and his jaw tensed with some strong emotion. "I hate terrorists. If my intelligence can eliminate a few of them, well . . . that's why I joined the SEALs." A grin teased his mouth and a blush bloomed on his freckled face. "Plus, I like the way SEALs push the limits on physical stamina. A buff body and girls. I can't deny there's an attraction in that."

Madrene smiled, and then, at his urging, told him about her life, starting with the days when her entire large family lived on a Norse farmstead up till her meeting the seals in the Arab lands.

It was then that Geek explained what it meant when these men called themselves seals. They didn't mean animals. The letters stood for SEa, Air and Land.

Then she continued talking about her life.

Geek laughed out loud at some times . . . when she described her method for deflating male parts, her futile attempts to learn scarf dancing in a sultan's harem, milking a camel. At other times, he grew grim, squeezing her hand, especially when she talked about the deaths of one member of her family after another.

After they were done eating and talking and cleaning up the kitchen, Geek said, "Let's go boot up Ian's computer and see what we can find out about . . . what did you call it, Hordaland?"

She nodded, even though she did not understand half of what he said.

Soon she sat on a stool and Geek on a chair in front of a square box on a piece of furniture called a desk. The box was a come-pewter, and Geek claimed it held information about everything in the world.

In the next half hour, Geek had obtained so much information that it made her brain fuzzy. In truth, the more he told her, the more she wanted to know. And, actually, his brow was becoming as furrowed as hers.

"This just doesn't make sense," he told her as his finger tapped on little buttons set into a tray. "I can find a country called Hordaland, but it's an archaic name. Hordaland does not exist today."

"What do you mean?"

"Hordaland more or less became the country called Norway. Is that where you're from? Norway?"

"Nay. Leastways, I never heard it called such. But I am Norse. So perhaps . . . I just don't understand."

"You're not the only one," he muttered.

Next he put the letters for Birka and Hedeby in. Then pronounced, "Same thing. Old names for places that no longer exist. Birka was in what is called Sweden today. Hedeby was in what is called Germany today."

"Can this magic box show me a picture of where these places are . . . were? A map?"

"Sure."

Within a few moments, she was studying several maps . . . something she'd had no need to learn in the past. Geek had to read the names printed on the map for the various countries and waterways. Finally she said, "It does look faintly familiar." She looked up at him. "I must be from Norway, then. Leastways, a country known as Norway here but Hordaland to its inhabitants."

He looked skeptical.

"Now can you show me how far it is from here to . . . Norway?"

"Sure."

Seconds later, her shoulders slumped with dismay. It was so far away. Daunting to think she would have to raise an army and then transport them there. Mayhap she should raise the funds here, travel to Saxon lands and raise an army there to travel with her to Norstead. No matter what the obstacles, it was a mission she refused to consider impossible.

Just then, they heard the front door open. They both sat up, alert. Who could it be? Surely it was not one of the terrorists this soon. Geek reached for the weapon, called a piss-toll, which he carried with him at all times.

The mystery was soon solved.

From down the hall, possibly from the kitchen, they heard Ian shout at the top of his lungs, "*Mad-die!*"

Her magic fingers did what? . . .

Ian was in a foul mood.

He'd hope to calm his temper on the ride home. No such luck! Anger bubbled in him just below the surface. He needed to hit something or he would explode.

Truth be told, Ian was as hurt as he was angry.

How could she?

He'd stormed into the house, seen no one in the living room. In the kitchen he saw evidence of Maddic's reading lessons. His eyebrows lifted at the book Geek was using. It was titled *See Jane Run*, but it was not like any primer he'd ever seen in school. On the cover was Jane, who looked a bit like Barbie. She wore spandex shorts and top and she was running, all right, with Ken hot on her tail.

He shook his head and hollered once again, *"Mad-die!"*

"You do not have to yell. I am right here," she said. "Why are you here?"

She strolled into the kitchen big as you please. Geek had the good sense to disappear back into the office.

Ian tried hard not to notice her body in a tanktop and shorts; she was barefooted. He tried not to recall every bit of that body he'd explored last night. *"Why are you here?" she had asked. The nerve! This is my house.* "Didn't you miss me?" he asked icily.

"No," she answered with her usual bluntness. "You said you would not be back till eventide."

He scowled at her. "What? Did you have plans for another foray outside? Naked foray, that is?"

She frowned for a second. "Oh, that is what this is all about." She waved a hand dismissively. "I just went for a swim. It was such a beautiful day. The sun warm. And I . . ." Her words trailed off as she noticed his scowl.

"I ordered you to stay inside," he said, pausing at each word. While he spoke he backed her up against the cabinets, fists on either side of her on the counter.

"I do not take orders from you or anyone else," she said in the same slow manner, emphasizing each word. Ducking under his arm, she returned his glower, then remarked, "The vein in your forehead is throbbing."

Aaarrgh! "You are under my protection. I have every right to tell you what to do. I order. You follow orders. That's just the way it is."

"That is your opinion."

"I'll shackle you to the bed." Immediately he wished he hadn't used that word, especially when her wrist and ankle and back scars were visible to him.

She looked wounded for a moment.

"Maddie," he said more softly now, crowding her toward the laundry room. When he got her inside, he slammed the door shut with the back of his foot. "I thought after last night . . . well . . . you know?"

She cocked her head to the side, and her face turned pink. At first he thought it was from embarrassment, but, nope, it was anger. "You thought that because I spread my thighs for you that I would suddenly turn biddable outside the bedchamber?"

"No, but—"

She was the one crowding him now. With a finger jabbing at his chest, she said, "Understand me well. Seal or not seal. Warrior or not warrior. Husband or not husband. I am my own person. I have suffered too much to give my freedom over to any man. What have men done but leave me, set me aside, betray me, beat me, attempt to break my pride? I do not trust men, least of all you."

That hurt. That really hurt. Anger seeped out of Ian and was replaced with regret that she lumped him in with all those tyrants. And it really hurt when he saw her wipe at a tear and proclaim, "I never cry. Do not dare to think I am crying."

She lifted her chin, refusing to look at him, instead staring with great interest at a box of detergent. Once again, he had the sudden feeling that he had seen her before. He'd had a similar feeling back in Iraq. The skin on the back of his neck prickled. He had met her before, he just knew he had. His instincts never failed him on something like this. "Have we ever met before, Maddie? In the past. Like a few years ago?"

She still would not look at him. "Nay. If we had, I would have remembered such an ill-tempered son of a weasel as you."

He almost grinned.

"It is not funny. You are an overbearing beast."

"I'm sorry," he said.

"You should be." She sniffled.

"I'm not used to people disobeying my orders."

"Get used to it."

"You were naked, for chrissake!"

She arched her eyebrows at the Tide. "And that signifies how? Didst expect me to get my new clothing wet?"

"You shouldn't swim naked in public. Surely you didn't do that where you come from."

"Yea, I did. What fool swims fully clothed?" If anything, her chin went even higher.

"How old were you then?"

"Five. Not that it matters."

He grinned. *Five? And she honest-to-God thought she could convince him that what she did at five was okay at her age? She was . . . something else.* "Let's kiss and make up," he suggested, reaching for her.

She swatted his hands aside and said, "Go swive yourself!" He could tell by the expression on her face that she was unaccustomed to such expletives . . . archaic as it was.

"I would rather . . . swive you."

She gasped and glanced down at the bulge in his

running shorts. "Oh, nay! Nay, nay, nay! You are not going to tamp my anger down with bedsport."

"More like laundry sport, baby." He was already shrugging out of his shorts and jockstrap.

She looked at his erection and waggled her fingers at it. At first he didn't understand what she was doing. But then he did. With a hoot of laughter, he told her, "Honey, you are not talking, mocking or waggling down this hard-on. There's only one way to do that." And he told her explicitly what that was.

"You are a vulgar, vulgar man."

"Yeah. Don't you love it?"

Spouting some mumbo-jumbo now, she continued to waggle her fingers.

He just grew bigger.

"It works. It really does," she cried out. "Your tupping days will soon be over."

"Tupping, huh?" He laughed and took her face in his hands, forcing her to look at him. "I thought about you all morning," he said huskily.

"I did not think of you at all."

"Out of sight, out of mind, eh?" He was nibbling at her neck, and she wasn't shoving him away. "Perhaps I need to do a better job so I'll be on your mind, too." He ground his hips against her belly.

He saw stars.

She still glared. But the pink on her face had moved down her neck. He knew when a woman was aroused. She was.

He kissed her.

She kept saying "no, no, no" against his mouth. At the same time, her hands had crept around his neck and pulled him closer. He moved his chest back and forth across her breasts. He hoped to God that the abrasion of cloth on cloth, chest on breasts, felt as good to her as it did to him. When the nos turned into a moan, he put his hands inside the elastic waistbands of both her shorts and panties and let them drop to the floor.

She looked up at him, her eyes droopy, her kiss-swollen lips parted, and murmured, "I'm still angry with you."

"I know," he said. "We can fight later. Let's make up first."

"Truce before the war?" She laughed, but it was only a short laugh because he'd perched her on the edge of the washer, spread her legs and slammed into her. He closed his eyes and saw bright red sparks. When he opened them, he saw that Maddie had closed her eyes, too. Leaning back, holding on to the edge of the machine, she spread herself wider for him. He looked down and saw her blond curls intermingled with his dark ones . . . and almost lost it.

It was short and sweet . . . emphasis on sweet. She came. He came. A dustpan, plastic bucket and box of detergent had gone flying off the shelf at the force of their lovemaking. Now he pulled his shorts back on and helped Maddie with hers.

He did not like the look on her face. It was definitely that of a woman who was well satisfied and looking for more . . . but something else, too. They went into the kitchen, which was fortunately empty. Geek must still be in the computer room. Ian soon found out what was on her mind.

Maddie turned to him. Her braid had come half unbraided. She did indeed have whisker burns on every visible surface of skin. And her nipples were standing out like sentinels. But she was staring at him with . . . determination.

Little alarm bells went off in his head.

"Do not give me orders again," she said.

That's my job, sweetheart. Leaders give orders. But she is not going to like hearing that. At first he refused to answer. Then he said, "I'll try." *That is such a lie.*

"One more thing."

"Uh-oh."

"Since we are getting along so well, does that mean you will help me raise an army to regain Norstead?"

Norstead again! Raise an army? Who does she think I am? "Be reasonable."

"Reason has no place in a quest for vengeance."

"That sounds like one of my motivational quotes." He laughed.

She did not laugh. "Say me aye or nay, but do not muddle about with half-answers. Are you going to help me raise an army?"

"Hell, no."

She exhaled loudly with disgust. "So be it. That was the last time we will make love, then. It cannot happen ever again."

"If raising an army is the price, then you're damn straight it's the last time."

She looked at him as if he'd just killed her cat. He felt as if he'd just killed her cat.

Sam walked into the kitchen just then, her belly dragging on the floor like a mop. She seemed to study Maddie, then him, then made a hissing sound as if to say, *Dumb, dumb, dumb!*

Chapter Thirteen

War of the (Viking) roses . . .

One sennight later, Madrene was sitting on the solar carpet with Pretty Boy, eating a delicacy called popcorn, and watching repeats of *Sex and the City* on the magic tea-vee box. A snoring Sam had wrapped herself around Madrene's shoulders like a mantle.

The tea-vee box was enthralling. She did not care what anyone said; there were actual people inside the box, acting out parts. Some of those plays were deliciously scandalous, like this one. She was learning *soooo* much.

She had given Luke—that was Slick's real name—her ten jewels to sell, and it appeared that she would gain a huge amount of coins for her mission.

Cage, bless the rascal, had told her of *Mercenary* magazine, and read her notices of hired soldiers willing to go anywhere.

Geek worked endlessly when he was here, teaching her to read and write, as well as map out a path she might take back to Norstead.

She and Omar had become quite the cooking experts. She taught him some Norse dishes; he taught her about spicy Arab foods.

Despite all this—the tea-vee, the jewels, the hired warriors, her reading and writing, and the cooking—Madrene was miserable. For one whole sennight, Ian had not spoken to her. Of course, she had not spoken to him, either, but that was not relevant, in her opinion.

He should have attempted to speak with her about their mutual decision to halt their lovemaking. Not that she would change her mind. Nay, regaining Norstead had to be her priority. She could not let sex with Ian distract her. He would try to change her mind, she knew he would.

Oh, my gods and goddesses! Look at that. Samantha is naked—Samantha, the naked woman, not the cat—and so is the young man. And he is swiving her in front of one and all. Loudly. And so hard the bed is moving. She put a hand to her flushed cheek and looked at Cage. He just winked at her.

Of course, Ian chose that moment to walk in.

His eyes went wide as he took in her and Cage sitting on the floor next to each other with their backs against the sofa, shook his head at Sam snoring on her shoulders, blinked several times at the program on the tea-vee—*Honest to Odin! I never knew two people could do* THAT?—and returned his attention to the two of them. He was wearing his brown uniform, and he looked so handsome Madrene could have swooned. Dropping his leather case to the floor, he addressed Cage. "This is how you guard her? You're here to work, not play."

At the sound of Ian's voice, Sam raised her head, saw it was only her "father" and went back to sleep.

Despite Ian's vile tone, Cage responded brightly, "Hey, I've got my AK-47 on the end table and a pistol in my pocket. There are motion detectors on every door and window. Sly and JAM are outside. We've got everything covered, man."

Ian shook his head at Cage and said, "Come into the kitchen. I want to update you on the latest happenings."

He walked away from them then. Without even greeting Madrene at all. *The boorish oaf!*

"Guess you should come, too," Cage said to her.

She eased Sam off her shoulders and gave her a little kiss before standing. Ian hadn't specifically invited her, but if his news involved her, she had every right to be present.

She hoped he didn't yell at her.

She was very worried about that vein.

The two men poured themselves goblets of that bitter brew, cough-he, and she got herself a Pepsi. Ian sat at one end of the table, she at the other, and Cage in between.

Ian didn't even acknowledge she was there.

Well, that wasn't quite true. There was a tic going in his right jaw, and the vein emerged, too. He was aware of her, for a certainty. That gave her a strange sort of satisfaction.

She was aware of him, too. Excessively aware. She never should have made love with him. It made it that much harder to resist him now. Not that he was pursuing her.

At odd times, she noticed a sadness in his eyes that hadn't been there before.

"Earth to Maddie. Earth to Maddie," Cage said.

She was jolted back to the present. "What?"

"Ian asked me if you were staying away from windows and doorways."

"Tell him yes. Tell him that message has been drilled into me. Tell him he is being childish and immature and a boor."

"Tell her she's a liar if she says I was boring with her."

"Tell the dolt I said boor . . . a rough clod . . . not boring."

Cage's head kept swinging back and forth between the two of them. He was grinning.

"Tell her I will be glad when this mission is over."

Madrene's eyes shot to Ian. *Does he really mean that? Will he be happy when I am gone? I do not care. I should not care. Why does it hurt so much?* "Tell him I will be out of here the instant the terrorists are caught."

Ian looked directly at her, too. He seemed hurt, as well, but only for an instant. Then he reverted to his usual crude self. "Tell her that her nipples are showing."

Cage made a choking sound.

"Tell him that his manpart is not all that impressive."

"Enough already!" Ian stood, almost knocking all of his documents to the floor. "While this is great entertainment, we have business to take care of here."

"Agreed," Cage said.

They both looked at Maddie.

She nodded her agreement, reluctantly. Madrene

had never been one to stop in the middle of an argument, and it rankled her to do so now.

"The tangos are in town," Ian announced as he sat back down.

Everyone grew silent at that news. It had been expected, of course. But now the dangerous part of the mission would start.

"How many?" Cage asked.

"Not sure. At least a dozen. Our informant tells us they're alternately skeptical that Maddie knows anything and outraged that a mere woman might reveal their secrets."

"How do they know I am here?" she asked.

For once, Ian talked to her directly. "That dirtbag Dan Sullivan took a picture of us together at our so-called wedding in Baghdad. Putting two and two together, they figured the U.S. government and its Navy have you under lock and SEAL."

"Can I see the picture?" From Ian's and Cage's startled looks, she could tell her question was odd, considering the more important information he'd relayed. She didn't care what they thought. Lifting her chin, she stared them both down.

"What's the plan?" Cage asked.

"First of all, more guards. I need to go into the base every day, to give the impression of normality. Once we get some intel on where they are and put some shadows on them . . . then we may or may not take her outside to draw them out for a showdown."

"Why can't we do it right away, and get this over with?"

Ian stiffened as if she'd just slapped him. "Don't worry, sweetheart, I'm as anxious to have you out of here as you are to leave."

Madrene felt as if a fist had just clenched her heart. That wasn't at all what she'd meant. But what did she say? "The instant this is over, I will be gone."

"Good riddance."

They glared at each other. Ian looked as angry as she felt.

"Let me ask you a question," she said.

"Be my guest."

"I have asked you and I ask you again: When this is over, would you lead a small army to my homeland to recapture Norstead?"

"You are crazy!"

"And you wonder why I will not lie with you anymore."

"Who asked you to?"

She growled.

He growled.

Cage stood and laughed as he said, "You two are so suited it's eerie."

Gotcha! . . .

It was two a.m., and Ian was still unable to fall asleep.

He sprawled out on his back, his favorite position. Didn't work. Tried one side, then the other. Nada. Even face down proved fruitless.

Maybe he should let Sam sleep in the bed again, like she used to, instead of being banished to the living-room sofa. Maybe he slept better before because he'd been lulled by the rhythm of her cat breathing.

Nah!

He attributed his insomnia to stress over this mission. He'd never been so personally involved in an assignment before. Or it could be the infuriating, tempting woman who lay on the other side of the bed, about a mile away.

It was pitch-black in the room, but he could picture her over there. The image of her naked body was imprinted on his brain forever. *Wonder if she's sleeping nude, like she did that first night. I like to think so. No, I don't. Who am I kidding? Shit!* Disgusted with himself, and his lack of sleep, he rolled over one more time.

"Ian," she said softly.

He froze. "What?" he barked. He hadn't meant to be so gruff; it just came out that way.

"I hear you moving. What are you doing over there?"

Great! Now we're going to chit-chat. Next she'll ask me what I'm thinking. "Guess."

She made a small sound of surprise. "Pleasuring yourself?"

Oh, my God! I didn't mean that. "Yeah." *That ought to shut her up.*

There was a loud silence before Maddie said, "Me, too."

This I gotta see. Ian sat up and turned on the bedside lamp.

She was lying on her side facing him, both hands folded under her cheek, prayer style. And there was a big ol' smirk on her face.

Ian got out of bed and stomped into the bathroom. He was going to take a long, cold shower.

Beware of women with plans . . .

Madrene had an unexpected visitor the next day.

There were not supposed to be any visitors, especially ones who had to knock before coming in. Cage was her inside guard today, and he immediately took out his piss-toll and checked it over. Then, pistol in hand, he picked up an ear piece which somehow connected him to the outside seals. After a short conversation, he put the gun down and told her, "It's okay."

Cage opened the door and said, "Admiral, we didn't expect you. Ian's not here."

"I know he's not here. I came to see his wife."

"No shit? I mean, absolutely, Admiral, sir."

Me? Why me? Madrene looked at the dignified gentleman who walked into the living room where they were sitting. He was dressed all in white, with short-clipped gray hair. There were many colored brooches on his chest and shoulders. She did not need to be told he must be an important military man.

Cage led the man in and said, "Admiral, this is Maddie Olgadottir . . . I mean, Maddie MacLean . . . oh, hell, I don't know what I mean."

Turning to her, his face beet red, Cage said, "Maddie, this is Admiral Thomas MacLean. Ian's father."

She was shocked.

He reached out a hand to shake hers. It was the custom in this country to greet each other by shaking hands.

"I'm pleased to meet you," the man said to her.

Once they were all sitting in the living room, Cage acting as if Odin himself had come to visit, the man gave her an all-over scrutiny. And smiled. "You'll do."

"For what?"

"Ian's wife."

"I'm not really Ian's wife."

"Oh?"

"It's just a temporary arrangement, as you well

know," Madrene snapped. All this false niceness was wearing thin with her. "And frankly, I am glad you have come to visit. There are a few things I would like to say to you. How dare you treat Ian the way you do?"

"I beg your pardon."

"You should beg *Ian's* pardon."

Ian's father looked as if he was either choking on his tongue or choking back laughter.

"A father should love his children above all else."

"I do."

"Hah! Not according to Ian. Nothing he does is good enough for you. Push, push, push, that is what you do. Well, someday you may push so hard you lose a son. You may have already."

"You are a brassy miss."

"Yea, I am, and do not forget it. Do not look down your nose at me. I carry the blood of Norse kings in my body."

"Okay, young lady, why don't you tell me what you think I have done."

Madrene did just that. It was a long and nagging lecture, even for her. When she stopped to take a breath, she noticed that both the admiral and Cage were gaping at her. Her lectures often had that effect on people . . . mostly men. "Well, it's the truth," she concluded.

Ian's father threw his head back then, slapped his knees and burst out laughing. So hard that tears filled his eyes, and he had to wipe them with a spotless linen he pulled from his pocket. "You'll do, missy."

Now that she'd spoken her mind, she asked, "Would you care for a beverage?"

"Actually, yes. Any beer in the house?"

"There is always mead here. Seals suck it up like air."

The old man grinned at her. Then he stood and held out his hand to pull her up. When he did, he tugged her into a hard hug and said, "Yes, you will do."

Madrene looked at Cage over the admiral's shoulder, pleading for help. He just grinned and said, "I'll go get the . . . mead."

When did his life become such a mess? . . .

Ian was in the SEAL headquarters catching up on some paperwork. His cell phone rang. He looked at the caller i.d. and groaned.

"Hi," Cage said in sort of a whisper.

"Hi yourself. Do not dare ask me if I know what my wife is doing now."

There was a long silence.

"Are you there?"

"Yep. I'm in the head. Don't wanna be overheard." He was still talking in a whisper.

Ian exhaled with a loud whoosh. "I give in. What is my wife doing now?"

"Well, it's not so much what she's doing. It's the visitor who came to see her."

"*What?*" Ian shouted into the phone.

"Really, *cher*, you've gotta work on your phone personality. My eardrums are developing a ring."

"Tell . . . me . . ." he gritted out.

"Your father came to visit Maddie."

This was the absolute last thing Ian expected to hear. He was angry with Maddie, but, God, his father would make mincemeat of her. "Why did he come?"

"Not sure. Guess he wanted to look over your better half."

Ian snorted his opinion.

"Man, you woulda been proud of her. She laid into your dad like some kinda warrior princess. She was a pit bull for you."

For me? Why would she defend me? Interfering witch! "And what did my father do?"

"He hugged her."

Hugged her? I think I will go slit my wrists. "Where is he . . . she . . . now?"

"They're sharing a *mead* in the kitchen and exchanging family secrets. I didn't know you peed the bed till you were three. Ha, ha, ha. What's that noise I hear?"

"My head banging on the desk."

Wacky or woo-woo? . . .

Ian was ambushed three days later as he left the mess hall. Geek, Omar and Pretty Boy stood in his path.

"We need to talk to you about Maddie. She—" Geek started to say.

"The last thing we need to talk about is Maddie," Ian interrupted. He put up both hands to halt them. "Unless she has flown the coop *again*, unless her life is in danger, unless your lives are in danger *from her*, I don't want to hear it."

"You should hear this," Omar said.

"No. My nerves are strung so tight, they could slinky me down the steps of the Washington Monument."

"Frustration will do that to you every time," Pretty Boy opined.

"Bite me!" Ian said succinctly. "Get back to work. All of you."

The three of them just looked at him, said "Okay" as one, and turned to walk away into the mess hall.

"Shit!" They were actually going to leave without telling him the latest on Maddie. Forget about the fact he'd told them he didn't want to know. They should have told him anyway. With a sigh of resignation, he called, "Wait!"

The three stooges turned and smiled at him, as if they'd known he would be curious. Soon they were sitting down to coffee.

Geek started first. "There is something really strange about Maddie."

Ian raised his eyebrows. "Tell me something I don't know."

"Seriously, Mac, it's not just the way she talks," Omar said. "And believe me, some of the random words in her speech are more like the tenth or eleventh century than today. In fact, I've heard Icelanders speak the way she does."

"Iceland!" he said with disgust.

"Yep. And the Icelandic language is similar to Old Norse."

"Norse! Oh, hell! This reminds me of Magnusson and all the Viking crap he used to spout." Max was Torolf Magnusson's nickname. "Where is Max these days?" He directed that last question to Cage, who was usually Max's team partner. Max had been the biggest pain in Ian's butt three years ago when Ian had been his instructor in BUD/S training.

"Still in Afghanistan working with a combined special forces team trying to teach fighting skills to guys who ride camels." Cage grinned. "He should be back next week or the week after."

Actually, Ian knew Max would be back by then. His sister was married to Max's brother, Ragnor. In fact, there was a big shindig being planned at Blue Dragon Vineyard in two weeks to celebrate some event related to grapes.

"There's more," Geek said, his voice too serious for Ian's comfort. "Hordaland . . . that country where Maddie says Norstead is . . . well, I couldn't find Norstead anywhere, but Hordaland was a region of southwest Norway about a thousand or so years ago. It wasn't called Norway then. There was a king called Olaf . . . you know, the guy she says was her grandfather's brother. Birka was a market town in Sweden, and Hedeby was a market town in Germany, though they weren't called Sweden or Germany then." Geek paused, not because he was done with his spiel, but because he wanted Ian's reaction. Apparently, he'd already discussed his discoveries with Omar and Pretty Boy.

Ian was dumbfounded.

His silence gave Pretty Boy an opportunity to offer his input. "On an everyday level, she's clueless. She honest-to-God never heard of a TV, a blender, a camera, the telephone, birth control, breast implants, things everyone knows."

Ian homed in on one thing. "Why would you be discussing birth control with my . . . with Maddie?"

Pretty Boy shrugged. "She asked. Guess you must have shown her a condom. Right?" The dunce grinned.

Ian refused to answer. "And breast implants? Don't try to tell me she asked about that?"

"Nope. I asked her."

"What?" he yelled.

"Come on, Mac. Even you wondered in the beginning."

"What did she say?" Cage inquired. Geek seemed even more interested.

"Get a life!" Ian advised them all before Pretty Boy could respond. After glaring at each of them in turn, he asked, "So what do you think all this means?"

"I think she's a time-traveler," Geek said.

Ian's jaw dropped.

"Nah! I think she might have a slight mental problem," Omar said. "Maybe even a split personality."

Ian's eyes widened.

"Uh-uh!" Pretty Boy said. "Gotta be reincarnation."

They all looked at Ian to see what he thought.

"I think you all have lost your freakin' minds," he said. "And I think I need to get knee-walking drunk."

As he walked away, he heard Cage say to the others, "Personally, I think he needs to get laid . . . again."

Yep!

Beware of pre-menstrual women . . .

Madrene had come to several conclusions.

One, time was of the essence. Soon the seals' mission here would be completed, and she would embark on her own mission. She could not do it alone, even if she hired mercenaries. She needed someone from this country to help her find her way back to hers. 'Twas a sorry fact.

Two, if she might die any day now, or if she didn't die and had to go home alone, she was bloody hell going to enjoy herself in the meantime. That meant sex. With the troll. Lots of it.

Three, as unpalatable as it might be, she would use sex to gain her noble goal.

Oh, she knew she was changing her mind in midstream. Technically, she was the one who had called off the bedsport. But her body ached for the man, despite all her good resolutions. It was probably because it was several days before her monthly flux, and she was always different at that time . . . some might even say difficult. Or mayhap it was because the bedsport had been so good with him. Or it might be all that *Sex and the City* watching that gave her ideas.

Whatever the reason, she was now on a mission. Seduce the man to her way of thinking.

No problem!

On the other hand, there might be a small problem. She had no idea how to go about seducing a man. Perhaps she needed help. She wished there were a woman she could ask. But there was not. Should she ask Cage for advice? Or Pretty Boy? Or Slick? She was almost afraid of what he would say; he was such a dark and secretive man. But Omar probably knew unusual stuff since he came from both an Arab and Indian background. And Geek, and JAM, and Sly.

Bloody hell! I guess I'll have to ask them all.

You want to do WHAT? . . .

Slick was the first seal that Madrene was able to corner about her particular problem.

Slick rarely came into the house. Usually he was one of the outside guards, or stayed back at the base. The man made her a little uncomfortable, he was so quiet, and he had these dark, piercing eyes. When he looked at you, well, you felt as if he saw too much.

But Madrene had never been one to cower when she had something to say. "What can I do to seduce Ian?" she asked as Slick was pouring himself a cup of coffee.

She knew he heard her because he stopped in the middle of pouring. But he didn't say anything. At first. Then he turned, very slowly, and looked at her. A long time. Then he said, "Breathe."

Hah! A lot of good that advice was. *Breathe and the troll would be seduced. I . . . do . . . not . . . think . . . so.* She walked huffily out of the room.

Next day, she asked Geek. The poor boy just blushed and stammered before saying, "Can't you just ask him to . . . uh, make love with you?"

"Of course not. I want him to think he is the one doing the seducing."

"Oh, I see," Geek said. But he clearly didn't see.

Next, Sly told her to flash him. She hesitated to ask him what he meant because of the grin on his face, but she did. *I should have known better.* Then he demonstrated by putting both fists at the center of his tea-*shert* and jerking his arms outward.

What? He expects me to expose my breasts. "There is no subtlety in that."

"Believe me, men don't need subtlety."

JAM was not subtle, either. He said, "A blow job."

At first she didn't understand what he meant. When she did, her jaw dropped. "A priest recommends such a thing? I am . . . shocked."

He grinned and said, "An almost-priest. I never took holy orders."

"And that makes a difference. How?"

He laughed and told her, "Even St. Augustine said he wanted to be good . . . but not yet."

Omar suggested she try belly dancing and actually showed her how. "The trick is to be wearing very little clothing," he said. "Preferably, a few sheer scarves."

"Oh, now I know what you mean. They used to do these dances in the harems."

Omar just rolled his eyes at her. They all did when she mentioned the harems.

Pretty Boy had some of the best ideas. Tight jeans, a boosty-air and red lip rouge. He was going to bring them for her tomorrow.

Cage, the rascal, just laughed and laughed. In the end, he suggested a place called Victoria's Secret, and said they could order some garments, delivered overnight, from the Inner-net.

So Maddie was all set. Too bad Ian was in such a bad temper when he got home. Oh, well. She needed a little time anyhow, to bolster her nerve.

But tomorrow, he'd better watch out.

Chapter Fourteen

She hit him with her best shot . . .

Ian came home early the next day.

The net was drawing in on the tangos. All of Team Thirteen was now involved in the mission. CIA operatives were all over the place, as well. These were mean sons-of-bitches that had been sent to either kidnap or take Maddie down. The SEALs could have eliminated a few of the more careless ones already, but they were going for the whole bunch of tangos. So it was a high-stakes waiting game.

You'd never know anything was up inside his home, though. There was a sort of normalcy here . . . although any space with Maddie in it could hardly be called normal. He used the remote garage-door opener, drove into the garage, then used a key to enter the house through the side door of the kitchen. Immediately he was hit with the tantalizing smell of something good cooking on the stove . . . probably

Cage's famous crab gumbo, since he was the SEAL assigned inside today. Yep, home sweet home.

Maybe I should just yell out, "Honey, I'm home."

On the other hand, considering her mood lately, I don't think so.

Still, there was a part of him that wondered what it would be like to come home to a wife . . . and a kid or two. And what if that wife were Maddie? And what if those kids looked just like a combination of the two of them? And what if they were happy as hell to see him?

Do I really want that?

Hell, no! Commit myself to a woman who might very well be a time-traveler, mental patient, reincarnated dingbat, or God only knows what? Hell, no!

On the other hand, hell, yes! I can't stop thinking about her. She puts me in my place. She makes me happy. She surprises me all the time. I never know what's going to come out of her mouth. She screws my brains out, then pulls the plug on sex. Well, we both pulled that plug, but who cares? A plug is a plug.

Sam came up and rubbed herself against his leg. That was a surprise. Sam had been ignoring him ever since Maddie came on the scene. He reached down and ruffled the cat's fur. "Guess it's you and me, babe. When this is all over, it will be back to you and me." Sam looked as sad as he felt.

Ian went over to the stove and took off the lid. Yep, crab gumbo. He took a wooden spoon and tasted. Ummm. Cage knew what he was doing when it came to Cajun cooking.

Ian heard soft voices from down the hall. They were probably in his office surfing the net again. "Yo, Cage," he yelled out.

The talking stopped. Then Cage said, "Be right there."

A few minutes later, when he came to the kitchen where Ian had already opened a bottle of beer, Cage had Pretty Boy tagging after him. Ian's brow furrowed with confusion. "What are you doing here?"

"I had a day off," Pretty Boy said, "and decided to drop by."

"Why?" *He'd better not be hustling Maddie.*

"Why not?" Pretty Boy said, then looked at Cage. "You comin'? Since Mac's back, you probably don't have to stay."

They both looked at Ian, and he nodded. "Go. I have paperwork to do, and it can be done here as well as at the base."

"Are you sure?" Cage asked. "We could stay."

"Yeah, I'm dying for some crab gumbo," Pretty Boy said.

Cage elbowed Pretty Boy.

"You two are acting dingy. What's up?"

"Nothing," they both said at the same time.

"Maybe we'd better go," Cage said.

"Yeah," Pretty Boy agreed dolefully.

Ian noticed that they practically dragged their feet as they picked up their weapons and put them in special carry-alls that disguised their contents from any tangos watching the house. Finally, after dawdling for five minutes more, they left.

Ian took his beer and briefcase into the living room. He picked up the remote and turned on the TV, channel surfed till he found a ball game, then spread his papers out on the coffee table.

Where's Maddie? he thought as another ten minutes went by, and there was no noise coming from down the hall.

Maybe she's taking a nap. Yeah, that must be it.

He worked for another few minutes, then threw his pen down in disgust. *I am not thinking about her on the bed. And I am definitely not thinking about a little Afternoon Delight.*

He took a long swallow from the long neck, put his hands behind his neck, leaned back and contemplated the fireplace. *She has a hell of a nerve cutting me off, demanding my help in exchange for sex. Like she's that special. Chicks are a dime a dozen. I could go down to the Wet and Wild, even now in the middle of the day, and chances are I could pick up a hot number. A one-nighter, that's what I need.* Why that idea had no appeal, he couldn't say. Actually, he could say. He'd been sick of one-nighters long before Maddie came on the scene. Now that she had come, he felt sick to his stomach even considering such a thing.

Sam jumped up on the couch and sat next to him. He could swear the cat looked sad. *Misery loves company, I guess.* Ian closed his eyes and sighed. *My life sucks.*

He heard Maddie coming down the hall, her heels clicking on the hardwood floor. His eyes flew open. *Clicking? High heels click. Not sandals or sneakers, which is all she has. Uh-oh.*

Sitting up straighter, he watched as Maddie stepped onto the living room carpet. He was speechless. That was all. Utterly, friggin', out-of-this-world speechless.

She wore the tightest pair of black jeans ever plastered on to a woman's body. She must have lain down on the floor to get them on. Even then, she had to have had help. *Cage and Pretty Boy! I'll kill them.*

On her feet were red, high-heeled, toeless shoes . . . stilettos, he thought they were called. Her toenails had been painted red to match. Where the hell did she get those shoes, and who painted her toenails? *Cage and Pretty Boy! I'll kill them.*

Up top—*be still my heart*—she wore a black leather bustier that left her arms, shoulders and half her chest bare, right down to a pair of uplifted breasts that just might pop the laces. *If those two jerks helped or watched her put this on, I'll definitely kill them.*

Even her face and hair were different. Her hair was loose and mussed. In fact, it looked as if someone had curled the long strands. *Where in God's name did those two men learn how to do that to a woman's hair?*

She wore red lipstick, too. And makeup, he was pretty sure. At least there was dark stuff on her eyelashes.

All this passed through his mind as she paused in the doorway. She licked her lips nervously.

A Blue Steeler popped right up in his pants.

She walked over to the chair across from the sofa and attempted to sit down. He should have been laughing at how difficult it was for her to bend, but there was nothing funny when your erection was about to burst the zipper at your crotch.

Finally she perched on the edge, looked over at him and said, cool as you please, "What's up?" She must have learned that expression from her two bozo makeover artists.

In answer to her question, he looked down at his lap.

She had the grace to blush. Damn straight she should blush.

"What's up with you, Madonna?"

Her shoulders slumped. "You think I look like the mother of God? Pfff. Cage and Pretty Boy said . . ." She let her words trail off as she realized she was revealing too much.

He hadn't been giving her words full attention, at first. He was too busy watching the rise and fall of her incredible breasts. Apparently, she was having trouble breathing. He started to grin, then stopped himself. "No, I didn't mean *that* Madonna. I meant the other one with the cone-shaped breast things."

"What is a cone?"

"Never mind. So, what's new?"

"Well, I learned to shag today."

"What?"

"You do not have to yell. I am right here. And, by the by, there comes that vein again. Really, you should do something about that. I knew a trader once who—"

"Who did you shag?" he asked icily.

She frowned at him. "Who? I did not shag anyone. I *did* the shag with someone. Cage. He really is a good dancer. Are you a good dancer?"

"No."

"You should ask Cage to teach you. He even knows how to dip. Do you dip?"

Ian put his face in one hand and counted to ten. Then he looked at her. "Am I supposed to interpret this outfit as an invitation?"

Her body went stiff as a board, or as much as was possible in her hooker outfit. "Why would I invite you to anything? I told you that you are no longer welcome to . . . you know. Have you changed your mind about helping me to raise an army?"

"Hell, no!"

"Then I have nothing more to say to you. Mayhap you should call Slick to come over so that I may ask him if would be willing to help me raise an army."

"No way!" he bellowed.

"You do not give me orders. How many times do I have to tell you that?"

"You are not meeting with any other man in that . . . that outfit," he sputtered.

"What's wrong with my apparel?"

"That outfit is sex bait, pure and simple."

"So?"

"Why are you wearing it if you're not inviting me?"

"Practice."

Aaarrgh! "Practice for what?"

"For when I leave here. I must needs make my way in the world when I interview candidates for my army."

"And who, pray tell, are these men you are going to interview in that *attire?*"

"Mercenaries."

Not in this lifetime!

"There are men who fight for money, you know."

"I know, but where is the money coming from?" *As soon as she leaves the room, I am going to hunt out those frickin' jewels of hers and hide them till she gives up the ludicrous idea of a personal army.*

"I have nothing more to say to you." She raised her chin haughtily and proceeded to walk away, and once again he had the niggling feeling he had seen her before. But then he didn't think any more because he almost lost it just looking at her ass in those tight jeans.

Ian decided to take a cold shower . . . *again*. He was beginning to develop prune skin.

A half hour later he came down to the kitchen, where Maddie was standing before the stove, stirring the gumbo. A rock station was on the radio and she was doing this kind of shimmy as she danced in place to "Wild Thing." Apparently, Cage had taught her more than the Cajun two-step and the shag. He spun around and returned for another cold shower. After that he shut himself in his office and did his work there. Good thing, too. His cell phone rang constantly with messages related to the upcoming trap being set.

It must have been five o'clock before he heard a soft rap on the door. "Yeah?"

Maddie cracked the door open and said, "You don't have to bark at me." She was wearing the same enticing outfit, but she'd ditched the high heels—her feet had probably been killing her—and her lipstick had worn off. "Dinner is ready if you're interested. But don't consider that an '*invitation*.' I've already eaten."

He started to apologize for snapping at her. His distress wasn't her fault. Well, actually, it was her fault for dressing like that. It wouldn't do any good to apologize anyway, because she was already sashaying down the hall. *Lordy, lordy!*

"By the by," she said, turning and walking backward. "Do you like blow jobs?"

Ian almost swallowed his tongue. He would kill whoever taught her that phrase. Or maybe he wouldn't. "Yeah. Why?"

"Because you're never getting one from me." She turned and continued walking away from him.

Amazing!

In the empty kitchen, which he noticed that Maddie kept spotlessly clean, he scooped some gumbo and white rice onto a place, then added a couple of slices of French bread. He walked to the table and was about to sit down, but decided he wasn't hungry after all.

He went to the living room, where Maddie was stretched out on the couch, all five feet ten inches of hot stuff. She was watching—Ian checked and had to grin—the weather channel.

He went over to the side of the couch and stared down at her. "Maddie?"

"What?" she asked, not even looking up at him.

"Let's cut the crap. I want you. You want me. Let's go to bed and screw each other's brains out." *I have the charm of a slug.*

"Who says I want you?" She looked up at him now.

"I say so." He hunkered down beside her and took her hand in both of his. "Come on, sweetie. You win."

"I do?" she said brightly, turning on her side. When she did, her breasts almost fell out of the leather bustier, and his heart almost stopped. "Does that mean you'll help me raise an army to go back to Norstead?"

He rolled his eyes. "No, it doesn't mean that. Is that the only way you'll let me in?"

She nodded.

"Sounds a little bit like prostitution to me." That sounded crude, even to his own ears.

But Maddie didn't seem offended, just angry. She slapped his hand away. "Let me tell you something.

If spreading my thighs for that beast Steinolf would have saved Norstead, I would have done it in a trice. If that be prostitution, so be it."

"Are you putting me in the same class as that monster?"

She sighed tiredly. "No. No, I'm not. I'm just trying to explain how important regaining Norstead is to me. I'll do anything to accomplish it."

"Even sleep with me?"

She nodded. "Even that."

"It's not much of a compliment."

She shrugged. "When I started this seduction game . . ."

Seduction game? Is that what this is? Why didn't someone tell me? I don't mind being seduced.

". . . I had a two-fold purpose."

You've got my attention, baby. This oughta be good.

"I wanted to change your mind about helping me raise an army . . ."

I am sick to my eyeballs of hearing about this fictional, never-gonna-happen army of hers.

". . . but I also tried to seduce you just because . . ."

I'd like to think . . . but no, you never can predict what she'll come out with next.

". . . because you make me all fluttery *all the time.*"

A slow smile crept onto his mouth, and he didn't even try to stop it. "That's a good thing, Maddie. Why do you look so sad?"

She sat up. Since he was still hunkered down, they were eye to eye. "You are a military man. How important is honor to you?"

Huh? We were talking about sex. "Very important. Why?"

"Because it is equally important to me. If I made love to you again, knowing how little regard you have for my quest, then I would be without honor."

That is the most fantastic bit of female illogic I have ever heard. "I don't see it that way."

"I know you do not," she said sadly.

Now he was growing angry because, frankly, he was beginning to understand that he wasn't getting any tonight. "How much honor is there in trying to seduce me to your way of thinking?"

She seemed to actually ponder his argument, then shook her head. "If your refusal to help me was a point of honor, then it would be dishonorable of me to try to seduce you. But since your refusal is based on mere muleheadedness and lack of trust and belief in me"—she shrugged—"my method was fair."

He threw his hands up in disgust. "You are crazy. That's it. No more begging. There are other fish in the sea."

Walking away from her, he thought he heard a stifled sob, but he was probably mistaken. Talk about muleheadedness . . . she took the prize there.

Ian had never been so twisted out of shape by a woman before . . . not even by Jennifer when she left. In fact, there had been a bit of relief when she'd skipped out on him; he'd already begun to suspect his feelings for her weren't that deep. It was probably why she'd cheated on him. But now, if he didn't know better . . . no, it wasn't possible . . . but what if . . .

Holy hell, I am in bigger trouble than I thought.

I have fallen in love with a looneybird.

Heartbreak Hotel . . . uh, Home . . .

Madrene stood under the hot shower for a long time that night.

She was crying and could not stop. She'd always known that if she started to let the tears escape, there would be a flood. And that was just what was happening.

She cried for the loss of Norstead and the death of so many of her people. She wept for the women who had been raped by Steinolf's men. She sobbed aloud when she pictured herself in the longship departing from the Norselands. She moaned the death of all her family members. There were tears, too, for the two long years in Arab lands, always, always determined that she would go back one day and unseat Steinolf. She even threw in her anguish over being barren.

But mostly, she cried for Ian because she truly wanted him to believe in her. Unrealistically, she had half expected him to be so enthralled with her that he would acquiesce.

I love him, she admitted to herself. *For the first time in my life, I have fallen in love. And it cannot be. It cannot be.*

With her forehead pressed against the shower tiles, with the hot water turning tepid, she sobbed her heart out where no one could see or hear her. It would be the last time she allowed herself the female weakness of tears, but for now she just let go of all her grief.

So engrossed was she that she didn't hear the door open.

Ian had stepped into the shower, wearing a pair of

his running shorts. He held her from behind, his arms wrapped around her middle, his chin resting on her shoulder. "Shhhh, don't cry, sweetie. Everything will turn out all right. I promise it will. Please don't cry."

Ian's heart was breaking over this strong, broken woman in his arms. He'd been in his office when he heard her go into the shower at least a half hour ago. When the running water had continued for such a long time, he'd gotten up and walked to the bathroom door. He'd rapped and got no answer. Then he'd opened the door a crack and heard her heartwrenching sobs.

"I am not crying," she cried.

"I know, honey. You never cry."

"And I am not cry . . . being sad over you."

"I hope not. I'm not worth it."

"You are so."

"Okay."

"I will never bear children, you know."

"That's what this is all about? Children?"

"Nay! I just thought I would mention that." Another sob escaped her. "Do you plan on having children someday?"

Now, there's a loaded question if I ever heard one. "I don't know. Finding someone to love would be more important than finding a mother for my children."

He turned off the shower and pulled an oversized towel off the rack behind him. Wrapping her in it, he picked her up and carried her into the bedroom. Sitting down on the side of the bed, he began to move his fingers through her wet hair like a comb so it was off her face.

For a few minutes she allowed him to minister to

her and make soothing sounds to stop her crying, but then she began to struggle. Her arms were bound at her sides by the towel. "Let me out," she demanded when he just held tighter. "I am over my . . . self-pity . . ."

Self-pity? Hah! More like all-out bawling.

". . . I am back to myself again. Let me go."

"No. I don't think so."

Her head shot up. "What do you mean?"

God, she was beautiful. Even with red-rimmed blue eyes. "I mean, I like you in this position. You're easier to talk to this way."

She squirmed.

He chuckled. "Give it up, baby. I've got you now."

She narrowed her eyes at him. "What are you going to do?"

"I'm not sure. Perhaps I'll start here." He lowered his mouth to hers and kissed her startled lips.

She was startled for only a second, before she squirmed some more.

"Have you any idea what your squirming is doing to my . . . lap?"

She stopped instantly, probably feeling his erection through the towel. Her cheeks flushed and she turned on him. "You would take me against my wishes?"

"No. Never. You'll be willing."

"Troll."

"You say that like an endearment. I've decided that every time you call me troll, you are really saying, 'Darling.' " He kissed her then, in earnest. Long, drugging kisses that went on forever. He kept his tongue in check at first, figuring she might just take a bite out of him. But when she moaned and opened for him, he entered the hot wetness of her mouth, and moaned himself.

He never knew there were so many ways to kiss a woman. Truthfully, he was probably inventing a few new ones. A woman like Maddie made a man creative.

While she was being so compliant, he lifted her off his lap and onto the bed. As he lay on his side, leaning over her, she stared up at him from the pillow. "Are you going to help me when this is over?" Her eyes were wide and sad as she waited for his response.

"Probably," he said. "Are you going to make love with me, regardless of what I would do for you in the future?"

"Probably," she said with a long sigh.

Probably. She said probably. When a woman says probably, she usually means yes. Holy cow! We're gonna make love again. And all I had to say was probably. He allowed himself to smile then.

"Stop smiling," she ordered. "You know what your smiles do to me."

He continued to smile, of course.

"Release me from this towel. Now that you got your way, you don't have to restrain me."

"You got your way, too, Maddie. And, no, I am not going to release you."

"Why?"

"Stop asking so many questions. I'm going exploring."

"Exploring what?"

He made a tsk-ing sound at her continuing questions. "You." With that, he moved down the bed, knelt over her legs, which were spread as far as they would go, then shoved the towel up to her waist. That allowed him to spread her legs wider and move between her legs. Her arms were still held by the towel.

"Eeeeeek! What are you doing down there?"

"Exploring."

"With your tongue?" she shrieked. "This is embarrassing."

"No, it's not. Besides, you asked me if I like oral sex."

"I didn't mean *this*. JAM described something entirely different when he explained oral sex to me."

Note to self. Kill JAM. "Be quiet, Maddie, or I'll stuff a washcloth in your mouth."

"You wouldn't dare. Oooooooh! What did you just do?"

You don't wanna know, sweetheart. "You're right. I wouldn't put a gag in your mouth, but I might do something perverted."

"Seems to me you are already doing something perverted."

"Not even close, baby."

She went still.

He put both hands under her buttocks and touched her *there*.

She bucked up and screeched. "I'll be quiet," she promised.

"Good. But, for the record, that wasn't perverted. You can trust me, Maddie." She was quiet; so he asked, "You do trust me, don't you?"

"Maybe."

That was good enough, for now.

He got down to business then, and what a delicious business it was. By the light of both bedside lamps, he was able to see Maddie's sweet spot and all its surrounding pink folds. She was only slightly aroused now. He looked forward to changing that situation.

It all came together quicker than he'd expected, but not quick enough as far as his own raging libido was concerned. Maddie was so cute—okay, not cute; more like hot damn sexy—when she made those little whoofing sounds as she came closer and closer to climax. And then she arched her hips off the bed, tried to bring her legs together, which he wouldn't allow, then howled as she came . . . and came . . . and came. Like everything else his Maddie did, she gave it her all and then some.

And, yes, he was thinking of her as his.

Before she had a chance to catch a breath, he moved up and over her and eased himself into her still spasming inner muscles. He was the one who felt like howling now.

"Ian?" she said.

Oh, God, oh, God, oh, God! She's going to talk now! He was gritting his teeth and could not respond.

"Troll?"

Didn't I just tell her, about an orgasm ago, that I would interpret troll as darling in future? Yeah, I did. He unclenched his teeth and grinned down at her. "What, sweetie?"

"If you don't unwrap me, you will never, ever be reciprocated for . . . what you just did." Her face was pink with embarrassment. At least she wasn't red from crying.

"That is a threat worth heeding."

Still embedded deep inside her, he managed to pull the ends of the towel out from under her, releasing not just her arms but those magnificent breasts.

"Why are you leering at my breasts?" she groused.

"Because I like what I see." *And because I consider them mine now. No other man is going to see you . . . them . . . like me.* "Did you like what I did to you?"

"Nay."

Her inner muscles belied her by clutching him even tighter. He would have teased her about that, but he was suddenly overcome with such love for her. The emotion was so powerful it made him breathless, and not just because a part of her was embracing him like it would never let go. There was an expression he'd heard one time about "loving someone to distraction." That was exactly how he felt. She mixed him all up. She nagged and berated him, refused his orders, gave him orders, turned him inside out and upside down with anger and frustration. Then, in the midst of it all, she told him that his smile made her fluttery.

He wanted desperately to tell her that he loved her, but he was afraid it was too soon. She would interpret his declaration as pity, coming so hard on her cry fest. And she would also tie it in somehow with her irrational quest for an army.

So he couldn't tell her. But he could show her how much he loved her.

"Move off me, you big lout, so I can make love to you."

"Not yet, sweetheart," he said, nuzzling her neck. And then he made slow, slow love to her. With each long stroke in and out of her slickness, he gave her soft words of praise and explicit whispers about what he was about to do or wanted to do. He worshiped her.

And she returned the favor tenfold. She caressed his face and shoulders and back. She murmured what she liked and told him what she wanted. She kissed him, alternating between coaxing and hunger. She offered him her breasts with her own hands. She reached between where they were joined and touched him and herself at the same scorching moment.

When they came together in an ever-increasing spiral of sweet agony, he wished he could tell her what was on his mind. *I love you, Maddie. Forever.*

You can't deny love . . .

Maddie was never one to hold her tongue.

So when Ian eased himself out of her and rolled to his side, taking her with him in a gentle embrace, she raised her head and looked down at him. "Ian?"

"Uh-oh! We're going to start talking, aren't we?"

"What's wrong with talking?"

"There's a time and a place for everything. And right now I want to make love to you. Over and over."

She liked the sound of that. Still . . . "Be that as it may. Ian, I have a question for you."

He groaned, leaned over her and kissed her softly on the lips, then dropped back down to the pillow. "Okay, spill, baby."

She twirled his chest hairs nervously, then looked him steadily in the eyes. "Do you think you could ever love a woman like me?"

He just stared at her for a very long moment. Then he whispered in a husky voice, "Do you read minds now, too?"

Confused, she tilted her head.

"Maddie, I love you. I honest to God do. I probably did the moment I saw you with that Phyllis Diller hair and camel stink on you. I think I will love you always."

"Oh, Ian." She began to cry. "I am not crying," she quickly said.

He brushed some hair off her face. "Why are you not-crying?"

"Because I love you so much it scares me."

Ian blinked several times, as if he might have tears rising, too. Then he pulled her down for a kiss that lasted this side of forever.

"What are we going to do about this love?" she asked him when they came up for air.

"I don't know, but one thing is certain, wife . . ."

It was the first time he'd addressed her that way, and a thrill rippled through her. *I am his wife. Truly. And he is my husband.*

"Are you listening, Maddie? I am *never* going to let you go."

His words sounded a little bit autocratic, as he often was with her. But this time, she liked the sound of it. Betimes it was all right to love a tyrant, Madrene decided.

Chapter Fifteen

People are not always what they seem . . .

Madrene was floating in a haze of love that morning when Ian left for the base and Geek came to take his place. She felt the same way all morning as she performed what had become routine chores for her. She could tell she was making Geek uncomfortable with her incessant smiling.

Then everything came crashing down.

Ian returned at lunchtime, and he had five seals and a *woman* with him. "Maddie, meet Maddie," he said cheerfully. He must have noticed the glare on her face, because he quickly explained, "Everything is going down today, and I found a way to protect you . . . keep you out of harm's way."

She folded her arms across her chest. "Did I ask you for protection?"

Ian's seal comrades began hooting with laughter and making remarks at the interplay between them, such as, "Give him hell, Xena." Let them make mirth. She did not care.

"No, but I'm giving it anyway. It's my job, sweetie."

"Sweetie?" she saw Cage mouth to Pretty Boy before the two of them raised their right hands high and clapped them against each other.

Ian seemed taken aback when she said, "Do not even try to soften me with endearments. Speak plainly and tell me what this is all about."

"This is Joan Askey. She's with the CIA, and she's going to impersonate you today. You won't even have to leave the house."

Madrene made a low growling sound before turning to the woman, who extended her hand for a shake. Madrene complied, but only because it would have been inhospitable not to. Then she surveyed the woman from head to toe. She had red hair, a small nose and mouth and no bosom to speak of. The only similarity between them was their height.

She looked at Ian and said, "She does not resemble me at all."

"She will, honey . . . when we're done fixing her up." He reached to squeeze her shoulder.

She ducked away. "Do not call me honey."

He frowned, the vein popping out in his forehead. "What bug crawled up your ass?"

"Not you, that is for certain," she replied, matching him crudity for crudity. "I am Madrene Olgadottir. I come from a bloodline of fierce fighting men and noble kings. Ne'er do I pay scutage to another to fight my battles."

Ian's jaw dropped. "Are you saying you want to

do the job yourself . . . that you want to risk possible death?"

"That is precisely what I am saying."

"Everyone," he shouted, waving to all the others in the room, "scram!"

They all left, reluctantly, even the woman, who had been staring at Madrene as if she were demented. She felt a bit demented.

"You said you loved me," he said, looking wounded.

She was wounded herself. Where was the euphoria she'd been experiencing all morning? "You said you loved me, too. But you do not know me if you think I can accept another taking my place in the front line of a battle."

"Maddie, be reasonable."

"There is no room for reason when honor is involved."

He rolled his eyes. "I don't have time to argue about this. We'll talk about this tonight." He leaned down to kiss her, and she turned her face to the side.

He gave her a hard look, then turned away, going down the hall to join his comrades.

Madrene sat brooding in the solar. Sam hopped up and nestled against her leg, meowing her commiseration, probably saying, *Men! Dumb dolts, all of them!* Geek was going to give her some reading and writing lessons this afternoon. She doubted she would be able to concentrate now that she knew Ian would be out facing danger. Anger warred with worry, and her concern for the overbearing brute won out. But only for a moment.

Ian and the seals came from down the hall, grinning. When they got to the archway of the solar, Ian asked, "What do you think?" He stepped aside and Madrene got an eye-popping look at the woman who presumably looked like her.

Joan wore a long blond wig that looked remarkably like Madrene's own hair. She had applied a large amount of lip rouge which made her appear to have a larger mouth. She had on tight jeans and a red sleeveless top. She carried a long-sleeved jacket of the same denim fabric. But there was one thing that really stood out. Joan had somehow developed a bosom that was huge. *Huge!*

"You are all a bunch of blind lackwits if you think I am *that* big."

"I don't know about that," Ian said, winking at her.

She knew he was just teasing, but she was in no mood for his jests. "She looks like the prow of a longship my lackwit brother once built."

"Okay, guys, weapons ready," Ian told the men. "Joan already has her body armor on."

Oh. So that's what all that padding is. Still, they had deliberately made her voluptuous.

All the men were taking off their shirts, putting on what she knew were called flak jackets, then putting the shirts back on. Concealed weapons were strapped onto every concealed part of their bodies. The larger weapons were broken down and carefully packed in special carrying bags.

Geek, who would be staying behind with her, was equally well armed, though he did not wear the protective armor. The young man was just as chagrined at being excluded from the mission as she was. Babysitting, he called it.

Everyone was ready to go. In fact, Ian checked

each of them in turn and said, "Good to go!" And Pretty Boy yelled out, "Yee-haw!" Madrene figured that must be a seal battle cry, like "Hoo-yah" which they also often said.

Ian looked at her, probably expecting her to melt, but she was too stubborn for that. He just nodded his disappointment with a clenched jaw, and turned away. Five of the seals went out the front door to their cars. They would pretend to be returning to the military base. Ian and Joan headed out the kitchen door to his car in the garage. They would pretend to go on a pick-knack . . . that was a kind of outdoor meal. She heard the door shut, softly but ominously.

Madrene stared at the empty space where Ian had been. *What is wrong with me, that I cannot bend, even for the man I love? I have had to act the man for too many years. That must be why I insisted on . . .* Her eyes shot up.

Ian had come back. He stomped up to her, picked her up so her feet barely touched the floor and kissed her handily. Then he left, though still stomping.

Not a word had been exchanged, but they'd both said much.

Men will be men . . .

For the next three hours, Ian didn't think about Maddie at all. He couldn't. When a SEAL, or any special forces operative, went into battle mode, his focus had to be centered on one thing and one thing only: the enemy.

He and Joan went into the park, which was not by any means empty of people. Everyone there was either CIA or SEAL, even that man and woman wheeling a baby carriage, which held not an infant but an AK-47. He and Joan set up a blanket and opened a picnic basket. Ian uncorked a bottle of wine and leaned over to kiss Joan, as if they were lovers enjoying a day in the sun. Joan set out an assortment of cheeses and fruits and smiled up at him.

Then all hell broke loose.

A gunshot, which came from north of the park behind the restrooms, hit Joan in the shoulder and knocked her backward. The shot was probably intended for him, because they would surely want Maddie alive. He pulled out his own pistol and threw himself over Joan, covering her with his body. It was hard to tell from his vantage point who was shooting at whom now, so loud and rapid was the gunfire. He could tell from the firing sounds what kinds of weapons they were, but who was firing, he was in no position to judge. These days, the tangos had just as sophisticated weapons as the U.S. military, thanks to profitable underground arms sales.

Ian would have liked to be up and actively participating in the action, but he would only get in the way at this point. The gunfight lasted only fifteen minutes or so. Even once it was over, he and Joan lay low. They both pulled concealed weapons out and snaked themselves on their bellies over to a thick bush.

In the end, three tangos were dead, two were seriously injured and captured, and two more were in custody for questioning. A successful operation, as far as he could tell. Dozens of SEALs, CIA, police and special ops guys from the other services crowded the park.

He and the other SEALs in his squad stood about

for a long time afterward, patting each other on the back. Recounting every aspect of the op and what they'd done right and wrong.

They all went back to the base together and spent another hour or more with the SEAL commander, once again discussing every aspect of their mission, what they might have done differently, what they needed to study for future reference.

After that, he and his squad members went to the Wet and Wild to celebrate and once again pat themselves on the back and wind down from the adrenaline rush that accompanied any op, whether local or OUTCONUS. Cage had called Geek hours ago to tell him that the mission had been successful.

Now, after two beers, Ian decided he wanted to celebrate in the best way possible. With Maddie.

The tango was more than a dance . . .

Madrene was happy and angry at the same time.

Geek had told her hours ago that the mission had been successful, and, except for a wound in Joan's shoulder and some abrasions on Sly's face from pieces of flying metal, everyone was all right on their side. That was a good thing, of course. But she was still fuming over not having been included. She was going to make the brute pay for that chauvinistic move, but not too long. Her relief at his safety made any other emotion petty.

But one hour went by, then two, then three. Still, Ian had not come home.

"They're probably at the Wet and Wild," Geek told her.

She arched her brows in question.

"It's a bar where lots of the military guys hang out. Drink a few beers. Listen to the music. Dance." Geek must have realized his mistake the minute the word came out. "I mean, after an op, the men like to wind down and rehash—"

"Dance? There are women there?"

"Yeah, but—"

"I'm going for a walk."

"I don't think that's a good idea. I have orders to keep you here."

"Then leave me alone or I fear I may wring your neck since you are the only male in sight."

"You sure you don't want to practice your letters some more?"

She sliced him with a look that told him exactly what she thought of that suggestion.

"I guess not." He ducked his head and went to the office to play with his come-pewter.

Madrene sat at the kitchen table drinking a cup of the pungent tea Omar had brought her yestermorn. She had much to plan now that the mission was over. Ian had said that he would help her . . . well, *probably* help her. With or without him, she needed to either buy a longship or arrange transport to the Norselands; and raise an army, either here or in the Saxon lands. Madrene was hoping, perhaps unrealistically, that Ian would convince his other seals to go with them. That small number of expert fighting men would be better than a far larger number of regular warriors.

A slight knocking noise from the garage door drew her attention. Mayhap it was just the wind, although there was no wind to speak of and certainly not in the garage. When the sound was repeated, she got up and looked down the hall to the closed office door. Geek was probably sulking over her harsh words. Since the danger was over, she walked up to the door and squinted her eyes at the peephole. A man stood there. He had the short cut many military men wore in this place and his long sleeved tea-*shert* had the letters "U.S. Navy SEAL" on the front. So she opened the door.

"Ensign John Smith here," he said briskly. "Mac asked me to bring you over to the base. The commander wants to talk to both of you."

"Oh," she said. That made sense. "Why didn't Ian come himself?"

"He's already in meetings."

Madrene glanced into the garage, where the mow-tore was running on Ian's red car. He must have sent this man in his vehicle to get her. She nodded and said, "Let me tell Geek where I'm going."

"He already knows," the ensign said, taking her by the elbow. "Hurry. There's not much time."

Madrene was puzzled. Why the rush when the danger was over? And another thing: As the end-sign helped buckle her in the seat and backed out of the garage at a rapid pace, she noticed that the interior of the car was different.

"Why is the leather of these seats brown? I thought it was black. And why are you driving north? I thought the base was . . ." A number of observations came crashing over her then, one after another. The man's hands were a different color from his face and neck. He was wearing makeup, she realized with amazement; she had learned about makeup from Pretty Boy. She was fairly certain that the end-sign's hair and eyebrows were not this blond color naturally. In fact, she was beginning to notice some Arabic features, particularly in the shape of the eyes and nose. "Who are you?"

"Shut up, bitch!" the end-sign snarled in Arabic and pulled a weapon . . . a piss-tole . . . out of his shirt. "You will to be our bargaining tool for getting Jamal released. You will spill your guts for us as you did for the See-eye-aye."

"Why doesn't anyone believe me when I say that I know nothing?" she answered him in Arabic, throwing her hands up in disgust. "You overvalue my usefulness in your ransom attempt. In truth, the people here do not care much for me, except for Ian, and even that is in question. So, if I were you, I would turn around and take me back. Ian might not lop your head off if you reconsider now. But later, who knows what—"

The end-sign used a very, very foul word—a Saxon one—then raised the handle of his weapon to hit her on the back of the head. Her last thought before blackness came over her was, *'Twould seem I am going to take part in the action after all.*

Sometimes the road of life has a few speed bumps . . .

Ian stood and laid some bills on the table at the Wet and Wild for his part of the tab. The adrenaline pumping through his body now was of an entirely different kind. He was ready for battle again, but this time there would be no guns involved. He hoped.

"Running home to the little woman, are you?" Omar asked, grinning at him.

"Pussy-whipped already," Cage proclaimed.

"Bet you have the 'I love you, baby, please forgive me' spiel down pat," JAM said.

"Better have." Pretty Boy nodded. "Maddie was royally pissed over being left behind."

"Sure you don't wanna stay here and see what kind of action you can rack up?" Sly inquired. "Oops, I forgot. You've got action central going for you back home."

Ian refused to rise to their bait. There was a time he might have been irritated, even angry, that they would dare to speculate on his personal life. But right now, all he cared about was getting home to Maddie and getting on with the rest of his life.

"Uh-oh," Cage said, glancing over Ian's shoulder.

Ian turned and said the same thing aloud. "Uh-oh."

It was Jennifer, his ex-fiancée, and she was headed toward him like a guided missile. He stood his ground and waited for her to come to him.

"Ian," she said in a husky voice he'd once thought sexy, but which now seemed kind of pathetic. Being of average height, she had to go on tiptoes to reach up and kiss him. He turned his face at the last moment so that her lips grazed his cheek, not his mouth where they were aimed.

The smell of her perfume he would recognize anywhere. A light flowery scent that was not unpleasant, but it held no allure for him now.

She looked at him with a puzzled expression on her face. "Can we talk?"

"I'm in a hurry, Jen. Can we make it some other time?"

"There was a time when you would have fit me in." She pouted, which she probably thought was attractive.

He shrugged. "Those days are long gone."

"Really?" She sidled up closer to him so that her breasts pressed against his chest and he felt her breath close to his chin.

"Really," he said and put her several feet away from him.

He could tell she was shocked. It wasn't the first time she'd tried to hook up with him since her divorce, but it was the first time she'd gotten this close. "Is there someone else?"

He didn't even have to think. "Oh, yeah!"

"You loved me once."

"I wonder."

"What the hell does that mean?"

"It means, sweetheart, that now I've found the real thing, I think what we had was a poor imitation. In fact, I have a lot to thank you for."

She folded her arms over her chest, probably embarrassed and angry at the same time.

"I think Maddie is the first woman I've ever really loved. Oh, and did I mention, Maddie is my wife."

Jennifer looked as if she might say something nasty to him, but she spun on her heel and stormed away.

He did not care, not one bit.

As he walked toward the exit, his cell phone rang.

"Mac?"

"Yeah."

It was Geek.

"If you ask me if I know what my wife is doing, I think I might scream," he teased.

"She's gone," Geek said without preamble.

"What do you mean, 'gone'?" He raked his fingers through his hair and felt like pulling it out by the roots. The woman just could not stay put.

"I think she was taken," Geek went on.

The blood drained from his head and extremities and he had to lean on the wall for support.

The other guys came up beside him, noticing his distress.

"I was in the office," Geek continued. "You told me the danger was over hours ago. Then I heard your car come into the garage, and I heard Maddie talking to someone, then the sound of the door closing and the car taking off."

"It was not my car," he said icily.

"I know that now. I saw the license plate. It had New York plates. I called you as soon as I realized what happened. Dammit, Mac, this is all my fault. I wouldn't blame you if you recommended me out of SEALs. What a fuck-up!"

"Take it easy, Geek. It's more my fault than yours. If I had come home right away, or if I'd taken her along like she wanted, none of this would have happened. I'm on my way home. Call the commander and tell him to send some of those CIA super sleuths, as well. They claim they can track anyone. Let's hope that's true."

Ian hung up and looked at his buddies. He didn't have to explain what had happened. As they made plans to go back to the base and regroup while he returned home, there was only one thing Ian could think:

Where are you, Maddie?

If only she had her favorite sword . . .

Five days later, Madrene was bored to the point of barminess.

Oh, these miscreants had slapped her face back and forth a few times, and one of them had kicked her in the thigh, and one of them even punched her in the jaw, not to mention the large lump on her head from the piss-tole blow that first day in the car. But those various aches and pains were naught compared to what could have happened, or might still happen.

They questioned and questioned and questioned her about her knowledge of terrorist secrets. No matter how many times she told them she knew nothing, they refused to believe her.

The Shepherds of Allah—the name they gave themselves—were waiting for word from some important villain in their terrorist group. She shivered to think what methods he might use to get her to answer the ridiculous questions. He was coming here by airplane from a country called Eye-ran.

In the meantime, she had been moved from an upstairs bedchamber to this small storage room in the basement. Her captors claimed her constant nagging was giving them a headache. She told them they were giving her an arse ache. That was when she'd been kicked.

She was unrestrained down here because there were no windows, but upstairs her hands had been tied behind her back. She'd learned something interesting while up there. They were in a house in Ian's neighborhood. Although the man who'd captured her had driven away from this area, he must have been trying to confuse her. Once she was unconscious he must have doubled back.

She had been blessed with one bit of good luck. The reason why the shepherds were not molesting her or harming her was because they believed she was pregnant, and men of their religion revered breeding women. Little did they know, and she was not about to tell them, that she was barren. Who ever would have thought she would be thankful for a weak stomach, but she had been vomiting since that first day, probably due to the head blow. And her stomach had been roiling since then at the unpalatable food they gave her and the fetid air. They put so much garlic in every dish they cooked that the house fairly reeked with it.

All of the men had felt the need to touch her breasts to see if they were real—*there was something about men and breasts*—and one of the lackwits proclaimed that they must be so big because they were filling with milk for the babe. Men were such halfbrains betimes. This reprieve would not last forever, of course, especially if she got her monthly flux whilst in captivity.

Why do things like this always happen to me?

Where is Ian? Is he worried about me? Is he searching? Of course he would search in the beginning, but has he given up?

I wish I had not been so cold when he was leaving.

At this rate, I will never get back to Norstead.

She closed her eyes and tried to visualize Ian standing in his solar. *Come to me, dearling. Here I am. Please come.*

There are surprises and then there are SURPRISES . . .

It had been a week and there was still no sign of Maddie. In fact, the CIA and SEAL command were talking about giving up the search. The D word was not used, but Ian knew they thought that Maddie must be dead.

Operating on coffee and very little sleep, Ian made his way into the base and went out for a solitary five-mile run on the beach. But today, even the mindlessness of long-distance jogging did nothing for him.

He showered, then tried to get some paperwork done in his office. He just kept staring at the picture of himself and Maddie which had been taken by Dan Sullivan in Baghdad. When he'd received it in the mail two days ago, probably from the slimeball, he'd slipped it into the frame which had previously held a picture of himself and his sister and two brothers.

His father, to his surprise, had been a rock for him. Somehow, the man who had been so hard on him seemed to understand his feelings for Maddie. His father had finally flown back to D.C. last night, but he'd pulled every string he could to keep the search going.

Ian heard a soft knock on the door.

"Max! When did you get back?" It was his sister's brother-in-law, Torolf Magnusson. Normally Cage's partner, Max had been a pain in the butt to Ian during BUD/S training, and, although he had become a colleague since then, Ian found his constant clowning an irritation. But then Ian suspected he was far too serious himself.

"This morning. Holy crap! I just heard everything that's been going on here. You got married?"

"Yeah. Unfortunately, you probably also heard that I couldn't hold on to the woman." He figured he'd better throw that in before Max made a joke of the situation.

"Don't go blaming yourself."

Ian shrugged. Everyone told him that, but it didn't make him feel any better.

"Is that her?" Max asked, walking up to the side of the desk.

"That's Maddie," he said, handing Max the framed photo to look at.

"Oh, my God! Oh, my God! *Oh, my God!*" Max cried out, alternately hugging the picture to his chest and gazing at it with incredulity. "It's impossible. Yes, it's possible, but, oh, my God! After all these years!"

Ian stood and came around the side of the desk to stand before him. "What's the problem?"

"Problem? It's no problem. It's a miracle." Max swiped at the tears that were welling in his eyes. "That's my sister, Madrene."

Ian felt as if he'd been sucker punched. "No! She said her name was Madrene Olgadottir, not Magnusson." *What an idiotic thing to say!* Then, he thought of something else. *Wouldn't it be really ironic if I was now related to this bozo by marriage? Ironic? More like hellish.*

Max shook his head. "Women take their mother's names in my country."

"Oh." *Another great brainiac observation!* Suddenly Ian remembered what had been niggling at his memory from the first time he'd met Maddie. An eerie prickle rippled over his skin. There was a perfect image in his mind of the mesmerizing Norse noblewoman in the painting at Blue Dragon Vineyard. He'd seen the artwork done by Dagny Magnusson, another sister, when he'd attended his sister Alison's wedding three years ago at the vineyard estate.

Maddie was the woman in the painting.

The Vikings are coming . . . and coming . . . and coming . . .

Within twenty-four hours, Ian felt as if he were living in a Viking psycho ward.

It started the morning after his meeting with Max. He was awakened before dawn from a deep sleep, the first he'd had in a week. And he'd been having a strange dream, too. Maddie had been calling to him, "Come to me, dearling."

Was she really dead, as others concluded, and calling to him to join her in death? Or was it one of those telepathic messages some people believed in?

Whichever! He made his way out of bed and stumbled groggily to the front door, where a loud pounding was going on nonstop. When he opened it, he jumped back. Five big, fierce-looking men stood there, wearing weird leather battle armor. They carried big-ass swords and battle-axes.

He knew who they all were, having met them before, but they scared him nonetheless. It was like a bad Halloween nightmare. Torolf and Jorund Magnusson, Maddie's brothers, stood in the back, but up front and way too much in his face were Magnus, Jorund and Geirolf Ericsson, Maddie's father and uncles, respectively.

"What have you done with my baby?" Magnus asked him gruffly as he faced him nose to nose, backing him up against the foyer wall. Ian was tall, but this guy had to be six-foot-six, and he had a hundred pounds on him. He was *big*.

"Are you referring to my wife?" *Good Lord! I must have a death wish.*

"That remains to be proved," one of the uncles proclaimed.

Uh-oh!

"We're here to help find her," the other uncle said.

With swords? Oops! Hope I didn't say that out loud.

Max and Ragnor were grinning at him.

Magnus came into the hall, dropped his sword and battle-ax to the floor, probably breaking some tiles, and took Ian into a tight bear hug which lifted him on tiptoes. "Do not be afeared, son. We will find Madrene."

Ian wasn't sure if the tears in his eyes were from relief or from being crushed by Attila the Viking.

But then, at the same ungodly hour, his father showed up. He was out of uniform, which was in itself a rarity. He took Ian by the shoulders and said, "I had to come. I couldn't just sit on my ass in Washington without trying to help." His father going outside the strictures of military protocol—it was a miracle to Ian, or a nightmare.

Of course, his SEAL buddies showed up, too. What was going on here? Was he sending out psychic messages for help? There were so many people at his house by six a.m. that Ian could barely move. Cage and Omar were cooking scrambled eggs and bacon. Geek was in Ian's office, showing Ragnor and the uncles the work they'd done so far on locating Maddie. Sly, JAM and Slick were doing sit-ups in the living room. Pretty Boy was making Magnus laugh over Maddie's makeover. Everyone was drinking beer, at this ungodly hour. One of them, Geirolf, was eating Oreos with his beer.

To top off his nightmare, Sam was behaving really

weird. She kept coming up to him and meowing like crazy. He let her outside a dozen times, which he normally didn't do, but she would immediately scratch to come back in. Like right now. She was screeching like a banshee at the front door. Maybe she was in heat or something. If she got pregnant, he would kill himself. He was pretty sure Jen had had her fixed, but God only knew if that was true; Jen had told him so many lies.

In the midst of all the chaos, Ian went to his bedroom and closed the door firmly. He needed some time to himself. Of course, Sam, who was on her outside rotation, came up to the sliding door on the deck, meowing for entrance. "Make up your mind. In or out," he grumbled as he let the cat in.

Sam just gave him her look.

Ian flopped down on the bed and folded his arms beneath his neck, staring at the ceiling. "Please, God, let me find Maddie." He wondered if he should promise to be good, or offer some bribe. He hadn't done much praying in his sorry life. He settled for just a simple plea. "I don't know for sure if You're up there, or if I deserve Your help, but please." Just for insurance, he added, "You, too, Odin."

Sam chose that moment to jump onto the bed—which was a real feat for such a fat cat—then walk up his body from thigh to stomach to chest. Putting her cat face right in front of his, she meowed dolefully.

"You miss her, too, don't you?"

Sam hissed as if she were exasperated with him. She scratched at his chest with one paw, gently, then started to walk away. Looking back at him, she meowed some more. Then she came back and repeated the exercise. Pawing at his chest, walking away, looking at him, then coming back. Sitting up and furrowing his brow, he asked the cat—*That was a sign of how far gone he was . . . talking to a cat!*—"Do you want me to follow you?"

He could swear Sam rolled her eyes and meowed, "At last."

Ian got up, let Sam out, then followed her around to the front of the house. Every couple of feet, Sam would stop and look back at him to see if he was following; then she would continue on her trek. She was probably taking him to a fish store or something. But no, Sam went down the street, crossed over, then started to walk behind a small Cape Cod-style house with an overgrown lawn and shabby exterior.

"Sam, come back here," he said in a loud whisper, not wanting to wake anyone who might still be asleep in the house. There didn't seem to be any activity around the place, but he'd seen a red car in the garage through the small glass windows of the door.

Red car? Holy shit! Geek had said the tangos took Maddie away in a red car. No, it was impossible. This would be too much of a coincidence. But then he remembered his prayer less than an hour ago. He glanced skyward and thought, *I've heard of the power of prayer. If this is what I think it is, You have made me a believer.*

He followed Sam to the back of the house, where she sat near the back corner, meowing. There was no basement that he could see, at least no basement windows, but Sam seemed to sense something there.

"Is Maddie down there?" he asked Sam. *I'm either crazy or really smart, not only talking to a cat, but expecting an answer.*

Sam meowed.

From inside the house, Ian thought he heard someone complain, "It's that damn cat again."

Another person said, "I'm going to shoot it."

Ian looked at Sam, whose ears perked up. Then she shot away toward home.

"No, you're not. You can't attract any attention from the neighbors."

Then another person must have entered the room. This one spoke in Arabic.

Ian's heart began racing and his heart lifted hopefully. He walked carefully toward the front. Then he took a chance and peered into the garage. Yep, a red Mustang convertible. Sam was sitting there waiting for him on the front sidewalk.

With a joyous spirit, he ran off, a surprisingly agile Sam beside him. When he got back to his house, he rushed into the kitchen, where the whole bunch of them were sitting at his table or standing around, all of them scarfing down the gourmet meal of eggs and beer. The motley bunch looked at him expectantly.

Ian smiled, for the first time in what seemed like forever, and said, "I've found Maddie."

Inside, though, he had one last prayer: "Please, God, let her still be alive."

Chapter Sixteen

She gave new meaning to the term "senior citizen" . . .

Madrene was beginning to loathe garlic.

She was lying on a blanket on the floor, having emptied her stomach once again into a smelly bucket in the corner. That was when she heard a tap-tap-tapping noise on the upper part of the wall.

It must be a mouse. She rolled over and tried to think of more pleasant times, to get her mind off her nausea. Of course, Ian came immediately to mind. She forced herself to go back farther into her memory, to those times when she and her family had all been alive and safe in their homeland.

The tapping started again. This time, the sound seemed to have a pattern to it. Tap, tap . . . tap, tap, tap, tap . . . tap, tap . . . tap, tap, tap, tap. She stood and walk over to the wall, peering up. That was when she heard the most joyful thing.

"Maddie? Are you there? Maddie?" a voice said in a loud whisper.

It had to be Ian.

"I'm here," she yelled. Then caught herself. "I'm here," she repeated in a low voice.

"Stay put, babe."

She wasn't able to do anything else.

"We're coming after you." Then there was silence.

Madrene had much to worry about then . . . and not just her own well-being. Musab Khazim, the man who'd arrived last night, was more vicious than the rest. When she'd not given him the answers he wanted, he showed her pictures on the tea-vee of people having their heads chopped off by other "shepherds" in their Arab lands. Madrene had no taste for head-lopping, and had never done it herself, not having the strength to heave a broadsword so strongly, but she had witnessed it more than once. She was not as shocked as these brutes expected her to be.

So the new man had stripped her naked and interrogated her more. Apparently, he did not share his comrades' qualms about harming a breeding woman, if his slaps were any indication. And what was it about men and their need to strip women of their clothing for purposes of humiliation? It was getting tiresome, to say the least. And chilly. But they'd let her put her jeans and tea-*shert* back on last night when she'd been banished to the basement again.

The knaves upstairs were heavily armed with weapons that resembled the guns and piss-toles she'd seen the seals carry. But Ian and his seals, who she presumed were with him, would be armed, as well. She had to trust in Ian.

Still, she worried.

Then she heard gunfire upstairs. Lots of gunfire.

She dropped to her knees and prayed as she never had before. "Please, God . . . please, Thor, god of battle . . . protect this man I love. Please, please, please."

She heard a hard object hit her locked door, even as the gunfire continued upstairs. She backed up against the far wall as the object hit once again and came barreling into the room.

The object was Ian.

He smiled grimly at her, swore softly at the bruises on her face, then lifted her into his arms. "Thank God!" was all he said, against her neck. She thought she felt a wetness there.

"Are you hurt? Do you need to go to the hospital?"

She shook her head.

"Did they . . . rape you?" he choked out.

Again she shook her head.

He carried her out in a rush, reaching the back yard through a separate basement exit. When they were free, he ran with her in his arms to a stand of trees at the end of the yard. He dropped down to his knees, then laid her gently down. Kissing her softly, he said, "I'll be right back, sweetheart." He rose then, picked up the large weapon that hung from a sling over his shoulder and ran back to join the fight.

Madrene realized belatedly that she hadn't uttered one word to Ian. *Me, speechless?* She smiled and thought there were some people who would find that a miracle.

The gunfire continued for a short while. It was early morning and she could see neighborhood people coming out of their houses, but the terrorist house was cordoned off with yellow ribbon. There were many armed men outside the house, as well as inside, and not all of them were seals. Some of them wore helmets.

The gunfire tapered off, then stopped. First, Ian's seal comrades came out of the house, talking excitedly. They turned as one and waved at her, huge smiles on their faces. She waved back. *Who knew I would be so happy to see a seal?* she joked to herself.

She stood when she saw Ian reel out to the front yard, punching and rolling on the ground with Musab, the one who had been so nasty to her last night. Was Ian pummeling the brute on her behalf? Probably. In the end, Ian had to be pulled off of the evil varmint by several of the helmeted men. As Musab was escorted by two of the helmeted men to a nearby square vehicle, Ian bent over at the waist, as if trying to get his temper under control.

Before long, he walked over and began talking to a group of several big men, even taller than he was. They all glanced her way, then one of them broke away from the group and started to walk toward her.

All the fine hairs stood out on Madrene's body, and she started to weep. *No! It is impossible. I am dreaming. But Ian is there smiling at me. It can't be a dream.*

What a cruel jest for Loki, the jester god, to play on me after all I have survived!

But what if it is not a dream or a jest?

A hiccoughing sob escaped her lips. She, who never cried, was making a habit of leaking eyes lately. Heart pounding wildly, she began to walk slowly, then faster toward the big, weeping man. *Weeping? He is weeping, too?* He had long blond hair with strands of gray at the sides, woven into war braids. *War braids?* And he had big ears. *Big ears?* There was only one man she knew with ears like that.

"Father?" she asked just before he lifted her into a tight, tight hug.

"Thank the gods, you have finally come home, Madrene. We have missed you mightily." Her father noticed the scars on her neck then and touched them tenderly. "The brute who did this to you will pay, that I promise you."

Madrene felt like a little girl again. No need to worry about anything. Her father would take care of everything. Ah, that wasn't quite true. Even as a youthling, Madrene had been taking over household duties. It was a nice fantasy, though.

Next came Ragnor, whom she swatted on the arm for having left her alone at Norstead, and Torolf, who told her an amazing story about his being a Navy SEAL. Then her uncles Jorund and Geirolf came to her for warm embraces. Her father told her that her other brothers and sisters were at a vineyard where they lived. Her father had remarried and had another child. Her Uncle Jorund had remarried, too, and had both his own and stepchildren. Uncle Geirolf was married for the first time and had his own family. Jorund and Geirolf lived in the faraway countries of Tax-us and Main. Even more amazing, Ian's sister Alison was married to her brother Ragnor.

Madrene felt dizzy with confusion and happiness. "I do not understand. How can this be?" she asked her father. "How did you all land in this same magic land? And for shame! You did not tell those of us left behind that you were alive. Can you understand the agony we went through? Really, what were you thinking? Yea, it is good to see you all again, but what you need is a sound walloping with a broom, if you ask me. And furthermore—"

"Ever the shrew, eh, Madrene?" Her father threw his head back and laughed uproariously. Then he held her at arm's length from himself. "Did you not know, child? Have you not figured it out? You have time-traveled."

It was her turn to laugh now.

" 'Tis true." Her father's face turned serious.

"Nooooooo," she said, shaking her head with disbelief.

"Believe it!" Ragnor said. "It is a thousand years into the future. I had trouble believing it, too."

"Nooooooo," she continued to protest. But already many things were beginning to make sense to her—if time-travel could ever be construed as sensible. The flameless lights, the cars, the metal travel birds, the guns, birth control, food marts, books, tea-vee, everything. She had credited these marvels to magic . . . to a strange magical land, much like the legendary land of trolls and dragons. Now it appeared as if these marvels could be explained by time-travel, if one was to believe it was possible.

Sudden alarming thoughts occurred to her. *How does Ian fit into this picture? Can he love a woman who is—holy Frigg!—a thousand years old?* She glanced toward the front yard to see how he was handling this family reunion.

Ian was gone.

Wedding bell blues . . .

Ian drove back to the base in his car, taking Cage, Pretty Boy and Geek with him; their weapons were crammed beside them every which way they could fit. They followed the other SEALs, the command staff, his father and the CIA field ops. The four tangos were in a highly secure van in the midst of them all, including the one Ian almost killed with his fists for making a vile remark about Maddie's body, which he must have seen naked.

"Do you think that's all of them?" Cage asked.

"Seems so," Ian answered. "At least, that's what Sullivan told me."

"He is such a creep," Pretty Boy said.

The rest of them agreed, "Yeah!"

"He asked me if you were nailing Maddie." Pretty Boy exhaled with disgust. "In the midst of gunfire, with her safety still in question, he asked a question like that."

"What did you answer?" Ian looked over at Cage, who was covered with dirt and perspiration. They all were.

"I told him to go screw himself."

"Good answer."

"Man, this has been a helluva couple weeks," Cage said. And it had been. Capturing Jamal in Iraq, marrying Maddie, setting up the trap in the park, Maddie being nabbed by the remaining tangos, the rescue, and the reunion with her family.

"Is it always like this?" Geek wanted to know.

"Yeah," the three of them lied and smiled at each other.

"What are you going to do about Maddie?" Pretty Boy asked from the back seat.

"Hell if I know." *But I know what I want.* "For now, her family is going back to my house to catch up on all the news. I didn't get the whole story, but Ragnor said they've been separated from her for years, and she thought they were dead."

"That's what she kept telling us all along," Geek pointed out.

But none of us would listen. "I'll know more when our meetings are over at the base, and I can get back and talk to her." *Alone. Definitely alone.*

"What do you think her family will say about your marriage?" Pretty Boy asked.

"That is the question."

Actually, there is a more important question. What will Maddie think of our marriage now that she's reunited with her family? Will I be extraneous?

She said she loves me.

Ian was hit with unexpected news just before he went into the debriefing. JAM pulled him aside and said, "Uh, I have something to tell you that you're not going to like."

Now what? "I got a piece of mail today that had originally been sent to my Virginia apartment, forwarded, then lost in dead mail for almost a year. I mean, I should have checked, but I didn't think it was necessary. And now . . . oh, hell!" JAM was clearly avoiding telling him what was on his mind. What? Was he still a priest, or almost-priest, and hadn't been released from his vows or whatever they called it?

"Spit it out."

"You're not married."

Ian inhaled sharply with shock. That was the last thing he'd expected JAM to say. "What do you mean?"

"The Church doesn't like its priests or almost-priests to continue with priestly duties. Apparently, the Vatican came out with a new edict that now disallows men like me from performing marriages."

"Not even civil ones?"

JAM shook his head. "I would have to apply for a special license and everything."

The back of Ian's neck prickled, a sure sign something suspicious was going on. "The CIA must have known this when they were being so accommodating about the marriage and Maddie leaving Baghdad without a passport."

"Maybe. Probably."

"Sonofabitch!" Ian felt like hitting someone or something. Not JAM—it wasn't his fault. But a nice wall would come in handy about now.

"Don't tell anyone about this, okay?"

JAM bit his bottom lip with reluctance. "All right. For now, my lips are sealed."

They went into the meeting then, but all Ian could think about was Maddie. How was he going to keep Maddie without the marriage binding them together? He had no hold over her now, with the marriage being null and her family here to protect her . . . nothing except love.

The question was: Would love be enough?

Daddy's little girl . . . not! . . .

Madrene was surrounded by mayhem.

Thirteen years might have gone by since they were all together, but some things never changed. Everyone talked at once. They teased each other mercilessly. The men thought women were to be protected and pampered.

"Pampered? Are you all demented? I have been running the farmstead and then Norstead for a long time. And I did it admirably, if I must say so myself, until . . . until Steinolf came." She stopped then and pondered what she had said. "I failed then. I was unable to hold Norstead from the invaders. Mayhap you are all correct. Mayhap a man would have done a better job."

"You are not to berate yourself, Madrene," her father said. They were all sitting around Ian's solar drinking beer and eating Dome-nose pizzas which Torolf had ordered delivered to the house. What a bunch of handsome men they were, she thought, even her father and uncles who were of an advanced age . . . more than fifty. And big! The large solar seemed small with all of them inside. "Are you listening, child?"

Child? I am thirty-one years old. Long past childhood.

"You did a magnificent job of defending Norstead," her father continued. "As good as any man. Steinolf is a devious warrior, and betimes good soldiers lose to evil forces when they choose the honorable way."

"I must needs raise an army and go back to fight him," Madrene told them. "It is my quest, and I have told Ian and his comrades so on many an occasion. In fact, I have sold the jewels I took from the harems, and raised almost a million dollars. Not that I know what dollars are."

Ragnor, who sat beside her on the sofa, grinned. Well, actually, he sat next to Sam, who sat next to her. Sam had taken to her family like a cat on a barrel of lutefisk. "You in a harem? I can hardly credit that. You must have driven the sultans mad with your nagging."

She reached over Sam and punched Ragnor on the arm. Sam hissed at him to back her up. Grinning, she said, "Nay. I drove them mad with my cock-wilting talents."

"Madrene!" her father chided her, but he was laughing like all the rest.

"You cannot say that and stop," her Uncle Geirolf said. "Explain yourself."

And she did, demonstrating the finger waggle and the "uhm-uhm" chant she'd perfected. They were all howling with laughter by the time she finished.

She turned to Ragnor. "Speaking of soft manparts, can I presume that you have regained your 'enthusiasm' for the bedsport?"

Ragnor's face turned red. "I never had trouble getting it hard," he tried to tell his hooting family members. He would never live this down, thanks to her jibe. "I just did not want to." He looked at her then and said, "I will never forgive you for this."

She made a face at him.

"About the army business," her Uncle Jorund said, "even if you are able to raise the manpower, what makes you think you, let alone a small army, could travel back in time?"

Everyone grew silent.

"First, I never heard about this time-travel notion till today. Two, I am not sure I believe in it. Three, if a person can travel forward in time, there must be a way to travel back."

"Personally, I don't even try to explain time-travel, I just accept it," Torolf said.

"Now, me, I just believe it is a miracle," her father said. "My mind cannot wrap around any explanation for time-travel, but I do believe in miracles. God, or the gods, destined me to be here in this time and place."

They all nodded, except for Madrene, who was still skeptical.

"And what's this about a marriage?" Torolf, waggling his eyebrows at her, was back to teasing. "I cannot picture my sister, the shrew, hooking up with the lean mean Mac machine. A loathsome lout if I ever met one."

"Yeah, you always said you wouldn't marry again," Ragnor reminded her.

"I hardly had any say in the matter," she told them.

"And now? Would you have the marriage annulled?" her father inquired, his eyes studying her sharply. She must have blushed, because her father said, "I see."

"Maaaa-dreeene! I am shocked," said Ragnor, who was anything but shocked. "It would seem you regained some enthusiasm, too."

"I did not know she ever had any. Not with that prick Karl." It was Torolf chiming in now.

She was not sure what a prick was, but she could pretty well guess, and, yea, it was a good description. "What? You thought only those with dangly parts could have the sap rise? Well, let me tell you, women get lustsome on occasion, too. I have been watching *Sex and the City*, and women definitely can match men when it comes to lust. And, by the by, why is it that I had to come to another country . . . or time . . . to learn about oral sex?"

"That will be enough," her father said. Everyone else was gaping at her. Ragnor put his face in his hand, and his body was shaking with laughter. Sometimes Madrene surprised even herself with her bluntness.

Her father coughed to compose himself. "The question then, daughter, is whether you wish for a divorce or to stay married to the loathsome lout."

"I want to remain married," she said without hesitation. *The more important question is whether Ian will want me once he learns of the time-travel nonsense. Or whether he will want to be linked to my barmy family.*

Her father tilted his head in question. "And why is that?"

"Because I love the loathsome lout."

"Spoken like a true Norsewoman," her father proclaimed.

She made him an offer he couldn't refuse . . .

Ian's nerves were shot by the time his meetings ended three hours later. He was worried about Maddie.

"I'm worried about you," his commander told him as they walked across the O-course.

It's not me you should be worried about. Ian's eyebrows arched.

"You haven't been to counseling since your Iraq mission ended. The other guys have, but not you."

All SEALs were required to meet with the base psychologist after every field op, the theory being that killing people can affect the mind. *Like anyone who's ever killed another human being doesn't know that!* The Navy did not want its men going bonkers from lack of proper mental care.

"I'll make an appointment for next week," he promised.

"We need to talk about this so-called marriage of yours, too."

There's nothing "so-called" about it in my mind. "I will not discuss my personal life with you or anyone else."

"Your personal life is the Navy's business, whether you like it or not."

Ian bit his tongue to stop himself from saying more. He didn't give a rat's ass what the commander, or the Navy, or the whole freakin' world thought about his marriage. It was real, or it would be as soon as he could make it legal.

He said good-bye to the commander, then turned away. As he started driving his car across the Silver Strand, his cell phone rang. Recognizing his home phone number on the caller i.d., he groaned. *Please, God, not someone asking me if I know what my wife is doing.*

"Ian?"

"Maddie?"

He was surprised, never having known Maddie to use a telephone before.

"I'm calling you on the tell-off-own," she told him.

"I know." He smiled. "I love you." Why he felt the need to say that, he didn't know. Well, yes, he did. JAM's news had put the fear of God in him.

"I love you, too," she whispered.

"Where are you?"

"In the closet?"

The closet? "Why?"

"Torolf showed me how to dial the tell-off-own, but I wanted privacy."

"Are you all right?"

"Nay, I am not all right."

He sat up straighter as he drove. "What's happened? Maybe you should go to the hospital for a checkup, just in case. I thought you'd be okay with your family. I thought you would want this extra time with them."

"I am fine, physically, but I must tell you, Ian, an hour with my family and I begin to feel suffocated Three hours and I am ready to go back to the harems."

"Same thing when I'm around my father. Not the harems, but the suffocation."

"Can you meet me someplace, outside the house?"

"Like where? I don't want you going out somewhere by yourself where you might get lost."

"The beach behind your house," she suggested.

"I'll be there in fifteen minutes."

He heard a rustling sound, then a loud bang in his ear as she obviously dropped the phone. "What are you doing?"

"Taking off my underwear."

"Make that five minutes."

Goin' for a dirty swim . . .

Madrene was walking along the beach some distance down the shore from Ian's house. The cold foam of the surf came and went over her bare feet. A soft breeze whipped her gauzy, ankle-length skirt about her. The late-afternoon sun still felt warm on her shoulders . . . or what part of her shoulders was exposed by her tanktop.

Her family, especially her father, was outraged over the welts that crisscrossed her back. She hadn't realized when she put on the tanktop that part of them would be visible. Torolf was the one who said, "The bastard will pay."

But Madrene could not care about all that now. She was at peace for the first time in forever. It was one of those moments out of time that a person comes back to over and over in her mind, a time when all the world seems to be in step. *I'm happy. Pure and simple. I am happy and in love and glad to be alive.*

She started to walk out a little deeper, up to her knees. Like a child she reveled in the splash of the water against her body. It was then, as she twirled about, that she saw Ian coming down the beach. He was taking off his *shert* as he walked and smiling wickedly at her. Once the *shert* was dropped to the sand, he toed off his shoes, then pulled off his socks. He was at the water's edge directly in front of her when he began to undo his *braies*.

She backed up a bit.

He walked in as he continued to work on his *braies*. The water covered him up to his waist when he scooted down, tugged his *braies* off and tossed them back to the shore. He was left in only white small clothes. She could see how much he already wanted her.

"No underwear, eh?" he said when he reached her.

She just smiled.

A large wave broke, wetting them totally. So they swam out past the breaking wave to still water. At this time of day, it was only waist high. He pulled her into an embrace with her legs wrapped around his waist. They bobbed about with the ripple of the current, just smiling at each other.

"Greetings, husband," she said.

An odd look crossed his face, but then he replied, "Hello, wife." Giving her a quick kiss on the lips, he murmured against her mouth, "So, do you have something to reward me for coming home so quickly?"

She laughed and undulated her hips against him,

belly hitting belly. "I was hoping it was the other way around. That you had something for me."

"Do I ever!" Without any foresport, he lifted her skirt and settled her on his upraised, very hard staff. "Oh, baby!" he said, closing his eyes for a second. "You make me breathless."

Madrene was not a playful person, and certainly had never been playful in the bed furs, but she was now. "Well, mayhap I should jump off this pole, then. I would not want to kill you for lack of breath."

He nipped her chin with his teeth. "Don't you dare move." Taking her buttocks firmly in hand, he eased his fingers under and forward so he was touching her in her nether folds, which held him in their clasp.

"Oh."

"Oh? That is all?" He grinned at her.

"Now I am breathless. Mayhap you will kill me with pleasure."

"Have you ever heard of the little death?" he whispered against her ear.

"Nooooo."

"Well, then, I guess I'd better show you."

And he did.

Three times.

Then he died himself, so to speak.

Ian said the oddest thing to her a short time later, after he'd donned his garments. They were walking across the sand back toward the house when he stopped and looked her directly in the eyes. "Please don't ever leave me . . . no matter what."

It was odd because men left her, not the other way around.

The beginning of the end . . .

Maddie was leaving him.

Oh, she said she was going to Blue Dragon for a short visit with her family, but Ian just knew she would never come back. Every instinct in his body screamed, *Make her stay!* But he didn't, of course. Besides, the entire SEAL Team Thirteen, which also included Torolf, was leaving on Monday for San Clemente Island, where they would engage in extreme terrorist training.

"Why don't you come with us for a few days?" she asked. They were standing in a loose embrace at his open front door. Torolf was at the wheel of an Expedition van out front which would take Maddie, her father and the two uncles back to the vineyard today, where a massive family reunion was being planned for the weekend. The motor was running, and soon the horn would be blowing. Sam was rubbing her body against Maddie's jeans-clad leg, meowing in one long whine; the cat obviously sensed she was leaving.

"You know I can't. Today's Friday. We're leaving Monday for training. Just not enough time." That was a lie, actually. If he'd really wanted to, he could have gone by plane and spent a day there, even two. But this was her time with her family, and he didn't want to intrude. More important, he was scared spitless that someone would find out they weren't really married before he was ready to tell Maddie. He was going to see how they could straighten out this mess while she was gone.

She nodded. "I'm afraid. Don't look at me like that. I know I've said I have no fear, but I do where you're concerned. What if you find someone else while I'm gone? What if your former betrothed wants you back?"

Something must have shown on his face.

"She already has expressed such a wish?" Maddie bristled. "When did you see her last?"

"The day you were taken, actually."

Maddie tried to pull out of his arms, but he wouldn't let her go. "While I was here waiting with Geek . . . while those brutes kidnapped me, you were off cavorting with your betrothed? And she told you she wants you back?"

He nodded. "I told her I'm not interested. I told her I am married."

"Oh," she said and ceased her struggles. "I miss you already."

He kissed her softly. *Stay. Please stay. Feel how much I want you to stay. I'm selfish. I know I am. But stay.*

She didn't read his mind.

Ian hated the fact that he was keeping a secret from Maddie . . . that they were not really married.

The truth shall set you free, he told himself.

Then immediately answered, *Bullshit!*

Surely Maddie would understand when he finally told her . . . say, a year or five from now. "Maddie, what would you think about us going to Las Vegas when you get back and getting married again?"

She cocked her head to the side, studying him. "Why?"

He wet his lips nervously. "It seems like maybe we should start this marriage over in the right way, instead of our being forced into it."

"What a romantic idea!"

I am such an ass.

"Perhaps my family could come, too. And your family. And the seals."

"No, no, no! It would be private, just you and me."

"Hmmm. I like that." She put a hand to his cheek. "I love you."

"I know," he said, grinning at her.

She swatted him playfully.

"I love you, too, babe. Come back soon."

With a last kiss for him and a quick ruffle of Sam's fur, she was gone.

And thus began the first day of the rest of Ian's empty life.

Chapter Seventeen

Be careful what you wish for . . .

Madrene was overwhelmed and scared. All these years she had yearned for her family, picturing life the way it used to be. But her family had changed. She had changed.

These strangers were polished, the rough edges of their Viking culture filed off. They still had Norse features, and bits of their language retained the old manner of speaking. Still, she hardly knew them.

Of course, she was happy to discover that her family members were alive and well, but she wished she were back in Sandy-egg-go. She missed Ian. She missed his cat. She missed the seals, which were not really seals.

He should have come with me.

Or I should have waited till he could come with me.

Her discomfort started as they were driving in a large white wheeled box to the vineyard owned by her father's new wife. Well, not exactly new, since they'd been wed for eleven years, but new to her.

"Why are you so quiet, sweetling?" her father asked from the front passenger seat. She was sitting in the second seat, alone, and her uncles were in the third seat, where they could stretch out their long legs. Torolf had work to do with his seals, but would come to the vineyard next week.

"It has been quite an eventful week for me," she explained. "Everything that has happened is just starting to sink in. *I wish Ian were here. He is my anchor in this land. Without him I feel lost.*

"Post-traumatic-stress disorder might hit you soon," Ragnor said from the driver's seat. "You should probably see a psychiatrist."

Ragnor ever was the one to use big words and show off his intellect. Madrene did not understand what he said, not one bit. "A sigh-kite-tryst?" *More words I do not understand.*

"A shrink." Ragnor laughed. "A head doctor."

Surely he is not suggesting I have some healer shrink my head. Is he jesting with me? Probably. "My head feels fine."

Ragnor laughed again. "Never mind."

Madrene had noticed that people in this country said "never mind" whenever they didn't want to explain something to her.

Uncle Rolf leaned forward over the seat and squeezed her shoulder. "Give it time, Madrene. We all went through this period of adjustment."

That was another thing. Madrene could not accept the notion that she had traveled through time a thousand years to land here. But then, she supposed it was no more far-fetched than her earlier belief that she was in a fantasy land of magical things.

"My wife is a head doctor," Uncle Jorund said. "Mayhap you would like to talk to her."

"About my head?" Madrene turned in the seat to look at her uncle.

He tweaked her cheek like he used to do when she was a child. Odd how she recalled that now. And what a handsome man he was still! In truth, all three of the brothers were of superior good looks, including her father. Only a little gray threaded through their long, brown-and-blond hair. But they wore modern clothing—denim *braies* and tea-shirts—which made them seem strangers to her. In truth, she'd never seen her Uncle Jorund without a sword, or Uncle Rolf without his shipbuilding tools, or her father without a hay rake nearby.

"You seem different," Ragnor said, looking at her in a small mirror attached to the glass front. "You were always nagging me before."

"Hah! She nagged everyone who got within her hearing range. A shrew, that is what she was," her father added, as if it were something to be proud of.

She shrugged. "I still am."

"I don't know about that. Looooove has made her soft." Ragnor made a face at her in the mirror. Really, the rogue was thirty years old, only one year younger than she was, and he still acted the fool.

"You are driving too fast, Ragnor. Slow down. There is no hurry. Dost think the sky will fall down if we get there a few minutes later? And, by the by, you need your hair clipped. It is too long and unruly. I am glad you have regained your 'enthusiasm,' but, whew, that Svein Forkbeard had his face hairs in a twist over you not marrying his daughter Inga. Men will be men, you always said. But methinks you are just a dunderhead who cannot keep his dangly part in his *braies*."

Everyone burst out laughing.

And Ragnor said, "Good ol' Madrene. A shrew to the end."

"And how does your husband feel about your shrewishness?" her father asked in a teasing fashion.

Before she could answer, Ragnor said, "Hah! They are a perfect match. Mac is as ill-tempered as she is. And nag? You would think he invented the word."

Madrene leaned forward and smacked her brother on the side of the head, even though she agreed. She and Ian were a good match, but not because of the nagging.

There was no time for teasing or anything else then, because the white box was traveling up a narrow lane, lined on either side by a low stone wall and magnificent old oak trees. At intervals were large clay pots overflowing with red flowers. Wildflowers filled the lawns that stretched out to a stream which fed into a small lake. Behind the house as far as the eye could see, there were dozens of neat rows of grapevines.

Madrene decided to gather some of the wildflower seeds before she left. They would look nice in her kitchen garden at Norstead.

That thought caught her up short. *Will I be going back to Norstead? Can I travel back? Do I want to go back? What about Ian? Honor says I must be avenged . . . my entire family must be avenged, in fact . . . but how will I manage all that?* She sighed loudly and answered her own question. *Like I always do. With bullheaded determination.*

"Look, Madrene, look up ahead," her father said excitedly.

There was a large keep with a porch that wrapped around all sides. In its courtyard stood many people, young and old. They were laughing and waving at her, as if they knew her well, and she did not recognize a one of them. She blinked her eyes rapidly several times. *I will not weep.*

Once they exited from the vehicle, her father guided her by the elbow toward the crowd, which now hushed. "This is my beloved daughter, Madrene, whom most of you know so well," he announced.

Since when did I become beloved to my father? He always called me a pestsome wench because I nagged him so. Ah, well, I always called him a hopeless libertine, and I still loved him.

The crowd formed itself into a line and Magnus introduced her to the family, one at a time.

"This is my daughter Marie, who was born after I left the Norselands." He put a hand on the shoulder of a black-haired girl of about thirteen who looked at her father with adoration and at Madrene with question.

Madrene felt a stab of jealousy that this stranger was held in such high regard by their father, which was mean-spirited, she knew. But there it was. She had no idea what to do, so she extended a hand to shake.

Marie stared at her hand, and Madrene realized it must have been an inappropriate thing to do.

Next, her father moved to a blond mophead of a girl with dancing blue eyes. She was probably a few years older than Marie. "You remember Lida, don't you?"

Madrene's eyes widened and she smiled. "The little smelly baby? She was not even one year old last time I saw her." She ruffled the girl's curls and moved on.

"I remember you," a young man of about seventeen said.

She cocked her head.

"Kolbein."

She gave him a kiss on the cheek. "You were such a needy mite, always following Father around like a shadow."

"Kolbein is thinking about becoming a priest. Can you imagine that? A Viking priest?" her father asked.

Madrene studied Kolbein and saw the same quiet demeanor he'd had as a boy. Yea, she could see him in the religious life.

"This is Hamr."

Madrene clapped her hands together and laughed. "Did you ever get the bow and arrow you always wanted?"

Hamr, as tall and burly as their father at . . . what? . . . nineteen? . . . gave her a fierce hug. "Oh, yeah. A long time ago."

"But he is more interested in football and wenches now than archery," her father joshed.

Madrene looked down the long line of people waiting to meet her and felt overwhelmed.

"Jogeir, dance for your sister," her father said then to a handsome man of about twenty years.

"Father!" Jogeir protested, but came forward, lifted her in his arms and twirled her about.

When he set her back on the ground, Madrene recalled that Jogeir had been lame. She glanced down at his straight leg in question and understood her father's odd request that Jogeir dance for her.

"He had an operation to fix his leg," her father explained. "So fit is he now that he is a runner in the Olympics when he is not studying farming in college."

Madrene smiled, not understanding half of what he said. The gist, though, was that Jogeir was no longer lame, he could run well, and he still wanted to be a farmer.

Njal, ever the mischievous one, came next. Wearing what she recognized as a Navy uniform, he winked before giving her a loud kiss on the mouth.

Storvald, at twenty-seven, worked as a craftsman at Uncle Rolf's Viking village, Rosestead.

And next was Dagny, who stood staring at her with tear-filled eyes. Her father had said she was a talented painter. They hugged warmly, but Madrene did not know this young woman of twenty-five. Last time she'd seen her, Dagny had been twelve and Madrene seventeen.

The woman next to her, only one year older, had to be Kirsten. It was Madrene who hugged fiercely now. Kirsten and Madrene, even at a young age, had often been left to manage the large household when one nursemaid after another left in a huff. Kirsten told her that she was a teacher at a large university, which was a school for adults.

That comprised her immediate family, and Madrene's head was swimming with all the new faces. None of her brothers and sisters had married yet, except for Ragnor.

Finally, her father introduced her to his wife, Angela, who took both her hands in hers and said with great sincerity, "Welcome home, honey. This is your home, as long as you want."

Madrene glanced about. It was a pretty place, but it did not feel like home to her.

She also met Angela's eighty-nine-year-old grandmother; Ragnor's wife Alison, who was Ian's sister—Madrene wanted to speak with her later; Uncle Rolf's wife Meredith and their children Foster and Rose; Uncle Jorund's wife Maggie amd their children Eric and the twins, Magnus and Mikkel, along with his stepchildren, another set of twins, Suzy and Beth, who were studying medicine.

After that, mayhem ruled . . . just like it had back at Norstead. Everyone talking at once. Laughter. Rough play among the boys. Shrieks from the girls. An occasional shout from one of the men. Loud music in the background. Pots and pans clattering. The only thing different was there were no babies crying, but that would come in time. Madrene realized in that instant that she had become accustomed to a peaceful, ordered life.

Can I live in such noisy chaos again?

I hope I don't have to.

As if sensing her discomfort, Angela took Madrene by the elbow and said, "Let me show you to your room." They went into the house, but before they went up the stairs to her sleeping chamber, Angela led her into a solar where a large portrait hung over the fireplace mantel. It depicted a stunning woman with long blond hair, dressed in regal Norse attire.

"That's you," Angela told her. "Dagny painted it from memory."

"Me?" Madrene, who had never had a mirror till

she came to this country, was shocked. A polished piece of brass sufficed back in the Norselands. *Praise the gods! Does my bosom really look like that? No wonder men stare at me!* She recognized the gown, but she did not know that woman in the portrait. Worse, she was beginning to suspect she did not know the woman she had become.

I am truly lost.

When great minds gather, make sure there's enough beer . . .

It was late at night, and everyone was asleep at Blue Dragon except for the Ericsson and Magnusson men, who sat about the kitchen table making important plans. Beer . . . not wine . . . flowed in abundance.

Even Torolf had managed to fly in for the night, and would return to the base and his training expedition early the next day. Which brought to mind Ian, who was glaringly missing. If Torolf had come, Ian could have, too.

Ah, well, Magnus thought, he probably wanted Madrene to have private time with her family.

So the five of them were about to make an important decision: Magnus, Jorund, Rolf, Ragnor and Torolf.

"Madrene is going to be pissed that we didn't include her," Ragnor said after taking a swig from his long-neck bottle.

They all nodded their heads. Madrene could peel the rust off a broadsword with her sharp tongue when she went off on one of her tirades.

"Dad . . . all of you. . . . you should know something," Torolf began. He had everyone's attention.

"Madrene told you that she was able to hold off invaders at Norstead for one year until Steinolf sailed his many longships up the fjord. And I know she told us, sketchily, how she went from one harem to another over the following two years." He smiled to himself. "I know she even told us of her creative method for keeping those horny sultans from raping her. But what you don't know is what happened to her before Steinolf sent her away."

Magnus felt blood rush to his head. "The slimy codsucker! Did he rape Madrene?"

"No. No. It was almost worse than that," Torolf said. "First, he killed all the warriors and cotters who resisted the invasion. It was a mass slaughter because he slithered in during the darkness of night and caught them unprepared. They had just fought off an invasion of pirates a sennight before and were not as alert as they should have been. Some were able to escape to the hills. Steinolf believed that, if Madrene would marry him, all her people would return and—"

"—he could slay them under a flag of surrender," Jorund finished for him. At one time, Jorund had been a far-famed warrior. "I am familiar with Steinolf. He is a *nithing* . . . a man with no honor."

Sensing that Torolf had not yet finished, Magnus prodded him, "Go on."

"Madrene refused, knowing full well that the marriage would result not only in her death but in the death of all our people."

"What did the bastard do?" Rolf asked icily, sensing what was to come.

Torolf took a deep breath and disclosed, "He had her whipped repeatedly over a period of three days.

On the last day, they led her by a neck tether through the great hall, afore two hundred fighting men. Naked."

Tears welled in Magnus's eyes and he started to stand.

Torolf put up a halting hand. "Let me finish while I can. I know that we saw those scars on Madrene's shoulders, but we did not see it all. Ian told me that she carries welts from neck to buttocks, dozens of them . . . scars that will never go away. That beast broke the skin and drew blood with each of his blows."

Magnus did stand then, and pulled at his own hair. With a bellow of rage, he went berserk for a moment. They all understood a father's fury at learning his daughter had been violated so. When he sat back down, his shoulders sank. "'Tis my fault. I never should have left the Norselands."

"Nay. 'Tis my fault for leaving Norstead to search for Rolf," Jorund said.

"Well, if anyone is to blame, 'tis me," Rolf said. "I was the first to leave. I started this nightmare."

They all argued at once then, getting louder and louder. Finally, Ragnor stood and shouted, *"No!"* When they quieted and turned to listen to him, he said, "I was the last. I did not need to go off to war with Svein. 'Twas I who left Madrene alone. I will ne'er forgive myself for that. But I know how to make amends. I will go back to Norstead and regain our family home. 'Tis the least I can do."

"Dost think it is possible to go back?" Magnus asked.

"I do not know, but it seems to me there must be a way. Perhaps, going back to the present-day site of

Norstead would be the way to begin." Ragnor had always been the smartest in the family, and everyone heeded his words.

They all sat silently then, pondering what would be best.

"I am her father. I should be the one to avenge her," Magnus said.

"I am the warrior in the family. I would be best able to avenge her," Jorund said. No one mentioned that he had not been a fighting man for nigh on fifteen years. His body was still hard, but his skills must be rusty.

"I am absolutely the one to go," Ragnor said, "because I was the last to leave her alone."

"Mayhap we should all go," Magnus offered, but no one seemed enthusiastic about that plan. Too many family members would be left alone here.

Torolf stood then. He had seen thirty and some winters, and he was in peak condition. The SEALs training had truly made him into a skillful soldier in the war on terror, not just in body but in honor, too.

To each of them in turn, Torolf said, "No. No. No. No." Then he addressed Magnus. "Father, I am the only adult male in our family with no wife or children. I will go."

Thus it was that a U.S. Navy SEAL made plans to go back in time. Some people said that SEALs were a little bit crazy. Torolf would for damn sure prove that to be true . . . or die trying.

Everyone needs to be needed . . .

Madrene felt useless.

There was nothing for her to do, especially since

she'd been told in no uncertain terms that Torolf would be the one to go back to Norstead, that she was no longer needed to raise an army. "That beast Steinolf will be dead by year's end, that I guarantee," her father had told her with a patronizing pat on the back.

She was not all that upset about not going back to her own time. If she did not have Ian, it would be another story. Then, for a certainty, she would return to run the royal estate alongside Torolf.

For now, everyone told her to just relax. Well, she was relaxed up to her bloody eyebrows. She wanted . . . nay, needed . . . work to do.

But when she offered to help oversee the household, Angela and her grandmother told her kindly that they had a housekeeper to take care of that.

"How about cooking?" she asked.

Turned out the housekeeper cooked, too. And used vast quantities of garlic. Angela came from an Eye-tally-on family which cherished the garlic cloves in most of their food. And once again, the garlic turned her stomach. Several times, she'd had to rush, without causing attention, to the bathing chamber to throw up the contents of her stomach into the toy-let. She must have developed some kind of bodily reaction to garlic, she supposed, just like Hilda the Dour used to break out in a rash when she ate strawberries.

Her father, Kolbein, Hamr, Jogeir and Njal were out in the vineyards trimming back the vines. When she'd offered to help, they told her it was man's work. That outrageous statement caused her to lash them with her tongue good and loud. It did her no good. In the end, they went off without her.

The uncles and their families had gone back to their respective homes, along with Storvald. Ragnor and Alison planned to drive back to Coronado this afternoon, where Alison was a doctor—the modern word for a healer—and Ragnor worked in Sandy-egg-go with computers, just like Geek. At one time Ragnor had planned to become a SEAL, too, but he'd decided he preferred working with his mind.

"Take me back with you," she said to Ragnor.

It was the first time she'd even hinted of her unhappiness here with her family.

Ragnor, who was helping his wife pack a leather carrying bag, looked up at her with surprise.

"Of course you can come, Madrene," Alison said, "but you know that Ian won't be back until the weekend."

"It matters not. At least I would have something to do. I could clean his house, even if he keeps it spotless. I could rearrange his socks and underbraies so that the vein pops out in his forehead when he sees they are not in their usual places. I could play with the cat."

"Have you told Father or Angela that you need something to occupy you?"

"Yea, I have. They tell me to relax."

They left without her, finally, when her father promised to go out on the morrow and buy her a loom to weave some fabrics. *A loom! For the love of Frigg! I need a man, not a loom.*

She went upstairs and sat on the bed, waiting for Ian's nightly call. Then she got a whiff of the red sauce cooking down in the kitchen . . . the red sauce highly seasoned with garlic . . . and ran for the bathing chamber.

At least it gave her something to do.

I've got a secret . . .

When Ian called Maddie that night, she kept blubbering stuff about looms, and garlic, and bullheaded men, and a family that no longer needed her.

"Slow down, sweetie, and tell me what's wrong."

"All these years I dreamed about how it would be if my family were still with me. What I failed to recall is what my father's households are like—full of disorder and noise and people and things I do not understand."

"What do you want to do?"

"I want to go home."

Ian's heart stopped. He had to ask, but he didn't want to. "What home?"

"Your home, of course. What did you think I meant, you lunkhead?"

Ian didn't care that she called him a lunkhead. He leaned against the wall with a goofy grin on his face. "I miss you."

"You'd better miss me. And you'd better not have run into your former betrothed again."

"Maddie, I'm on an island."

"Hah! You would be surprised what lengths some women will go to to get a man. I might just have to come there and whack her on the head with a rock if she keeps chasing after you. I know how to do that, you know. Whack someone with a rock, I mean."

"I know that too well, babe. How about I come and pick you up on Saturday?"

She was silent for a moment, then said, "That is three days away. I cannot wait that long. Methinks I will demand that my father take me back tomorrow."

"You would be all alone at the house."

"Nay, I would not. Sam would be there."

He smiled at that image. "Actually, it would be kinda nice coming home to you."

"I can even greet you in that garment I never got to wear."

"What garment is that?"

"When I was trying to think of ways to seduce you—"

"Yeah?"

"Cage bought me a red silk teddy from Victoria's Secret. Would you like to see it?"

"Definitely."

"I'm feeling fluttery right now. I have my hand on my belly and I swear it is actually fluttering."

"Oh, Maddie, you are incredible."

"Do you ever flutter?"

"Oh, yeah."

"I did not know my bosom was so big."

"Huh?"

"The picture on the wall here . . . 'tis the first time I have ever seen myself as others do. I had no idea I looked that big. Kirsten tells me there is a procedure that a doctor can do to make them smaller."

"Whoa, whoa, whoa! You're not too big, and don't even think about breast-reduction surgery. It's dangerous. And besides, most women would die to have a body like yours."

"Really?"

"Yep. I'll prove it when I see you on Saturday. Do you want me to bring you something? Candy? Flowers?"

"A vibrator."

Ian practically swallowed his tongue. "Wh-what did you say?"

"I want a vibrator. Carrie on *Sex and the City* said a vibrator is a woman's best friend."

He shook his head and grinned. "Honey, do you even know what a vibrator is?"

"Nay, but you can show me. Can't you?"

"Absolutely. Hey, I've gotta go. There's a guy behind me who wants to use the phone. One last thing. There's a secret I've been keeping from you. I need to tell you when I get back."

"I have a secret, too. I have been afraid to tell you about it. It's . . . it's a big one."

She probably wants to tell me that Luke sold the jewels for her. I already know that. "It can't be any bigger than mine."

"I would not wager on that."

Chapter Eighteen

When in doubt, go shopping . . .

One day at a time, that was Madrene's new credo.

She could not continue to contemplate the complexity of time-travel and whether she had or had not, lest she go mad. She had no idea what her future held, either here or with Ian. She had no idea if she should go back to Norstead with Torolf or not.

And so she had chosen to live for the moment, not thinking about the future, which was contrary to the way she always used to live. Everything had a plan then. Her life was organized and well thought out.

And look where that got me.

Now the only thing she could say for certain was that she loved Ian. She knew that without a doubt.

But what will he think when I tell him about the time-travel? Will he still love me then?

She had no answer.

Initially her father had balked at bringing her back to Sandy-egg-go, but he finally gave in when

Madrene railed at him. She knew he was hurt that she didn't want to spend more time in his company, but she was a grown woman now, and there would be plenty of time later for them to reminisce. Since coming back, she had cleaned and polished Ian's home from floor to ceiling, even though it was not all that dirty. She polished doorknobs and metal fixtures in the kitchen and bathing chamber. Windows sparkled from her vinegar cleansing. She picked cat hair off the furniture piece by piece.

Ian would be back tomorrow. She planned to tell him her secret right off. Then what would be, would be. The fates had brought her here. The fates would decide whether she should stay.

She had gained a friend in Polly, the lady who lived in the keep next to Ian's and who cared for Sam in Ian's absence. Polly's husband was serving on a ship somewhere whilst Polly stayed home and cared for their two small children.

"Gone a-Viking?" Madrene had asked her.

Polly had laughed. "You could say that."

They were going shopping together at the food mart today.

Madrene had plenty of money since Slick had sold her jewels. She kept the parchment money in three leather traveling bags in back of Ian's closet. She had told Slick she preferred coin, but he'd grinned and said, "No, you don't." As she eased herself down into Polly's bug—that was what she called her small yellow vehicle—she asked, "Is this enough money?" She pulled out the small sheets of parchment from her pocket.

Polly stared at her in astonishment, as if questioning whether she was serious or not. "Five hundred dollars should be more than enough money for the supermarket, honey. Besides, we can't buy too much, or it won't fit in the bug."

As they drove toward the market place, Madrene turned in her seat and entertained the two children in their own special seats . . . one-year-old Sharon and two-year-old Jonathan.

"They are beautiful children," Madrene said with a sigh.

"Yeah, they are," Polly said with unabashed pride. "Do you and Ian plan to have children?"

"No."

"No?" Polly was clearly surprised. "But Ian adores children. I've seen him play with mine. He would be such a good father. I'm sorry. It's none of my business."

"I am barren."

"Are you sure? Have you been to a doctor?"

"Nay. 'Twould serve no purpose to consult a healer on such a matter. For more than five years my husband tried to plant his seed in me. It would not take."

"Did it ever occur to you that it might have been his fault?"

Madrene shook her head. "No sooner did he wed another than she became big with child." She shrugged. "I have become resigned to my misfortune."

Polly drove her bug into a parking slot and stopped. Turning to face Madrene directly, she put a hand on hers and said, "Number one, the fact that your jerk of a husband couldn't impregnate you doesn't mean another man couldn't. It happens all the time. Two, even if it is your problem, there are things doctors can do today. It might be as simple as a tipped uterus. Three, you could try artificial insemination. Four, if all that fails, you could adopt a child."

Madrene did not understand most of what Polly had said, but she got the gist of it . . . modern medicine might have an answer for her. She doubted it, but it was worth pondering, she supposed. Later, she would ask for a further explanation.

Inside the food mart—a different place from the one Ian had taken her to—Madrene pushed a cart with Jonathan in front and Polly pushed another with Sharon in front.

"I cannot read," she confessed to Polly, who looked shocked. "I am learning," she was quick to add, "but in the meantime, I cannot prepare many of the foods here because I cannot read the directions on the boxes. So you must help me pick out things that I can make, without needing special instructions. For example, I can bake bread if you will show me where the flour and fat renderings are."

"You mean lard, or Crisco. Don't you need yeast, too?" When she saw Madrene frown, Polly added, "A leavening agent so the bread will rise."

"I usually make manchet bread . . . a type of flat bread . . . but I could try the yeast, too, if you tell me how."

Madrene bought fresh fruit and vegetables and several kinds of meat and fish. She made a wonderful smoked cod in dill sauce that people usually liked.

When they got to the personal products aisle—that was what Polly called it—Polly put two objects in her cart. Tamp-axe and co-tax. When Polly explained their purpose, Madrene clapped her hands with glee. *What a wonderful country this is that they have such products!* She put several in her cart.

While in that section of the mart, Polly picked up her favorite body cream, which smelled of almonds. Madrene picked up one of the tubes, too, but she bought the one that smelled like lilies of the valley.

She could tell that Polly was baffled by her ignorance of so many everyday things in this country. *I wonder what she would say if I told her I have time-traveled. Hah! She was shocked that I cannot read. She would probably think I am a demented person.*

When she got home, she made bread. It was one thing, at least, that did not require education. She made half of the dough into flat bread and the other half with the leavening. Setting the oven as Polly had directed, she baked the manchet bread first and let the other rise in a sunny place on the cabinet top. Was there anything in the world like the smell of fresh bread baking?

Sam settled herself at the base of the stove, attracted by the warmth. Just like her Rose at Norstead, who liked nothing more than sleeping before the fireplace. Madrene stilled for a moment, wondering if Rose had found a good home. She hoped so.

After that, she opened a can in the manner Omar had taught her. Pleased with herself that she was adjusting so well, she took her bowl of chicken noodle soup into the solar and ate whilst she watched Doctor Fill on the tea-vee.

Later, she took a shower, shampooed her hair, shaved her legs and armpits and smeared herself all over with her new cream. *I smell like a bloody flower,* she thought, grinning. She was not tired but she went to bed anyhow, knowing that the sooner she slept, the sooner tomorrow would come and Ian would be home.

As she lay in bed, she thought about all that had happened to her. The assault by Steinolf on Norstead, her living in the Arab lands, meeting Ian, then being reunited with her family. *Is there a reason why I was sent here? Did everything that happened to me need to occur before this fate could be completed? If so, why?* Her father had mentioned miracles. That, she might be able to accept. Even then, why? An idea came to her unbidden. Just before she'd fled from Fakhir's holding, she had said a prayer to the gods, asking for help. Could it be that simple? "Ask and you shall receive." That was a line her grandmother, Lady Asgar, used to quote from her Christian Bible.

She inhaled deeply, enjoying the scent of her body cream. She would have to wash the bed linens in the morning, before Ian got home, lest he think he was sleeping in a garden. 'Twould not be manly.

Finally she fell asleep.

Honey, I'm home . . .

Ian got home at two a.m. after hopping an early flight back to the base.

As he entered the quiet house, Sam came up and meowed a greeting against his leg, then went back to the sofa to sleep again . . . the sofa she was not supposed to get up on. He shook his head at the hopelessness of trying to teach a cat anything.

Dropping his duffel bag on the hall floor, he

walked into the kitchen, where the most delicious smell filled the air. Fresh-baked bread, he soon realized. Cutting off a hunk for himself and slathering it with butter, he glanced around the room. Not only was it spotlessly clean, but he would swear every aluminum fixture in the place shone like silver. Maddie had been a busy beaver.

He turned off the kitchen light and went down the hall. Opening the door to his bedroom, he could see by the hall light that Maddie was sacked out under a sheet. Possibly naked, if her bare shoulders were any indication. He felt an unexplainable pleasure just knowing she slept naked in his bed even when he wasn't there.

The room was humid, and the sliding door to the deck was opened to the ocean air. She probably didn't know how to turn the air conditioner on. He sniffed the air then. Holy hell! It smelled like a funeral parlor in here. Seeing no cut flowers around, he figured she must have sprayed air freshener . . . enough to wipe out the whole ozone layer.

Should he hop into bed and give her a little early-morning hello, or should he shower first? He opted for the latter. Closing the door carefully, he went into the bathroom, where once again everything shone; even the tiles appeared to be polished. He was anal about things being orderly and clean, probably due to his military background. Either Maddie was the same, or she had done all this for him. Either way, he was grateful. He would show her how grateful after the shortest shower in history.

Honey, I'm home, he thought a few minutes later as he eased himself onto the bed and under the sheet. *I've got something for you.*

Dream lover . . .

Madrene was having an erotic dream.

She knew about such things, having grown up in a household with many virile men who thought nothing of speaking of intimate things in front of women. Apparently, men, especially young ones, had dreams all the time that were so carnal, they spilled their seed into the bed linens. Madrene wasn't spilling anything, but she definitely felt a carnal ripple or two.

She stretched and arched her back at the exquisite rub of the bed linen across her sensitive nipples. All these years she had never known her breasts could be a source of such pleasure. Ian had taught her that.

Her lower body felt sensitized, too. Almost as if butterfly wings were passing over the nether hair, back and forth, till she opened her legs, wanting the wings to touch her in that special spot. And they did. Sweet merciful Valkyries! The yearning in her body turned red hot and urgent. She wanted so badly to be touched . . . touched till the fire crackled through and she exploded.

She had never touched herself before. Never had any inclination to. But in this dream state, she did now.

In her mind, it was Ian caressing her, readying her for mating.

The ultimate male fantasy . . .

Oh . . . my . . . God!

Ian had crept into the bed wanting to surprise Maddie. He'd thought a few whispery caresses would arouse her into wakefulness. There was nothing like entering a woman still warm from sleep. Instead—*oh my God*—she was going to masturbate. In her sleep. In front of him. Without knowing he was there.

He knelt on the bed at her side.

Should I stop her? the nice-guy side of his brain asked.

Are you nuts? the horny-guy side replied.

I'll just watch for a little while.

Yeah, right!

She won't mind.

You hope.

She shoved the sheet down to her waist, exposing her breasts, then kicked the rest of the sheet aside. Her breasts were full and firm and beautiful, the pink nipples already hard points which she teased further by rubbing her closed fingers up and down over them in washboard fashion. They got even harder and bigger. Her lips parted on a long sigh, and she arched her body up, squeezing the entire breasts, then flicking a forefinger over the nubs, till she was moaning.

While he was biting his lip, trying to keep himself from leaving before the gospel, so to speak, she moved her hand lower, exploring her belly and navel and then her pubic hair. He really was going to need another cold shower before he made love with her.

She raised her knees, then spread them. She lowered her finger till she found what she was looking for and keened, "Aaaaaahhhh!"

He figured it was time to get out of Dodge. She would be embarrassed at his witnessing this, as beautiful as it was. It took the skill of a Navy SEAL to extract himself from the bed without her noticing.

Looking down at the Blue Steeler that pointed the way out of the bedroom, he murmured, "Hold on, buddy. You'll get your turn."

Strangers in the night . . .

Something awakened Madrene in the middle of the night. She had been having the most incredible dream. And then . . .

Sitting up in the bed, she tried to orient herself. Water, that was what she'd heard. And not the sound of the ocean. It was coming from the bathing chamber. Carefully she got out of bed and took a piss-toll out of the bedside drawer—not that she knew how to use a piss-toll, but her intruder wouldn't know that. With weapon raised, she crept out of the bedroom toward the bathroom door, which she opened quietly.

She didn't know who was more shocked, she or Ian in the showering stall.

"Ian!" she shouted, putting a hand over her fast-beating heart.

"Maddie!"

"You rat!" she said. He should have told her he'd come back early. It had scared her spitless thinking a stranger was in the house.

"Don't shoot! I didn't want to wake you. I only watched for a little while."

What is he talking about? "I thought you were an intruder." She lowered the pistol and set it on the sink, then tilted her head in puzzlement. Her eyes went wide, and she gasped when she realized what he meant. "You watched? Oh, you are a loathsome lout! How could you?"

She turned and ran from the room. He caught up

with her at the end of the hall, grabbing her from behind and wrapping his arms around her so her back was against his wet chest. She squirmed but he wouldn't release her, just rested his chin on her shoulder and kissed her neck.

"I was sleeping."

"I know."

"I've never done *that* before."

"I could tell."

"You shouldn't have watched."

"I couldn't help myself."

"Liar."

"Okay, I watched because I wanted to. Will you do it again?"

"Hah! Not bloody likely! Not even in my dreams!"

"I would do it for you."

She felt his chest shaking then, and turned in his arms. "You're laughing at me? You really are a wretch."

"No, no, sweetie. I'm not laughing about that. I'm laughing at the thought of you facing an intruder, naked, with a pistol. The poor guy would have probably stopped whatever he was doing just to look at you."

She tried to swat him on the face but he grabbed her hand and kissed her palm. Before she had a chance to hit him with the other hand, he lifted her off her feet, high in his arms, which were wrapped around her waist. Then he walked back to the sleeping chamber. He probably didn't have sleep in mind, if the hardness poking her thigh was any indication.

"I missed you," he said.

"You're looking at my breasts when you say that."

He just smiled.

With a wild whoop, he threw her onto the bed. She landed flat on her back with her head on the pillow, and he leaned over her.

"I missed you, too," she admitted.

"You're looking at my cock when you say that."

She just smiled.

Lovin' you ain't easy . . .

It was almost dawn. They'd screwed each other's brains out. Now it was time for the big bang.

"I have to tell you something, Maddie," he said, dreading it more than anything he could think of. He'd rather run the O-course a thousand times than tell Maddie they were not married.

"Me, too," she said. Turning in his arms, she looked up at him, and she was clearly scared. *Maddie scared? It must be really bad.*

"You go first," he said.

She sat up in the bed, cross-legged and naked, which made his eyes do cartwheels in his head. The woman just did not have the usual feminine anxiety about her body. You had to love her for that alone. He sat up, too.

She inhaled and exhaled as if for courage. "I'm a time-traveler."

That was not what he'd expected. That she came from Russia and was a cossack, maybe. Or a freedom fighter in the North Pole, yeah. But a time-traveler? He started to laugh.

She stared at him, absolutely serious.

"Come on, Maddie. What's the joke?"

She shook her head. "I do not jest." She told him the year of her birth, about her family living in some royal estate in the Norselands, that all of her looney-bird family had time-traveled, too, that everything she'd told him so far about Steinolf and the invasion and the harems was true, except those events took place long, long ago.

"That's over a thousand years ago. Give me a break!"

" 'Tis true. I swear it is. Leastways, I think it is."

He put a hand to his chin and rubbed. He needed a shave. He looked at her again as she gazed at him expectantly. What did she expect? That he would tell her, "It's all right if you're a thousand years old, I still love you." *Shit! How do I tell her she needs to see a shrink if that's what she really thinks. But she can't think that. It's gotta be a joke.*

"Do you think you could still love me if I am a time-traveler?"

"Sweetheart, I would love you if you were an alien from outer space." He leaned over and kissed her lightly on her kiss-bruised lips. *First thing this morning, I'm calling Dr. Feingold at the base to get his advice. This is bizarre.*

"You don't believe me, do you?"

"No, but it doesn't matter."

"What is your secret?" she asked then.

Oh, God! I forgot. There was nothing to do but brave it out. "We're not married."

She gasped and jerked backward as if he'd punched her.

He took both of her hands in his and tried to explain. "It's just a technicality. We can go get married somewhere private. Las Vegas, Reno, city hall, I don't care. It doesn't mean anything."

"We are not married?" She looked crushed.

"Turns out JAM's license to perform marriages had been taken away without his knowing it. But, please, don't look like that. I feel as if we're married. We will be married. Today, if you want."

"It does matter," she said in a dead voice. "How long have you known?"

He felt his face heat up. "A few days."

She shook her head at him. "The question is, will you be willing to wed a thousand-year-old woman?"

"That's silly."

"No, it's not. Tell me this, can a person get married in this country with no identity? Do they just marry anybody?"

"Well, no. You need a birth certificate at least, I would think. I don't know for sure. I was never married."

"And where are you going to find one for me?"

He was getting tired of this game. "Hell if I know! You've given me so many countries that you're from."

"Madrene Olgadottir, born in the Norselands in the year 982, daughter of Olga Gerdsson and Magnus Ericsson, former wife of Karl Ivarsson." She lifted her chin, daring him to contradict her.

What could he say to that? Deep down, he wondered if she wasn't just coming up with this goofball story to get out of marrying him . . . again. Well, he was not going to beg. With a grunt of disgust, he got out of bed and pulled on a pair of jogging shorts, then sat back down to put on socks and athletic shoes.

"Where are you going?" she asked. She was still sitting on the bed behind him.

"Running." He stood and looked down at her. There were tears in her eyes. He wished she would rail at him like she usually did. Shrewishness he could handle. Tears would do him in.

"Why?"

"I need to clear my head. I'm in love with a wacko. That's gonna take a little getting used to."

She winced at his words. Before he could take them back, she said, "Running away will not solve anything."

"I'm not running away." But inside, he wondered if that wasn't exactly what he was doing.

For more than an hour, he ran on the beach. It had started to rain, but he didn't care—he needed a cold shower. By the time he'd made the return run, he'd come to a conclusion: He would take Maddie any way he could get her. Even if she claimed to be Cleopatra coming down the Mississippi on a barge, he loved her, pure and simple. She could get psychological help, or not . . . he didn't care.

But when he got back to the house, it was deathly silent.

Maddie was gone.

Chapter Nineteen

Freedom is just another word for . . .

Ian needed running to clear his head. Madrene needed absence to clear her head.

For two weeks, Madrene had been staying alone in a temporarily vacant apartment in Coronado which Ragnor and Alison had found for her. Hiding out would be a more appropriate description, since no one but the two of them knew she was there. With Ragnor's help, she'd left a short message on the answering machines at Ian's home and Blue Dragon, stating that she was all right but needed time alone to think. She'd sworn Ragnor and Alison to secrecy.

The apartment was merely the living quarters on the second floor of a house owned by a lovely elderly woman named Lillian, who had an adorable horse of a dog named Sam, the same name as Ian's cat, except this animal really was a male. Apparently, Alison had lived here before marrying her brother. Now they owned a house in another part of town.

Since Ragnor was out of town at some kind of come-pewter meeting, Alison had come over to spend the afternoon with her. She was not on duty at the base hospitium on Saturdays, although she could be called in an emergency. They planned to watch a tape on the tea-vee of *Sex and the City* repeats. Alison was a fan of the old show, too.

"How are the lessons going?" Alison asked as they sat down in the kitchen, which overlooked the backyard. The apartment was sparsely furnished, but it served Madrene's purposes for now.

"Very well." Ragnor had hired a tutor to work with her three hours a day, not just teaching her reading and writing, but history and biology, and geography, and numbers, and so many other important things. "I don't know how Ragnor, and all the rest of my family, did it. My mind gets fuzzy at all there is to know just to live here."

"Ragnor has only been here three years, and look how well he's adjusted. He speaks like a native," Alison pointed out.

"Pfff. Ragnor always was more intelligent than the rest of us."

Alison patted her hand. "It will come to you, too."

"I love this apartment and its location," she told Alison. "I can walk everywhere. To the ocean. To the bay. Downtown Coronado and all its shops. Even the base, if I wanted to." Which she did not want to do, for fear she might run into Ian.

As if reading her mind, Alison asked, "Are you ready to talk about my brother yet?"

Madrene had refused to discuss Ian or her reasons for leaving him. Apparently, Ian had been just as close-mouthed.

She had deliberately not allowed herself to ask before, but she had to now. "How is he?"

"Not good. Even Sam has gone into total meltdown. Won't eat, hisses at Ian all the time, keeps going to the closet where a shirt of yours still hangs."

Madrene tried to smile but could not. A lump formed in her throat. "Tell me about Ian."

"He's devastated. This is way worse than when Jennifer left him. I honest to God think he was relieved then. But now, it's as if someone—you—cut out his heart. The worst part is that he has totally shut down his emotions. He won't talk about it. Claims he doesn't care."

"I did not mean to hurt him."

"I'm sure he didn't mean to hurt you, either. Can't you two work this out?"

"I don't know. I hope so." She looked at her sister-by-marriage who had become such a good friend to her. "We are not married," she confessed.

"Really? I had no idea. I mean, everyone said you were married in Baghdad."

"We were, but it was not legal."

"And my brother the rat refused to marry you again," she concluded. "Wait till I get ahold of him. I'll wring his stupid neck."

Madrene laughed. "No need for that. Ian did want to get married again . . . in a place called Lost-vague-ass. But I could not do it as long as he refuses to believe I have time-traveled."

"Oh, Maddie, he might not ever do that. I know I still have trouble accepting it."

"And Ragnor does not mind?"

"Sweetie, your brother would take me any way he

could get me. And if he didn't, I would force him to." She grinned. "Another thing. Dad has been here, and he's been badgering Ian to get off his ass and find you."

Madrene groaned. "That is just wonderful. If anything will make Ian do the opposite, it is an order from his father."

"You know Ian well. But he's too hard on Dad, in my opinion. Our father is overbearing and he has been especially hard on Ian, but his heart is in the right place. Ian just can't see that . . . yet."

"I had the same impression of your father."

"It's stuffy in here," Alison said. "Do you mind if I open the window?"

"No. Go ahead. I am so accustomed to the cold of the North that warmth like this is a treasure to me, as it was in the Arab lands. And, believe you me, that was the only thing I liked about the Arab lands."

"Yummmmmm. Smell that. Lillian must be making her famous lasagna."

"Garlic," Madrene said with alarm as her stomach roiled and she ran for the toy-let.

When she came back out, Alison remarked, "Still have a reaction to garlic, huh? Maybe you should get a checkup. It might be an allergy or something."

"Nay, it is only garlic that affects me so. As long as I avoid it, there is no problem."

"So, what are you going to do about you and Ian?"

"I need a little more time. I am relishing this time alone, with more freedom than I have ever had. It is only as I have had time to contemplate that I realized my life has been akilter for a long time. I have fought and fought and fought against one stricture or another. I am tired of fighting."

"You also need some time to heal from all the physical and emotional batterings you've had."

Madrene nodded.

"But in the end, being the eternal optimist, I am confident that love will win."

"I hope you are right," Madrene said, because there was something else she had realized in this time of reflection.

Freedom was not everything.

Never provoke a woman in public . . .

It had been three weeks since Maddie had left, and Ian was royally ticked.

At first, he had been worried about her. Maddie was clueless about finding her way around the block, let alone a big city.

Then the devastation had set in. Hurt was too small a word. He had loved her beyond anything he'd ever thought possible, and she'd just sloughed him off like he was nothing to her.

Anger came next. She had a hell of a nerve leaving him without any message other than she was all right. He deserved a lot more than that. No one had any idea where she was, or if she was indeed all right.

And that time-travel crap! *Give me a break!*

Well, today was the first day of the rest of his life. He had just met Laura Madison for lunch at a little outdoor cafe in Coronado. She was a nurse at the same hospital where his sister worked. He was in uniform, as she was, since he had to return to the base in an hour or so. She was attractive and smart and wasn't a psycho time-traveler. *She also doesn't have breasts that merit a* Penthouse *gig. Shit. I am not going to think about that. Not, not, not!*

They were halfway through their Caesar salads and Laura was telling him about a recent scuba-diving vacation in the Bahamas when Ian glanced to the right, then did a double take. *Torpedo time!*

There came Maddie sashaying down the street as if she hadn't a care in the world. Her hair hung in one long braid. Sunglasses were on her eyes. And she wore a tight white tanktop tucked into a jeans skirt. At the bottom of her long bare legs were sandals. She was carrying a small shopping bag from a nearby clothing shop.

His heart started beating wildly and a lump formed in his throat. All this time he'd been searching for her, she'd been right here, practically in his own back yard. His sister lived in Coronado. He would bet his left nut that she had something to do with this.

She looks great. Apparently our separation hasn't affected her at all.

He saw the moment she spotted him. She stopped dead in her tracks, took off the sunglasses, then smiled. She actually had the balls to smile. The smile lasted only a nanosecond . . . till she spotted Laura at his table.

"Uh-oh!"

"What's wrong?" Laura asked, turning in her seat to look at Maddie storming toward them like Attila the Hun.

Before he had a chance to warn Laura, Maddie reached their table. "What are you doing with my husband?"

"Hu . . . husband?" Laura's eyes darted to him.

He would have said that he wasn't Maddie's husband, not anymore, not ever, but Maddie was on a tear. "Some women do not have the sense to stay in their own bowers. They must go sniffing around the bed furs of men who are already wed. And you . . ." She turned to him, her blue eyes flashing like diamonds, ". . . you cannot keep your dangly part in your *braies* even for a short time—"

"Three weeks," he reminded her. *Holy shit! I must be as crazy as she is. I feel like smiling . . . because I've missed her nagging.*

She threw her hands in the air. "Three weeks. Three hours. Same thing!"

"Not to me!"

Now she was back to addressing Laura, whose mouth hung open with astonishment. She also kept checking out Maddie's breasts . . . even women tended to do that. "Men! They are ever fickle, do you not agree? I do not know why I thought Ian was any different. Methinks I will go buy myself a dog. At least they are loyal. And, by the by, Ian, your vein is about to pop."

I even like her commenting on my vein. "Maddie, you're causing a scene," he told her. And, man, was she! Not just because of her tirade, but about three dozen people, mostly men, had their eyes glued on Maddie's breasts. *I wonder if she's wearing a bra.*

Did she listen to his warning about causing a scene? Hardly. She sat down at an empty seat between him and Laura, linked her fingers together, setting her forearms on the edge of the table, and looked at him with those soulful blue eyes of hers.

"You're angry," she observed with surprise.

"No kidding."

"I told you I was all right."

"Big deal!"

"You knew I would come back eventually."

"Oh, really? And how in hell was I supposed to know that?" He barely restrained himself from reaching over and shaking her. "For all I knew, you could be dead."

"I told you I love you. Didst think I say that to everyone . . . or anyone, for that matter? You should have known I would not leave you."

She still loves me. Oh, God! I should not care, but I do. I want to wring her neck and kiss her at the same time. "What planet do you come from?"

"No planet. Just time—"

"Don't even say it. I am not in the mood for that time-travel crap."

She shrugged, as if to suggest that time-travel needn't be an important issue between them. Then she sniffed several times and said, pointing to their dishes, "Is that garlic I smell?"

Huh? "Yeah, there's some garlic in this salad." Actually, there was quite a bit, now that she mentioned it.

She did the oddest thing then. She clapped a hand over her mouth as she began to retch. Then she ran away from them, presumably to find a ladies' room.

He looked at Laura. She looked at him. "Go," she said.

Placing a twenty on the table, he squeezed her hand and said, "Thanks. And, for the record, she's not my wife."

Laura grinned at him. "She should be."

He grinned back. "Yeah."

Halfway down the block, he caught up with Maddie, who was heading into an alley. He grabbed one hand, the one that still clutched the shopping bag, and stopped her so that she turned to face him. She still had one hand over her mouth.

"Are you sick?" *She does look kind of pale.*

She shook her head, took several deep breaths, then said, "It was just the garlic."

"Garlic? I thought maybe it was me." *Maybe I should apologize. I don't know what for, but I'll say I'm sorry for just about anything if she'll come back. How pathetic is that?*

She didn't react to his words. "Ever since those terrorists kidnapped me and did so much cooking with garlic, I have developed this . . . reaction."

Oh. Well, I'll be damned if I'll apologize for garlic. Even I am not that pathetic. He had backed her up against the brick wall in the alley. She smelled like flowers . . . the same scent that had hit him the last night he'd been with her. She'd told him it was body lotion. "I've never heard of garlic doing that to a person."

"You look awful," she said.

"Thanks a bunch."

"There are circles under your eyes and you look thinner."

"Well, you look great. In fact, you're glow . . ." His words trailed off as the most bizarre idea occurred to him, and several facts flipped through his mind like a deck of cards: how glowing she'd looked walking down the street, and how white her face was now; and the retching.

Is it possible?

Nah!

But what if . . . ?

"Why are looking at me so funny?"

He linked his fingers with hers and said, "Come with me."

The whole time as he dragged her along to the drug store and selected and paid for his purchase, she berated him, "You are such a low-down, good-for-nothing weasel. What were you doing with that woman? Oh! You had better not have tupped her. If you tupped her, I just might lop off your head. Better yet, another body part. Where are we going? You are walking too fast. I'm hungry of a sudden. Can we go back and get a cheeseburger, French fries and a chocolate milk shake? Oh, you are a tyrant to starve me so!"

He stopped abruptly

She ran into him.

"Where are you living?"

He could see that she considered not telling him, but she must have noticed the "No mercy" expression on his face. She gave him the address, which was only two blocks away. Yep, Alison and Ragnor had a lot to answer for. He recognized the address as Allie's old second-floor apartment in a Coronado Victorian house.

He began pulling her along again, walking briskly. When they got to the house, she asked, "Are you going to beat me? If you even try, I swear I will kill you . . . mayhap not right away . . . but sometime in your sleep perhaps."

He still held her hand firmly, but he put the other hand to her cheek and said, "Oh, Maddie, don't you know? I would never, ever hit you. Never."

"Well, I don't understand what all the hurry is

about, then," she grumbled as they made their way up the stairs.

"Sweetheart, I am pretty damn sure I am going to make your day."

Pink or blue, baby . . .

Ian had lost his mind.

That was the only conclusion Madrene could come to as he shoved her inside her apartment and tugged her toward the bathing chamber. "Pee in this cup," he said, handing her one of those disposable cups that hung in a special case on the wall.

"I beg your pardon." *He must have gone barmy. 'Tis my fault. I made him demented.*

"Pee in the damn cup." He had the nerve then to lift her skirt, pull down her panties and shove her onto the toy-let seat. Then he shoved the cup between her legs.

"Have you lost your mind?"

"Undoubtedly. I'm not leaving till you do it."

Despite her mortification, she did as he ordered. "You'd better not be planning that perverted thing in bedsport that they did on *Sex and the City*. There are some things that I will not do. For a certainty, *that* crosses the line."

His mouth gaped open like a blowfish, and then he laughed.

After she got up and adjusted her clothing and washed her hands, he barred her from leaving. "What is going on with you?" she asked.

He had taken out the box he'd purchased downtown. It had the letters E, P and T on it. She tried to sound it out, but the word made no sense.

Taking an object out of the box, he stuck it in the urine. *He truly is demented. Should I suggest he see a head doctor?*

Then he took her in his arms and hugged her tightly to him. In a voice so soft she hardly heard him, he whispered against her ear, "I think you're pregnant. This is a test that will tell us for sure."

"No!" she cried out, trying to struggle out of his embrace. "It is so cruel of you to tease me on that subject. How could you? How could you?" Madrene's legs gave way, and her heart nigh burst with agony.

He still held her tightly, making soothing noises as he stroked her hair. "You've asked me to believe in miracles . . . time-travel, for God's sake. Can't you believe in miracles, too?"

"Do not do this to me. I beg you," she cried.

"If time-travel could happen, maybe you're not barren like you think, or at least not with me."

She was sobbing loudly now. The pain was crushing her lungs. She could barely breathe.

Ian was no better.

He was taking a huge gamble. He could see how badly Maddie was taking his suggestion, but he had to go on. This might very well be a make-or-break point in their relationship. *Hey, Lord, if You're up there, I could use a little help. Please don't let me have set her up for a crushing disappointment.* "Where's my brave girl who fights off Viking invaders, Arab sultans and Navy SEALs? She doesn't even have the nerve to take a pregnancy test? I don't think so!"

She pulled her head back to look at him. There was hope in her eyes. Glancing over at the pregnancy test, she asked, "What does it say?"

He let her go. Now he was the one losing his

nerve. He picked it up, looked at it, then closed his eyes. Finally he turned around. With tears burning in his eyes, he held his arms open to her.

Then he smiled.

Epilogue

Anything worth doing is worth doing well . . .

Two weeks later, on a Saturday, Ian and Maddie were sleeping late in his bed, with Sam curled up at the bottom of their bare feet.

In that dream state, halfway between sleep and wakefulness, Ian smiled to himself. Today was going to be his wedding day. They'd obtained a license, thanks to a forged birth certificate for Maddie given to them by Slick. Ian didn't want to know how Slick had gotten it. They had a noon appointment today at City Hall, where they would officially become husband and wife.

It would be a private affair. He and Maddie had both insisted on that, despite her family's suggestion that they hold a fancy big-ass wedding and reception at Blue Dragon, and despite his fellow SEALs' urging that they hold a wild big-ass party/wedding here near the base. Actually, they both felt as if they were already married, and the wedding rites were just a technicality.

He should have known it couldn't be that easy.

Just as he was about to open his eyes and wake Maddie with a kiss, and something more, a loud explosion went off out on the beach.

He jackknifed to a sitting position and then stood. Sam almost hit the ceiling with a screeching meow. Maddie screamed. Another explosion went off, but now he realized it was more a rat-a-tat series of explosions.

Grabbing a pistol from the bedside table and a rifle from the closet, he rushed out to the deck, not bothering to dress. His jaw dropped practically to his chest. "Sonofabitch!"

It was Cage out on the beach, setting off firecrackers. And he was all decked out in dress whites. Up in the sky, some skywriter, probably Pretty Boy, was spelling out *Ian Loves Maddie.* Another plane followed the skywriter, and out dropped at least ten skydivers, all in dress uniforms. As they landed, he was able to identify them: his squad members, Ragnor, his commander, his XO and, unbelievably, his brothers and father. They shucked their chutes and harnesses, and the whole bunch of them joined Cage and started walking toward him. As one, they gave him a little wave.

He gave them the finger.

"Nice duds!" Cage called out with a laugh.

He looked down and saw that he was naked. Not that he cared. Oops! Maybe he did care. Glancing to the side of his house, he saw some women. His sister, Polly, the Magnusson and Ericsson women with their men, and lots of others.

Quickly he ducked inside the bedroom, where Maddie was staring with horror at the scene unfolding before them. At least she'd had the sense to don a robe.

There was a short rap on the open sliding door. It was Cage. "Don't hit me," he said, grinning. "I just wanted to explain."

"There isn't any explanation that would stop me from hitting you." Ian pulled on a pair of sweatpants.

"Remember how you always said, 'Anything worth doing is worth doing well.' Well, we SEALs and your family and her family decided it would be a shame not to give you a suitable sendoff."

"Do not dare throw my own words back at me. I am so pissed at you . . . all of you. I told you we wanted this to be private."

Cage shrugged. "My MeeMaw, she allus said, some folks jist doan know whass good for 'em."

"What are those people doing out there?" Maddie screeched in Ian's ear. She was standing right behind them.

"I think they're the caterers," Cage said.

A dozen people outside were arranging chairs and tables and a freakin' tent big enough to hold a circus. In another section of the beach, a rose-covered trellis or archway or something was being erected. And—oh, no!—a red carpet.

He and Maddie both glowered at Cage.

Throwing his hands up in the air, Cage said, "Don't blame me. It was your father." He was speaking to Maddie now. "Whew! When Magnus says he wants to do something, you don't argue with him. Especially when he's carrying that sword. He said,

'There is going to be a Viking wedding. By Odin, I swear it will be so.' What could we do?"

A Viking wedding?

A sword?

Ian groaned.

"My father! I should have known!" Maddie shrieked. "Let me go out there. I will tell him what I think of his highhanded methods. Yea, I will. How dare he! E'er did he treat me like a child, even when I was married."

Just in time, Ian put his hands on her shoulders to hold her back. They needed to think this out and be calm . . . before they kicked ass.

"I don't have my dress whites. They're at the dry cleaners." *What a pitiful excuse for not having a wedding!*

"No problem," Cage said with a wide smile. "Geek picked them up yesterday."

"The city will never let us have a wedding on the beach."

"Slick knows somebody who knows somebody. It's all taken care of."

"How long have you been planning this?"

"A week."

"How many of you were involved in planning this . . . nightmare?"

Cage pretended to be counting on his fingers, then announced, "Twenty-five."

"Twe-twenty-five?" Ian sputtered out.

Maddie had seemed to be in shock, but now she spoke up. "I cannot get married here. I have naught to wear."

What a pitiful excuse for not having a wedding!

"Well, actually," a feminine voice said from the

doorway, where Maddie's sister Kirsten stood. She and Dagny brought in a very unusual dress . . . in fact, it appeared to be identical to the one she was wearing in the portrait at Blue Dragon.

Maddie started to weep. For a woman who never cried, she was doing an awful lot of that lately.

"It's out of our hands now, honey," Ian said, squeezing her shoulder. But into her ear, he whispered, "We have our own special secret that we are not sharing with anyone. Let them have their fun. We have this."

She put a hand over her belly and smiled at him, gloriously.

With a final laugh, Ian walked off to help plan the biggest blowout wedding he and Maddie never wanted.

A SEAL farmer? I . . . don't . . . think . . . so! . . .

In the end, Madrene and Ian had to admit it was the best wedding any couple could have ever asked for.

When Madrene walked down the red carpet, through an archway of swords held by the SEALs and the men of her Viking family, everyone sighed at the romantic picture she made. The way she carried herself, some said she looked like an ancient princess. She said the only prince she wanted was standing beside her.

Ian's father came up to Ian at one point and said, "I am proud of you, son." Before a stunned Ian could say a word, his father pulled him into a fierce bear hug.

JAM, who had somehow renewed his license, married them . . . again.

Torolf gave Madrene an extra hug near the end of

the day. He would be taking a leave from the SEALs shortly and departing for Norway and the site of long-ago Norstead in hopes of returning to the past and ousting Steinolf. Madrene understood his need to do so, but in some ways she hoped he failed. Sometimes it was best to put the past to rest, she thought.

When they had all eaten their fill, and danced till they dropped, and the musicians had gone home, Magnus came up to his daughter and his new son-by-marriage. "I have a little gift for you, child," he told Madrene and handed her a document. Madrene gave it to Ian to read.

"A farm? In the Imperial Valley? It's a deed to a five-hundred-acre farm." Ian was clearly confused and turned to Madrene to say, "What would we do with a farm?"

But then he saw her face.

"A farm!" she cried with glee, clapping her hands together. "With horses, and cows, and pigs, and chickens?"

Her father nodded.

"Whoa, whoa, whoa!" Ian said. "Be reasonable, Maddie. What would we do with a farm?"

"It's not for now," her father explained. "It will be taken care of till the time you tire of the military and want to please your wife."

After her father walked away, Ian asked Madrene, "A farm? With cow manure? And mean ol' bulls? And milking? And all that hard work? You want to live on a freakin' farm?"

"Yea, but we don't have to. I will be happy wherever you are. We can give it back to my father. Whatever you want."

Yeah, right! When a woman says that, it means she'll get her way eventually. But a farm? Holy shit! A farm?

When they were finally alone, in bed, with Sam, Ian said, "I didn't have time to buy you a wedding gift, honey."

She rolled over in his arms, kissing him softly on the lips. Then she put his palm on her bare belly. "This is the greatest gift you could have given me."

Ian had trouble speaking over the lump in his throat. But finally he said, "No, sweetheart, it is a gift you are giving me."

A little later, when Ian was almost asleep, Madrene leaned over and whispered in his ear, "I forgot. I have a gift for you, dearling."

Uh-oh! It better not have anything to do with farms.

"Have you ever heard of the Viking S-Spot?"

Some claimed that forever after, Ian was said to remark on many an occasion, "God bless Vikings!"

AUTHOR'S NOTE

Dear Readers:

So many of you wrote requesting Ian and Madrene's story. I hope you enjoyed *Hot & Heavy*. Personally, I think both characters turned out well...her a shrew and him overly serious. I especially liked the way Madrene turned Ian's orderly life upside down and inside out.

Of course, time-travel is a fantasy, and the only way I am able to suspend disbelief is by saying that miracles do happen. Other than that, I did try to make my books as accurate as possible, both in contemporary and historical settings. Having said that, I admit unabashedly that I have taken some license. For example, I know that a SEAL squad leader would never leave his team, and that SEALs would not talk so much on their inter-team radio while on a mission, and an assault rifle probably wouldn't go off the way it did, and that a real SEAL would not have told a stranger that he was a SEAL.

As an indication of how much I like Vikings, this is my eleventh book about those amazing Norsemen, and my second placing them in a Navy SEALs environment.

I have the greatest admiration for Navy SEALs, more so every day as our nation faces such dire terrorist threats. They are the guys who do the dirty, dangerous jobs that keep us all a little bit safer. These elite special forces are physically fit, intelligent, loyal and patriotic. My SEALs go a few steps farther. They are handsome, have a wonderful sense of humor, cherish family, and are great lovers. Perhaps all SEALs are that way. Who knows? And, as I've said before, isn't it remarkable how many similarities there are between SEALs and Vikings?

If this is your first time reading a Sandra Hill book, please know that *Hot & Heavy* is the fifth book in a loosely linked series (can be read out of order) that began with *The Last Viking* (Geirolf), *Truly Madly Viking* (Jorund), *The Very Virile Viking* (Magnus) and *Wet & Wild* (Ragnor).

In addition, I have another Viking series, which is a combination of time-travels and straight historical novels. They include: *The Reluctant Viking* (Thork), *The Outlaw Viking* (Selik), *The Tarnished Lady* (Eirik), *The Bewitched Viking* (Tykir), *The Blue Viking* (Rurik), *My Fair Viking* (Adam) and *A Tale of Two Vikings* (Vagn and Toste).

Most of these books are still available new, either through a full-service bookstore or Dorchester Publishing, 1-800-481-9191.

Please visit my website to sign up for my mailing list and the occasional contest. I only send out email newsletters before each book.

As always, I wish you smiles in your reading. And I thank you all for your continuing support.

Fondly,

Sandra Hill
P.O. Box 604
State College, PA 16804
shill733@aol.com
www.sandrahill.net